# EMMA DARCY

# OUTBACK

## Heroes

# CONTENTS

7 - 129

# The Outback
# Marriage Ransom

# PROLOGUE

*First day at Gundamurra*

THE PLANE WAS heading down to a red dirt airstrip. Apart from the cluster of buildings that marked the sheep station of Gundamurra, there was no other habitation in sight between here and the horizon—a huge empty landscape dotted with scrubby trees. Ric wished he still had the camera he'd stolen. He could take some unbelievable shots here.

'The middle of nowhere,' Mitch Tyler muttered. 'I'm beginning to think I made the wrong choice.'

'Nah,' Johnny Ellis drawled. 'Anything's better than being locked up. At least we can breathe out here.'

'What? Dust?' Mitch mocked.

The plane landed, kicking up a cloud of it.

'Welcome to the great Australian Outback,' the cop escorting them said derisively. 'And just remember…if you three city smart-arses want to survive, there's nowhere to run.'

All three of them ignored him. They were sixteen. Regardless of what life threw at them, they were going to survive. And Johnny had it right, Ric thought. Six months working on a sheep station, had to be better than a year in a juvenile jail. Ric, for one, couldn't stand overbearing authority. He hoped the guy who ran this place wasn't some kind of tyrant, getting off on having three slaves to do his bidding.

What had the judge said at the sentencing? Something about getting back to ground values. A program that would teach them what real life was about. In other words, you worked to live, not skim off other people. Easy for him to say, sitting behind his bench in a cushy chair, safe with his silver-tailed government income.

There was no *security* in Ric's world.

Never had been.

Thieving what you wanted was the only way to get it. And there was a lot Ric wanted. Though stealing the Porsche to impress Lara Seymour had been stupid. He'd lost her now. That was certain. A girl with her privileged background wouldn't even consider a convicted criminal for a boyfriend.

The plane taxied back to where a guy was waiting beside a four-wheel drive Cherokee. Big guy—broad-shouldered, barrel-chested, craggy weathered face, iron-grey hair. Had to be over fifty but still looking tough and formidable. Not someone to buck in a hurry, Ric decided, though size didn't automatically command his respect. If the guy laid a hand on him...

'John Wayne rides again,' Mitch muttered in the mocking tone he habitually used. Sour on the whole world was Mitch. Could become a real drag, living with him at close quarters.

'No horse,' Johnny remarked with a grin.

He was going to be much easier to get on with, Ric thought.

Johnny Ellis had probably cultivated an affable manner as his stock-in-trade, as well as a protective shield, though he was big enough and strong enough to match anyone in a punch-up. He had friendly hazel eyes, a ready grin, and sun-streaked brown hair that tended to flop over his forehead. He'd been caught dealing in marijuana, though he swore it was only to musicians who'd get it from someone else anyway.

Mitch Tyler was a very different kettle of fish, charged with a serious assault on a guy who, he claimed, had date-raped his sister. Though he hadn't put that defence forward in court. Didn't want his sister dragged into it. He was lean and mean, dark hair, biting blue eyes, and Ric had the sense that violence was simmering under his surface all the time.

Ric, himself, was darker still in colouring. Typical Italian heritage.

Black curly hair, almost black eyes, olive skin, with the kind of Latin good looks that attracted the girls. Any girl he wanted. Even Lara. But looks weren't enough in the long run. He had to have money. And all the things money could buy. It was the only way to beat the class difference.

The plane came to a halt.

The cop told them to get their duffle bags from under the back seats. A few minutes later he was leading them out to a way of life which was far, far removed from anything the three of them had known before.

The initial introduction had Ric instantly tensing up.

'Here are your boys, Mister Maguire. Straight off the city streets for you to whip into shape.'

The big old guy—and he sure was big close up—gave the cop a steely look. 'That's not how we do things out here.' The words were softly spoken but they carried a confident authority that scorned any need for physical abuse.

He nodded to them, offering a measure of respect. 'I'm Patrick Maguire. Welcome to Gundamurra. In the Aboriginal language, that means "Good day." I hope you will all eventually feel it was a good day when you first set foot on my place.'

Ric found himself willing to give it a chance.

Fighting it wasn't going to do him any good anyway.

'And you are...?' Patrick Maguire held out a massive hand to Mitch who looked suspiciously at it as though it were a bone-cruncher.

'Mitch Tyler,' he answered, thrusting his own hand out in defiant challenge.

'Good to meet you, Mitch.'

A normal handshake, no attempt to dominate.

Johnny's hand came out with no hesitation. 'Johnny Ellis. Good to meet you, Mister Maguire.' Big smile to the old man, pouring out the charm. Getting onside fast was Johnny.

A weighing look in the steely grey gaze, plus a hint of amusement. No one's fool this, Ric thought, as he himself was targeted by eyes that had probably seen through all the facades people put up.

'Ric Donato,' he said, taking the offered hand, feeling the strength in it, and oddly enough a warmth that took away some of the sense of alienation that was deep in Ric's bones.

'Ready to go?' the old man asked.

'Yeah. I'm ready,' Ric said more aggressively than he meant to.

Ready to take on the whole damned world one day.

And come out on top.

Maybe even win Lara in the end.

He still couldn't get her out of his head. Probably never would. Class... that's what she had. Unattainable for Ric right now but he'd get there. One way or another, he'd make it to where he wanted to be.

# CHAPTER ONE

*Eighteen years later...*

RIC DONATO SAT with his executive assistant, Kathryn Ledger, in the Sydney office, checking photographs that had come in, most of them featuring celebrities at the Australian Film Industry Awards. That was the big number this week. Freelance photographers—some reputable, some paparazzi—sent them to his agency via the Internet. His staff sifted through them, choosing the highlights to be sold to magazines around the world.

Always class, Ric reflected with considerable irony. That was what his network of agencies sold—here in Australia, Los Angeles, New York, London, his contacts legion now, all of them eager to jump on his red carpet ride.

The grim realities he'd shot as a photo-journalist covering war zones had won prizes and respect in some quarters but the appeal of those photographs had been very limited. He'd learnt the hard way that it was pretty pictures that sold everywhere. People wanted to see class. They revelled in it, if only vicariously. They turned away from suffering.

Focusing on class had paid off, at both ends of the market. The rich and famous liked his guarantee that nothing negative would be brokered through his agencies. They even alerted his staff about photo opportunities, happy to supply the demands of the media as long as the shots were positive publicity for them. And the magazines lapped up what he could provide, paying mega-dollars for exclusives.

Everybody happy.

The magic formula for success.

Class...

It was the password to paradise, at least in terms of wealth and acceptability into even the highest social strata. He'd known that instinctively at sixteen, forgotten it in his twenties when he'd pursued other quests, learnt it again in time to build up what had turned into a multimillion dollar business.

Kathryn downloaded yet another photograph from the airport—more Hollywood stars departing, Ric thought, idly watching until one of the faces being revealed galvanised his attention.

Lara?

Her head was ducked down. She was wearing sunglasses. Was that discolouration beside her left cheekbone part of a black eye? Her mouth was puffy as though she'd taken a hit there, as well.

He switched his gaze to the man accompanying her. That was Gary Chappel all right—the guy she'd married—heir and current CEO to the Nursing Home empire his father had built. Born to huge wealth and with the kind of clean-cut handsome looks that could have made him a pin-up model if he'd been so inclined.

But he wasn't looking so attractive in this photo, his mouth thinned into grim lines, hooded eyes emanating a vicious threat. He had one arm wrapped tightly around Lara's shoulders. His other hand had a tight grip on her arm which was tucked between them. Bruisingly tight.

'Wow! There's fodder for the gossip pages,' Kathryn remarked.

Gary and Lara Chappel—definitely an A-list couple in Australian high society, usually photographed as two of the most beautiful people. Ric had seen plenty of shots of them before, but never like this.

'Delete?' Kathryn checked with him before carrying out the action.

'No!' It came out forcefully.

Kathryn looked her surprise. 'It's not a happy snap, Ric.'

'Print it for me and buy the copyright.'

'But...'

'If we don't buy it someone else will. As you said, it's prime fodder for gossip pages and I don't want it printed publicly,' he said decisively, acting on his gut instinct which was too strong for him to ignore.

'It's not our business to protect, Ric,' Kathryn reminded him, her eyes searching his for the reason.

He'd trained her to handle all the business that came into the Sydney office. She was in charge when he was elsewhere. He trusted her judgment. But this was personal. Deeply personal. And he couldn't let it go.

Funny after all these years and having had no contact with Lara Seymour since he'd been taken to Gundamurra...yet the sight of her, looking as though she was the victim of physical abuse by her husband, got to Ric.

And here was Kathryn, looking at him with eyes that questioned if he'd suddenly lost his marbles—green eyes, auburn hair cut in a short chic style, pretty face, trim figure always smartly dressed in a business suit—all in all a very attractive package, housing a brain that invariably displayed a quick intelligence. He liked her, wished her well in the marriage she was planning with her boyfriend who was a hot-shot dealer in a merchant bank.

In fact, he liked her very much and wasn't sure her fiancé was good enough for her. Yet he'd never *wanted* Kathryn himself, not how he'd wanted Lara Seymour.

To him she'd been the embodiment of perfect femininity; softly slender, idyllically proportioned, a wonderful flowing curtain of shiny blond hair, a face of features drawn with delicate distinction, eyes the sparkling blue of summer skies, a beautiful smile that was both shy and inviting, smooth unblemished skin that glowed with a sheen he had ached to touch, to stroke. He'd understood the phrase, a swanlike neck, in the way she moved her head. And she'd walked like a dancer, innately graceful.

Every aspect of her had given him intense riveting pleasure, yet she'd also embodied the mystique of the unattainable, compelling him to... but that was far in the past.

'Lara and I go way back, Kathryn,' he said quietly. 'She would hate having this exposed.'

'You...and Lara Chappel?' She looked astounded.

'Lara Seymour...'

'Is *she* why...' An embarrassed flush flooded up her neck and burned her cheeks. Her gaze was hastily switched to the computer screen. 'I'll do a print for you,' she muttered.

'Why what?' Ric pursued the point, curious to know what she was thinking.

A rueful glance. 'Not my business, Ric.'

'Say it anyway.'

A shrug that disowned any personal interest. 'People talk about you. Let's face it…you'd have to be one of the most eligible bachelors in the world. You could have your pick of beautiful women, yet…'

'Yet?'

She finally gave him a direct look. 'You never seem to have a serious relationship.'

His smile was wry. 'I lead a busy life, Kathryn.'

'Of course.' She nodded and busied herself producing a print of the photograph on glossy paper.

Ric pondered the question she'd raised.

Yes, it was easy enough to get dates with women he found attractive. Somehow the attraction never lasted very long. It usually ended up feeling false, with him becoming too conscious of how pleased the women were with what he could provide. They didn't *know* him. They just wanted the part of him that emanated the power of huge success and big money.

He'd certainly fulfilled his ambition of making it to the top. The world was more or less his oyster. He owned apartments in London and New York—prime properties—as well as in Sydney, with a magnificent harbour view. He also had classy cars in each city; a Jaguar in London, a Lamborghini in New York, a Ferrari here.

The Porsche he'd once stolen to impress Lara flitted through his mind. He could have bought one. Didn't want to. Why remind himself of frustration…defeat? Although he wasn't that boy anymore…was he?

Did anyone ever really escape the past?

Kathryn handed him the printed photograph and he stared down at it, feeling the past grab him back to that time and place when being with Lara Seymour had seemed more important than anything else. Somehow she'd been the fulfilment of all he'd craved for himself.

'Got an envelope for this?' he asked, knowing he was going to act on it.

Kathryn opened a desk drawer, gave him one.

'Print five more copies…' His instincts insisted on the precaution. 'Lock them in the safe. Then delete.'

She nodded, frowning over the unusual commands. 'What should I pay for the copyright?'

'I don't care.' He slid the photo into the envelope, sealed it, stood up. 'Negotiate the best price you can.' He threw her a look of reckless determination as he headed for the door. 'The bottom line is... I don't care how much it costs. Just do it.'

'Right!' she said, accepting the task without any further questions, though her eyes were full of them.

Ric didn't care. He could afford a stupid self-indulgence if that's what it was. It looked to him as though Lara was in a bad situation with Gary Chappel. The photo had been taken at the airport. Had she been attempting to run away from her husband?

Domestic abuse could occur in any household and all too often it was hidden through shame. And fear of more punishment. His own mother had been a victim of it—dying from ruptured kidneys when Ric was only a kid. He'd been too little to protect her, getting beatings for trying. At least his father had gone to jail for it, but Ric had never forgotten the fear of testifying against him in court.

If Lara was living in that kind of fear...

Ric found his hands clenching as he rode the elevator down to the basement car park. It wasn't his fight. He had no rights in this matter. Nevertheless, he couldn't ignore it. His heart burned with the need to act. And in his mind flared a wildly wanton exultation in having the power to do it—the power to do anything he chose to do.

He wasn't a street kid anymore.

He was a rich guy.

With class in spades.

And money to burn any way he liked.

In that respect, he could more than match Gary Chappel.

He was glad he'd dressed in his favourite Armani suit this morning, more for meeting Mitch Tyler for lunch in the city than for business. Barristers always dressed in suits and Mitch was a top-line barrister these days. He'd made it to where he wanted to be. Johnny Ellis had, as well, going platinum on quite a few of his country and western songs. Even after all these years since their time at Gundamurra, the three of them still connected when they were in the same place.

None of them had married.

As Ric got in his Ferrari, he wondered if Mitch and Johnny had the same problem with the women they dated, finding themselves more outside the relationship than in it after a while. The three of them probably understood each other more than any woman could. In fact, he might need Mitch to sort out Gary Chappel if that was what Lara wanted.

He drove out of the car park for the office building at Circular Quay and headed for the Eastern Suburbs. The envelope containing the photograph was on the passenger seat beside him—a major weapon in a war he could wage if Lara wanted to be free.

He knew where she lived. Not that he'd ever kept tabs on her. There'd been a splash of publicity when Gary Chappel had acquired the fifteen million dollar mansion on the harbour foreshore at Vaucluse—a photospread of Lara showing off the refurbishings they'd subsequently done.

The perfect hostess for her station in life, Ric had thought then. He hadn't imagined for one moment that her station in life might be miserable in private. It had seemed to him she was blessed with everything...and still unattainable as far as he was concerned. No point in manipulating a meeting with her. Leave the past in the past, he'd argued to himself. No good could come of it...only more frustration and defeat.

So why was he butting in now?

Because the picture he'd always had of her charmed life was askew.

What did he hope to achieve by intervention? Who did he think he was? Super-guy to the rescue?

Well, it might turn out as a black joke on him, but Ric knew he wouldn't rest easy until he knew the truth behind that photograph.

Determination drove him to Vaucluse. Determination took him up to the massively colonnaded front porch and pressed the doorbell. Determination made him endure the long wait for the door to be opened—not by Lara, but by a middle-aged woman. The permed grey hair and royal blue button-through uniform dress instantly cast her as staff in Ric's mind. Probably the housekeeper.

'My name is Ric Donato. I've come to visit Mrs. Chappel,' he declared with even more determination.

'I'm sorry, Mr. Donato. Mrs. Chappel isn't receiving visitors today,' came the totally uncompromising statement. But it did reveal Lara was here.

'She'll see me,' he replied grimly, holding out the envelope. 'Please give this to Mrs. Chappel and tell her Ric Donato has come to discuss its contents with her. I'll wait for her reply.'

'Very well, sir.'

She took the envelope and closed the door in his face.

He waited.

In a way, it was blackmail. Lara would know it wasn't the only copy of the photograph. She would be afraid of what use he might make of it. Fear would open this door to him. Then he would be entering her life again.

For how long he didn't know.

He thought of it only as...something he couldn't turn away from.

# CHAPTER TWO

LARA SAT IN the nursery, her feet automatically tipping the rocking chair back and forth in a rhythm that was supposed to soothe, although she knew nothing was going to lift the depression of being imprisoned in this life with Gary. She had to escape it. Had to. But how?

She stared bleakly at the empty cot, the empty pram, the empty everything she'd bought for the baby she didn't have. Stillborn. She wished she'd died with it. The ultimate escape. Probably the only one. Gary was too watchful of her to let her get away. Watchers everywhere.

All the same, she had to go before he made her pregnant again. She desperately hoped it hadn't happened last night. That would be unbearable. She'd managed to get a packet of contraceptive pills from a pharmacy in Kings Cross, lying about leaving her prescription at home, promising to bring it in the next day. But she'd only been taking them for two weeks and wasn't sure they would work yet.

Having a child would trap her in this marriage forever. Impossible to flee. Gary would have the law after her in no time flat, getting custody. Everything within her cringed from the thought of leaving a child in his keeping. That couldn't be allowed to happen.

Marian Keith appeared at the doorway, holding a large white envelope. She was Gary's choice of housekeeper, a widow in her fifties who'd run into financial difficulties, having sons who needed helping through university and very grateful for the generous wage she earned here.

All the domestic staff were Gary's choices and they answered to him, not his wife. Yet occasionally Lara did catch a flash of sympathetic concern in the housekeeper's eyes. More than anyone else, Marian Keith saw what went on in this house. Not that she saw much. Gary was careful to keep his brand of tyranny private.

'Excuse me, Mrs. Chappel, there's a gentleman at the door...'

'You know I can't see visitors today, Mrs. Keith,' she said wearily, rocking on, her gaze drifting to the Walt Disney motifs printed on the wall. Snow White. Lara grimaced. She'd certainly eaten a poisoned apple when she'd married Gary Chappel. And there was no one to rescue her. No one.

'He was very insistent. A Mister Ric Donato...'

Shock slammed into Lara's heart. Her gaze jerked back to the housekeeper. 'Who?' she asked, not ready to accept what she'd heard.

'He said his name was Ric Donato.'

Unbelievable after all these years! Her mind spun back to the past. How many times had she looked for him then, hoping he'd turn up, wanting to be with him again, not caring who he was or what he didn't have. Ric Donato. Ricardo...

A lost dream.

One she'd buried as the years went by with no sight of him, no contact with him. Too late now. Impossible to let him see her like this.

'He asked me to give this to you.' Marian Keith came into the nursery, holding out the envelope. 'He's waiting at the door. He said you'd want to discuss the contents with him, Mrs. Chappel.'

Lara shook her head but she took the envelope and slit the flap open with her finger, curious to see what was inside. She only half removed the glossy sheet of paper, another more fearful shock hitting her at the sight of the faces printed on it.

Her hand instinctively shoved the sheet back in the envelope to keep it hidden. For several moments her mind froze in sheer terror of the consequences if the photograph was released to any form of the media.

'What should I tell him, Mrs. Chappel?'

*Him...* Ric Donato waiting at the door...prepared to discuss the contents...

She had no choice.

It was either see him or...

Her heart fluttered. Her chest was unbearably tight. She sucked in air and made the only decision that might save her from Gary's rage. 'Show Mister Donato out to the patio, Mrs. Keith. I'll see him there.'

Hesitation. Worry. 'Are you sure, Mrs. Chappel?'

Gary would find out she'd had a visitor. No escaping that. She would have to confess why. Dear God! There was no way out. But better to stop this from going public and take the punishment for causing the scene that had been so graphically captured by someone's camera.

'I'm sure, Mrs. Keith,' she said with far more confidence than she felt.

'Very well.' A nod of wary acquiescence and a brisk departure.

Lara couldn't bring herself to move. The envelope gripped in her hand felt like dynamite, the fuse already lit and nothing was going to stop it burning to a dreadful explosion. Even if she was able to block publication of the photo, Gary would hate anyone knowing about it and Ric Donato knew. She shrank from facing the knowledge in his eyes—dark eyes—like dark brown velvet, she had once thought, caressing her, making her feel...

She shuddered, automatically trying to shake off the memory. No point in it. Too much water under the bridge since then. She'd only been fifteen, Ric sixteen. It had been a wildly romantic fixation...a crazy dream...Romeo and Juliet...ending because it had never had a chance of surviving in the real world.

And surviving was what it was all about, Lara thought grimly.

She pushed herself out of the rocking chair. Mentally bracing herself for the inevitable meeting with Ric Donato, she made a quick trip to the downstairs powder room to check her appearance. Make-up almost hid the discolouration around her eye. Carefully drawn lipstick minimised the puffiness of her mouth. Her long blond hair, as always, was a smooth, shiny fall to her shoulders. Even around the house, Gary expected her to maintain an impeccable appearance.

She wore stone-coloured designer jeans and a long-sleeved brown and white striped shirt. The cuff covered the bruise around her wrist. Nothing showed except...she put on a pair of sunglasses—perfectly reasonable to wear them on the patio, considering the sun glare from the swimming pool.

Probably stupid pride, she mocked herself. Ric Donato was not about to be deceived. He hadn't come to be fobbed off, either, though why he had come...Lara took a deep breath in a desperate attempt to calm her inner agitation. He had to be faced, regardless of what motivation had brought him here.

She carried the envelope and its too revealing contents out to the patio, trying to quell the fear that was making mincemeat of her stomach. He was already there, standing under the sails that shaded the outdoors dining setting, gazing out at the sparkling blue waters of Sydney Harbour.

She was surprised to see him wearing a suit. The fabric and cut of it sharply reminded her of who Ric Donato was now—a man who could afford as many beautifully designed and tailored suits as he cared to own—a man who had the power to broadcast her private secrets to a gossip-hungry world. Over the years she'd read quite a few articles about him—prize-winning photo-journalist, moving into business with a network of photographic agencies around the world.

Yet she found herself staring at the black curly hair that was still worn long enough to dip over the back of his collar, remembering a much younger Ric Donato, remembering her fingers threading through the tight corkscrew curls...

One kiss.

That's all there'd been between them.

Just one kiss...

He turned abruptly as though suddenly sensing her presence. She couldn't look into his eyes—eyes that had to know where *she* was at now. Shame curled around her heart, squeezing unmercifully. How had her life come down to this hopeless prison of fear? It had been like a slippery slide...once on it, no way back.

'Hello, Lara.'

The soft deep voice caused her pulse to flutter. Still she couldn't bring herself to meet his gaze. She stared at his mouth—a full lower lip and an emphatically curved upper one. Sexy and sensual. An oddly compelling contrast to the strong chisel chin and the very masculine Roman nose.

She remembered how he'd kissed her...slowly, and oh so seductively, wooing the romantic soul she'd had then. If only she could go back to the past, make different choices, take different paths...

'Ric...' she forced herself to say with an acknowledging nod.

He gestured to the envelope in her hand. 'It was taken at the airport and sent to my Sydney Agency this morning. For sale to anyone interested in buying.'

'You haven't sold it on yet?' she pleaded in a frantic rush, unable to contain the flooding well of panic.

'No. And I won't, Lara,' he assured her. 'In fact, I've just called my executive assistant who told me she's secured the copyright.'

'I'll pay whatever the price was.'

He shook his head. 'It's irrelevant.'

Lara gestured haplessly. 'I don't understand. Why have you come if not to...'

'Make good on my investment?' His mouth quirked into an ironic grimace. 'Oddly enough, I came for you.'

'Me?' It came out as a squeak. Her throat was almost choked by a huge lump of chaotic emotion. She dragged her gaze up to his. Was it caring in his eyes? They burned with some indefinable purpose which certainly encompassed her, making her feel weirdly skittish.

'Take your sunglasses off, Lara. You don't have to hide from me.'

'I'm not...' She bit down on the lie, but to show her naked face...it was too humiliating. 'Can't you leave me with some pride, Ric?'

'This isn't about pride. It's about truth. Just between you and me,' he stated quietly, giving a promise she instinctively believed.

Besides, he had the photograph. Which he'd effectively quashed from publication. Didn't that prove he was keeping her situation under wraps?

With a defeated little shrug of resignation, she removed the glasses, revealing the swelling that reduced one of her eyes to a narrow, bloodshot slit. 'Black truth,' she said self-mockingly, fighting back the pricking of tears.

He nodded. 'I never told you my mother was a battered wife.'

Lara flinched at the brutal labelling of what he was seeing.

'She died of injuries my father inflicted when I was eight,' he went on, hammering home what could happen. 'As many times as I tried to protect her, to get in the way, to deflect his violence, I couldn't save her.'

'I'm sorry. I...' She shook her head, swallowing hard to hold back the threatening tears. 'No, you never told me,' she choked out, trying desperately to hang on to some dignity.

'But I can save *you*, Lara. If you want me to.'

'Oh, God!' Control was beyond her. She moved blindly to the closest chair, dragged it out from the table, collapsed onto it, and covered
her face with her hands, propping her elbows on the table for some solid
support as she wept over the impossible prospect of being *saved* from a
husband who was never going to let her go.

She was horribly conscious of Ric Donato watching her, waiting. At
least he didn't try to touch her or speak comforting words, which would
have been unbearable. He remained on the other side of the table, as still
as a statue, saying nothing, doing nothing, just giving her time to get
herself together again. Which she did eventually, pride in terrible tatters, but as Ric had already said, this wasn't about pride.

'Thank you. But there's nothing you can do.' She lifted her head, letting him see that stark truth in her eyes. 'Except what you've done...
with the photograph. I'm very grateful to you for...for blocking it, Ric.'

Still that dark burning in his eyes. 'At the airport...you were running from him?'

'I failed,' she admitted wretchedly. 'Everyone here...they all report
to him. I can't go anywhere...without his knowing.'

'No support from your family, Lara?' he asked, frowning over her
helplessness.

'My father suffered a stroke.' Her eyes mirrored the bleak irony of the
situation. 'He's in one of the Chappel nursing homes. My mother doesn't
want to hear anything against Gary. It's too...threatening...'

She didn't go on. Ric knew she was an only child. No siblings to turn
to. As for friends, Gary chose them. She'd lost touch with the girlfriends
who'd shared her modelling years.

'But you do want to leave him,' he pressed.

'Oh, yes.' She flashed him a derisive look. 'I'm not a masochist, Ric.'

'How much, Lara?' he challenged. 'How far would you be willing to
go to have Gary Chappel out of your life?'

She shook her head defeatedly. 'It's not possible.'

'Yes, it is,' he said with such arrogant confidence it goaded her into a
reply that snapped with a mountain of miserable frustration.

'Do you think I haven't tested what can and can't be done?'

'Would you spend a year on an Outback sheep station, away from
everything you've known?'

The Outback? She'd never thought of that as an escape route. Had never been there. Knew no one there. Was completely ignorant of how people lived there. But they did *live*. And she'd be free of the fear—fear she knew all too intimately, ever constant.

'Yes,' she said, defying any other judgment he might make from the rich and privileged lifestyle that had always been her environment. Desperation bred desperate measures.

'Are you prepared to walk out with me now? No baggage. Just you, walking out and leaving all this behind.'

'With...you?'

Her mind whirled with this further shock. Ric Donato wasn't posing some theoretical situation. He was actually asking her...and she didn't know the man he was now. How could she agree to such drastic action when her only personal experience with him had become a teenager's romantic memory? That had been...eighteen years ago!

'I'm your safe passage, Lara,' he stated without so much as a flicker of an eyelash. 'I can get you to Gundamurra where you'll be protected from any possible pursuit by your husband. You'll have safe refuge there for the year it takes to get a divorce.'

Gundamurra...it sounded like the end of the earth...primitive...

'It's best if you choose quickly,' he coolly advised. 'If what you say is true, and everyone here reports to your husband, he may already know of my visit and be suspicious of it.'

'How can I trust you to do what you say you'll do?' she cried, the fear of consequences paralysing any decision-making process.

'I'm here. I'm offering. What have you got to lose by trusting me?'

'If you fail, it will be much, much worse.'

'I won't fail.'

'Gary said he'd have a man watching me. Watching the house. Watching where I go.'

'My car is parked at your front door. I have the resources to evade anyone who follows us.'

He spoke calmly, with an indomitable self-assurance that actually calmed the surge of panic that was screaming through her mind. In its place came a wild litany of hope. Could he do it? Could he really? Get her away to a safe place where Gary couldn't reach her?

An Outback sheep station.

Why not?

It had to be more *civilised* than living like this.

'It's your choice, Lara. It will be a different life, but at least a life where you can always breathe easy.'

She took a deep breath. 'This Gundamurra...it belongs to you?'

'No. But I have lived there. And you'll be made welcome. It's where you can get your head straight...if you want to.'

Freedom was all she could think about, but freedom might also have a price tag.

'If we do this...and succeed in getting there... I'll owe you big-time, Ric.'

His mouth softened into a whimsical little smile. 'This isn't a money issue.'

Money? She hadn't even thought of money. Looking at the man he'd become—powerful enough to challenge Gary, and feeling his power reaching out and winding around her...what did *he* want of her?

Was it only compassion for her situation moving him to offer help? What if he was like Gary, taking without caring what she wanted? No, he couldn't be like that or he wouldn't have spoken about his mother. She was letting fear screw up her instincts.

'You can always pay me back whatever you think you owe me after you get a divorce,' he dropped into her fretful silence.

'How will I manage a divorce if I'm...?'

'I know just the guy who can do that for you. Don't worry about it, Lara. Mitch will nail Gary Chappel to the wall so there'll be no comeback from your *ex*-husband.'

She shook her head incredulously. This was all happening so fast—promises being held out that she desperately wanted to grab. 'Are you sure about this?'

'Absolutely.' His dark eyes glittered with more than determined purpose as he stepped forward and picked up the envelope she'd laid on the table. 'This photograph will be used to gain fair compensation for what you've suffered at Gary Chappel's hands.'

She stared at him, and the feeling that she'd had about Ric Donato as a teenager came flooding back—a driving, unstoppable force. But he had been stopped then...by the police for stealing a car.

No need for him to steal now. He had the wealth and power to make him unstoppable in any enterprise he chose to take on. With that recognition, hope grew in Lara's heart. Rightly or wrongly, she did trust him. Whatever the risk, his offer was worth taking. At least she should try it.

She scraped her chair back and stood up, adrenalin shooting new energy through her. 'I'll go and get ready.'

Decision made.

He nodded, acknowledging it, approving it. 'Bring nothing more than an ordinary handbag, Lara. Purse, driver's licence, what you'd normally carry on an outing. Okay?'

She was acutely aware of the sense in that instruction—nothing to suggest a final departure. 'I'll only be a couple of minutes, Ric. Wait here for me?'

'Yes. You can put your sunglasses on again.'

She did, then amazingly she found herself smiling at him, the heady promise of freedom lifting her heart. 'Thank you, Ric.'

He smiled back. 'I always wanted to be a white knight coming to the rescue of a fair damsel in distress. It feels good to be at your service, Lara. That's enough for me.'

It was a reassurance that she was safe with him.

He wouldn't demand anything of her.

Maybe fairy stories could happen in real life, Lara thought light-headedly, hurrying off to get a bag. Though she couldn't see Ric Donato as a white knight. More a dark prince.

But dark was good when it came to hiding.

If he could keep her safe from Gary, he would indeed be a prince.

# CHAPTER THREE

THE MINUTES TICKED BY, every second excruciatingly long for Ric. He paced up and down the patio, willing Lara not to change her mind, not to give in to a burst of panic over her decision. He kept checking his watch. Time was critical. If someone had reported his visit to Gary Chappel…if he came home…a face-to-face confrontation before they could get away might scuttle everything.

Footsteps coming…

He moved to meet them, his whole body wound tight with tension.

Lara…wearing a brown shoulder-bag now and carrying a hat. 'Ready,' she declared, determination in her voice, and with a slight lilt of excitement.

'Let's go,' he said, and there was not the slightest hesitation from her, much to Ric's relief.

The housekeeper was in the foyer. She looked anxiously at the two of them. 'Mrs. Chappel…?'

'I'm just going out for a while,' Lara answered, heading straight for the front door. 'We won't be long, Mrs. Keith.'

The housekeeper beat her to the door. 'Mrs. Chappel…' It was a plea for Lara to reconsider.

She knew what went on here, Ric thought, and didn't like it. He laid a hand on the housekeeper's shoulder, drawing her gaze to his. 'Don't worry. I'll look after her.'

She shook her head slightly but stepped back, letting them go without further protest.

'It's a conspicuous car, Ric,' Lara remarked fearfully as he loaded her into it.

'We won't be in it for long,' he assured her.

It was good to get behind the driver's wheel and fire the engine up. He had Lara in his custody now and nothing was going to stop him from flying her to Gundamurra. The temptation to leave in a burst of speed was strong, but the wiser course was to drive sedately, watching for the watchers.

He was no sooner out of the private driveway to Chappel's mansion, than a grey sedan, parked at the kerb on the street, started up and pulled out, quickly catching up to the Ferrari, sitting just behind it. A male driver, wearing sunglasses and a baseball cap.

Ric had no intention of shaking him. That was better done when the follower least expected it. At the first red light, he used his car phone to contact his office at Circular Quay. It only took a few moments for Kathryn to come on line. He spoke to her as he drove on.

'Kathryn, I'm heading back to the office. I have Lara Chappel with me and I need your help. Clear your desk for the next couple of hours, grab your bag and car keys and be waiting for me in the basement car park. We should be there in about ten minutes. Okay?'

'I'll be standing by, Ric.'

'Tell your secretary you're off to a business meeting with a magazine editor and won't be back until after lunch.'

'Will do.'

'Thank you.'

'Who's Kathryn?' Lara instantly asked, her hands curling in her lap, clearly apprehensive about anyone knowing what they were doing.

'Kathryn Ledger. My executive assistant in the Sydney office. She has both my confidence and my trust.'

'Is she the one who bought the photo?'

'Yes.'

Lara took a deep breath. 'I take it we'll be switching cars.'

'Necessary. Don't jerk around in your seat to look. We're being followed by a guy in a grey sedan.'

The hands curled into white-knuckled fists.

Ric wondered just how many escape attempts had been thwarted. And punished. Irrelevant, he told himself. That was the past. He had to secure Lara's future.

At the next red light, he punched out the numbers for Bankstown Airport and made contact with the guy in charge of Johnny's Cessna.

'Ric Donato. I'll be taking Johnny's plane on a flight to Bourke. Can you get it on the tarmac with a flight plan lodged as soon as possible, please. I should be there in an hour or so.'

'I'll do my best, Mr. Donato. Want some refreshments on board?'

'Yes. There'll only be two of us.'

'No problem.'

He heard Lara take another deep breath. 'A private plane?' she asked tentatively.

He nodded. 'It belongs to a friend of mine. I have the authority to take it any time I want. Johnny's in the U.S. He won't be using it for a while.'

'You can fly?' An odd wonderment in her voice.

He threw her a confident smile. 'Don't worry. I have a pilot's licence and I've logged thousands of hours in the air.'

'Bourke...?'

'First stop. We'll get you some clothes before moving on.'

'I don't have much money with me. But I do have credit cards. If Gary doesn't...'

'No. No credit cards. You can be traced through using them. I'll supply the money. Consider it a loan.'

She didn't protest.

Ric was glad she had the presence of mind to take in the ramifications and not make any fuss over the plan he was still formulating. He was getting quite a buzz from it. Reminded him of his years in war zones when fast action and planning on the run were critical for survival. Lots of adrenalin rushes in those days. This was a different kind of battle but a battle nonetheless. Lara's life was at stake.

No doubt in his mind on that score. The black eye, the gut-wrenching weeping, the expressions of utter despair...that was more than enough to put Ric in fighting mode. The evidence of the guy following them sealed the truth of what Lara had told him. The Vaucluse mansion had been a prison and Gary Chappel deserved to lose his wife.

Whether the bastard had wrought irreparable damage on Lara, only time would tell. Ric was intent on giving her that time. Strange, after all these years, he still felt a strong tie to her. His first love. His only love, if it could be called that. More a fantasy, he told himself and Gary Chappel had more or less fitted into that fantasy. Except the truth of their marriage was very, very different to what he had imagined and Ric felt a hard cold fury toward the man who had brought Lara this low.

He glanced at her clenched hands, saw that she'd taken off her rings. A brave act, given her fear. Also a huge measure of her trust that he could, indeed, deliver what he'd promised. Which surely meant she did feel some positive connection to him. Perhaps a hangover from the past, remembering an *innocent* relationship between them.

Whatever...she had come with him and Ric was not about to abuse that trust in any shape or form. First and foremost she needed to feel safe. Then a swift, clean end to her marriage had to be accomplished. Which reminded him of his lunch date.

He called Mitch's chambers and left a message with his clerk, cancelling the luncheon and saying he'd contact him tonight. 'That's the barrister I spoke about,' he explained to Lara. 'Mitch will know how best to handle your divorce.'

'A barrister...' She glanced curiously at him. 'You have some very handy friends, Ric.'

Many friends, but only a few he could absolutely count on in this situation. 'Johnny and Mitch shared my time at Gundamurra,' he said matter-of-factly. 'And the man who owns the sheep station, Patrick Maguire, was like a father to us at a critical time in our lives. Each one of these men would do everything in their power to protect you, Lara.'

'Because you ask them to?'

He shook his head. 'Because they don't like people being hurt and not one of them would be intimidated by anything your husband could do.'

She heaved a ragged sigh. 'That might be a tall order.'

He threw her a devil-may-care grin. 'They're all tall men.'

It evoked a wry smile from her. 'You, too.' Then with a worried frown. 'I don't want Gary to cut you down. He's used to getting his own way, Ric. There will be...repercussions...from helping me.'

Amazing that she could be concerned for him and his friends when her own survival was on the line. 'There are times when a stand must be made, Lara,' he said quietly. 'And we are lesser people if we don't do it.'

There were so many injustices in the world. For years he had shown them through his camera, but the shots he had taken hadn't made any difference. They were simply a record of man's inhumanity to man. Maybe that was part of what was driving him today—the need to make a difference, if only to Lara's life.

He drove into the basement car park, using his office passcard to lift the barrier. 'Gary's guy can't follow us in here by car. We have time to make the swap. We'll both have to hunker down in Kathryn's car so he won't see us going out. You okay with that?'

'Yes.'

Kathryn was waiting.

The escape ran smoothly. No hitches anywhere along the line. By midafternoon they were in Bourke. Ric set up an account in a local bank, made Lara a signatory to it, withdrew several thousand dollars, gave the money to her and sent her shopping by herself. He also gave her the keys to the car he'd hired at the airport, now parked in Oxford Street. She could load her shopping bags in it whenever she wanted to.

'What will I need, Ric?' she asked anxiously. 'This is foreign territory for me. I want to fit in.'

Good positive attitude.

Ric was glad she had accepted the challenge of a year in the Outback, showing no traces of being a spoiled rich bitch who'd continually kick against the life. He wondered how she'd cope with the isolation, whether she'd welcome it or hate it. Only time would tell.

'Shorts, jeans, shirts, good walking shoes, sandals,' he rolled out. 'You'll need a warm jacket. A couple of sweaters. It can get cold at night out here. Think casual. Nothing too classy.' He shrugged. 'Look around you. See what the local people are wearing.'

Not that she'd be seeing any of them for the next couple of months. It was the end of February, still the wet season, and the road to Gundamurra would be washed out, impassable. The only way in and out was by plane. Even if Gary Chappel discovered where she was, he'd find it impossible to get to her. Patrick Maguire would see to that.

'You'll have to be quick, Lara,' he warned. 'We need to leave here by five o'clock if we're to land at Gundamurra before sunset.'

'I'll be quick,' she promised, then suddenly grinned. 'No one's going to care what I look like, are they?'

It was her first carefree expression. Ric felt his own heart lift with pleasure. 'No one will give a damn. You're not judged by clothes in the Outback. It's the person you are that counts, Lara.'

'The person...' She sobered, grimaced. 'I lost the girl you once knew, Ric.'

He nodded. Impossible to go back. They'd both grown beyond what they'd been as teenagers. 'This is a chance to find out who you are now,' he said, waving her on to do her shopping. 'I'll meet you at the car at five.'

He watched her quick jaunty walk up the street, knew she was revelling in the first taste of freedom. It was good, seeing her without the fear, seeing *the difference*. Reward enough for what he'd done.

The next step was to warn Patrick of their imminent arrival. He went to the post office to use the public telephone, wary of any record of the call being traced through his mobile. Luckily Patrick was in his home office not out in the paddocks.

'It's Ric,' he announced. 'I'm in Bourke. I'll be flying in to Gundamurra before sunset.'

'Great! I'll meet you at the airstrip.' Warm pleasure in his voice.

'Patrick, I'm bringing someone with me and I've promised she can be your house guest for a year.'

'A year?' Startled by the length of time.

Ric quickly explained the circumstances. Patrick listened, making no comment until everything had been told.

'This is your Lara, Ric?' he asked. 'The girl you stole the car for?'

*His* Lara. She'd never been *his*. Wasn't now. Yet... 'I had to rescue her, Patrick. Will you keep her safe for me? She needs the time to put her marriage behind her.'

'It may not work out the way you want, son,' came the serious warning. 'No good her walking out of one prison into another, if that's how she feels about Gundamurra. But she's welcome here for as long as she's happy to stay.'

'That's all I ask.' The choice was Lara's. He couldn't—didn't want to—make her do anything against her will.

'Fair enough.'

'Thanks, Patrick.'

'I look forward to meeting her.'

*It may not work out the way you want...* Ric pondered those words as he strolled down the street to the Gecko Café where he could buy a coffee while he waited for Lara.

What did he want from this?

He knew what he didn't want—Lara being a battered wife.

But beyond setting her free from Gary Chappel...he wanted to see joy in her eyes...to recapture something of the girl that had once made every moment spent with her unbelievably special.

Magic.

Or was that a youthful dream, reaching for stars that were unreachable?

He shook his head, accepting Patrick's dictum that it may not work out how he wanted.

But it didn't kill the latent hope in his heart.

# CHAPTER FOUR

RIC WAS LEANING against the hood of the hire car, arms folded in a posture of relaxed patience. He'd left his suitcoat and tie in the plane. His shirt collar was open, sleeves rolled up his forearms.

Lara paused in her rush to the car. Seeing him like this, at a slight distance, she realised he had a more powerfully built physique than Gary. His arms were very muscular and his shoulders were still broad without any clever tailoring to make them seem so. He'd filled out quite a lot from the boy she remembered.

She'd never thought of a photographer as leading a hard physical life, but of course it could hardly have been a picnic in war zones. And if Ric had also worked on an Outback sheep station...

Though how had he come to Gundamurra in the first place?

An odd choice for a city boy.

He might be very wealthy now but he was certainly a different breed to the men she knew. That hadn't changed about Ric Donato. He was different and she still liked the difference. She'd never been afraid of it. It was attractive, exciting. But more than that, she knew instinctively he would never knowingly hurt her.

Was that because of seeing his mother hurt and hating it?

Even as a teenager he'd treated her as though she were some precious being to be handled with care, given every courtesy. Like a princess...

Well, she was little more than a beggar maid now, and what's more, she never wanted to be viewed as a princess again. She resumed walking, happy with the clothes she'd bought. No artifice about them. No stylish elegance. Now that she was free of Gary, she was going to be a person, not a clothes horse to be shown off as a man's possession.

Ric caught sight of her and snapped upright, ready to move. Action man, she thought with almost giddy joy, still amazed at how he had so personally effected her escape, even to flying her away in a private plane. Though they hadn't yet arrived at their final destination, she hastily reminded herself. Even so, she no longer cared where it was or what it was. Ric said it would be safe there and she believed him.

She believed him even more as they approached the landing strip at Gundamurra. The Australian expression—*out the back of Bourke*—took on real meaning as she gazed down at a vast flat landscape, seemingly endless inland plains, far from civilisation.

'How big is Gundamurra?' she asked.

'A hundred and sixty thousand acres,' came the mind-boggling reply. 'Patrick runs forty thousand sheep on it.'

Lara did the maths. 'You mean each sheep gets four acres to itself?'

He nodded. 'The feed can get very sparse out here.'

'How does Patrick get around such a huge property?'

'Plane, truck, horse, motorbike. Depends on what has to be done.'

'The buildings...it looks like a little village down there.'

'Homestead, overseer's house, jackeroos' quarters, the mess and the cook's house, shearing shed, maintenance sheds, station office, school. There's usually a staff of twelve. With families, there are about thirty people living on the station. You'll have ready company, though not what you're used to, and it is isolated. Mail comes and goes once a week. By plane.'

Like an island, sufficient unto itself, she thought, except it was surrounded by land, not water. 'What brought you to Gundamurra, Ric?' How had he even heard of it?

He shrugged. 'When I was convicted of stealing the Porsche, the judge gave me a choice—time in a juvenile detention centre or working on an Outback station.'

So that was what had happened to him!

'Patrick had set up the work program as an alternative for kids who

were prepared to give it a go,' Ric went on. 'At our first meeting he told
us that Gundamurra meant "Good day" in the Aboriginal language, and
he hoped we would always remember our arrival there as a good day in
our lives.'

'And it was for you?'

'Very much so.'

She sighed in rueful memory of the night the police had caught them
in the Porsche. Ric had cleared her of any complicity in the theft and
her father... 'My parents shuttled me straight off to boarding school and
watched over me like a hawk after we were caught.'

He threw her a sardonic look. 'No more undesirable connections?'

'None without the *proper* connections,' she mocked right back. 'Every
school vacation I was taken to a fashionable resort, away from any chance
of meeting up with you. Or someone like you.'

'I did write to you from Gundamurra. Several letters.'

His voice was flat, non-judgmental, but she sensed the deep disappointment he would have felt at no reply. 'I didn't receive them, Ric.'

'No. I guessed not.'

'I'm sorry. My parents must have kept them from me. Destroyed
them.'

'You were only fifteen, Lara,' he said wryly. 'I was no good for you
then.'

'Yes, you were.' The words came out with such fierce emphasis, it
drew a quizzical glance from him. 'I don't mean about the car,' she hastily explained, flustered by her own outburst. 'I really liked being with
you, Ric.'

His mouth softened into a smile. His eyes softened, too...dark caressing velvet. 'I liked being with you, too,' he murmured, then switched his
gaze back to the dirt airstrip where he had to land the plane.

She lapsed into silence, shaken by the strength of feeling that had so
swiftly seized her. How could she *want* any man after her experience with
Gary? Utter madness. Ric was her safe passage away from an abusive and
destructive marriage. Being grateful to him, appreciating the fantastic
effectiveness of his resources and the generosity behind his every act on
her behalf...that was warranted. But *wanting* him...?

No. She was emotionally overwrought, off-balance. More likely she
wanted to be cocooned by his protective strength. The clawing desire to

feel safe was attached to him. But she had to detach it now. They were landing at Gundamurra. It was to be her safe haven, not Ric Donato. Somehow she had to regain at least some sense of who she was before she could even consider forming any relationship at all.

Gary's superficial charm had wooed her into marriage. Her parents' overwhelming approval of the match had also had its influence. Immense wealth had promised security and all the good things in life. But all those shining promises had been false and she had swallowed them. What did that say about her?

Time to take stock.

And this place certainly gave her the opportunity to do it.

Focus on Patrick Maguire, she sternly told herself. He was the constant around which her life on Gundamurra would revolve. A father figure to Ric. Maybe a benevolent father figure to her, too. She could do with a lot of benevolence.

He was waiting for them, a big man—huge—a giant of a man, standing by a four-wheel drive Land Rover as Ric taxied the plane back down the runway. 'Is he expecting me? Have you told him?' Lara suddenly thought to ask, the reality of actually being here rushing in on her, putting her nerves on edge.

'Yes. While you were shopping.' He gave her a reassuring smile. 'It's okay, Lara. You're welcome.'

She took a deep, calming breath. Ric had taken care of it, just as he'd taken care of everything else. She realised her mind had been in a fog of unreality all the way from Vaucluse to Bourke, not quite believing in what was happening, more letting it happen, taking the ride—any ride, as long as it was away from Gary.

Now she had to think, to act on her own behalf, to hopefully make a good impression on the man who was granting her space in his home until she could legally free herself from her disastrous marriage—a man whose protection she could count on, Ric had said—protection given to a woman he didn't even know. It was a gift she hadn't done anything to deserve. Maybe she could do some useful work here, at least earn it.

Her mind was a whirl of wild anxiety again by the time she and Ric emerged from the plane, both of them carrying her shopping bags. Did it look as though she'd bought too much? Been too extravagant? She was horribly conscious of the designer outfit she was wearing, wishing she'd thought to change into the more appropriate clothes in the bags.

Patrick Maguire lifted the hatch at the back of the Land Rover so they could load the bags straight into the vehicle. 'Lara had to leave with nothing. We bought this stuff in Bourke,' Ric explained.

The old man nodded, making no comment. He had to be in his sixties or seventies, though he wore his age well. The shock of white hair was still thick. There were deep lines in his face, particularly the crow's feet at the corners of his eyes, but there wasn't much loose skin. Strong bones, sharply delineated, though well-fleshed. Nothing scrawny or weak about this man of the land. His eyes were a steely grey and Lara could feel her insides quailing under their patient observation.

Ric closed the hatch door and made a formal introduction. 'Lara, this is Patrick Maguire. Patrick, Lara Chappel.'

'You're very welcome, Lara,' he said in a deep quiet voice, offering his hand.

'Thank you for...for taking me in.'

A slight frown drew his brows together and she realised her sunglasses made eye contact with her impossible. Worried that he might think her rude, she whipped them off.

'Sorry. I didn't mean to...' Hot embarrassment flooded up her neck and burned her cheeks as his eyes narrowed at the damage the glasses had hidden. She grimaced. 'I'm a bit of a mess. Please forgive the glasses.' She shoved them back on in an agony of self-consciousness.

He gently squeezed her hand, imparting a comforting warmth. 'Don't worry about it, Lara. You'll mend,' he said simply.

'I don't want to be a free-loader, Patrick,' she rushed out. 'I'll do whatever I can to earn my keep here.'

He nodded, giving her the sense he approved, though his reply was a measured one. 'Time for that when you find your feet. No need for you to feel anxious.'

'I just think...it would be good to be busy with something.'

Again he nodded. 'We'll talk about it after you've settled in. Okay?'

'Yes,' she quickly agreed, not wanting to seem demanding. This was such unfamiliar territory, she didn't know how to act.

Patrick released her hand, but he didn't move to usher her into his vehicle. He regarded them both with a distinct air of challenge, then stated, 'You should both know there have already been aggressive moves made to find you.'

Tension screamed through Lara. *Aggressive* meant…she could feel the blood starting to drain from her face, beads of sweat breaking out on her forehead as fear clamped its chilling grip on her heart.

'How do you know?' Ric asked.

'Mitch called earlier this afternoon, asking me if I'd heard from you. I hadn't and told him so.'

'Mitch…' Lara clutched at the name, trying to steady herself. 'The barrister Ric knows?'

Patrick nodded.

'Why would he call here?' Ric asked sharply.

'He wanted to make contact with you and thought you might be heading to Gundamurra. He said no more at that point. After your call from Bourke, I realised there had to be trouble—maybe at your Sydney office—so I got in touch with Mitch and discussed the situation with him.'

'Oh God!' Lara groaned, turning anguished eyes to the man who'd put himself at risk for her. 'I did tell you. Gary won't let go, Ric. He's… he's…'

'I know what he is,' he flashed at her, his gaze returning to Patrick. 'What trouble?'

'No, you don't know,' she cried, plucking at his arm in frantic urgency. 'You haven't lived with him. I haven't told you. It won't stop, Ric. He'll go after you if he can't get at me. I shouldn't have let you do this. I shouldn't have…' She shook her head, realising she'd blinded herself to consequences for Ric in her need to believe escape was possible. 'I have to go back.'

'No!'

It was a violent negative, and she ached to give in to it, hide behind him as long as she could, but it wasn't fair. 'I don't want you to suffer because of me,' she shot back at him just as violently. 'It's all my fault for…for being such a fool to marry Gary in the first place.'

His dark eyes burned with the unshakeable purpose he'd shown before. 'I won't let you be his victim again, Lara.'

'You don't understand. He'll victimise you and your people. If he's already been to your office…'

'Kathryn must have gone to Mitch.' His gaze jerked back to Patrick. 'How was it handled?'

'Kathryn kept the situation contained. That will probably last until tomorrow. But to keep Lara safely hidden here, you'll have to leave, Ric, lay a trail elsewhere and let yourself be the target for pursuit.'

'No...no...' Lara protested, tortured by the trouble she was causing him.

Patrick kept on speaking, punching out the current problem. 'That will give Kathryn a legitimate line for her to take, to halt any further harassment at the Sydney office. Mitch will call tonight. He wants to speak to both of you. I'm telling you this now to give you time to prepare for what's coming.'

'It's not right,' she pleaded with Patrick, wanting him to see how wrong it was. 'I got myself into this.'

'Lara...' The steely grey eyes locked onto hers and while she saw compassion for her anguish, they also reflected the same steadfast purpose in Ric's. 'There is no going back,' he stated quietly. 'Ric has chosen his course. And I agree with it.'

'But... I didn't mean to...to...'

He smiled at her, and it was like a warm blanket of approval enfolding her, welcoming her into his world. 'You're a woman who cares for others. Which is right and good. But understand there are times when a man must act according to his sense of rightness. In the end, we all have to live with ourselves.'

Even the chaotic mess in her mind cleared enough to recognise the truth he had spoken.

It was an inarguable argument.

The decision was made.

Come what might, there was no going back.

# CHAPTER FIVE

HAVING SEEN LARA to the guest suite Patrick had designated—there were four of them in the huge homestead which had been built to house the Maguire family and provide hospitality to any visitors—Ric left her to settle in and refresh herself before dinner.

Patrick had told her she was welcome to borrow any clothes from his daughters' rooms, if she found herself short of anything. They wouldn't mind. All three of them were pursuing careers elsewhere but they came home from time to time to check on Dad. Their mother had died from cancer a few years ago.

This information had been affably offered as they drove up from the airstrip, along with a quick, potted history of Gundamurra. Its obvious purpose had been to allay any fears Lara had about accepting a virtual stranger's hospitality. But there were other fears to be dealt with and Ric drove straight to the point when he joined Patrick in the sitting room.

'You were testing her.'

It was a flat statement, not open to question, and Ric searched the old man's eyes for the reasons why he had revealed what he had at the airstrip instead of waiting for a private man-to-man talk.

'It's been eighteen years. A youthful fixation might have impaired your judgment. I wanted to know if she was worth what bringing her here will cost you.'

'It's not a matter of price to me.'

'I know that, Ric. But you're not the only one involved in this now and I had to feel right about it.'

'Do you?'

'Yes. There was a chance she was just using you for her own ends. I remember your letters were never answered.'

'She never got them. Her parents...' He waved a dismissal of that issue. It was far in the past. It was the present and future that concerned him. 'Give me the details of what Mitch told you.'

'Apparently Gary Chappel stormed into your office during the lunch hour, demanding to know where you were. No one could tell him. He waited for Kathryn to return from her meeting. She told him you had a lunch date with an old friend and didn't know when or if you'd return to the office. He said your car was in the basement parking area. She said you had probably walked to the restaurant. He insisted on being given the name of the restaurant and she saw no harm in telling him. It got rid of him so she could contact Mitch for instructions.'

Ric nodded. 'That was my advice to her if Gary Chappel came to the office.'

'Mitch got the message during a court recess. He called her, got a run-down on what had happened, and immediately sent two of his people to escort Kathryn to the courtroom where he was arguing a case. When I last called, he was in his chambers and Kathryn was still with him.'

'Best I talk to him now then.'

Patrick nodded. 'Use my office.'

It worried Ric that Mitch had decided on protective measures for Kathryn. To his mind, the better course was for her to be innocently going about her work, as though nothing untoward had happened. Ric was not based in Sydney. He came. He went. He spent most of his time in London. To take Kathryn out of the office actually pinpointed her as knowing more than she had admitted. It put her under a constant threat which was not what Ric had intended.

The moment he heard Mitch's voice on the other end of the line, he spilled out his concern. 'Mitch, have you still got Kathryn with you?'

'Yes. She's right here.'

'Why? I thought I'd left her covered. Won't this excessive caution make her a target?'

A pause.

Ric's nerves screwed up to piano-wire tightness.

'My gut feeling is that Gary Chappel will make her one,' came the measured reply. 'We're not dealing with a reasonable guy, Ric. I've seen the photograph. You did right to take Lara out. I'm behind this action one hundred percent.'

'I'm glad you agree. But Kathryn shouldn't be in danger. This isn't her fight.'

'Any way you look at it she's a link to you.'

His stomach churned. 'Can you keep her safe?'

'That's what I'm doing. But I need your cooperation, Ric. And Lara's. Especially Lara's. I take it she wants a divorce.'

'Yes.'

'I need to speak to her. Get the legal paperwork going as fast as possible. But first, it's best you get out of the area, Ric.'

'Patrick has already passed on that advice.'

'Good! Fly to Brisbane or Cairns tomorrow. Don't come back to Sydney.'

He'd have to arrange for Johnny's plane to be flown back to Bankstown Airport since he couldn't do it himself. Shouldn't be a problem.

'Catch the first available flight out,' Mitch went on. 'At the last minute, notify your office where you're going so it can be passed on to anyone who asks. It will distract attention from Kathryn who'll be taking a sick day tomorrow.'

'But when it's discovered I travelled alone...'

'It gives me time to put wheels in motion, Ric. Trust me. I'll handle this end of it.'

Ric took a deep breath to ease the tightness in his chest. 'I doubt legal paperwork will stop him, Mitch.'

'It stops an accusation of abduction. He can't get the law onside with him.'

'But it doesn't remove the threat he poses.'

'As soon as I've spoken to Lara, I intend to courier a copy of the photograph to Gary Chappel's father with a message to contact me.'

The tactic momentarily blew Ric's mind. 'Blackmail?'

'A manoeuvre,' Mitch corrected him. 'He'll come with his lawyer.

We'll talk. Victor Chappel holds the reins of power in that family. If anyone can restrain his son, he's the man.'

'Counterthreats.' It might restore some balance to the situation, Ric thought hopefully.

'My reading is Victor Chappel will want to put a lid on this.'

'Will it work?'

'To a degree. My guess is it will move Gary into a covert operation. He'll be furious and his kind don't give up, Ric. You're going to have to watch your back. You took his wife from him.'

Ric frowned. Surely there would be an end to it one day. How long did fury last? He accepted having to go into exile, away from Lara, accepted he might be in danger for a while and he'd take steps to safeguard against it, but a lifelong vendetta? Only time would tell, he thought grimly. Meanwhile...

'What about Kathryn?'

'I think she'll be safe. I'll state the case very strongly to Victor Chappel that any further harassment of your office staff will have very public consequences.'

Ric breathed a huge sigh of relief.

'By this time tomorrow I should have things settled down at this end,' Mitch assured him.

'Thank you. I appreciate your help...more than I can say.'

Another pause. Mitch cleared his throat but his voice was uncharacteristically gruff when he spoke again. 'Patrick said...this is your Lara... from the old days.'

Ric closed his eyes, remembering how he'd talked about her in the bunkhouse at night. A boy's idyllic fantasy. Until the hard reality of getting no reply to his letters had straightened him up and forced him to face the truth that he could never be acceptable to her as he was.

Was he acceptable to her now? As more than just a white knight who had come to her rescue?

He shook his head. This wasn't the time to think about that.

'Yes. But that was a long time ago, Mitch,' he answered.

A heavy sigh. 'I would have told you about Gary Chappel if I'd known about her marrying him.'

'Told me what?'

'A guy like that doesn't change his attitude to women. It's not generally known but he has a history of abuse.'

Covered up, no doubt.

Ric felt his jaw clench. The power of wealth could hide a multitude of sins. But no power on earth was going to put Lara back in Gary Chappel's clutches. Over my dead body, Ric thought with a ferocity that tightened every muscle in his body to battle readiness.

'I'll do everything I can to contain him through legal means,' Mitch went on. 'You can count on that. I'm only sorry your Lara's caught in the middle of it.'

Ric managed to loosen his mouth enough to say, 'At least she's safe here.'

'Yes. And I'll keep Kathryn with me tonight.'

'What about her fiancé?

'He's in Melbourne on business.'

'Put Kathryn on for a moment, please Mitch.'

A pause while the receiver was handed over.

'I'm okay with all this, Ric,' she instantly assured him. 'And let me tell you I don't blame Lara Chappel for running. Her husband is one scary guy.'

'Promise me you'll do everything Mitch tells you, Kathryn. Take nothing for granted.'

'I will.'

'Good. And thank you again for your help. I'll be in contact once I reach L.A.'

'Take care.'

'You, too.'

She handed back to Mitch who immediately asked, 'Will Lara talk to me now?'

'Give me fifteen minutes. I'll call you back and put her on.'

Was Lara calm enough to give Mitch the information he needed? Time was clearly of the essence. Hoping she'd have the presence of mind to co-operate fully in telling Mitch all he needed to know, Ric strode around the veranda to the guest wing, hating the necessity to put her through this.

She'd already been through too much with her husband. Her fear of Chappel and what he could do was obviously based on experience that Ric could only guess at. *A history of abuse...* God only knew what that encompassed. Her white-faced panic over what Patrick had told them at the airstrip was sickening in itself. Was it even possible for her to think straight at this juncture?

He knocked on her door, knowing he had to persuade her to talk, yet inwardly recoiling from pressing her into it. He savagely wished he could have achieved her release from torment by himself, not involving others—just her and him—but that was as futile a dream as wishing for everything to be different. It wasn't. Never would be.

She opened the door and he just stood there, looking at her, unable to say a word, rendered speechless by a chaotic torrent of powerful emotions. *His Lara...*

She wore blue jeans and a blue and white checked shirt that still had the creases from its packaging. Despite the swollen and bruised eye and the years that had gone by, she looked fifteen—young, terribly vulnerable, and he desperately wanted to take her in his arms and promise that life would be good to her. She was safe with him. He would love her as she should be loved. Nothing to fear.

But she wasn't fifteen, and the years that separated them carried a weight he couldn't shift. Not yet. Perhaps not ever. One step at a time, he told himself.

'Mitch needs to talk to you now, Lara,' he stated bluntly, incapable of bringing any finesse to *this step*. Concentrating on action was the only way to hold his feelings at bay.

Her carriage stiffened, shoulders going back, chin up. 'I'm ready,' she said, clearly determined on doing whatever was asked of her to redress a situation that now endangered others.

He gestured for her to accompany him, intensely relieved that she had at least accepted they had moved beyond her going back to her husband. She stepped out of her room, closed the door and fell into step beside him.

'You've spoken to Mitch, Ric?' Tension in her voice.

'Yes.'

'Is Kathryn...safe?'

'Yes. She's with him.'

Her throat moved convulsively. She managed a ghost of a smile. 'I liked her. Is she...special to you?'

'As a business associate and a person, I value Kathryn very much but we've never had a private relationship. She's engaged to be married.' It suddenly seemed important to add, 'While I, on the other hand, have no romantic commitment to anyone.'

'Oh! I just...' She ducked her head, her long hair veiling the rush of heat into her cheeks. 'You seemed to have a good rapport with her.'

'I trained her to take the position she has in my business. It's given her a keen understanding of what I'm about.'

A nod. 'You're sure she's safe?'

The threat Gary posed was weighing heavily on her mind. Ric gave her a quick rundown of what Mitch had already done and intended to do.

'Victor doesn't want to know,' she said in bitter comment. 'Gary is his only son.'

'Believe me, Lara. Mitch is not going to allow Victor to turn a blind eye to what his son is.'

'I begged him for help. He wouldn't listen. He brushed off everything, saying it was between me and Gary to work out our...our *differences*.' There was a world of painful disillusionment in that last word. Helpless frustration, too.

'Tell Mitch,' Ric gently advised. 'It will be far more effective put in a legal context.'

Her hands started fretting at each other. 'I'll tell him, but...' An anguished glance at him. 'I'd rather speak to him alone.'

'I'll wait outside the office door. You can call me in if Mitch needs to speak to me again.'

Her breath shuddered out on a sigh of deep relief. 'Thank you.'

Shame. He knew it was an integral part of what she'd been through and nothing he said would take it away. Right now she couldn't bear him to hear the worst. Ric knew it would make no difference to what he felt about her but she wouldn't believe that yet. Nevertheless, she had to understand and appreciate the need for honesty.

They reached Patrick's office and he ushered her inside, saw her seated in the chair by the telephone. Before he picked up the receiver, he paused to emphasise the gravity of the situation. 'Lara, I know you're going to hate this, but you must give Mitch all the ammunition you can for him to go into battle. The photograph is good but if you can give him more...'

She nodded, her gaze evading his, the heat of humiliation still staining her cheeks. 'I won't hold back anything, Ric. I owe it...to all of you.'

'No.' He frowned at the responsibility she was loading onto herself.

'You owe it to yourself,' he said emphatically. 'The truth is what will set you free, Lara. And it's the best weapon you can give to Mitch to use on your behalf.'

She flashed him a look of flinty courage. 'I won't spare myself when so much is being done—being risked—for me. Call him, Ric. I'm ready.'

He got through to Mitch again and left Lara to it.

Outside the office, he paced up and down the veranda, needing to expend some of the violent energy stirred by thoughts of what she might have suffered at Gary Chappel's hands. His own hands kept clenching. It was just as well that Mitch was handling the Sydney end because Ric wasn't sure he could trust himself to act rationally if he was anywhere near the Chappels.

Best that he get himself right out of the way, and not just to separate himself from Lara and draw attention away from where she was.

She needed space from him, too.

Patrick would be better company for her. A father figure. Someone who didn't want any more from her than her own well-being. She'd grow confident again with Patrick, not feel ashamed. Able to be herself. No sense of having to measure up to a memory of what she was before Gary Chappel.

Yes. He could see he had to go. Yet it felt like hell, having to leave her. She didn't need him, he told himself. In fact, he might be harmful to the process of healing. No choice, anyway. No choice. He had to go.

The office door opened. He had no idea how much time had passed. Lara beckoned him. 'Mitch wants a further word with you, Ric.'

She looked pale, sick to her soul, but there was no trace of tears. He strode back into the office, picked up the receiver. 'Have you got what you need?' he rapped out, wanting this torment to be at an end for Lara.

'All except a fax with Lara's signature, appointing me her legal representative.'

'We'll do that now. Thanks for everything, Mitch.'

'Just leave it with me, Ric. Take care of yourself.'

'You, too.'

He switched on the office computer, then flicked an apologetic look at Lara. 'Almost done. I'll just type out what Mitch needs—authority to act on your behalf—you sign it and I'll fax it to him. Okay?'

She nodded.

It only took him a couple of minutes. Her hand was surprisingly steady as she wrote her name on the printed sheet. She stood with him, watching it go through the fax machine. Before Ric was aware of what he was doing, his arm was around her shoulders in a comforting hug. She didn't flinch from his touch. She actually leaned into him, much to Ric's relief...and a burst of private pleasure.

'It's over for you now,' he assured her.

She released a shuddering sign and rested her head wearily on his shoulder. 'It's the start of something else, Ric,' she said sadly. 'I'm worried for you, and everyone else this is touching.'

He rubbed his cheek over her hair, unable to resist the close contact, a surge of tenderness tempering the desire to feel a much more intimate bond with her. 'Don't worry on my account. I'm a survivor from way back.' Before temptation could get the better of him, he quickly added, 'We'd better join Patrick. No doubt he's kept dinner waiting for us.'

'Yes,' she agreed, lifting her head and giving him a wobbly smile. 'You're one of a kind, Ric Donato. Did you know that?'

He wanted to read more into her comment than there probably was. He'd rescued her. That made him special in her eyes. He disciplined himself into returning a reassuring smile. 'You'll find that Patrick is one of a kind, too. He'll be good for you, Lara. Be at ease with him.'

Her mouth tilted wryly. 'A pity I wasn't sent here with you all those years ago. A different life...'

'Don't look back. Look forward. Okay?'

'I'll try,' she promised.

He walked her to the door, casually dropping his arm from her shoulders as he opened it to usher her out. Giving comfort was one thing. Pressing it too far was something else. Yet as they walked around the veranda to the main body of the homestead, he reached out and took her hand, holding it as he had held it when they'd walked together a lifetime ago.

Her fingers fluttered for a moment, then settled, content to accept the feeling of friendly companionship. She'd been alone too long, Ric told himself. She needed to be connected to someone who cared about her.

He cared.

# CHAPTER SIX

LARA COULDN'T SLEEP. Her mind kept churning over the events of the day. She knew whatever happened now was out of her control, not that she'd had control of anything much for a long time, but that had only affected her. She worried about Ric—what Gary might do to damage him and his business.

Almost unlimited wealth gave the Chappel family an insidious power. A corrupt power. And she didn't believe his father could stop his one and only son from using it. Victor didn't keep close tabs on Gary. He might think a caution from him—even a command from him—would be respected, but Lara knew better. Gary would agree up front, and do what he wanted behind Victor's back.

If she couldn't be got at, Ric would certainly be the object of his fury. Ric, who hadn't counted the cost when he'd rescued her. Ric, who'd held her hand tonight but would be gone tomorrow, a moving target for Gary to focus on. If something bad happened to him—her mind shied away from the all too possible outcomes—how could she bear it?

He'd been so good to her.

More than that, she felt...if Ric went out of her life again, there would be a terrible black hole that nothing could ever fill. There *was* a bond between them. She'd felt it growing again all day, strengthening, tunneling deep into her soul. It wasn't that she'd been so dependent on his initiatives. It was Ric himself. The way he was. The way he was to her—knowing intuitively what she needed, giving her his support, caring at a deeper level than she'd ever known before.

Her marriage had been completely barren of such caring, like a desert that bred only emotional nightmares, no oasis in sight. She was supposed to be at peace here, but how could she be with Ric going into danger because of her?

Sitting across from him at dinner tonight, watching him, listening to him talk to Patrick, she'd kept seeing the boy she'd known in the man, marvelling at how much he'd grown from that time, yet eerily staying the same—the expressions on his face, how he moved his hands, the cadence of his voice, his respectful manner toward her. Ric Donato...

He was certainly no disappointment to the memory she had of him. Far from it. If only...

No. It was stupid, futile to indulge in *if onlys*. She was here at Gundamurra, where Ric had found direction for his adult life. And it was an amazing place, not at all the primitive lifestyle she had imagined. There was even house staff to cook and clean.

The homestead was huge, constructed with four wings that enclosed a courtyard which, incredibly, had a fountain in the middle of its green lawn, not to mention garden beds in bloom and pepper trees to give shade.

A screened veranda ran around all four sides of the quadrangle and the rooms themselves were very civilised, indeed. Well kept antiques graced the sitting and dining rooms, and even in this guest suite the chest of drawers and dresser were beautifully polished cedar pieces, and the patchwork quilt on the queen size bed was a work of considerable artistry.

It all projected a sense of solid old-time values that would outlast anything a more sophisticated world would declare *in* as *must haves* if one was to be up to date with modern fashion. The refurbishing of the Vaucluse mansion had been an exercise in creating the *right* image—all for show, nothing to do with setting up a home that actually felt like a home.

Cold rooms. Almost clinically perfect, but no personality in them. How could they be anything else when they were the work of interior decorators who were never going to live there? And, of course, Gary had been the one they'd consulted with, not her. She'd very quickly learnt not to change anything, not to offer any input. Best to smile and agree to everything.

But that was over now.

Look forward, not back, Ric had told her.

Except looking forward encompassed Ric's departure tomorrow and she was frightened of what that might lead to. If she was safe here, why couldn't he stay, too? Why did he have to put himself at risk? Or was that hopelessly selfish thinking, wanting him to be with her?

Her life could be put in limbo at Gundamurra, but Ric had an international business to run, other people depending on him. It would be totally unfair of her to beg him to stay. He'd done more than enough for her. Yet if she lost him again...

Footsteps were coming along the veranda outside her suite. It had to be Ric. He'd be sleeping in this wing, too. After dinner, Patrick had suggested she retire, noting how tired and strained she looked. True enough, but she'd guessed the two men had much to say to each other in private so she'd left them to it, though she would have preferred their company to her own.

She did feel washed out physically. Mentally and emotionally, too. But her mind couldn't be shut down. Maybe it would some time in the night...and if she was still asleep when Ric left in the morning...

*Ric was going by now...*

She hurtled out of bed and raced to the door which opened onto the veranda, her heart pumping with an urgency that couldn't be denied. The footsteps had already gone past and when she stepped out she could only see the back of him walking away from her, a shadowy figure in the darkness—too shadowy when she desperately wanted the reality of him.

'Ric!'

He stopped. It seemed an aeon before he turned, making her wonder if she'd mistaken someone else for him. Riven with doubts, she shrank back against the doorway, acutely conscious of not having paused to put on the dressing gown she'd bought. While the cotton pyjamas were a decent enough covering, they were no armour for confronting a man in the middle of the night.

Her rioting nerves were somewhat soothed as she caught the silhouette of his profile. It *was* Ric, looking back at her, half turning, holding his distance but at least acknowledging her call.

'Do you need something, Lara?' he asked quietly.

*You. I need you.*

The words pounded through her mind.

She couldn't say them.

They asked too much.

She simply stood there staring at him, barely able to contain the turbulent yearning that pressed her to run to him, fling her arms around him, never let him go. Maybe the power of it tugged at him. After a pause that screamed for answers he slowly retraced his steps toward her, coming to a halt an arm's length away, looking at her with what felt like a fierce concentration of energy.

'Are you having trouble sleeping? Would you like me to...?'

'No. I mean yes...I can't sleep,' she gabbled.

'I doubt Patrick keeps sleeping pills in the medical kit. Perhaps a drink of hot chocolate...'

'No...no... I just...' She took a deep breath, trying to pull herself together, be reasonable.

'Are you frightened, Lara?' he asked softly.

The words burst from her before she could stop them. 'Will you hold me? For just this one night, Ric. Will you hold me?'

The raw plea *was* a cry of fear—fear that she might never have any more of him than this—fear that Gary might take Ric from her, too, along with everything else he had taken from her—fear that her life would always be dominated by the loss of what should have been.

She saw Ric's chest expand as he sucked in a deep breath. Her senses registered a harnessing of strength but she was too chaotically needful to discern if it was meant for giving or rejecting. She could only wait and hope, every nerve in her body tense with a desperation that craved the caring he had shown her.

'Lara...' Was that the sound of longing, too, borne on his gruff whisper? But he didn't move. He didn't reach out to her.

'Please...?' she begged, fighting the restraint her instincts were picking up. She plunged on with wild argument, her hands fluttering, reaching out to him in frantic appeal. 'It mightn't be sensible. It might be mad. But you'll be gone tomorrow and I...'

Ric couldn't stop himself. His feet responded before his brain even attempted to countermand them, stepping forward of their own accord, and his arms scooped her into his embrace, precluding any other course of action. Her soft, slender body sagged against his and her arms lifted to wind around his neck, locking him into holding her.

It was the strangeness of being in an alien environment, he told himself, feeling alone and frightened of what the future held for her. She needed comfort, reassurance. He was the only familiar person for her to hang on to. She wasn't asking for any sign of the flood of passionate possessiveness that was surging through him, dragging at the vestiges of reason he was clinging to. He had no right to claim her as his. *No right...*

She nestled her face against his bare throat. He hoped she couldn't feel the wild beating of his pulse. Her breasts were pressed against his chest. He had to fight off the temptation to slide his arms down and haul her closer, fitting her stomach and thighs to his, craving the feel of her entire femininity, the essence of what had always made her desirable to him.

He felt his own body stirring and spoke quickly to distract himself from the sexual arousal she couldn't want from him. 'You will be safe here, Lara. I promise you,' he said emphatically.

'I wish you could stay with me.'

The yearning murmur struck chords in him that threatened to overwhelm all common sense. The warmth of her mouth moving against his skin shot an insidiously exciting heat through his bloodstream.

'I'll be back,' he assured her, his voice terse with the strain of having to exert intense control. 'It's just a matter of time.'

'Time...' She heaved a sigh that played havoc with his good intentions. 'So much of it has already gone by, Ric. Years...years of missing you,' she whispered.

He sucked in a quick breath, desperate for a shot of oxygen to clear his brain of the wild exultation her words had triggered. She couldn't mean what she was saying. Surely she'd had a good life before she'd married Gary Chappel...a successful model, feted and admired...

'I don't want to lose you again,' she went on, her voice a throb of fierce passion, whipping up the desire that had to be contained.

'You don't have to worry. It will all work out,' he assured her, then driven to take some diversionary action, he moved her to his side, intent on walking her back into her room. 'Come on. When you wake up tomorrow, you'll feel like a free woman.'

He got her inside, meaning to tuck her into bed, sit with her for a while, but she stopped before they reached the bed, turning to him with a frantic rush of words. 'What if he takes you, too? He's taken so much from me. If he gets to you, Ric...do you think I could ever feel free?'

Was it simply fear for him, driving this violent emotion? He rested his hands on her shoulders, gently kneading the tense muscles there. 'Lara...it's best that I go.'

He saw the glitter of tears in her eyes. 'I can't bear it,' she cried and threw herself at him, wrapping her arms around his waist.

She was so close, it felt as though her heart was thumping against his. He couldn't think, didn't want to think. His hands traced the curve of her spine, the pit of her back, touching all he could allow himself to touch. His face buried itself in her silky hair, rubbing, kissing, breathing it in.

This was Lara...not a figment of his imagination but flesh and blood reality, setting him on fire for what he had missed over the years. He filled his senses with her, hoarding it all in his memory, craving more yet afraid of taking more than he should in this time and place.

As it was, there was no quelling the erection that telegraphed the desire he'd tried to hide. He expected her to ease away from him, expected a rush of mutual embarrassment that he'd somehow have to handle with some finesse, excusing it on some specious grounds that he'd have to bend his mind to. Soon...when she shifted...when it didn't feel right to her...

But she hung on so hard, it seemed she'd burrow right into him if she could, as though his warmth and strength was the elixir of life to her. She had to know he was reacting to it, reacting as a man, not as a chivalrous white knight whose only wish was to help. He was a man, burning to take her as his woman.

Her head lifted.

He didn't want to look her in the eye, didn't want her to see...

'Kiss me, Ric.'

His gaze sliced to hers, disbelief and rampant desire in instant battle. Had he misheard the soft whisper that echoed the deep ache in him?

'Please?' she pressed, her face tilted to his in open invitation. 'Kiss me like you did when we knew nothing else. Wipe out all the rest. Please?'

The memory came sharp and clear, banishing any resistance he might have mustered. His head bent to hers, the compulsion to recapture what had been lost directing the kiss he gave her, a gentle grazing of his lips over hers, a soft, slow tasting that was strangely bittersweet because he was so acutely aware of her vulnerability, the damage that had been done to her.

Innocence was forever gone. He couldn't bring it back, yet her tremulous, tentative response, her compliance to his initiatives, the hint of eagerness to explore more...eighteen years fell away and the love he'd wanted to show her at sixteen poured into his kiss.

He didn't intend it to change into something else. Did she spur it on? Or was it the years of sexual experience urging him to take her on a deeper journey where passion flared and hungered for more and more satisfaction? One kiss wasn't enough. One kiss incited an exhilarating ardour for more. And more.

She was travelling with him, her whole body telling him this was what she wanted too, her mouth barely leaving his for breath, intensely giving, her hands raking down his back, pulling him into her, her stomach rubbing against his erection as though wantonly stroking it, savouring his desire for her, revelling in it.

A crazy triumph was bubbling through his mind. Lara *was* his. She was giving herself to him. The sheer power of their need for each other made it right...didn't it? It had to. His body was screaming for the ultimate satisfaction of bonding intimately with hers. He moved them toward the bed, his hands sliding under the elastic waistband of her pyjama pants, getting ready to...

A bolt of sanity hit him, shocking him into an abrupt halt.

'Don't stop, Ric. Please?'

The feverish pleading seduced all reason for a moment...but he'd pledged her safety and to keep on going without...

'Lara...' Anguish writhed through him. 'I don't have any protection with me. We must stop.'

# CHAPTER SEVEN

*PROTECTION?*

Bubbles of hysteria fizzed through Lara's brain. There'd been no protection from Gary's loveless demands on her, and Ric was stopping because he was worried about getting her pregnant? If it was going to happen, it would have happened last night so what difference did it make?

The only difference—the huge difference—was she wanted this with Ric...wanted it with every atom of her being. This was how it should be...what she was feeling with him...and if she didn't have it now...

'It's all right. I'm on the pill,' she rushed out in reckless disregard for whether it would provide effective protection or not. Why should she let Ric care about it when Gary...

No, she wouldn't let herself think about last night.

This was tonight.

And she wanted her mind filled with Ric and the incredibly wonderful sensations of being loved instead of brutally used. She wanted to feel *his* hands moving over her again, caring hands, exciting sensual hands that knew how to caress, not hurt. And his mouth, kissing her with the heat of real passion—passion she could happily glory in because it felt so marvellous.

'I don't want to hurt you,' he said, his voice edged with strain. 'I'm sorry. I wasn't thinking...'

'You won't hurt me.' She believed that implicitly. It wasn't in him to hurt.

He shook his head, frowning more concern. 'If you have other bruising, Lara...'

'No. I stopped fighting,' she cried, desperate for his understanding. 'It was better not to fight. Oh God!' Her hands lifted in a desperate plea. 'Don't remind me. Don't let him come between us. Not between *us*. He always wins.'

But not this time. A feverish determination overrode the panic welling up. She had to stop Ric's retreat from her. Gary was not going to win tonight. Not tonight.

Her hands were trembling as she reached for the buttons on Ric's shirt, wildly intent on forcing another start to what had to be finished, her fingers fumbling but acting fast and obsessively focused. His tautly muscled chest rose and fell as she dragged the opening apart, then stood staring at what she'd laid bare, scarcely believing she'd been so bold.

He wasn't smooth-skinned like Gary. A nest of tight black curls arced between his nipples and arrowed down to the waistband of his trousers. Somehow it made him more elementally male—very different—not polished and sophisticated. A real man. A true man. The kind of man who protected his woman.

Except she didn't want to be protected from knowing all of Ric Donato. Did he understand now? Stunned by what she had already done, Lara was in a weird state of paralysis, still hanging on to the edges of Ric's shirt. It was an enormous relief when his hands covered hers, loosening their grip, carrying them down to her sides.

But did this mean he was about to step away?

Leave her?

She looked up in agonised protest. His face looked hard, tightly drawn, and his eyes glittered, as though ablaze from some inner fire.

'Are you sure about this, Lara?'

Firm command in his voice. Unshakable control.

He was giving her the choice, insisting she have it. Not like Gary. Not one bit like Gary. A leaden weight lifted from her heart. The tight ache in her chest eased. This wasn't rejection. It was a gift being offered and a wave of intense relief washed over the frantic worry that he saw something wrong in her...too wrong for him to get more deeply involved.

'I *am* sure,' she cried. No pause to reconsider. 'I want you, Ric. I need you.'

Doubts raged through his mind but denying her at this point was impossible. Need, desire, whatever it was for her...he could only hope it was right to go on, that it wouldn't turn out to be terribly wrong afterward.

He lifted her hands, pressed their palms against his bared chest, felt his heart hammering as though it wanted to break free of its cage of flesh and be held by her. He fiercely cautioned himself to move slowly, give her the chance to call a halt. The violence of his own need had to be contained, channelled into giving Lara as much pleasure as he could—pleasure to blot out whatever she had endured at her husband's hands.

He had to leave her with a good memory—one that gave her hope for the future—one that taught her all men were not the same as the bastard she'd married. She was asking this of him tonight, not somewhere down the track. Ric was acutely aware of the risk that he might simply be a turning point for her, yet if it was more than that...if she had missed him down the years...

It could be right.

He wanted it to be right.

He needed it to be right.

Without any haste, he undid the buttons on her pyjama top and drew it slowly over her shoulders, down her upper arms. She slid her hands down his chest, dropping them to let the garment fall to the floor. She stood absolutely motionless, tense with anticipation—or was it fear?—waiting to see how he would touch her.

Ric discarded his own shirt, making them equal, sharing the same amount of nakedness, the same vulnerability. Yet it wasn't the same because he was a man with a man's superior strength and that was all too obvious. He took her hands again, his fingers gently stroking reassurance, intertwining with hers. He felt her relaxing, looking at him with trust.

It was all right.

She wasn't afraid of him.

He caressed her arms with a feather-light touch, loving the satin smoothness of her skin. It gleamed with a pearly sheen in the darkness which no longer seemed so dark. He could see her quite clearly, the feminine slope of her shoulders, her long graceful neck, the proud thrust of her breasts.

He traced the curves of them, learning their shape, revelling in the freedom to do it, filling his hands with her beautiful softness, his thumbs tenderly grazing over her nipples, arousing an alluring tautness.

Her breathing quickened but she didn't stop him. In fact, she reached out, tentatively touching him, surprising him further with a husky plea. 'I want to see you, too, Ric. Know all of you.'

He was happy to oblige, removing the rest of his clothes, then her pyjama pants, gliding his fingertips back over her calves, behind her knees, up her thighs, feeling her quiver under his touch but not flinching away from it. He cupped the more voluptuous curves of her bottom and drew her into full body contact with him.

She came willingly, once more winding her arms around his neck, lifting her face to be kissed, and as he rained tender kisses around her temples, on her cheeks, nose, mouth, she swayed against him in a kind of shy, experimental manner, not deliberately sensual yet it was incredibly tantalising, stoking the desire he was battling to contain.

His passion for her flared again, whipping into urgency. It was difficult to think beyond the need surging through him. Yet he had to know she was ready, too, not just exploring how it felt with him. He moved them to the bed, lifting her onto it, sliding down beside her to avoid the most tempting contact.

He kissed her breasts as he slid his hand down to the apex of her thighs, stroking to see if she would open to him. No resistance. No reluctance. She welcomed his touch with a moist heat that drove his excitement higher.

Her fingers were scrabbling through his hair, tugging, pressing, and he moved to her erratic rhythm, drawing her nipples deep into his mouth, applying suction, releasing it. Her back arched up to him. She was breathing in quick little gasps.

He shifted his body, trailing kisses down her stomach, positioning himself between her legs, moving his mouth to the centre of her sexuality, wanting to deliver maximum excitement, using all the sexual expertise he had learnt over the years, needing to show her what she should feel, gently pushing her to the pinnacle of ultimate pleasure.

She moaned, arched higher, her inner muscles convulsing against the caress of his fingers as he worked what he knew was blissful magic—enthralling, ecstatic ripples of sensation that seized every bit of consciousness, honing it toward the only possible end, the climax of all a man and woman could feel together.

'Enough...enough...please... I want *you*, Ric.'

Her hands plucking at his shoulders, needing to drag him up, have him inside her. He didn't have to think anymore, didn't have to hold back. He surged forward, entering her with a swift plunge as he covered her wildly arcing body, exulting in her moan of satisfaction as she felt the full power of himself going deep, answering the sweet ache, releasing the built-up tension.

Having reached the innermost heart of her, he covered her mouth with his, kissing gently, asking the question, needing her response to be positive because he'd gone past the point of no return. Her tongue tangled with his in a slow wondrous dance, almost as though she was awed by the connection.

It was enough.

More than enough.

It was incredibly exhilarating feeling her body moving to match the rhythm of his, her legs goading him faster, giving herself entirely to the intensity of their union. To Ric it was the most powerfully moving act of his life—joining so intimately with Lara, feeling her welcoming him, wanting this with all her being, just as he did.

Aware she had already climaxed, Ric still held off his own as long as he could, revelling in the sensation of Lara giving herself to him with a totality that fulfilled every dream he'd ever had about her—a memory to cherish while he had to be away from her. When the tension inside him finally burst into release, Ric was riding the high of his life, and once it was over and he gathered Lara into his arms, holding her to his heart, he knew what happiness was.

Having this woman.

Holding her.

Loving her.

And feeling her love for him.

# CHAPTER EIGHT

A LOUD DRONING sound penetrated Lara's slumber and snapped her awake.

The plane!

Ric...gone from beside her...flying away!

She leapt out of bed, realised she was naked, grabbed the dressing-gown from the chair in front of the dresser, thrust her arms into its sleeves as fast as she could, and wrapped it around her as she rushed to the door that led onto the veranda.

Too late to say goodbye. The plane would already be in the sky now. But she wanted to see it, if only to feel Ric was safe in the pilot's seat and the flight was going smoothly. She just caught a glimpse of it passing overhead. Then it was gone beyond the roof of the homestead and all she could do was listen until the sound of it was gone, too.

'Safe journey, Ric,' she murmured, willing him to get beyond Gary's reach as fast as possible and remain safe.

A sad deflation hit her as she walked back into her room. It was impossible to project how long it would be before she saw Ric again. *If* she saw him again. Her heart cringed at that thought. He'd said he would come back. She had to believe he would because she was in a helpless position to change any of the circumstances for him or anyone else. Everything to do with Gary was out of her hands.

Much stronger hands than hers were dealing with it now, she told herself, but she was still frightened for Ric, despite all his reassurances. He'd been so good to her, good in every way, and she was fiercely glad she had the memory of how it had been with him—the loving of a man who knew how to love, making her feel beautiful and precious, intensely cherished and cared for.

Her gaze fell on the indentation left by his head on the pillow beside hers. She crawled across the bed and buried her face in it, wanting to breathe in whatever scent of him was left behind. She closed her eyes and concentrated on remembering all the pleasure he'd given her from the lightest tingling touch to the final crescendo of incredible sensation that had tipped her into a sea of ecstasy.

How long had she floated there in blissful contentment while Ric had simply held her? It had seemed like time itself had stopped and they were in a world of their own, complete unto itself. She remembered listening to his heartbeat, stroking *his* body with a sense of awe, wanting him to feel how he had made her feel—incredibly special—because he was.

She wished she'd told him that.

Somehow last night the feeling of sharing something totally overwhelming had been so strong, so deep, words had seemed trivial, useless for expressing what had gone beyond anything that could be described. The silent, physical communication had seemed more right—just being together.

Had Ric understood?

Should she have said something?

*Thank you* were the only words she had spoken. And his mouth and eyes had smiled. No other reply. None necessary. He'd given what she'd asked of him. He was happy she was satisfied. And she didn't have to be told the pleasure had been mutual.

So it had all been good.

No regrets on either side.

She sighed and rolled over, knowing she had to face this day—without Ric—and take whatever steps she could toward making a different life for herself.

*I won't let you down, Ric,* she silently promised. *No matter what happens, I will become a better, stronger person because of what you've done for me.*

Having made this resolution, Lara got up and moved purposefully to the ensuite bathroom. A clean start, she thought. As clean as she could make it. No looking back.

Half an hour later she was showered, dressed, hair brushed, a touch of make-up applied to diminish the discolouration around her eye which was much less swollen this morning, rooms tidied and bed made. She walked around the veranda to the main body of the house and found her way to the kitchen, a huge utility room where three women were busy rolling out pastry on marble slabs and the smell of freshly baked bread instantly whetted her appetite.

The women—all of them part Aboriginal—stopped chatting when they saw her. Lara smiled and said, 'Hi!' but they just stared back until Evelyn, the housekeeper, whom she'd met last night, took charge of introductions.

'You're looking a lot better this morning, Miss Lara,' she said approvingly. 'These are my helpers, Brenda and Gail.'

'We're making pies for the men,' Brenda declared, a young curly-haired woman, probably in her twenties, merry brown eyes.

'Lamb and potato,' Gail added. She was about the same age, darker skinned, rather wildly dyed red hair, and a grin that beamed an attitude of finding fun in everything. 'I told Mister Ric he was missing out by going so early.'

'He had a good breakfast before he flew off,' Evelyn stated firmly as though Lara needed to be assured of it. She was a big woman, her salt and pepper hair marking her as middle-aged but wearing her years well, her plump good-humoured face relatively unlined. 'Now what about you, Miss Lara? There's still some pancake mix or I could cook you some eggs. What would you like?'

'We've got plenty of eggs from the chicken run,' Brenda added as she saw Lara hesitate.

All three faces looked at her, beaming an eagerness to please. It assured Lara they were happy to welcome her amongst them and she relaxed, warming to the cosy atmosphere in the kitchen. 'What I'd really like is a couple of slices of your fresh bread. It smells wonderful.'

They laughed, inviting her to sit at the big kitchen table while they worked around her. Two thick slabs of bread were cut. A tub of butter and jars of honey, vegemite and fruit conserve were laid out for her use. A pot of tea—her preference—was quickly produced.

Lara enjoyed her breakfast and the conversation which revolved around good-humoured answers to her questions about Gundamurra. She wasn't asked any questions about herself. It seemed her presence was simply accepted and the women were happily intent on drawing her into their community.

Their husbands worked on the station, carrying out maintenance and moving the sheep from paddock to paddock. Their children went to school here, lessons supervised by the overseer's wife and directed by radio from The School Of The Air. While the Paroo River ran through the property, most of the water used came from bores. There were beef cattle, as well as sheep, though they were more a sideline to the main business which revolved around stud rams and first class wool.

'Where is Mister Maguire this morning?' she asked, wondering when she would meet her host again.

'In his office,' Evelyn replied. 'I am to show you through the homestead before taking you to him. Make sure you know where everything is.'

'Thank you.' She smiled. 'I must say every room I've been in is beautifully kept, Evelyn.'

The housekeeper beamed with pleasure. 'Mrs. Maguire trained me herself,' she stated proudly. 'I am training the girls, just as she told me.'

'Well, you do a great job, Evelyn.' It was on the tip of Lara's tongue to offer her own help, but decided it was best if she speak to Patrick first in case she'd be treading on the toes of the domestic staff, butting in where she shouldn't be.

The tour of the homestead gave her a broader appreciation of how life was lived here. Adjacent to the large laundry was a mud room, stocked with raincoats, akubra hats and boots, clearly the first and last stop for those working outside. A bathroom completed the facilities for cleaning up before moving into the main body of the house.

'Have you had much rain?' Lara inquired.

'Many storms this time of year. Which is good. We need the rain. It's hard to keep everything going in times of drought.'

Lara had seen television coverage on the devastation of long periods of drought in pastoral Australia. It had evoked both horror and sympathy but the visuals had been so far removed from her own life, the feelings had been only momentary. It would undoubtedly have more impact on her now she had entered this different world.

Though it was certainly not without many civilised amenities. The billiard room was also a library and music room, open for use to anyone on the station. Walls of shelves contained an amazing selection of fiction and non-fiction books, videos and CDs. A generator supplied electricity and a satellite disk gave them television and internet facilities.

'Mr. Johnny bought us the hi-fi system,' Evelyn informed her, grinning as she added, 'So we can play his music.'

'Johnny who?' Ric's friend who owned the plane?

Evelyn looked surprised. 'You don't know him? Johnny Ellis? He's a very famous country and western singer.' Then she laughed. 'They call him Johnny Charm. And he is.'

'Oh, yes! I've never met him but I do know of him.'

In fact, Johnny Ellis was really big on the country and western scene, having made a huge hit in America with his songs. He was also something of a pin-up boy—a gorgeous hunk, while still exuding a very earthy hometown charm.

'Long time ago he and Mr. Ric were at Gundamurra together,' Evelyn ran on. 'Two of Mr. Patrick's boys. Now they are both famous. Mr. Johnny comes back here a lot. He says we are his inspiration.'

Hence the plane, Lara thought. And Johnny Ellis must also have been convicted of something criminal when he was a teenager, and given the same choice as Ric—*two of Mr. Patrick's boys.* Lara wondered how many of them there had been over the years, how many had made good after being here. *I'll make good, too,* she promised herself.

The one other room which fascinated her was the sewing room. 'Mrs. Maguire made everything here,' Evelyn explained. 'The curtains and cushion covers and patchwork quilts. Tablecloths and serviettes, too. Dresses for the girls. She loved making up patterns.'

There were bolts of fabric stacked against the wall, boxes galore containing samples of materials. The whole room was set up very professionally with a central table for cutting out, good lighting, shelves of cotton reels in every shade of colour, a range of scissors.

'Do any of her daughters sew?' Lara asked.

'Not much. Only to fix things. The oldest one, Miss Jessie, has just become a doctor. She wants to work for The Royal Doctor Flying Service. Miss Emily is a helicopter pilot and does mustering up north. Always loved flying. The youngest one, Miss Megan, is studying at an agricultural college. I think she aims to take over from Mister Patrick and run Gundamurra.'

A woman...running this vast sheep station?

Why not?

Lara berated herself for her own limited thinking. Clearly Patrick Maguire's daughters were all determined achievers. She herself had never nurtured any ambition. Modelling had more or less happened to her. At seventeen she'd been *spotted* at a pop concert, approached by an agent for a model company and very quickly promoted into the international scene, much to the delight of her mother who had pushed the career with so much pride and enthusiasm, Lara hadn't considered anything else.

By the time she'd met Gary she had tired of the scene, the constant travelling, the long exhausting photographic sessions, the sense of always being on show, the clothes that were more bizarre display pieces than actually wearable in real life. Everything was a performance and she'd yearned to feel more grounded.

Getting married and having a family had felt the right step to take. Maybe working in a kind of dream factory had seriously impaired her judgment. Certainly the dream husband had set about crushing her illusions very quickly and becoming a part of *his* family had shown her that having babies was not the answer to anything.

She needed to do something productive with her own life, not just reflect or enhance what others did or wanted for themselves. All she'd been was a show pony. There was no sense of self-worth in that. Ric had given her the time and space to sort herself out while she was here, and this purpose was very much on her mind when Evelyn finally ushered her into Patrick's office.

He gave her a benevolent smile and invited her to sit down—this man who'd fathered three daughters now carving out their own paths in life—who'd been the father figure to boys who'd gone off the rails, setting them on their feet to go forward with confidence in their abilities to make something positive of their future. She saw kindness in his eyes, but knew there was a lot more than kindness in this man's makeup. He had to have a very shrewd knowledge of human nature and how it could be best put to work.

'You look better this morning,' he started.

*Less beaten,* she thought, determined on rising from the wretched ashes of her marriage to Gary Chappel. 'I won't let Ric down,' she said firmly.

Patrick frowned, gesturing a dismissal of her reply. 'I understand you're grateful to Ric, but Lara...don't hang what you do here on him. Ric wouldn't want you to measure this time by what he or anyone else might expect of you. It's your time. Make it belong to you, doing what you want because *you* want it.'

The slow, serious words struck a realisation that she'd spent far too many years pleasing others, firstly in a desire for their approval, then because if she didn't please, it meant getting hurt.

Clearly, Patrick Maguire was very different to her own father who'd had the habit of laying down the law with dictatorial impatience for any argument whatsoever. He'd never *listened* to her. She suspected he'd approved her modelling career and marriage because in his view, women were meant to look beautiful and marry well. Full stop. They weren't supposed to think or quarrel with the men who were in charge of them.

Even though he was paralysed by a stroke and cared for in a nursing home, her mother was still subservient to him. Her reply to everything Lara had told her was, 'Your father wouldn't have wanted...'

*Always your father...your father...your father....*

Lara's cry, 'What about me?' had never been heeded.

Eyeing Patrick curiously, she asked, 'Is this what you tell the boys who've come here? To shed the influences that have led them into trouble?'

'That's quite a leap,' he said appreciatively, settling back in the big leather chair behind his working desk—a man who was comfortable with himself, not needing to impress, yet all the more impressive because of it. His eyes twinkled. 'What did Ric tell you about his time here?'

'Not much. He explained the program you ran as an alternative to spending time in a detention centre. And when he spoke of you it was with enormous respect and trust.'

He nodded, a musing little smile softening his expression. 'Some boys responded to the challenge. Others just put in their time. Ric, Johnny and Mitch were like the three musketeers, determined to fight their way out of where they were.'

'Mitch, too?' Lara looked her surprise and confusion. 'I didn't think anyone with a criminal record could go into law.'

'Mitch was a special case. He didn't defend himself at the time. There were extenuating circumstances that were eventually put before the court.'

'Through your connections?'

'Yes and no.' He shrugged. 'Because of my program here I was listened to, but the outcome of the hearing depended on what Mitch put forward himself.'

Not a backroom power play. Lara was relieved to hear it. She didn't want to think of Patrick Maguire doing the kind of deals she knew Victor and Gary did—bribing their way to the outcome they wanted. She needed to know Mitch Tyler was straight, too, not dependent on others' influence.

'Don't worry about Mitch, Lara.' Patrick's smile had a touch of whimsy in its tilt. 'Justice is a burning issue to him. Always was. One way or another, he'll checkmate Gary Chappel.'

Lara wondered if her thoughts were transparent. Not that it mattered. She had her answer. 'Has there been...any news...this morning?'

He shook his head. 'Maybe tonight.'

Lara hoped Kathryn was safe.

Patrick shifted, leaning forward, resting his arms on the desk, regarding her with lively curiosity. 'I've always asked each boy who chose to come to Gundamurra...what would he like to have that would add personal pleasure to his time here?' He paused a moment, then softly asked, 'Is there something you would like, Lara?'

She hadn't thought about her own personal pleasure for a very long time. Even last night with Ric, wanting him...it had all been focused on what he could *give* her, not what she could give herself. Apart from undoing his shirt buttons, she had been more passive than active...letting it happen to her. That seemed to be the story of her life.

'What did Ric choose?' she asked.

'A camera.'

'Johnny?'

'A guitar.'

'And Mitch?'

'A chess set.'

They had known what they wanted. Why didn't she? Was she just a blob to be directed by others, having no direction of her own?

'You don't have to answer straightaway, Lara,' Patrick said kindly. 'Think about it. Let me know when...'

'There is something I'd like to try,' she burst out, liking the idea as it had raced into her mind. 'Evelyn showed me the sewing room. She said no one uses what's there anymore...all the different fabrics and cottons. Maybe I could design and make things...if you wouldn't mind.' She flushed as she realised she might be treading on private ground.

'My wife would have been pleased to share her hobby with another woman,' he said with warm encouragement. 'Please feel free to use whatever's in the sewing room.'

'Thank you.'

'You're welcome.' He pushed up from his chair, rising to his full formidable height. 'Now let me walk you around the station...meet the other women...get your bearings.'

Yes, Lara thought, she needed to get her bearings very straight in her mind, not for her new environment so much as for her own life. No one ever really got a clean new slate, but this, she decided, was as good a chance as she was ever likely to have. It was up to her to make the most of it.

# CHAPTER NINE

FOR THREE LONG months Ric had been moving around—Los Angeles, New York, London—going about his business, being alert for any trouble. As far as he knew there was none, not even with his Sydney office where Kathryn was still operating without any further problems. To his mind, Mitch had successfully quashed any move by Gary Chappel to raise more hell for Lara or anyone connected to her.

It was safe for him to go home.

He'd take every precaution not to be followed to Gundamurra. He was sure he could do it without endangering Lara. The desire—the need—to be with her again, to assure himself that everything was fine between them, had been building to such a pitch, he could barely concentrate on anything else.

For the past few weeks he'd been feeling something was wrong. When he'd first set up the private Internet site for them to correspond with absolute safety, Lara's messages had been like a daily diary, nothing deeply personal but full of her activities and written in an enthusiastic vein. He'd been satisfied she wasn't fretting and was communicating in a natural open way that he found very reassuring.

More recently her messages had tapered off into flat little reports. Maybe it was simply that the newness of her life on an Outback station had worn off. It wasn't surprising or adventurous or exciting anymore. Yet he sensed a depression that worried him, spurring him to act.

Gundamurra might not be the right place for her. He could bring her to London, watch over her himself. There were dozens of alternatives. All he needed was her compliance and he'd take her anywhere.

The first step was to talk to her, face-to-face, and that meant flying home. He'd written his intention of visiting Gundamurra last night. Her reply had to come this morning. He didn't want to leave his Knightsbridge apartment until it did. Impossible to set his mind to working in his London office today.

He forced himself to have some breakfast then checked his home computer again.

Yes...a message.

Ric stared at the monitor screen, feeling his heart squeeze into a painfully tight ball as he read Lara's reply over and over again, desperately trying to interpret it differently to what it said only too plainly.

*It's better for me if you don't come, Ric.*

No explanation.

Just the one line.

And his knotted gut was telling him it was because he'd had sex with her and she didn't want to be reminded of it. Didn't want him thinking it could be on again. Didn't want the hassle of a confrontation about it.

Mistake.

Huge mistake.

And he couldn't undo it.

So what the hell was his next step?

Ric pushed himself away from the computer with its dead-end message, refusing to believe he had no future with Lara. The connection between them had been too real, too strong. There had to be a way over this barrier.

He paced around his apartment, burning off the negative energy that pressed in on him—the old defeatism that had kept him away from her in the past. He *was* good for her. She'd wanted him to make love. And she couldn't now think of it as a bad experience. It had been great for both of them. He couldn't be mistaken about that.

Perhaps she was now ashamed of having had that need at the time. Linking him to Gary. Having had months of freedom to sort out what she wanted, she might well have developed a desire to be free of attachment to any man—an easier life, not complicated by relationships where more could be expected of her than she was willing to give. The short reports might mean she'd been weaning herself off any sense of dependence on him, subtly letting him know that maintaining a rapport with him held less and less importance.

A phase of detachment was not unreasonable in the circumstances. It meant more waiting, patience on his part. On the other hand, surely she knew he wouldn't do anything to hurt her. So why block him out?

*Better for me if you don't come.*

Did she feel *safer* with him away? Was the fear of Gary still uppermost in her mind? Had something happened he didn't know about?

Ric snatched up the telephone and called Mitch at home, where he should be since it was now well into the evening in Australia. The call was promptly answered by his old friend, much to Ric's relief.

'Is there any pressing reason why I shouldn't come home?' he blurted out.

Mitch weighed the question for a few moments, then replied, 'None that I know of, providing you exercise due care.'

'There's no overt threat from the Chappel front? Something that's worrying Lara?'

'All quiet there. Certainly Victor Chappel accepts there will be a divorce. I don't trust Gary not to seize any chance he can get to stop it so I would emphasise...don't lead him to Lara.'

'I can use Johnny's plane again to fly to Gundamurra.'

'That would be the best way if you *must* go, Ric.'

'You don't think I should?'

Another longer pause. 'It's not for me to judge. I've never seen the two of you together...'

'But...?' Ric pressed.

'Lara has been through a lot. More than you know, Ric, and I'm not at liberty to tell you.'

'You're saying my presence might be an unwelcome pressure.'

'I don't know. I do know that for other women who've been in a similar situation...it's not forgotten in three months. It's a long, uphill battle to put it behind them.'

Time...

As much as Ric wanted to leap over it, he couldn't ignore Mitch's advice nor Lara's own words. He resigned himself to more months of patience, ended the call to Mitch and went back to his computer. His fingers tapped out the message—

*As you wish, Lara.*

*As you wish...*

Tears welled into Lara's eyes as she stared at the words Ric had written back to her...giving words...so typical of everything he'd done for her...giving...

Yet his caring for her needs only added another burden to her torment. She'd asked too much of him and now she was damned for it.

Three months' pregnant...

Lara propped her elbows on the computer desk, buried her face in her hands and wept.

Outside the heavens opened again and dropped another load of drenching rain. It drummed on the tin roof of the homestead, drowning out the sound of her private grief. Not that anyone would be listening. Patrick had set aside this time in the office for her use. She was always left alone to write to Ric.

But how could she continue this link with him?

If the baby was Gary's...there would be no escaping the Chappel family, even with a divorce. She'd thought wildly of somehow arranging an abortion but she couldn't bring herself to go down that dark road, not having had a stillborn child. It was her baby, too. Every innocent life was precious.

And it might be Ric's child...a desperate hope that would at least save her from being connected to Gary again, yet dreadfully unfair to Ric, trapping him into fatherhood, giving him no choice about it.

Guilt writhed through her. How could Ric ever trust her word again? She'd let him believe that the contraceptive pill she'd been taking would protect her from pregnancy, recklessly pressing him into making love to her. He wouldn't have gone through with it otherwise. She had used him to drive Gary out of her mind—wantonly used him—not caring about anything but her own selfish needs.

The sheer dishonesty of it sickened her. It would surely sicken him, too. She couldn't even face him with the possibility that the child was his. The shame was too great.

No...she had to assume it was Gary's...live with the consequences... end the link with Ric now. It was the only fair thing to do. This wasn't his problem. It was hers and hers alone.

No forcing herself to write cheerful little messages to him. That was dishonest, too. She pulled herself together, stabbed a finger at the switch on the monitor screen, watched *As you wish, Lara* wink out into blank darkness, then shut the computer down.

It wasn't what she wished.

But there was no turning back the clock.

She left the office and stood on the veranda, watching the rain come down—almost blinding sheets of it. There'd been storms like this for the past few days, causing the river to rise, bringing the danger of flooding. All the men were working hard, moving the stock to safe paddocks. It had to be done by horseback. The ground had become too boggy for any motorised vehicles.

She knew everything about the life here now. It had a natural harmony that she liked. And there was nothing pretentious about the people on the station. What you saw was what you got. No hidden agendas.

She was the only person hiding something.

So far she'd managed to keep her pregnancy to herself. The loose shirts she wore covered her thickening waistline, and as with her last pregnancy, she didn't suffer bad morning sickness. No throwing up. Mostly the nausea receded when she ate something. And since she spent afternoons in the sewing room, it was easy to take a little nap there so no one knew of the fatigue that sometimes overwhelmed her.

She might be able to go another month before the truth was too obvious to hide any longer. What then? Sooner or later she would have to tell Patrick. Would he let her stay here? Have the baby here?

Would she have to tell Mitch Tyler, too?

A baby couldn't be kept a secret forever.

Ric would inevitably learn of it, one way or another...and he'd feel betrayed.

She was no good for him.

She'd never been good for him.

And there was no chance of redemption now.

No sunshine after the rain.

She took her misery to bed and listened to the constant beat of the rain on the roof, wanting it to beat out any more thought. Yet she kept hearing...

*As you wish...as you wish...as you wish...*

Back in Sydney, Gary Chappel was getting what *he'd* wished for...the mistake from Ric Donato that would lead him to his runaway wife. He'd paid through the nose for it, but his private investigator had finally come up with the goods from the illegal tap on Mitch Tyler's home telephone.

Gundamurra.

# CHAPTER TEN

THE SOUND OF a plane coming in woke Lara from her midafternoon nap. Ric, she thought, her heart kicking with instant apprehension. Had he changed his mind and come after all? But surely he would have let Patrick know of his intention. And he couldn't have got here this fast...could he?

He'd been in London three nights ago.

And he'd written, 'As you wish.'

Reason fought off the rush of frantic worry. No one could land, anyway. The airstrip wasn't firm enough after all the rain they'd had. Only a helicopter could make a safe landing and this was not the sound of a helicopter. But the pilot was flying very low.

Someone in trouble?

She was up and running.

People were yelling, 'It's coming down.'

Outside the homestead, it seemed everyone was running, knowing instinctively that help might be needed. They all saw it happen and could do nothing to stop it. The landing gear ploughed into the soggy ground. The nose of the plane went down. The tail flipped.

The shock of the crash stopped Lara in her tracks. Waves of nausea rolled through her. Frightened of fainting, she managed to stumble to a bench seat under one of the pepper trees and lowered her head to below her knees, trying to fight off the dizziness. Evelyn found her there and hauled her back to the kitchen, sitting her down at the table and making her a cup of tea.

'It wasn't Johnny's Cessna, was it?' Lara pleaded.

'No. None of our neighbours either. Looked like a charter,' Evelyn answered bruskly. 'Someone lost, most likely, and not even having the sense to call us on the radio about the condition of the airstrip.'

'Maybe they couldn't. Or were too low on fuel to go anywhere else.'

'That's not for you to worry about. It's men's work down there.' Evelyn gave her a knowing look. 'You have to be looking after yourself, Miss Lara. I've seen too many pregnant women not to recognise the signs.'

Another shock.

'If you want to keep it to yourself, that's fine, but you might as well know you're not fooling me. Now drink up your tea and off to bed with you. That plane crash won't be any business of yours.'

Lara felt too weak to argue. She did as she was told, grateful to slip into bed and not have to involve herself with the horror at the airstrip.

Yet in the end it was her business.

Patrick came into her room, drew a chair up beside her bed and regarded her with a gravity that had her nerves twitching in alarm. Had Evelyn told him of her pregnancy? Should she confess it now? Or did he have bad news about the plane crash?

It couldn't have been Ric...could it? Why would he charter a plane when he could use Johnny's? Her mind whirled in a frenzy of stress as she waited for Patrick to speak.

'Lara...your husband was in that plane.'

Gary?

The shock of it rendered her speechless. Her stomach churned as fear swept past the shock. Gary had come for her. He'd found out she was at Gundamurra, chartered a plane and...everything within her shrank from having to confront him. Yet there was nowhere to hide now. He *knew*...

'He was not strapped into a seat,' Patrick went on. 'There was nothing we could do for him.'

What did he mean...there was nothing they could do for him? It was Gary who had the power, who'd do whatever was needed to get his own way.

'He's dead, Lara.'

Dead?

Gary...dead?

Powerless to do...anything at all?

'He died before we could get to him. The impact of the crash...'

Dead...

Gone...

He could never touch her again...never direct any part of her life again...or her baby's...it was as though God was having mercy on her by taking him away.

*I'll be a good mother,* she silently promised, her hand moving protectively to the slight mound that held the new life inside. If she achieved nothing else with this second chance to be free of fear, she would ensure her child would know only love from her, regardless of who the father was.

'The pilot and a third man—a private investigator—have multiple injuries,' Patrick said, letting her know Gary had come with a backup man.

No doubt if conditions had been favourable, she would have been abducted back to Sydney, put into one of the Chappel medical clinics, classed as a mental breakdown needing psychiatric attention, and once it was discovered she was pregnant...but that couldn't happen now.

'A rescue helicopter will be arriving soon to fly them to Bourke for treatment. Gary's body will also be going. I have to ask...' Patrick heaved a sigh and quietly added, '...do you want to see him, Lara?'

She shook her head.

'I thought...you might want to be sure.'

She swallowed hard and forced herself to ask, 'Is there any doubt?'

'He carried identification and the private investigator confirmed it. There's no cause for doubt. The police in Bourke can contact his father.'

'Then I don't need...to see him.'

'Only if you want to.'

'No.' Instant and decisive. Better to think of him as completely gone than to have some awful last image of him stamped on her mind.

Patrick nodded and rose to his feet. 'I'll have Evelyn sit with you. If there's anything you need or want, just tell her.'

'Thank you.'

She closed her eyes.

The hunt was over.

Ric was not in danger anymore.

Set free.

*She* had to set him free, too.

Raising the possibility of fatherhood would not be fair. Even if the child was his, the responsibility was all hers. It would be terribly wrong to hang a lifelong commitment on him when he would have chosen differently. He'd done so much to give her freedom. To lean on him any more...to take his freedom from him...

If this baby was the result of a lie...

Better that Ric didn't know.

A lie was the worst possible foundation for a lifelong relationship.

And she wanted her baby to know only love.

# CHAPTER ELEVEN

RIC HAD COME into the Sydney office to work because he couldn't stand his own company. It was four months since he'd seen Lara and the only communication he'd received from her this past month had been relayed through Mitch—a request for him to stay clear. There would inevitably be—and had been—a media furore surrounding Gary Chappel's death, funeral and inquest, and she didn't want Ric spotlighted as a player in her life.

No scandal for the gossip pages.

She had been legally separated from her husband, pending a divorce. Irreconcilable differences. No other man involved.

In short, Ric had been effectively sidelined with no comeback in sight. The respectable widow walked alone. She didn't need or want his support. Mitch had assigned her a good solicitor to handle Gary's estate and Lara had reached some private settlement with Victor Chappel so there'd be no contest. Ric suspected a deal had been made—her silence on the nature her marriage—no slur cast on his son's character—and she'd be a wealthy woman for life.

He'd felt increasingly savage about the hypocrisy of it all.

Even more so over being left out of Lara's life.

She didn't *owe* him anything. He'd told her that repeatedly. And meant it. Yet the intimacy they had shared…he couldn't accept that *it* could be just swept aside as though it was now irrelevant. No way could he forget the night he'd spent with her…how *right* it had felt…and her words about missing him all these years…

He was at the point of wondering whether that had been a seductive lie to push him into doing what she wanted—wipe Gary out of her mind. Yet he'd believed, at the time, it had turned into more than that—a mutual loving that had gone so deep he couldn't tear it out of his system, couldn't set it aside and go on as though it made no difference to his life.

It did.

'Ric…'

The insistent tone in Kathryn's call of his name broke into his turbulent brooding. His gaze snapped up, his eyes stabbing her with all the angry resentment he felt over the situation with Lara. She was sitting on the other side of his desk and he saw the startled look on her face, realised what he'd done and swiftly rearranged his expression.

'Sorry. You were saying?'

She grimaced. 'Have you heard anything I've said, Ric?'

'No,' he admitted, shrugging off any care about his lack of concentration. 'Better leave your report with me, Kathryn. I'll read it later. I'm not in the mood for discussing business right now.'

'Okay.' She stood up and handed him the stapled pages she'd been using as a reference. 'I'll be in my office. Call me if you want to question anything.'

He had a million questions, but not about business.

'Has Lara Chappel made any contact with you?' he shot at her.

She straightened up, her hands linking in front of her as though needing to guard herself from attack. Her eyes were wary as she gave a slow, measured reply. 'No personal contact, Ric. However, she did send me a beautiful arrangement of flowers on her return to Sydney, with a note thanking me for my assistance.'

Flowers for Kathryn.

At least *her* involvement in the rescue and its aftermath had not been ignored.

Yet this acknowledgment felt like an even bigger slap in the face for Ric. No flowers for him. *Nothing* for him.

Kathryn's hands started fretting at each other.

His tension was obviously getting to her. Ric was about to wave her on her way when he noticed something missing. 'You're not wearing your engagement ring.'

'I gave it back to Jeremy,' she stated flatly.

It momentarily distracted him from Lara. He frowned his concern. Rejection was hell. 'Your decision or his, Kathryn?'

'Mine.' Her mouth tilted into a wry little smile. 'He wasn't the man I thought he was.'

'I'm sorry.' The guy must have let her down in some serious way.

'Don't be. I made a mistake. Better to find out before I married him.'

'Yes,' Ric agreed mockingly. 'Mistakes can be very costly.'

Like making love to Lara.

'I've actually been seeing Mitch Tyler,' Kathryn said in a rush.

'You...and Mitch?' He was surprised.

She flushed and he realised she was embarrassed about telling him, yet there was a sympathy in her eyes which instantly had him writhing inside. Kathryn and Mitch...discussing him and Lara.

'Good luck to you,' he said bruskly and gestured for her to go.

As soon as the door closed behind her he was up and pacing, unable to contain the violent energy coursing through him. To hell with standing back and doing nothing! He needed action. He wanted answers. Lara's silence was killing him. He snatched up the telephone and stabbed out the numbers for the Vaucluse mansion.

Though how Lara could go back there was another question that taunted him.

But she had. Within three days of Gary Chappel's death she had flown away from Gundamurra—lifted out by a helicopter which had been paid for by Victor Chappel. A very swift return to the life she'd left behind in Sydney. Couldn't wipe the dust of the Outback off her feet fast enough. No waiting for Ric Donato to escort her anywhere. Not wanting him with her, not for love nor money. No need for *his* money now. As for love...

'The Chappel residence.'

Not *her* voice. Had she kept on the housekeeper Gary had employed? All the staff that had been *his* watchers, reporting on her? Ric couldn't comprehend what Lara was about anymore.

'It's Ric Donato,' he snapped. 'And I'd like to speak with Lara Chappel.'

A pause, then, 'Please wait, Mr. Donato.'

Waiting for what? Ric thought viciously.

To be rejected point-blank?

At least that would be some satisfaction. He'd know exactly where he stood. Fantasy dead. Just another episode with Ric Donato put to rest. No *missing* him at all.

He waited.

And waited.

He was turning into stone while he waited.

'Hello, Ric.'

*Her* voice.

He could hardly believe his ears, having geared himself up to expect nothing. His mouth was completely dry. He had to work some moisture into it before he could reply.

'Lara...' His mind was blank. No other words came.

She broke the ensuing silence. 'It's good to hear from you.'

Good?

'I'm glad you feel that.' The remark flew out, edged with a sarcasm he instantly regretted. Maybe she had cogent reasons for not contacting him in person. Maybe she had cogent reasons for everything she'd done. If she was welcoming his call now...'It's been a long time,' he quickly added.

'Yes. Yes it has.'

No apology. No excuse for her silence.

'I was wondering if we could meet,' Ric tested. 'Have dinner together.'

A long pause, then with what sounded like forced brightness, she answered, 'What about lunch? Tomorrow, if it suits you.'

Not dinner. Not risking a night with him. Not *wanting* a night with him.

'Lunch. Tomorrow,' he repeated, gripped by a fierce determination to see this through. 'That's fine. Where would you like me to take you?'

'No.' Strongly decisive. 'This is on me, Ric. I'll book a table at the Osiris Restaurant. It's in the Radisson Hotel, quite close to Circular Quay so it won't be far from your office. Let's say we meet there at twelve-thirty.'

'Twelve-thirty,' he repeated, hating the obvious limitations she was putting on their meeting. 'I'll look forward to it,' he grimly added, wondering if he was a stupid masochist, begging for more pain.

'Until tomorrow then,' she said briskly, and ended the call.

He heard the click of disconnection.

It felt like a shot in the heart.

But he would go tomorrow.

He needed to say goodbye to her—face-to-face!

Lara barely got the receiver down before she choked up completely, tears welling into her eyes, spilling down her cheeks. She tried to dash them away with her hands as she bolted upstairs to her bedroom, savagely wishing she didn't have to go through the wretched torment of meeting Ric tomorrow.

But how could she not?

He'd sounded hurt...bitter...and she felt deeply ashamed of the cowardice that had kept postponing any contact with him, evading a confrontation that would only be painful. She couldn't tell him the truth and didn't want to be put in the position where only more lies would effect the necessary parting. But an outright snub on the telephone...she hadn't been able to cut him like that. It was indecent, given all he'd done for her.

She reached her room, closed the door and leaned back against it, hugging herself tightly in a desperate attempt to reduce the ache of loss that had started up from just talking to him. How could she manage tomorrow...sitting down face-to-face...the memories of how it had been with him brought vividly to mind by his physical presence?

He'd cared about her.

Really cared.

Would he still care if she spilled out the truth?

Even if the baby wasn't his?

A terrible yearning for Ric to hold her again gripped her mind, her heart, her entire body. But that was precisely how she had got herself into this hopeless dilemma...being selfish. Blindly, foolishly selfish. Caring only for what *she* wanted.

So what could she say tomorrow?

*Oh, by the way, Ric, I'm pregnant. Don't know if it's your baby or Gary's. Sorry about letting you think I was protected. I was wild for you at the time. But now it's come to this, how about standing by me for the rest of our lives? Love me, love my child, regardless of who the father is.*

A great reward that would be for all his giving!

She'd made this bed.

It was wrong to even flirt with the temptation of asking Ric to share it with her, to take on the load of fatherhood when she'd led him to believe there was no chance of it.

No.

Somehow she had to make him believe she wanted to lead an independent life. That she had plans which didn't include him. In all decency, she had to thank him graciously for freeing her to pursue her own goals, and effectively bow out of any further connection with him.

But it shouldn't be a bitter end.

Hopefully an understood one.

Though her heart bled for all the things that would have to remain unsaid.

Her arms slid down to hug the child within. The shock of the plane crash and Gary's death had worried her. She'd returned to Sydney as soon as she felt well enough to travel, anxious to see a doctor and have the baby checked. So far everything was all right. Last week's ultra-scan had revealed a perfectly healthy baby.

She needed this baby to live.

Something good to hang on to.

Tomorrow she had to say goodbye to Ric.

And let him go.

# CHAPTER TWELVE

RIC WALKED INTO the Radisson Hotel at twelve-fifteen. The entrance to the Osiris Restaurant was at one end of the lounge area in the foyer. He sat in an armchair which gave him a direct view of anyone arriving.

Taxis came and went on the street outside, unloading and picking up passengers. None of them was Lara. He tensed each time a chauffeured car pulled up, only to be disappointed when a stranger emerged from it. Time ticked on...past twelve-thirty, past twelve-thirty-five, past twelve-forty...

He wasn't paged to come to a telephone. No message explaining why she was late. After four months, any normal courtesy would demand punctuality for this meeting, or at least a call informing him of a delay. Everyone had mobile telephones these days. There was no excuse for leaving him hanging.

Was it deliberate?

A message in itself—*You're not important to me?*

An even more demeaning thought occurred to Ric. He strode into the restaurant to check if a booking had been made. If not, he'd been kissed goodbye in one of the most contemptible ways imaginable. He'd pushed for some civility from Lara and she hadn't even granted him that.

'A table booked for Chappel?' Ric demanded of the maître d'.

'Mr. Donato?' the man inquired, as though *he* had a message to deliver.

Ric seethed at the thought that Lara had arranged to pay for his lunch while not appearing herself. 'Yes,' he snapped.

'This way, sir.'

He led off, leaving Ric little choice but to follow him. They were moving toward the far end of the restaurant. Ric quickly scanned the spaciously arranged tables ahead of them, not recognising any of the diners. His jaw clenched as he spotted an empty table tucked behind a buttress beside one of the picture windows. He was not going to stay here and eat alone.

But the table wasn't unoccupied.

Lara sat in the chair that was hidden from general view by the buttress, her gaze turned to the view of the city beyond the window. Ric barely had time to absorb the shock of seeing her before the maître d' announced his arrival, swinging her attention straight to him.

He'd seen many photographs of Lara since her return to Sydney but none of them had prepared him for seeing her in the flesh—the breathtaking beauty of her undamaged face. Her eyes were a stunning blue. Her skin glowed. Her gleaming fair hair was softly looped up, gathered into a sophisticated topknot, somehow accentuating the delicate perfection of her features and the graceful length of her neck.

'Ric...' She smiled at him, rose to her feet, offered her hand.

No moving out to give him a kiss of greeting, just a polite smile, more nervous than projecting warmth, and a hand which he took as he nodded and forced himself to return her name.

'Lara...'

He couldn't bring himself to smile. He'd never felt less like smiling in his life. She wore black. The grieving widow? It was a black trouser-suit, undoubtedly designer wear, the jacket fitting snugly around her breasts then flaring out into a feminine A-line, skimming her waist and floating around her hips.

He released her hand after a light squeeze and she promptly resumed her seat. The maître d' held out the chair opposite hers and Ric sat, too, his gaze falling on the pearls Lara wore around her neck, three strands of perfectly graduated pearls. Probably worth a fortune. Booty from Chappel's wealth.

Well, what did he expect? Ric savagely mocked himself. She wouldn't come to this classy restaurant in jeans and cotton shirt. He matched her appearance, anyway, even down to Gucci shoes. He just didn't like her wearing what Chappel money had obviously bought for her, keeping up the image of her high status marriage when both of them knew what that image had hidden.

'I was waiting for you in the hotel foyer,' he stated, looking her straight in the eye again, still resenting the long futile watching for her to show up.

'I'm sorry. I did say the restaurant, Ric. I arrived early and came straight in.'

'Very early,' he couldn't stop himself from commenting. She had to have been seated here for over three quarters of an hour by now.

She flushed and tried to shrug it off. 'I didn't want to be late. With traffic the way it is...'

'My mistake,' he quickly granted and tried to relax as a waiter spread the starched white linen table napkin over his lap and handed him menus for food and wine. 'Have you already seen these?' he asked Lara.

She nodded. He quickly made a selection, not caring what he ate or drank, just wanting the waiter to go away and leave them alone. Lara added her order and the business of the meal was done. He sat back and set his mind to taking stock of the situation. She'd come even earlier than he had. What did that mean? Anxious not to miss a minute with him or getting herself settled before having to confront him?

She looked calm, composed, still a touch of warm colour in her cheeks but her eyes were regarding him steadily, taking in every detail of his appearance as though matching it to her memory of him—a one day/ one night memory that she'd made no attempt to revisit until he had taken this initiative. So what was she thinking now?

'You look well, Lara,' he said, which was no more than the truth.

'I've been looking after myself,' she returned, instantly striking an independent stance. She didn't need *him* to do that for her anymore.

'Good!' he said approvingly, then bluntly asked. 'You don't mind living in the Vaucluse mansion? No bad memories crowding in?'

Again she flushed, her gaze dropping to the cutlery on the table. She moved it aside in an agitated manner, then pulled a glass of water toward her. 'It's a big house,' she said jerkily. 'And all Gary's stuff has been taken away. I only live in part of it.'

Her gaze lifted in a flash of determination. 'It will go on the market soon. An estate agent is already preparing for it to be auctioned. Until it's sold it needs to be maintained.'

'Of course,' he murmured, though he knew money could easily achieve that. The place didn't have to be lived in. His apartments were all regularly serviced while he was away.

She sipped the glass of water.

'Same housekeeper?' he asked.

'Yes.' She looked defiantly at him. 'I managed to hire Mrs. Keith again. She left the day after I did. I'd told Mitch Tyler she was one of the people who might testify against Gary and that did prove true. She's a good person and needs the employment.'

But another reminder of the past, Ric thought. Did Lara want that understanding of her marriage from the people around her? For what purpose?

'Do you have any plans for where you will go once the house sells?'

'I haven't had time to look yet.'

'But you've thought about it,' he prompted.

'Yes.' She shrugged. 'Somewhere smaller.' A wisp of a smile. 'A place to call my own.'

Another pointer to complete independence.

'In Sydney?'

She nodded and sipped again.

'Any suburb in particular?'

'I want to be reasonably close to my mother.'

Her mother? Who hadn't listened to her problems? Who'd sided with Gary?

Ric found his jaw clenching and it took considerable willpower to unclench it. Lara was choosing to be near people who hadn't lifted a finger to help her, while *he* had been kept out on the perimeter, barely acknowledged by her. It made no sense to him.

Unless he was the most painful reminder of all she had been through—the one closest to it because of the intimacy she had begged of him.

But what of the feelings that had surfaced that night?

Was she now embarrassed by them?

Wishing she hadn't laid herself quite so bare with him?

'Is everything going well with you, Ric?' she asked, assuming an expression of bright interest.

'Business-wise, yes. On a personal level...' His gaze locked onto hers, searching, questioning. '... I've been missing you, Lara.'

His choice of words were pointedly deliberate and she flinched from them, tearing her gaze from his and dropping it to the glass of water which she turned around and around on the table. He felt no sympathy whatsoever for her tension. If she'd lied to him about *missing him all these years,* she deserved to stew in her lie.

'Mitch Tyler assured me that Gary hadn't done you any injury, either personally or professionally,' she said stiffly.

'No. I guess you could say I did him one.'

It startled her into looking up, a pained confusion in her eyes. 'What injury?'

'I did take you from him,' he reminded her, returning a look of black irony.

'I went willingly. I'd already tried...'

'Yes, I know. But then it was also me who gave him the lead to Gundamurra, which ended in his death.'

'You? I don't understand.'

He shrugged. 'I guess Mitch didn't tell you that Gary's private investigator had bugged his home telephone.'

She shook her head.

'After you e-mailed me not to come, I called Mitch to ask if he knew of any reason why I shouldn't go to Gundamurra, with all due care taken. That's how your husband found out where you were, Lara.'

'Oh!'

'Though I daresay all's well that ends well,' Ric mocked. 'You're not only completely free of him now, but also left a wealthy widow.'

She took offence at the mercenary aspect. 'I'll only be taking what I need to...to...'

Ric waved a dismissive gesture. 'You're entitled, Lara. God knows what you put up with as his wife.'

'It's not about money,' she stated with fierce pride.

'No,' he agreed. 'You've already made it clear it's about independence.'

'And setting things right,' she quickly added.

'Oh?' He raised his eyebrows. 'Is that what this lunch is for...setting things right with me?'

She stared at him, through him, her eyes becoming unfocused. She finally dropped her gaze, shook her head, and muttered, 'I don't know how to do that, Ric.'

The wine waiter arrived with the bottle of Chardonnay Ric had selected. There was the usual process of showing him the label, uncorking the bottle, pouring a taster. Ric gave his approval. The waiter moved to pour Lara some of the wine. She covered her glass with her hand.

'None for me, thank you. I'll stick to water.'

Wanted to keep her head, Ric instantly thought, *while I lose mine.*

The waiter filled his glass and left.

Ric didn't touch it. He'd ordered the wine automatically—an appropriate complement to the seafood they'd selected. If he'd known he'd be drinking it alone, he wouldn't have even glanced at the wine list. Lara's refusal of it felt like another point of separation—one less thing shared.

Was he overreacting...reading this all wrong?

If he put himself out to be charming instead of challenging, would it make any difference?

She *had come* to this lunch.

He tried to push his anger and frustration aside, tried to come at the situation through her mind. 'I'm sorry.' He managed a self-deprecating smile. 'I'm not making this easy, am I?'

She sighed. Her eyes reflected a weariness of spirit that held out no hope for him. 'It never was going to be easy, Ric.'

Undoubtedly the reason why she had evaded—postponed—any personal contact with him. He decided he might as well be direct.

'Why, Lara? Is it because of that night?'

Again she flushed and couldn't hold his gaze, dropping hers to the glass of water again.

'I remember it as good,' he stated quietly.

She closed her eyes.

No reply.

The memory was very vivid in his mind...how she had responded to everything he'd done. Not once had he moved on without being certain it was what she wanted and welcomed. And afterward...the sense of loving and being loved. No hint of regret. No second thoughts about its rightness. She'd snuggled up to him and fallen asleep in his arms.

'I thought it was good for you, too,' he murmured.

She shook her head. 'It was wrong,' she blurted out. 'I shouldn't have asked. Shouldn't have pressed.'

Her tone was pained, carrying thousands of regrets.

Shame...guilt...humiliation...were all those negative feelings attached to him now, making it difficult for her to look him in the face?

'It didn't feel wrong to me, Lara,' he softly assured her. 'I don't think any less of you for wanting what you did. It's a natural impulse to use sex as an affirmation of life.'

'Please...' She raised anguished eyes. 'I'd rather you didn't refer to it, Ric.'

She was skewering him, giving him no room to move. He frowned, certain now that this was at the heart of the problem she had with being in his company. 'You want me to sit here and pretend it never happened?'

'I can't do that, either,' she cried, the calm composure she'd greeted him with now in total tatters. 'I'm sorry. You've been so good to me but...' Her eyes pleaded. '... I want to close the door on it, Ric.'

Wipe it out.

He'd made love to her because she'd wanted to wipe out Gary.

She didn't need that anymore.

Gary was dead.

But Ric Donato was still alive and kicking...kicking hard against her wish to wipe him out of her life. Futile...if she'd made up her mind.

'I guess you'd better spell that out to me, Lara. Do you only want the door closed on what we shared in the past? Or do you also want it closed on any future we might have together?'

She took a deep breath. Her eyes looked sick but she said the words. 'There is no future for us, Ric.'

It was a flat, unequivocal denial of the bond he'd felt with her—a bond that had spanned eighteen years for him and would probably haunt the rest of his life.

He couldn't stop himself from asking, 'Are you sure about that?'

'Yes. I'm sure.'

No hesitation. No room for doubt.

He should move. Go. Couldn't make himself do it. It felt as though every atom of energy had drained out of his body. He stared at the glass of wine the waiter had poured. A cup of poison, he thought.

'I'm sorry,' she murmured. 'I owe you so much and there's no way I can repay...'

His gaze flicked to hers in savage derision. 'There's no debt. Everything I did...was what I *wanted* to do.'

Her cheeks were burning. 'I kept all the dockets from the clothes you bought me. I've written you a cheque. At least let me repay that, Ric.'

She reached down for her handbag.

He exploded onto his feet. 'Don't!'

She snapped back up without the bag. He glowered down at the strained appeal on her face. 'This isn't about money,' he grated, trying to contain the mountain of emotion erupting inside him. 'It never was. Though I tried to close the gap between us by stealing the Porsche. That was the blindness of a boy who thought he wasn't good enough for you. I don't know what your measure is, Lara, but I will not accept being paid off.'

He had the grim satisfaction of seeing her look shattered.

'Enjoy your freedom,' he said.

And walked away.

# CHAPTER THIRTEEN

RIC DIDN'T GO back to the office. He was in no mood to face Kathryn or anyone else. Having retrieved the Ferrari from the basement car park, he drove home to his Woolloomooloo apartment where no one would bother him.

The view of Sydney Harbour from the picture windows in his living room reminded him of Lara's view from the Vaucluse mansion. He'd barged into her life that morning—uninvited—and demanded that there be truth between them. Nothing hidden.

Was that why she couldn't live with him now?

Easier to hide?

Ric still couldn't get his mind around it. He told himself it was a futile exercise even trying to work it out. She'd stated categorically—no future together. There was no choice but to let her go. And that final insult, wanting to pay him...pointless to struggle for understanding when she clearly had no understanding of him.

The bond he'd felt had to be fantasy.

Time to close the door on it.

Get out of Sydney, too, right away from Lara.

New York. Things were always jumping in New York. A city where anything could happen. Easy enough to get back in the social swim there, maybe even find a woman who'd move him past Lara, give him a reality check.

He was reaching for the telephone to book a flight when it rang. He automatically snatched up the receiver, not remembering he didn't want to speak to anyone until he'd lifted it, and then it was too late. The voice of Johnny Ellis boomed into his ear.

'Hey, man! Glad I caught you somewhere! Here I am in downtown Sydney with a night to spare before I fly home to Gundamurra. Any chance of you joining up with Mitch and me for dinner tonight?'

Ric hesitated, hating the thought of having to speak of Lara, knowing she would inevitably be brought up somewhere in their conversation. He'd borrowed Johnny's plane for her escape. Mitch had been privy to the whole affair, though that was mostly confidential. But not Ric's part in it.

On the other hand, be damned if he'd shut the door on an old friendship because of her! Mitch and Johnny had proved true over the years. He could always count on them. And the three of them didn't get together much. Stupid to knock back this chance, letting Lara get in the way. Mitch and Johnny would still be figuring in his future, long after today.

'Sure, Johnny,' he answered strongly. 'That would be great. Have you got a restaurant lined up?'

'I called the Italian joint you like, just below your apartment. Otto's. Eight o'clock okay?'

'Fine! Look forward to it.'

The boys from Gundamurra...

To Johnny it was *home,* the only place where he felt a real sense of belonging. Like Ric he had no family, and the two of them always went to Gundamurra for Christmas, Johnny visiting more often during the year. They'd been made to feel part of the Maguire family, welcome whenever they wanted to come.

Ric wished he hadn't taken Lara there now, though it had seemed the right place at the time—in fact, the only place which could have guaranteed her safe refuge. Even if Gary's plane hadn't crashed, Patrick would not have allowed Lara to be taken. But that was all academic now. The problem was, Ric knew he'd never be able to go there again without thinking of her.

Get over it, he savagely told himself.

He'd done the right thing in rescuing her from an abusive husband.

What happened after that...well, it just hadn't worked out the way he wanted. Patrick had warned him of that, right from the beginning. So move on past it. You're a survivor, remember?

When he met up with Johnny and Mitch in Otto's that evening, Ric had managed to push Lara into a mental compartment with fortified walls. He ended up having to refer to her, as expected, but the emotion she'd stirred was safely contained. He brushed quickly over the whole issue, declaring it over and done with. Lara could resume her life. He could resume his. In fact, he was off to New York at the end of this week.

Mitch proved a ready ally in steering Johnny back to regaling them with tales of his music world and the evening was mostly filled with news of his most recent tour in the U.S., all amusingly told. Johnny had the knack of making fun out of everything. Ric even found himself laughing. No doubt the alcoholic haze of several bottles of great wine helped to relax him. And the company was good.

The next day he worked hard with Kathryn, tying up the managerial loose ends in the Sydney office. He'd be basing himself in New York for the next few months, flying out tomorrow afternoon. He wondered how Kathryn's new relationship with Mitch was working out but didn't ask. Personal business was personal business. Privately, he wished them both well. Good people.

The telephone in his apartment started ringing just as he opened the door. Frowning over who the caller might be—a glance at his watch showed six-fifteen—he kicked the door shut and strode quickly to the wall phone in the kitchen.

'Ric Donato,' he rapped out, wondering if Kathryn had thought of something he'd forgotten—more business to be attended to in the morning before he left.

'Johnny here, Ric.'

He was surprised. 'You didn't get to Gundamurra today?'

'Yes, I did. Flew in this afternoon. Sat in the kitchen with Evelyn while she fed me her carrot cake, freshly made and iced with cream cheese and walnuts.'

Ric smiled, picturing the scene. 'I trust you fully appreciated your welcome home.'

'Had three big slices. But that's not the point of this call, Ric.'

'What is?' Some problem at Gundamurra? Patrick not well?

'Well, I might be treading on sensitive ground here, but neither you nor Mitch mentioned it, and Patrick tells me he didn't know...'

'Know what?' Ric cut in impatiently, his gut contracting at the thought this might be something about Lara.

'I'm sorry if I'm out of line...'

'Get to the point, Johnny.'

A big breath. 'The point is... I remember that Lara Seymour was a big deal for you, Ric, and I figure, with all you did for her, getting her out of a bad marriage, bringing her here...well, I think you ought to know there could be a good reason why she didn't stick around for you to come and collect her after the guy got killed.'

'A reason,' Ric repeated flatly, fighting against rising to a bait that might give him false hope.

'Didn't make sense to me that she'd give you the flick,' came the painful remark. 'Anyway, I was chatting to Evelyn...'

Ric gritted his teeth. Of course, they would talk about him and Lara—the big drama on the station this year. He could see them sitting in the kitchen, eating carrot cake, tongues wagging between bites...

'Now you know nothing gets past Evelyn, Ric,' Johnny went on. 'And she told me straight-out that Lara was pregnant.'

*Pregnant!*

'Must have happened just before you got her away from her husband because Evelyn said she wasn't far along. Wasn't even showing—at least not obviously—when she left Gundamurra.'

Three months...four months now...seated at the restaurant, not wanting him to see her arrive...the loose jacket...not drinking any wine...

'Anyhow, Evelyn said the shock of the plane crash made Lara real sick. Looked like she was going to faint. Had to be put to bed. Evelyn was worried about the baby and she reckons Lara would have been, too, on account of her last baby had been stillborn.'

*Last baby?*

Ric's mind was reeling. He hadn't known Lara had given birth to a stillborn child. But when had they had the chance to talk about such things? In the limited time they'd spent together, she hadn't wanted to discuss her marriage with him. Her subsequent e-mails had contained only news of what she was doing at Gundamurra. And the cheerful chattiness of those had started dwindling off...

*When?*

It hit him like a sledgehammer.

*When she realised she had to be pregnant!*

'Ric...are you there?' Worried tone.

He realised he'd stopped breathing and expelled the air caught in his lungs. 'Yes, I'm still here, Johnny.'

'Is this news to you?'

'Yes.'

'Okay. Well, Evelyn's guess is, Lara went back to Sydney as soon as she was well enough to travel because she wanted a medical check on the baby. Which all makes sense to me.'

And to Ric.

Devastating sense.

'She might be rid of the guy,' Johnny went on. 'But she's having his baby, Ric. Puts her in a bit of a dilemma, doesn't it?'

'You could say that,' Ric answered grimly.

Was it Gary's child? Did Lara know that with absolute certainty?

'Just thought you should have the full picture. Mitch said...well, never mind that.'

The two of them had shared a taxi from the restaurant last night. Obviously they'd shared more than a ride.

'Hope I haven't trod where I shouldn't,' Johnny added apologetically. 'But if it was me... I'd want to know the ins and outs of it.'

Ric didn't hold anything against his old friends. They cared about him. He'd thought he hadn't showed he was hurting, but...

'It's okay, Johnny. You're right. It's better to know. Thank you.'

'Hard call to make. Take care of yourself, Ric.'

'Will do,' he answered automatically.

Yet his world was now tilting to a very different angle. Ric knew, even as he put the receiver down, he wouldn't be flying off to New York tomorrow.

Lara was pregnant.

He'd used no protection that night.

She might well have lied about taking contraceptive pills.

If she could be pregnant to Gary in that time-frame, she could be pregnant to him, too.

Either way, Ric wasn't about to go anywhere without settling that question first.

# CHAPTER FOURTEEN

LARA HAD TURNED the nanny's quarters, next to the nursery, into a sewing area. On the cutting table lay the squares of fabric she'd chosen for the patchwork quilt, all pretty prints in a variety of colours. A desperate need to block Ric Donato out of her mind had spurred her to spend most of yesterday arranging and rearranging the squares, trying to assess which combination would give her the most pleasing result. The quilt was to be only cot-size and Lara wanted it just right for her baby.

The ultra-scan had confirmed that her pregnancy was perfectly on the track. Amazing, seeing her baby on screen, being able to check that he or she was properly formed. Lara hadn't wanted to know whether it was a boy or girl. If something did go wrong—like last time—she was sure that knowing it was a son or daughter made the loss so much worse. Better to wait. Let it be a surprise.

Meeting Ric again had stirred up an aching desire for the child to be his. It had been so hard, sitting across from him in the restaurant, not telling him, feeling the blast of his anger and hurt, having to watch him walk out of her life.

It had left her quaking inside, agonising over whether she'd made the right decision. He had felt betrayed, anyhow. But, at least, this way, his involvement with her was something he could move past, free of any responsibility for what she herself had done.

All the same, she hoped the baby would look like him so she'd know. But if it didn't…well, it was her baby, anyway. And she had to get on with her life…without Ric.

Eyeing the quilt pattern on the table this morning, Lara decided she couldn't improve on it. The red border was right for it, too. Everything bright and beautiful. She gathered up the first row of squares and settled herself in front of the sewing machine, bought on her return to Sydney. During her months at Gundamurra, she'd found enormous pleasure in creating and making her own designs. She wanted to keep on with it, maybe develop a business later on.

The buzz of the machine blocked out any sounds from the rest of the house. This room was like a private little world—a world she'd take with her wherever she went after this house was sold. Ric had thought badly of her for staying on here, but the baby was her first concern. Best to move slowly, not get herself into a twist with decisions that made too many waves with the Chappel family.

Gary was gone. He couldn't hurt her anymore. And oddly enough, she felt sorry for Victor, losing the son he'd groomed to take over from him. He'd laid out a program of settlement with her on the agreement that she didn't publicly blacken Gary's character. Having no wish to give any details of her marriage to the media, Lara had accepted Victor's plan with no argument at all, against the advice of her solicitor who'd insisted she was entitled to a bigger cut of the estate.

The extra money wasn't important.

Freedom with no comebacks was.

Once everything was legally wound up, she'd be free to go her own way, financially independent—if she was careful—for the rest of her life. Ric could scorn her for taking the money as much as he liked, but she wanted it for her child—backup security in case she wasn't success-ful in setting herself up in business. Besides, if Gary was the father, she was certainly entitled to it.

Having finished sewing the first row of squares together, she moved back to the table to lay them down and pick up the next row. Her atten-tion was distracted by Mrs. Keith's voice, raised in protest, clearly speak-ing to someone else in the hall that led through this section of the house.

'I assure you, this is completely unnecessary!' She sounded upset.

Lara frowned, wondering who was overriding the housekeeper's sense of correct behaviour. Was it the real estate agent, insisting on some further inspection of the house?

The grimly determined voice that replied sent a whiplash through Lara's spine and thumped her heart into stopping dead.

'I will not be parked in some isolating room while Lara skips out a back door.'

Ric!

'Mrs. Chappel is a lady.' Outraged dignity.

'Who lies through her teeth,' came the fierce rejoinder. 'And if you're leading me astray, Mrs. Keith...'

'Don't you threaten me, Mr. Donato! Or Mrs. Chappel. I'll ring the police. It's only because you helped her before that I'm not on the phone to them right this minute.'

'Oh, I don't think Lara will want a fuss. In fact, I'm damned sure of it.'

'Well, we'll see what Mrs. Chappel says.'

The knock on her door kicked Lara out of her shocked paralysis. Her heart leapt into turbulent beating. She sucked in a quick breath. Her mind belatedly grasped that Ric thought she'd lied to him.

About what?

That was the big question!

She didn't have time to say, 'Come in.'

The door was thrust open.

'Mr. Donato...'

The shocked cry from Mrs. Keith was totally disregarded by Ric. He stepped inside the room, his savage gaze pinning Lara to where she stood by the table. The room seemed to flood with his anger, swirling around her in a storm of feeling that was just as quickly caught back, brought under control. She could see the effort it took him, his face tightening under the strain, his eyes glittering with fierce willpower.

He wouldn't physically hurt her.

Not Ric.

He never would.

But she knew he was hurting badly and she'd done it to him. Though she hadn't mean to. And somehow she had to make it better for him.

'It's all right, Mrs. Keith,' she assured the housekeeper, trying her utmost to make her voice come out with calm confidence. 'You can leave Mr. Donato here with me.'

'He wouldn't wait, Mrs. Chappel.'

Lara nodded to her. 'Don't worry about it. Please leave us alone now.'

With a disgruntled sigh, the housekeeper closed the door on them and left. Ric shifted to stand in front of it, deliberately blocking the exit from the room. His eyes ran mockingly over the clothes she wore— quite a dramatic change from the choice she'd made for their meeting at the restaurant.

Lara's nerves twanged in alarm as his gaze traversed her stomach. The stretch maternity jeans were comfortable around her thickened waist and the loose flannelette shirt hid the pot belly which was still small, cer- tainly not showing an obvious pregnancy. He couldn't see. He couldn't know, she frantically assured herself.

He was probably thinking these were the kind of clothes she'd worn at Gundamurra. There hadn't been any need to keep up a classy image at the Outback sheep station and Lara didn't feel any need to change that now. She wasn't going back to the socialite life. The outfit she'd bought for their lunch meeting had been like a coat of armour, deflecting any sense of how vulnerable she'd felt inside. Better for Ric to think she didn't need him for anything. Though that, too, was a lie.

Yet how did he know she'd been lying to him?

His roving gaze returned to hers, still with a hard mocking gleam. 'Have you told Victor Chappel you're carrying his grandchild?'

The words were shot at her like bullets, shredding her defences. She didn't reply. Couldn't. The shock was too great. She stared back at him in a helpless daze, trying to absorb the fact that her attempt to hide the truth from Ric Donato was now a totally lost cause. He knew. He wouldn't be acting like this if he was only guessing.

'Is that why you're still living here, Lara...playing the bereaved widow...making deals with your father-in-law...keeping him sweet so your child will have the chance of inheriting the lot?'

'No!' she cried, appalled that he should think her so calculating and mercenary.

'Then why hide your pregnancy from me?'

She could see how damning that was in his eyes. But the rest of it wasn't true. She shook her head. 'I haven't told Victor. I haven't told any- one. Only my doctor and he has a private practice, not attached to any of the Chappel medical clinics.'

'So...you're worried that the child might look like me,' he shot back at her. 'That would upset the applecart, wouldn't it?'

Lara felt herself shrivelling under the blast of his contempt. She had to swallow hard to work some moisture into her dry mouth. 'I wasn't going to claim Gary as the father,' she stated, but it came out shakily and Ric instantly pounced on it.

'Just let it be assumed...if there are no telltale pointers to me.'

She lifted her hands pleadingly. 'Gary could be the father, Ric. The night before you came to help me escape from him...' She stopped, flushing painfully as shame and guilt washed through her, seeing the sharp leap of realisation in Ric's eyes that this was what she'd wanted him to wipe out.

'You didn't want Gary to win,' he said flatly, recalling and repeating *her* words, damning her even further.

But that time with Ric had turned into much more. She desperately needed to tell him so and have him believe her, yet the words choked in her throat, strangled by all her actions since.

'So what was the plan, Lara?' he tossed at her derisively. 'To confuse the issue if you *had* fallen pregnant to Gary before you gave yourself to me? Say the baby was mine and not his?' He threw up his hands in disgust and moved to the end the table, pressing his balled fists onto it as he leaned toward her in biting challenge, 'Did you really imagine you could get away with that when DNA testing can prove paternity either way?'

'I didn't have a plan,' she cried. 'I was just...reacting.'

'Lying to me about protection,' he bored in.

'I didn't want you to stop.'

'And you didn't care about *my* rights, did you? I was just there to be used.'

'No!'

'And now that Gary's dead, *he* can't use the child to stay in your life, so it doesn't make any difference to you who the father is.' He glared at her in towering fury. 'Does it, Lara?' One hand lifted and sliced the air in savage dismissal. 'You can waltz off and do what you like with the child, without any interference.'

She closed her eyes, unable to bear seeing the dreadful pain she had given him with her deceit. 'It's my responsibility, Ric,' was all she could say in her defence.

'Oh, I'm not disputing that, Lara. Look at me, damn you! Don't think you can shut me out now!'

She opened her eyes, feeling utterly helpless to fix what she'd done. To him it was all offensive. 'I don't know how to make it right,' she said hopelessly.

'The procedure from here is very simple,' he blazed at her. 'We go to a doctor of my choice—not your doctor, Lara, because I don't trust you anymore.'

She flinched. Even knowing she'd broken trust with him, it hurt to be the object of such bitter mistrust. 'I didn't plan getting you to make love to me,' she protested, needing to fight at least that accusation.

He straightened up, a tall powerful man, intensely formidable in his wounded pride. 'You called me back to you on the veranda, Lara. I'd already passed your room.'

'I was afraid I might be asleep when you left in the morning. I wanted...'

'You wanted me to lie with you.' His eyes mocked any innocent spin she could put on that.

She shook her head. 'It just all built from what I felt with you,' she said defeatedly.

'Whatever you *felt* with me, Lara, it obviously wasn't enough for you to consider sharing your life with me.'

Her chin lifted, defying this judgment of her. 'Trapping you into it with a child...after I'd assured you I was protected? Would you be pleased with that situation, Ric?'

'*You* made all the decisions,' came the counterpunch. 'The queen... disregarding the pawn...as though I had no part in the game at all. And believe me... I will disappear from it altogether if it's Gary's child. But if it's mine...'

His jaw tightened. His eyes beamed hard, ruthless determination. '...don't think for one millisecond that I can be turned out of my child's life. I'll fight you with everything I've got for appropriate visiting rights.'

Visiting rights.

Of course.

He wouldn't want her after this.

His opinion of her was so low, it was a wonder he wasn't threatening to sue for custody of the child.

If it was his.

'Make what arrangements you like for the DNA test,' she said dully, resigning herself to the inevitable. 'Let me know and I'll be there.'

'Do I have your word on that?' he grimly demanded.

'Yes.' Her eyes did their own mocking. 'If my word is worth anything.'

He frowned, mistrust flitting over his face again. 'I'll line up an appointment. On the day, I'll come and collect you for it,' he said decisively.

'No need for you to suffer my company any more than you have to, Ric. I'll turn up for the test. I want to know, too.' She summoned up a wry little smile. 'I couldn't bring myself to ask it of you before. But now...' She shrugged. '...you've made your position clear. I can't keep you free of it any longer.'

'No, you can't,' he whipped back.

All her torment over the decisions she'd made had been in vain. Ric hated and despised her for taking the course she had ultimately chosen—the worst possible outcome.

'I guess we should both hope the child is Gary's,' she said bleakly. 'Then you won't have any need to be involved with me anymore.'

'You *want* the child to be Gary's?'

His intonation implied that such a wish should be anathema to her—wanting the child of a man who had abused her. Yet it was the one *out* for him, his only chance of being free from a lifelong commitment to a child he wouldn't have chosen to have.

'Don't *you* want that, Ric?'

His eyes flared with some violent emotion. When he spoke, it was with a bitter edge that cut into all she'd done wrong. 'You know something, Lara? You've never once asked me what I want. It's all been about what you want...which I've tried to give you. But I'm not giving any more. I'll do what's right for me. And I hope you'll have the decency to acknowledge what's right.'

She bowed her head, mortally ashamed of having taken so much from him and giving nothing in return. Though God knew she'd meant to... his freedom for hers. But he was never going to see it that way.

'I'll call you about the appointment,' he said bruskly.

And left.

Lara stared at the closed door for a long time, wishing she could open it again, do it all differently. Ric Donato had come back into her life—the one man who might have been her soul mate—and she had messed up the chance of their ever getting together in a happy and loving relationship.

She found herself fiercely hoping that the child was his. Then he wouldn't walk away. He'd claim visiting rights as the father and maybe somewhere down the line of the future they'd be forced to share, she might be able to change his opinion of her.

It all depended on the DNA test.

A knock on the door startled her. Her first thought was Ric had come back and she quickly called, 'Yes,' not caring if he berated her on some further issue. Any chance to correct his totally negative view of her was welcome, regardless of how painful it might be.

It was the housekeeper, returning to check on her. 'Are you all right, Mrs. Chappel?'

'Yes.' She managed a rueful smile. 'Sorry you were troubled, Mrs. Keith.'

The housekeeper frowned, not satisfied with having this matter brushed off. 'That Mr. Donato…he came in like a storm and went out like one, too, not waiting for me to show him the door.'

'It won't happen again, Mrs. Keith,' Lara assured her, turning her attention to picking up the next row of squares to show everything was back to normal.

It struck her that she was playing another deceit, hiding the truth. Gary had taught her to do that—maintain the image that nothing was wrong or there'd be consequences she wouldn't like. But she had no reason to hide anything now.

'I'm pregnant,' she blurted out.

'Good heavens!'

The housekeeper's shock was testament to how well Lara had hidden her true situation. At least, over the pregnancy. She hadn't been able to completely hide how Gary had conducted their marriage.

'Mr. Donato was upset because I hadn't told him…and he has reason to believe the child I'm carrying might be his.'

'Oh, my dear!' The shock melted into sympathy. 'Do you know…is it your husband's?'

Lara grimaced. 'It could be, Mrs. Keith. That's why…' She heaved a sigh that carried the whole miserable weight of her dilemma. 'Anyway, I've agreed to a DNA test to settle the question one way or another.'

The housekeeper nodded. 'It must be very difficult for you,' she said sadly. 'Can I bring you something? Tea and cake?'

'Yes. Thank you.'

Tea and cake...it reminded Lara of... *Evelyn!*

She hadn't asked Ric how he'd learnt of her pregnancy. *How* had been irrelevant when his very first words had expressed certain knowledge. While she had never actually admitted it to Evelyn, hadn't discussed her situation at all, there was no one else who could have been Ric's source on this.

Gundamurra...

Lara sank onto the chair in front of the sewing machine. Her gaze dropped to the squares of fabric she'd picked up and was still holding. Pieces of a pattern. At least she was in control of the quilt pattern. She wasn't sure she'd ever been in control of the pattern of her life.

At Gundamurra, she'd decided she would take responsibility for what she'd done, steer her own course, stick to what she thought was right, make her own way forward. But that decision had been tainted by the deceit it had forced her to maintain with Ric.

Deceit was never good. Even with the best of intentions, it was never good. Next time she met Ric...there might be only one more time if the child wasn't his. She crossed her hands over her stomach, closed her eyes and fervently prayed...

*Please let it be his...please let it be...*

# CHAPTER FIFTEEN

LARA WAS ALREADY waiting in the obstetrician's rooms when Ric arrived. She looked up from reading a magazine as he entered, her gaze connecting directly with his, affirming that her word was good. She *had* turned up. In good time, too. It was still ten minutes short of the appointment he'd made.

Ric gave her a brief nod of acknowledgment as he strode to the receptionist's desk, his inner tension easing somewhat with the assurance of her presence here. Having had his name checked on the waiting list, he strolled over to the corner where Lara sat and settled on the bench seat adjacent to hers, not crowding her but close enough for them to speak privately.

Not that he had anything to say.

Sitting next to her was more a courtesy thing since they'd be seeing the obstetrician together. All the same, it was a mistake, making him aware of her in ways he needed to forget. He could even smell the perfume she was wearing, some insidiously floral scent that teased him into remembering the sweet sensuality of kissing her hair, her ears...

'Hello.'

The simple word of greeting from her, as though they were teenage kids again, had him gritting his teeth. She'd closed the magazine. Her eyes were fastened on him, eyes as blue as summer skies. He hated her...

yet she could still get to him, making him want what they'd shared before...before he'd realised how she'd used him...and discarded him.

'Did you consider aborting this child?' he shot at her.

She flinched, but recovered quickly, her chin tilting up defiantly. 'No, I didn't.'

'If Gary hadn't died, it would have brought you trouble,' he tersely reminded her.

Pain in her eyes. 'I had a baby...just three months before you took me to Gundamurra. It was...stillborn. I couldn't take this baby's life, Ric. No matter what.'

'Fair enough,' he clipped out, and reached for a magazine from the coffee table in front of them, needing distraction from the way she was affecting him.

It was a fortnight since he'd rampaged into her house, forcing her to admit what he knew. He'd been so chewed up about her rejection of him—even as the father of her child—he'd been barely aware of anything else. Today was different. She'd submitted to his demand. And she was so stunningly beautiful, it hurt.

He flicked through the pages of the magazine but couldn't focus on reading. He kept remembering how her e-mail messages to him had tapered off into flat little reports on her life at Gundamurra, once she'd known she had to be pregnant. No doubt there'd been many conflicts in her mind. This past week, he'd been mad enough to think she might want to keep the baby because it could be his, but it really had nothing to do with him. It was obviously a maternal need.

'Losing a baby is a terrible thing, Ric,' she said quietly.

He didn't want to feel sympathy for her. 'Right!' he said, giving her a hard look. 'Then you understand I won't want to lose any child of *mine*.'

She nodded.

He saw her throat move convulsively.

Her voice was husky, her eyes filled with eloquent appeal as she blurted out, 'I'm sorry I didn't tell you.'

Was she? Ric stared at her, searching for some further layer of deceit.

'It wasn't because I didn't want you in my life,' she rushed out. 'It was because...it wasn't fair to tie you to a lifelong commitment when you would have chosen not to risk it.'

She looked sincere.

Ric frowned and returned his gaze to the opened pages of the magazine. He had no ready reply to what she'd said. Of course he'd been concerned about protection. A decent guy didn't just take a woman without caring about the consequences of sexual intimacy. Lara should not have lied about that. But...in all honesty...he hadn't wanted to stop. And given that moment again...if the truth had been told and she'd still urged him on...

'I had started taking contraceptive pills,' she added, an anxious pleading in her voice. 'Secretly, because Gary was determined on trying for another child and I didn't want it to happen, but I'd only been taking them for two weeks, so... I guess it was too soon for them to work.'

Was this another lie?

It certainly made sense that she wouldn't want to fall pregnant to Gary again—an unbreakable tie to him for life with the possibility of the child suffering abuse, as well. If she had been taking pills...even for a short time...he could understand her wanting them to be effective. Which would mean she hadn't told an out-and-out lie about being protected. More a desperate hope.

And the hope had died some six weeks into her stay at Gundamurra.

Maybe she'd been in such hell about it, she couldn't think straight... cutting him out because the child might be Gary's, and that would mean there was no ultimate escape from the man. Endless fear. And feeling she had no right to drag Ric into her hell.

He could accept that kind of reasoning. But once Gary was dead... no, he couldn't forgive her for cutting him out then. Paying him off...

'You should have wanted a DNA test, anyway,' he stated coldly. 'If the child was another man's, Gary wouldn't have had any lever to force an ongoing relationship.'

'Then he would have known I'd been with you,' she answered so quickly, it must have been played through her mind many times. 'He might have killed you...or had you killed,' she added grimly. 'Gary was very, very possessive.'

'But he ended up dead, Lara,' he shot back at her. 'And you still proceeded to push me away from you.'

Anguish in her eyes. Hot patches of colour burning in her cheeks. He wrenched his gaze from her and directed it firmly to the magazine.

'There's no point in this conversation,' he declared almost viciously, fighting the crazy impulse to sweep her up into his arms and promise everything was all right now.

It wasn't.

'If the results of the test prove the child is mine, we'll have something to talk about,' he added, deliberately limiting the focus of any further conversation with her.

The ensuing silence told him it had been effective.

Yet he couldn't stop himself from brooding over her attempts to clear up various pertinent issues with him. His mind kept returning to her claim that she didn't feel it was fair to tie him into a lifelong commitment when he hadn't chosen to risk having a child with her.

The fatherhood trap.

Except he would never have regarded it as a trap.

And she hadn't asked him.

Maybe because *she* didn't want to be trapped with another man. Which didn't say much for any positive feelings toward him. Yet…how could she have responded so positively when they'd made love if she didn't have good feelings with him, snuggling up so contentedly afterward?

The receptionist called their names.

Ric swiftly set the magazine aside and rose to his feet, instinctively moving to help Lara up, though she wasn't cumbersome with her pregnancy. In fact, the clothes she wore—a navy blue skirt and jacket, teamed with a smart overblouse in navy, white and red—disguised the fact she was pregnant at all, and she stood with the innate fluid grace he'd always associated with her.

Nevertheless, his hand stayed glued to her elbow as they were ushered into their meeting with the obstetrician, some latent sense of possession grabbing hold of his emotions, wanting her to be *his* Lara, the mother of *his* child. It was impossible to shake off the feeling that they did share a bond and somehow the child was a natural outcome of it.

Two chairs had been placed for them in front of the doctor's desk. The enforced separation helped Ric to concentrate on the purpose that had brought them here. The paternity testing was explained. Ric chose to give a small blood sample. Lara chose to do so, as well, but she also had to undergo a procedure called amniocentesis, where a needle was inserted through the abdominal wall to extract some amniotic fluid. This was necessary to perform cytogenic analysis. The tests on the samples usually took five days and the results would be express-couriered to both parties.

Once Ric's blood sample was taken, he waited outside for Lara's procedure to be completed, hoping she wouldn't be upset by it. A needle was just a needle. Nothing to worry about. But she might be supersensitive about anything to do with the baby, having had a stillborn child. He didn't like the idea of her worrying about this one. Which led him into having a few worries himself.

Was she taking appropriate care?

Shouldn't she be bigger at four and a half months?

Was she eating properly?

What had *her* doctor said about the pregnancy?

Ric was champing at the bit by the time Lara emerged from the obstetrician's office. 'I'll drive you home,' he said, taking hold of her arm again and steering her through the waiting room.

'The fee...' She made a fluttery gesture toward the receptionist.

'I've paid it.' He gave her a searching look. 'Are you okay?'

She flushed, lashes sweeping down. 'Yes, of course. It was...nothing. Just a pinprick.'

'Some people get shaky about having needles. I'll see you safely home, Lara.'

She didn't protest.

He waited until he had her tucked into the passenger seat of the Ferrari and the car was moving before mentally pausing to take stock of where he wanted to go with Lara from here. He hated taking her back to the house that Chappel had bought, but it was her choice to stay there until it was sold. He found it bitterly ironic that the last time she'd been in this car, she'd trusted him to get her away from that bastard. Here he was, returning her to *the gilded prison,* possibly pregnant with her husband's child.

Though it might be his.

He *wanted* it to be his.

No denying that, whatever grief it might bring him.

'I presume you've had your pregnancy checked,' he tossed at her, keeping his eyes firmly planted on the road ahead.

'Yes. I've had an ultra-scan. There's no...no abnormality.'

'Everything's going well then?'

'The doctor says so.'

'Do you know the sex?'

'I didn't want to know. If something goes wrong...' She took a deep breath. 'Last time I knew it was a daughter. I'd even named her. She was already a person to me...'

Ric's hands tightened around the driving wheel. The sadness in her voice...the need to protect herself from more grief...she'd been through so much...it struck him he should have been taking far more into consideration than he had in judging and condemning her for pushing him away. A wounded animal holes up by itself, warding off friend and enemy alike, only seeing a world filled with pain.

'You have nothing to fear from me, Lara,' he said quietly. 'If the child is mine, I'll take a supportive role. I don't want there to be any conflict between us.'

She didn't reply.

A sideways glance caught her hands fretting at each other in her lap, revealing the depth of her inner tension.

'Lara?' he pressed, needing to satisfy himself that she was not regarding him as a tyrant who would continually make demands on her. He wasn't like that. He'd be reasonable, try to fit in with what she wanted as best he could. Providing she was reasonable, too. No way was he going to be shut out of his son's or his daughter's life. He'd had a rotten father himself. But he'd be a good one, being there when he should, giving love instead of abuse.

A heavy sigh signalled a dark weight on Lara's heart. *'If the child is yours,'* she repeated in a flat, defeated tone. 'Yes, I expect you will take a supportive role, Ric, given that you're the father. And no, I'm not afraid of you.'

He could hear the line of logic left unsaid—no support at all if the child was Gary's. She envisaged him walking out of her life as abruptly as he had walked into it. No future together.

Her previous actions had implied that was what *she* had decided upon— for him to be right out of her life. But he sensed now it wasn't what she wanted. Or was he fooling himself?

It wasn't her fault if she was carrying Gary's child. No doubt it had been forced upon her. No choice. Though she had chosen *him* to wipe her husband out of her mind. How much did that mean?

'You won't mind my having visiting rights?' he asked warily.

Another sigh. 'No, I won't mind. I know you'd make a good father, Ric.'

But was he big enough to be a father to another man's child? A man he despised?

Either way, the baby was Lara's. She wanted it, no matter what. The critical question was...did she want him, putting aside everything else? Her previous rejection of him suggested that she didn't. Or that the whole situation was just too difficult for her to sort out. Easier to turn her back on it and go her own way. Which also meant he wasn't important enough for her to fight for. Or maybe she'd had a gutful of fighting in her marriage and couldn't summon the will to make another stand.

Ric found himself driving up to the front door of the Vaucluse mansion with this torment still raging in his mind. Lara bent forward, picked up her handbag from the floor near her feet, opened it, found the keys that would lock him out of her life again. Every muscle in his body tensed, aggression pumping through him. He braked more abruptly than he should have, the tyres of the Ferrari spraying gravel as they ground to a halt.

She waited for him to let her out of the car. He did it reluctantly, watching the silky fall of her hair flow forward as she ducked her head, stepping out. His gut was in knot. The urge to fight for this woman's love was like a madness in his brain, yet a vestige of sanity insisted it couldn't be forced. Love was either there or it wasn't.

He closed the car door and accompanied her up the steps to the colonnaded porch. She said nothing. He said nothing. They stopped in front of the door. She looked down at the keys in her hand.

'Thank you for bringing me home, Ric,' she murmured. 'I guess... I guess this is goodbye...unless the DNA test proves you're the father.'

Her hesitant tone seemed to carry a sad yearning for a different outcome. It was encouragement enough for Ric to seize the moment and ask, 'Do you want it to be goodbye, Lara?'

Slowly, very slowly, her eyelashes lifted and the poignant feeling reflected in the beautiful blue eyes pierced his heart. 'I couldn't bear it... if you didn't care for my baby, Ric.'

There it was.

She shook her head, tore her gaze from his, inserted the key in the lock, opened the door, stepped inside and shut him out.

He'd hung everything on its being his child.

And it wasn't enough.

# CHAPTER SIXTEEN

It was the sixth day.

The obstetrician had said the tests usually took five days.

So today should bring the courier to her door.

As on every other morning, Lara doggedly went to the sewing room, determined on keeping busy, doing what she would have done if Ric had never learnt about her pregnancy. But she'd finished the cot quilt yesterday, and didn't have the heart to start something else, not when the courier could arrive at any minute.

She forced herself to sift through fabrics that might be good for cushion covers—a futile exercise. Her mind could not focus on anything other than the news she was waiting for—the news that would either bring Ric Donato back into her life or keep him out of it forever.

He'd cared about her, more than she had ever expected anyone would, and her heart bled over the loss of Ric's caring. She'd killed it by trying to set him free and he'd taken her decision as meaning it didn't matter to her. *He* didn't matter to her. And that was the biggest lie of all.

She left the sewing room and wandered listlessly into the nursery, stared at the newly finished quilt that was now spread over the cot, ready for her baby. The desire for it to be Ric's child was desperate now. She knew he would pour all his caring into being a good father, and maybe... maybe somewhere in the future, his caring for their child would spill over onto her and she'd feel it again…the feeling of being *his woman,* so special to him he'd do anything for her. As he had.

Tears blurred her eyes. There was no chance of any future with him if he wasn't the father. He'd made that all too clear. And she couldn't blame anyone but herself, hiding the truth, too ashamed to lay it all out to him. Too late when she did. Though he might never have accepted the child, anyway, if he wasn't the father.

She had to hang on to that thought.

It was her only protection from breaking up entirely. She had to stay strong for her baby, let Ric go if she had to.

'Mrs. Chappel…?' The housekeeper, not finding her in the sewing room.

'I'm in here, Mrs. Keith. Admiring my quilt,' she added in wry explanation.

The nursery door was open. Lara blinked hard to erase the film of moisture in her eyes and turned to face the housekeeper who took only a few moments to walk the extra metres along the hall. She appeared in the doorway, holding an official looking envelope, and Lara's heart instantly kicked into a fearful gallop.

'This has just come for you, Mrs. Chappel. I've signed for it.'

Signed…courier…it had to be…

Lara couldn't bring herself to move, to actually take it, knowing its contents would decide her future. Mrs. Keith had to enter the room to hand it to her, forcing an acceptance of it. The envelope hung between Lara's fingers and thumb, just a sliver of paper, yet it sent pins and needles over her entire body. She stared down at the official printing on its top left-hand corner—DNA Diagnostics Centre.

'Shall I bring your morning tea up here, Mrs. Chappel?'

She barely heard the words. Her ears were filled with the drumbeat of Fate rolling inexorably over her.

'No.' Even her own voice sounded far away. 'I'll have it out on the patio near the swimming pool, Mrs. Keith. Sit in the sun for a while.' Though it was unlikely to warm her. The chill in her bones went too deep.

The housekeeper nodded and left, giving Lara immediate privacy. Because she had to know what the envelope meant. Tea and sympathy, Lara thought, though nothing would be said. Mrs. Keith would wait to be told what could be expected in the future—a part-time father for the baby to be born...or none at all.

The question could be answered right now. All Lara had to do was open the envelope, read the results of the DNA test. Do it, she told herself, but her fingers wouldn't obey the order. They felt numb, not connected to her brain. Or there was a bank of resistance in her mind, overriding the dictate.

She walked downstairs and out to the patio, carrying the still sealed envelope with her. The sky was blue. Not a cloud in it. The harbour lay glittering in front of her. It could have been a summer's day, except for the slight nip in the air. But there was winter in her soul and the sunshine did nothing to dispel it.

She set the envelope on the table, where she had sat and wept when Ric had forced her to tell the truth about her marriage. He'd had to do that all along—forcing truth from her. Even now she couldn't look at it—the truth of the DNA test. After Mrs. Keith had served the tea, she told herself. Then she'd be alone with it, more ready to cope with whatever it meant to her.

The memory of Ric standing out here that first morning drew her over to where he had stood, taking in the view. Had he actually been looking at it, or seeing only the memories he had of her—memories of a far more innocent time when it had felt as though they'd been born for each other.

Even then she'd hidden the truth, avoiding telling her parents about Ric, knowing they would disapprove of any relationship with him and move to cut him out of her life. And that, in turn had led Ric into believing he wasn't good enough for her, stealing the Porsche...

It was she who wasn't good enough for him.

He'd grown into a man that any woman in the world would be proud to have at her side, and not just because he was handsome and wealthy. He was so much more than that...so much more. And she hadn't even had the wits to see through Gary Chappel's charming facade to the cold, cruelly calculating heart within.

She didn't deserve Ric, didn't deserve his caring. It was enough—more than enough—that he'd freed her from Gary so she could make something positive out of her life.

And taking her to Gundamurra. That had been good for her, too. She had a lot to be grateful for. Although none of it eased the ache inside her.

She hugged herself, trying to make it go away. The baby would make up for the painful sense of loss. Her baby...

Footsteps on the patio behind her...the housekeeper bringing out a tray of morning tea things...the sealed envelope still on the table. What were Marie Antoinette's infamous words before she was condemned to the guillotine? *Let them eat cake?*

'Just set it down, thank you, Mrs. Keith,' Lara instructed without turning around. 'I'll serve myself when I'm ready.'

No reply.

No sound of the tray being set on the glass surface of the outdoors table.

No footsteps going away.

Absolute silence.

Was the housekeeper staring at the unopened envelope?

Well, at least it transmitted a message that Lara had nothing to talk about yet. Being the soul of discretion, Mrs. Keith would follow instructions and discreetly withdraw. Any moment now. Then it was up to Lara to face what had to be faced. No more hiding from it.

'You still don't know.'

The deep timbre of that voice—Ric's voice!—vibrated through every cell in Lara's body. Ric...here...! Dear God, did that mean...?

Her heart leapt with joy. A cocktail of hope fizzed through her mind. She swung around, giddy with the prospect of having Ric in her life on a continuing basis. He had to be the father of her baby. He wouldn't have come otherwise.

But his grim face made her check the burst of pleasure at seeing him. The dark velvet eyes burned like hard coals, and she felt their fire searing her soul, no quarter given in the search for a truth he was determined on having.

'I don't know, either,' he said, reaching inside his jacket and withdrawing the envelope that matched hers. He tossed it onto the table. It hadn't been opened.

Lara stared at it in shocked confusion. She didn't understand this. He'd wanted the proof of paternity, either way. Demanded it of her. It made no sense that he'd come here without first checking the results of the test. She wrenched her stunned gaze from the incontrovertible evidence that he hadn't, and forced it up to meet the blaze of purpose in his.

'Why, Ric?' she asked simply.

'Because you matter more, Lara,' came the heart-jolting reply. 'I would accept...and love...any child of yours...because it's part of you.'

*Love*...her reeling mind clung to that one word. She couldn't quite take in the rest but she thought it meant he still cared about her, that she *was* special to him.

'The question is...' he went on slowly, searchingly '...am I deluding myself about what you feel for me?'

She couldn't speak. There was a massive lump of emotion blocking her throat. He moved toward her. It didn't occur to her to move toward him. Every atom of her energy was focused on watching him, trying to feel what he was feeling. The yearning inside her was so huge, she wasn't sure if she was misreading the same need in him...the need to have and to hold because despite all the differences between them—in the past and right now—they touched something in each other that blotted out the rest of the world.

Her hands were linked in front of her, instinctively protective of the baby in her womb. He gently drew them apart and lifted them to his shoulders. Her heart fluttered in wild hope. Everything inside her quivered at the sheer force of the desire he stirred.

'When we made love...' he murmured, his eyes softer now, molten liquid flowing into her, warming the blood in her veins, making it race to a chaotic beat. '...it was me, you wanted, wasn't it, Lara? Not just because I was there...and I could answer your need?'

Somehow she forced her voice to work. 'Only you could have done that, Ric,' she answered, and the truth of that night, which she'd kept dammed up inside her, burst its banks and came pouring out. 'And the need...the need was to have you. At least once in my life. Because I might lose you again. And I couldn't bear...not to have known you like that while I still could.'

He drew in a deep breath, his chest expanding with it. She could feel his tension in the rigid shoulder muscles, knew that what she'd said had hit him hard. But it was the truth and she fiercely willed him to believe her.

'It wasn't about...wiping out what Gary had done?'

'That, too,' she admitted. 'But I would have said anything to make you give me...what you did, Ric. I'm sorry it got so complicated...with the pregnancy.'

'It doesn't matter,' he said gruffly.

'It wasn't fair...'

He placed a silencing finger on her lips. 'There's nothing fair in love and war, Lara. We just have to survive the hard patches. And believe in what we're doing.'

The finger moved, trailing across her cheek, tracing its contours before shifting the fall of her hair back behind her ear. Lara stood mesmerised by its touch, feeling her skin come alive under the brush of his. It had always been this way with Ric—holding hands when they were teenagers...sharing that one kiss...the total experience of intimacy with him...

'I couldn't bear for you to be a battered wife,' he said softly. 'Not my Lara...'

*His?* Did he still think of her as his?

'You remained an unattainable dream to me until the day I saw that photo,' he went on, his voice furred with deep emotion. 'But what I feel for you now is very real. And if what you feel for me is real...'

The need in his eyes swelled the tidal wave of need rampaging through her. His hands cradled her face as his own came nearer and nearer. When his lips touched hers...covered them...moved them...the sweet bliss of connecting with him again triggered an overwhelming response. She kissed him back with all her heart, her soul, and her mind danced with the sheer joy of it... Ric wanting her, no matter what.

She loved this man. Loved all that he was. Her hands hugged his head, holding him to her. Her mouth expressed all the passion she felt for him. Her body strained against his, revelling in the closeness that was not going to be taken away. He was going to stay with her...love her...love her baby.

And in between the kisses his eyes shone down at hers, seeing, believing. It *was* real...this feeling they had together. He held her, his hands moving over her possessively, tenderly, lovingly, passionately, and the sunshine of his touch seeped into her bones, a brilliant heat that chased winter away.

'Come home with me, Lara,' he murmured. 'I need you to be with me.'

Not here with the shadows of her marriage. In a space they could own together. 'Yes,' she happily agreed, wanting what he wanted, yearning for it.

He smiled, drew back, took her hand. She looked down at this simplest form of being joined to him, remembering, feeling it again...the bond that seemed to link their lives to a magical place that belonged only to them.

'We used to walk like this,' she said, smiling back at him.

'I remember.'

'It's not a fantasy, Ric.'

'No. It's not.' He rubbed his thumb over her bare third finger. 'Will you wear my wedding ring, Lara?'

The breath caught in her throat momentarily. A kind of ecstatic incredulity billowed through her mind. So much...so soon? Yet the determined purpose that had brought him here still burned in his eyes, a simmering glow now, but telling her unequivocally the words were meant.

'I'd feel very honoured to wear it, Ric,' she said soberly.

'Then I think we should get married as soon as possible. Before the baby is born.'

'The baby...' Her gaze swung to the envelopes, still lying on the table. Her hand convulsively squeezed his as anxiety flooded through her. 'Ric, you have to know...'

'No. Leave it. I promise you it won't make any difference.'

'But it does. I haven't told Victor Chappel about my pregnancy, but if I have a baby who looks like Gary, or anyone in his family...' She shook her head worriedly. 'He won't let it go, Ric. And if you marry me, you'll be caught up in the fight, too.'

'Lara...your fight is my fight. I won't let you stand alone against Victor Chappel,' he said calmly.

'He won't give up. It will be ongoing...' The fear seized her brilliant bubble of happiness and started tearing it to shreds. 'He'll get some legal order preventing me from leaving the country with the child. Which wouldn't matter if I was on my own. But your business takes you overseas, Ric, and I wouldn't be able to accompany you. I won't go and leave...'

'The business can be run by others,' he argued. 'I can start something else.'

His confidence in resolving any and every problem soothed some of her agitation. But she couldn't help feeling it was asking too much of him. He hadn't lived with the Chappels as she had. Her gaze shifted to the envelopes again, drawn by a dreadful sense of inevitability that she'd bring trouble to Ric.

'Victor will insist on a DNA test, anyway,' she muttered. 'I have to know what I'm getting you into. I won't hide from this. I won't.' She lifted pleading eyes to his. 'If you want me to go forward with you, Ric, it has to be with the truth, both of us knowing what we'll be dealing with. That's fair, isn't it?'

He weighed her argument then slowly answered, 'As long as you understand I won't let you back out of marrying me, Lara. Whatever it takes for us to be together... I'm your man.'

Her man.

Yes, he was.

In every sense.

Whatever the future held, she would never undervalue his feeling for her, or hers for him.

'Thank you,' she said, acknowledging the extraordinary gift of his love. 'Thank you for coming back into my life. Thank you for rescuing me and making me feel like a worthwhile person. Thank you for letting me be one with you. I promise you I'll never turn away from that, Ric. No matter what.'

He drew a deep breath and gestured to the table. 'Then let's deal with the truth.'

She looked at the sealed envelopes. They held no power to hurt, she told herself. She and Ric had moved past that place. Determined to prove it, she stepped over to the table, picked up the closest envelope, tore it open, extracted the contents and read the results of the testing.

And it felt as though the world shifted.

All the conflicts she'd feared just...winked out of any possible existence. She looked at Ric—seeing him as the driving force behind everything that was now right for her. Even this. Especially this.

'It's you. You're the father of my baby.'

'Our baby,' he corrected her.

She laughed. And then she was crying. But they were happy tears, not tears to be hidden. Ric kissed them away and they smiled at each other.

'Come home with me now?' he asked.

'I am home with you, Ric. That's how it feels.'

'Yes. That's how it feels for me, too.'

# CHAPTER SEVENTEEN

*Christmas at Gundamurra...*

RIC WAS LOOKING forward to it.

'Got to show you off to Patrick,' he told the baby who was cradled in his arms, eyes closed, not so much as a flutter from the thick black lashes.

The rocking motion of the swing-lounge always did the trick—stopped the crying, put the baby to sleep. Ric automatically used his feet to keep the swing going as his gaze roved over the view from where he sat. To his mind, this deck outside the main living room was one of the best features of the house he'd bought for Lara. It faced north, catching the sun all winter, and the view over the bay at Balmoral with the Norfolk pines edging the beach and the marina full of yachts, coming and going, made sitting out here a constant pleasure.

Lara loved everything about the house and was still getting the furnishings *just right* for it, taking enormous delight in choosing exactly what she thought made it a home for them. It made Ric happy, simply to see her so happy. And Balmoral was just across the harbour from Circular Quay, not far at all for him to buzz into the office when he had to. Though he was taking time out for a while, enjoying being a father, giving himself paternity leave.

Right now it was his job to mind the baby while Lara and Mrs. Keith packed for the trip to Gundamurra. 'I'm a top-notch rocker, kid,' he told his charge whose perfect contentment confirmed the claim.

The self-indulgent boast brought Johnny to mind—king of rock when it came to country music. Ric grinned as he remembered Johnny rolling up to the hospital to view the new Donato, bringing his guitar with him, and singing the ballad he'd written about the boy from Gundamurra... 'His spirit would not rest...till he'd brought his woman home.'

There were many verses but that was the chorus, repeated so often, the whole hospital ward had ended up gathered outside Lara's room, listening to Johnny sing and joining in with him on those two lines. Totally embarrassing. But Lara had loved it. And Mitch had egged Johnny on to get the song recorded, give them all a copy of it for Christmas. No doubt Evelyn would love it too, play it endlessly, especially with having Gundamurra mentioned in the lyrics.

Patrick would smile.

Patrick...the only real father the three of them had ever known. Always there for them if they needed him for anything. Always coming through for them when asked.

'I'm going to be like him,' Ric promised his own child. 'You can count on me to plant your feet on the ground so you know how to choose your own path, get it right. And I'll always be there to back you up, lend a helping hand...'

He was glad he'd taken Lara to Gundamurra, that she'd spent those months with Patrick. Although she had established a better relationship with her mother, and even Ric was now acceptable to Andrea Seymour, there'd been no argument over where they'd go for Christmas. The Outback sheep station was now a special place for both of them.

It was going to be great this year. Mitch was coming, too, bringing Kathryn Ledger with him, which was certainly a sign that the relationship between them was getting serious. Though Mitch was a deep one. He didn't give much away. He might simply be taking Kathryn to Gundamurra to see how she reacted to it. A test. Mitch had a habit of cross-examining everything—a barrister by nature as well as by profession.

If it was a test, Ric hoped Kathryn would pass it. He liked her. Lara liked her, too. Though love was something else, as he well knew. If

Johnny and Mitch ever got married, he wished for them the same kind of love he'd found with Lara. It made such a huge difference to his life.

'Mrs. Donato is ready for the baby now,' Mrs. Keith called out to him.

'Okay. We're coming,' Ric answered, pausing the swing-lounge and moving off it without a jolt.

The housekeeper was holding the door open for him to pass inside. She smiled at the two of them and he grinned back at her. 'Fast asleep,' he crowed, nodding down at the babe. 'See what a father's touch can do?'

She arched an amused eyebrow. 'Nothing to do with the swing, of course, Mr. Donato.'

'It's knowing the right rhythm, Mrs. Keith.'

'An instinctive knowledge,' she agreed, her eyes twinkling.

Definitely a good woman to have with the family, Ric thought. Lara had been right about that. A very helpful and pleasant presence in the house. Gave Lara support with the baby, as well, having had plenty of experience with her own children.

He walked through to the nursery where he knew Lara would be getting ready to feed the baby. She was laying out fresh clothes on the change table when he entered. She turned to him, smiling as she quickly unbuttoned her blouse and unhooked the maternity bra.

'We're all packed and ready to go. As soon as I've fed the baby, we can leave.'

'No big hurry,' he assured her. 'Johnny will wait for us.'

Her beautiful blue eyes sparkled with excitement. 'Just as well we're travelling in his private plane. I've got so many Christmas gifts to take.'

'This is the best one,' Ric said, smiling down at their son... Patrick Alexander Donato.

'And it's so right that he'll be spending his first Christmas at Gundamurra,' Lara happily declared.

'He won't remember it.'

'But *we* will. You've got your camera ready, haven't you?'

'Of course.'

'Then I know you'll capture it all brilliantly, Ric.'

She took their son who came instantly awake at the change of contact, snuffling around at the smell of milk. Barely one month old and latching onto Lara's breast the moment it was bared. *That's my boy,* Ric thought with fatuous pride, watching Lara settle into the rocking chair where she liked to feed him.

My son...my wife...our home...and Gundamurra for Christmas.

Life couldn't be better than this.

Except...he hoped they'd have a daughter next time, make up for the one Lara had lost. And he'd give her the pleasure of naming their little girl.

She'd insisted that he name their son—Patrick for the man who'd saved both of them, Alexander because the world was out there to be conquered—in a strictly personal sense. He was going to teach his son that barriers were only in his mind.

He and Lara could have been together a long time ago if he hadn't put that *unattainable* barrier in his own mind. Would have saved a lot of grief, too. But he couldn't redo the past, only make the most of the present and the future...the rest of their lives.

Lara looked up at him, her eyes softly glowing. 'I love our life together, Ric. Thank you for making it happen.'

'It could only happen with you. I love you, Lara. Always will.'

'It's the same for me. You do know that, don't you, Ric?'

No mistaking the love in her eyes.

'Yes, I know.'

*His Lara...*

Always had been...

Always would be.

\* \* \* \* \*

133 - 261

# The Outback
# Wedding Takeover

# PROLOGUE

THE PLANE WAS heading down to a red dirt airstrip. Apart from the cluster of buildings that marked the sheep station of Gundamurra, there was no other habitation in sight between here and the horizon——a huge empty landscape dotted with scrubby trees.

'Wish I had my camera,' Ric Donato murmured.

Mitch Tyler frowned over the other boy's words. Apparently the stark visual impact of the place didn't intimidate Ric. But then the guy had been copped joyriding in a stolen Porsche. He probably got off on wide-open spaces, while Mitch had always been happiest with a book in his hands. No local library here to tap into.

'The middle of nowhere,' he muttered dispiritedly. 'I'm beginning to think I made the wrong choice.'

'Nah,' Johnny Ellis drawled. 'Anything's better than being locked up. At least we can breathe out here.'

'What? Dust?' Mitch mocked.

The plane landed, kicking up a cloud of it.

'Welcome to the great Australian Outback,' the cop escorting them said derisively. 'And just remember...if you three city smart-arses want to survive, there's nowhere to run.'

All three of them ignored him. They were sixteen. Regardless of what life threw at them, they were going to survive. And Johnny had it right,

Mitch thought. Six months working on a sheep station had to be better than a year in a juvenile jail.

It was half the time, for a start, and there were only two other guys with him, not a horde of criminals who would have established a pecking order. Mitch hated bullies with a passion. He'd learnt how to look after himself. No-one touched him anymore. But he sure didn't want to be incarcerated with a mob of power pushers.

He hoped the owner of this place wasn't some kind of little Hitler, exploiting the justice system to get a free labour force. Mitch decided he'd work out for himself what was fair and challenge anything that wasn't.

What had the judge said at the sentencing? Something about getting back to ground values. A program that would teach them what real life was about. Wouldn't teach him a damned thing about *real life,* Mitch had thought at the time. He'd majored in *real life,* ever since his father had walked out on his crippled wife, leaving him and his sister to look after their mother. The lion's share of that had fallen to Jenny, who'd only been eleven years old to his eight when their father had deserted them. Not that he'd been much help anyway, getting drunk every night, drowning his sorrows instead of facing up to them. A coward. That was what his father had been. A contemptible coward.

But not as contemptible as the guy who'd date-raped Jenny.

At least Mitch had had the satisfaction of facing that bastard with what he'd done.

There she'd been, all excited about being invited to a swish party, finally getting into a bit of social life, and to be treated like a disposable piece of meat...

He was glad he'd given that piece of slime a beating he'd remember for a long time. It might be primitive justice, and against the law, but better than letting him get away with it, no justice at all. Jenny had been too traumatised to press charges against him. The silver-spoon heir to a fortune would probably have got off anyway, with his mega-wealthy family having the power and influence to get anything excused.

Mitch felt no remorse over what he'd done. None whatsoever. Though he was sorry he wouldn't be at home to help for the next six months.

The plane taxied back to where a man—the owner?—was waiting beside a four-wheel drive Land Rover. Big man—broad-shouldered, barrel-chested, craggy weathered face, iron-grey hair. Had to be over fifty but still looking tough and formidable. Not someone to buck in a hurry, Mitch decided, though size didn't automatically command his respect.

'John Wayne rides again,' he mocked to cover his unease with the situation.

'No horse,' Johnny remarked with a grin.

Mitch found himself smiling back.

It looked like Johnny Ellis would provide some comic relief if life got grim here. He seemed to have the kind of affable nature that would avoid violence if it was avoidable, though even at sixteen his physique was big enough and strong enough to match anyone in a punch-up if forced into it.

Johnny and Ric were street kids. No family. And no doubt they'd worked out ways of looking after themselves. Mitch figured Johnny specialised in being everyone's mate. He had friendly hazel eyes, a ready grin, and sun-streaked brown hair that tended to flop over his forehead. He'd been caught dealing in marijuana, though he swore it was only to musicians who'd get it from someone else anyway.

Ric Donato was a very different kettle of fish. He had an intensity about him that could make him dangerous, Mitch thought. Was he a thief because he wanted too much, too obsessively? He seemed to have a very single-minded passion for the girl he'd stolen the Porsche for, wanting to match up to her rich life.

Mitch imagined that most girls would get a thrill out of Ric, just by being the focus of his attention. The guy had sex appeal in spades—mad, bad and dangerous, well-built without being hunky, and strikingly handsome in a very macho Italian way—black curly hair, almost black eyes, olive skin, and a face that Michelangelo might have carved for its masculine beauty. Perversely enough, the guy didn't seem to have tickets on himself at all. Like he'd been hit too many times to believe he'd been handed anything to feel good about.

Mitch felt okay with himself. Angry at what had been dealt out to his family, but okay with the person he was. He didn't have Ric's good looks but he was presentable enough—on the lean side but not a weakling, taller than most guys his age, and having blue eyes with almost black hair seemed to impress some girls.

Mitch would prefer them to be more impressed by the smart brain that had got him labelled as a nerd before he took up boxing at the local boys' club. He'd never understood why using his intelligence earned scornful remarks from the jocks. Anyhow, he wasn't called a nerd or a weed any more. He might not be liked but he'd made damned sure he was respected.

The plane came to a halt.

The cop told them to get their duffle-bags from under the back seats. A few minutes later he was leading them out to a way of life which was far, far removed from anything the three of them had known before.

The initial introduction had Mitch instantly tensing up.

'Here are your boys, Mister Maguire. Straight off the city streets for you to whip into shape.'

The big old man—and he sure was big close up—gave the cop a steely look. 'That's not how we do things out here.' The words were softly spoken but they carried a confident authority that scorned any need for bully-boy tactics.

He nodded to the three of them, offering a measure of respect. 'I'm Patrick Maguire. Welcome to Gundamurra. In the Aboriginal language, that means "Good day". I hope you will all eventually feel it was a good day when you first set foot on my place.'

Mitch felt reassured by this little speech. It had a welcoming ring to it, no punishment intended. As long as they were treated fairly, Mitch was prepared to cope with whatever work was thrown at them. He mostly lived in his mind, anyway.

'And you are...?' Patrick Maguire held out a massive hand that looked suspiciously like a bone-cruncher.

'Mitch Tyler,' he answered, thrusting his own hand out in defiant challenge.

'Good to meet you, Mitch.'

A normal hand-shake, no attempt to dominate.

Johnny's hand came out with no hesitation. 'Johnny Ellis. Good to meet you, Mister Maguire.' Big smile to the old man, pouring out the charm. Getting onside fast was Johnny.

A weighing look in the steely grey gaze, plus a hint of amusement. No-one's fool, Mitch thought, impressed by the shrewd intelligence of the man and watching him keenly as he moved on to Ric who looked every bit as keyed up as Mitch had been.

'Ric Donato.' It was a flat introduction, strained of any telltale emotion. Ric took the offered hand, feeling the strength in it, seeming to test what it might mean to him.

'Ready to go?' the old man asked.

'Yeah. I'm ready.' Aggression in this reply.

Ready to take on the whole damned world if he had to, Mitch interpreted. Ric Donato might not have tickets on himself but he sure had a huge chip on his shoulder. Mitch wondered if Patrick Maguire would somehow manage to remove it while they were here. Would he also be able to dig under Johnny's genial facade and discover what made Johnny tick?

The knowing grey eyes swept back to Mitch and he felt himself bristling defensively. Did this old man of the land have anything to teach him? Only about sheep, Mitch thought mockingly...yet six months was a long time, and for all he knew right now, he might end up feeling it was a 'good day' when he'd first set foot on Gundamurra.

# CHAPTER ONE

*Eighteen years later...*

THE IRON COMPOSURE of the woman in the witness stand finally cracked. Mitch knew his cross-examination had been merciless. At his lethal best. And totally justified in his mind. This woman had shown no mercy to her son who'd begged his mother for help which had been steadfastly refused, and not even his suicide had softened her heart toward her bereft daughter-in-law. He watched her break into weeping and felt no sympathy at all.

She wasn't weeping over her lost son.

She wasn't weeping over the torment he'd suffered.

She was weeping because she'd been faced with her own monstrous ego that had branded her son a failure for not living up to what *she* had required from him.

And now it was going to cost her, not only in having her character stripped bare in public, but also in an appropriate financial settlement for the cast-off daughter-in-law and her baby son.

His opposing counsel, Harriet Lowell, who also happened to be Mitch's recently excised partner in bed, requested a recess and the judge decided it was close enough to the lunch break to take it now, court to be resumed at two o'clock.

Harriet threw Mitch a dirty look as she moved to assist her client from the witness stand. He returned a steely gaze that promised more of the same after lunch if there was no agreement to the settlement he was demanding on behalf of his client.

Harriet could spit chips at how he was handling this case but he was going to win it hands down. Justice would be served. And he was glad it had come to this—payment in more than dollars. People who gave pain should feel it themselves. The trick was to find what actually hurt them, make them reconsider their position. And keep it all under a legal umbrella.

Use the system to get justice.

That's what Patrick Maguire had taught him.

It was a good system if it was used as it was meant to be used. Patrick had been right about that. Mitch had been studying the law ever since he'd left Gundamurra—eighteen years—orchestrating what was necessary to get his own juvenile conviction for assault set aside so he could enter the profession, working his way up to becoming a barrister with a formidable reputation for winning the cases he took on.

He believed in them. That was what made the difference. He never took on a case unless he believed he was fighting for right, and then he gave it everything he could bring to it. Harriet saw the law as a chess game—moves and counter-moves—but to Mitch the chessboard was always black and white, and he wasn't interested in playing black.

His clerk met him outside the courtroom, handing him a message from Ric Donato. He couldn't make lunch today. Disappointing. Mitch always enjoyed meeting up with Ric. And Johnny. Although their lives had travelled very different paths since their time at Gundamurra, the three of them had remained good friends over the years.

They shared the common bond of Patrick Maguire's influence in setting them on the paths they'd chosen—each to their own bent. And they understood where each other was coming from and why. Not too many people ever achieved that kind of understanding.

It came from living together in constant proximity for six months. There were few distractions in the outback. It was a place for talking, chewing over things, reflecting on what had meaning and what didn't, sharing each other's visions of the world. And dreams.

Ric had become an award-winning photo-journalist—amazing stuff he'd shot with his camera. Retired from the job now and running an international photographic agency. Very successfully.

Johnny was a star with his country music, currently touring the U.S.—a millionaire many times over with most of his recordings going platinum.

Mitch was the only one whose chosen career kept him in Australia. The halls of justice called to him and Sydney was his city. Still, it was great to catch up with the others when they were in town. He wondered what had caused Ric to miss their lunch today—had to be some business problem.

'Cancel the booking at the restaurant,' he instructed his clerk. 'I'll buy some sandwiches, eat in the park, get some fresh air.'

If he couldn't have Ric's company to dilute the cold nastiness of this case, he'd prefer to be outdoors, soaking up some sunshine.

Sitting in the park reminded Mitch of his own mother—the countless times he'd pushed her wheelchair to the small park near where they'd lived at Surry Hills. Every Saturday and Sunday if it was fine. Fresh air and sunshine, being outside, watching other people, spending time together, giving Jenny a break so she felt free to go and do her own thing—which was what his mother had always encouraged for both of them, hating the idea of her disability holding them back from pursuing goals of their own.

She hadn't tried to rule the lives of her children, not like the woman he'd just pilloried on the witness stand, meting out punishment when her son hadn't measured up to her predetermined mould for him. If anything, his own mother had been too self-effacing, not even wanting to ask for what was her rightful due.

It was good that she'd lived long enough to see him called to the bar. She'd been very proud of that achievement. And she'd seen Jenny married to a good guy, too. Both her children doing well for themselves. If he ever had children himself...well, that wasn't going to happen any time soon.

He'd dallied with the idea of marrying Harriet. They shared the same profession. She was a smart, witty woman and he'd generally enjoyed her company. Enjoyed the sex with her, too. Until he'd found out she was also having sex with one of the judges, laughing it off as simply a strategy to give her an edge in court. Winning was what Harriet was about. Winning at all costs. She'd probably thought winning him would be a feather in her cap. She'd certainly been angling for marriage.

No way now, Mitch thought. If he ever married, he'd want honesty in the relationship. Loyalty, too. As for love...well, Harriet had engaged his mind, but had she ever really engaged his heart? Mitch wasn't sure what love was between a man and a woman. Attraction, yes. A sexual high, yes. But love...maybe he'd become too disciplined in controlling emotion to feel a deep abiding passion for a woman.

He strolled back to the court house, gearing himself up for another competitive round with Harriet who'd no doubt be objecting to every tack he took with her client. His clerk met him on the steps with another message—this one from Ric's executive assistant in Sydney, a woman by the name of Kathryn Ledger, asking him to return her call on a matter of urgency.

Was Ric in trouble?

A broken lunch appointment, no excuse given.

Now an urgent call from his office.

Mitch glanced at his watch. Still ten minutes before he was due in court. He whipped out his mobile phone, retreated down the steps for a quick bit of privacy and called the number written on the message slip.

'Kathryn Ledger,' came the brisk response.

'Mitch Tyler. I don't have much time. What's the problem?'

'In a nutshell...Ric received photographic evidence this morning that a woman he knows is a battered wife. He went straight to her home and took her out of the situation. He's flown her off somewhere in Johnny Ellis's plane.'

'Good God!' Mitch muttered in disbelief.

'The husband was having her watched by a private investigator who lost their trail at our basement car park when Ric switched cars.' The incredible tale went on. 'Her husband has since turned up at our office, harassing the staff for information. I gave him the name of the restaurant where you and Ric were supposed to meet for lunch, but he's bound to come back when he doesn't find Ric there. My instructions were to call you if there was trouble.'

'A woman he knew?' Mitch queried.

'He called her Lara Seymour and said they went back a long way.'

Ric's Lara? From when he was sixteen?

Mitch's mind boggled.

Could a youthful passion last this long?

Stealing a Porsche to impress a girl was one thing. Stealing a married woman from her husband—eighteen years later!—was one hell of a leap.

'But the name isn't Lara Seymour now,' the informing voice went on. 'It's Lara Chappel...married to Gary Chappel, son of Victor Chappel. You know who I mean?'

Gary Chappel!

Mitch was momentarily poleaxed by shock.

'Mr Tyler? The Chappel medical clinic and nursing home empire? We're talking big money and power here. And we've got trouble.'

Mitch's trapped breath hissed out as his mind clicked to action stations. 'I know exactly what you mean, Ms Ledger. Do you still have this photographic evidence?'

'Yes. Five copies in the safe.'

'I'll be sending two security men to escort you to my chambers. Do not leave your office until they arrive. Bring one copy of the photograph with you. Once you are safely in my chambers, wait in my private office for me. I'll join you as soon as I'm free. I cannot emphasise enough... follow these instructions to the letter, Ms Ledger. Believe me, you have big trouble.'

'Thank you, Mr Tyler. Rest assured I'll follow your advice.'

'Good!'

Efficient and sensible, Mitch thought as he hurried back to his clerk. As she should be, given her executive position in Ric's business. All the same, he was impressed by her quick summary of the situation and her no-quibbling response to the course of action he'd outlined.

He told his clerk what he wanted done, adding, 'This is urgent business. Get the security men there pronto, and tell them Ms Ledger is carrying merchandise that is invaluable.'

Definitely *invaluable,* Mitch thought with grim satisfaction. Legal evidence against Gary Chappel! No way could that bastard wriggle out of this one. Or buy his way out. Not with Mitch Tyler having a controlling hand.

Harriet signalled him aside just as he was about to enter the courtroom. Even with a barrister's wig covering her silky blond hair, she still looked beautiful—flawless creamy skin, her full-lipped sensuous mouth painted a glossy red, a fine aristocratic nose breathing fire while her big grey eyes smoked with angry frustration.

'Where have you been?' she demanded.

Not at *her* beck and call any more.

He raised a mocking eyebrow. 'Out. Is your client ready to settle?'

'She's ready to deal.'

'The only deal on the table is what I nominated from the beginning.'

'She won't come at that.'

'Then I'll see you both in court.'

Harriet reached out and grabbed the sleeve of his robe, halting him. 'This is blackmail, Mitch.'

'No. It's exposure.'

Which was what Gary Chappel deserved, too.

Though it probably wouldn't work out that way.

Better to hold the sword over his head if the aim was to keep everyone free of trouble.

'You're painting this black and white, not accepting any greys. And there are greys,' Harriet insisted vehemently.

'Then prove it to the jury.'

'You know damned well you've got their sympathy.'

'I wonder why.'

With that mocking retort he pulled his robe free of her grasp and headed into the courtroom, prepared to fight on but suspecting he wouldn't have to. That little contretemps had sounded like a last-ditch effort to get him to bend a little, win something for her client, which, of course, would be a face-saving exercise for Harriet. Total defeat didn't sit well with her. Never would. Greys suited her better.

No sooner was everyone settled in the courtroom than Harriet made the request to approach the bench. In very short order, Mitch was informed that Harriet's client had conceded and full settlement was agreed upon. The case was over, bar the paperwork.

Normally Mitch would have felt enormously gratified by this result but he found himself impatient with having to tie up all the ends, deal with the media, and see his client off with the courtesy due to her. This fight had been won. Gary Chappel was now in the antagonist's corner and Mitch's mind was already occupied with the fight ahead.

Kathryn Ledger was no more than a name and a voice to him. He thought of her only as a source, bringing him the ammunition he'd use to attack. That she was also a woman held no relevance at all until he entered his private office and came face-to-face with her.

# CHAPTER TWO

IT WAS LIKE a bolt of electric energy charging into the room. Kathryn felt as though she'd been zapped off the chair she'd been sitting on, her body lifting onto her feet, straightening up, instinctively meeting the force of the man head on, while staring at him in wide-eyed shock.

This was Mitch Tyler?

A barrister?

She'd always thought of barristers as rather lofty and effete academics in fusty wigs, full of their own self-importance. Yet here she was, faced with a dynamic entity who literally bristled with masculinity, so much so her knees felt weak. And her heart was fluttering.

Tall, dark and handsome, but not like Ric Donato. Not like Ric at all. Any woman would call her boss drop-dead gorgeous, but this man didn't come out of any romantic mould. Power was the only word that came to Kathryn's dazed mind. He had a strong square jaw, very firmly delineated mouth, a sharp triangular shaped nose, straight black brows, and beneath them, stunning blue eyes that burned straight into Kathryn's like twin lasers, totally transfixing her.

She stared at him and he stared right back at her. Kathryn couldn't gather wits enough to say a word. The mutual stare went on so long, she began to wonder if he doubted her identity, though surely his clerk would have told him she was waiting in here where he'd told her to wait.

* * *

Mitch was thinking Ric must be mad. He had *this* woman right under his nose and he ran off with someone else?

She was like Tinkerbell…magic…a pixie face with those wonderful green eyes and the gamine hairstyle, like a flyaway cap of burnished copper, a lovely pouty mouth that was made for kissing, an hourglass figure poured into a curve-hugging green suit, the skirt delectably short enough to show off long, shapely legs…how could Ric be immune to such gut-tugging femininity? Mitch was struggling to remember this was a professional visit.

'Mr Tyler…?'

Her voice sounded husky, uncertain…and incredibly sexy.

'Mitch,' he said forcefully, deciding Kathryn Ledger was not his client and he didn't have to keep a professional distance. She was here on Ric's behalf. And Lara Chappel's. He propelled himself forward, offering his hand. 'Good to meet you, Kathryn.' Lovely name. Rolled off his tongue as though he'd been saying it for centuries.

'Mitch,' she repeated, looking at him wonderingly as her hand slipped into his.

The top of her head only came up to his chin so her face was tilted up. There were sparkly gold specks around the rim of her green irises like an explosion of fireworks. Her mouth was still slightly parted from having spoken his name and Mitch had to fight the urge to bend down and taste it. Her hand was soft, dainty, and he hung onto it because it was the only touch he could sensibly allow himself at this point. They'd barely met.

'No trouble coming here?' he asked, pushing his mind to get back on track—the whole purpose of her presence in his office.

'No. Thank you for the escorts.' A swift little smile. 'They certainly made me feel safe.'

'Good!' He smiled back, feeling a wild joy in having protected this woman. And he'd go on protecting her, whatever it took. 'You've brought the photo?'

'Yes. In my bag.'

She nodded to a many-zippered beige handbag resting by the chair she'd been sitting on. Mitch reluctantly released her hand, freeing her to get the critical photo for him. Losing the physical link made him realise how possessive he was feeling toward Kathryn Ledger—amazingly so. He couldn't recall any other woman ever having such an impact on him.

He watched her lift the bag onto his desk as he mentally examined the primitive instincts she stirred. Control was second nature to him. Only once in his life had he completely lost it, wanting to beat Jenny's rapist to a pulp, and he might well have done so if he hadn't been forcibly restrained.

Control the anger and channel the energy into more effective strategies, Patrick had advised. But this...what he was feeling now with Kathryn Ledger...was completely outside Mitch's experience and he couldn't find any control mechanisms for it. His entire body seemed to be buzzing with excitement.

Her left hand moved to open a zipper on the bag. It was like a punch in the heart, seeing the ring on her third finger. A ring with a flashy solitaire diamond. An engagement ring!

She was taken.

Another man had already claimed her as his.

Anger smashed through the shock. It wasn't right. It couldn't be right. He'd fight to...

No!

Mitch shook his head clear of the crazy surge of testosterone, enforcing reason. Kathryn Ledger had willingly given herself to someone else. Someone she obviously wanted to marry. Her choice was made. And, of course, Ric had respected it. She wasn't available to him any more than she was available to Mitch.

Checkmate!

He had to back off.

Never mind that it felt wrong.

She had come to him for help. Nothing more. He had to get his mind focused on the job and forget everything else.

Kathryn was trying desperately to get herself together. It didn't help that her hand was still tingling from Mitch Tyler's touch, that her legs felt shaky, and she could barely concentrate on opening her bag and extracting the telling photograph. She felt as though she'd been knocked completely out of kilter.

For a moment there, she'd even been wondering what it might be like if Mitch Tyler kissed her. Jeremy—her partner for the past year!—had been totally blotted out of her mind. The reason for being here in these legal chambers had been lost, too. It was as though she'd been caught up in some magnetic force-field that shut out everything else but the man holding her hand, and she was still quivering inside from the unbelievably strong tug of his attraction.

Her fingers closed over the photograph and she took a deep breath before turning to hand it to him. It was a relief that his gaze instantly fastened on the image of Lara and Gary Chappel, giving her more time to recover her composure. Better still when he stepped away from her, moving around to the other side of his desk, putting considerable distance between them, enough distance to ease the tightness in her chest.

'Thank you,' he said, flicking a look at her as he gestured to the chair she'd vacated. 'Please sit down again.'

She grabbed her bag off the desk and gratefully retreated even further, settling herself before risking another glance at him. He'd sat down, too, occupying the big leather chair behind his desk, studying the photograph she'd given him, his straight black brows lowered in a frown.

His dark hair was also straight, very thick and cut short in graduated layers to stay neat. He had neat ears, as well, almost no lobes like her own, but curved around the top, not pointy. He wouldn't have been teased about having pixie ears when he was a kid. She couldn't imagine anyone ever teasing Mitch Tyler. One look from those powerful blue eyes...

A convulsive little shiver ran down her spine. He had to be dynamite in a courtroom. She wondered how Ric had come to know him. They looked to be about the same age—mid-thirties—yet she couldn't see how their lives would have touched. As far as she knew, her boss had not gone through university. Maybe somewhere in his years as a photo-journalist he'd sought legal assistance. Whatever...Ric Donato trusted this man and Kathryn could see why he would. In any kind of fight, she'd want Mitch Tyler on her side.

He jackknifed forward, picked up the telephone from his desk, made a call, still frowning as he waited for a response which came within a few moments. 'Patrick, it's Mitch. Have you heard from Ric today?'

The reply must have been negative because he quickly ran on, 'I think he's heading your way. Took Johnny's plane out. If you hear from him would you please let me know?'

Another pause, a grimace, then, 'He left me with a problem and I'd appreciate more instructions. If he calls you, tell him to call me. Okay?'

Phone down. He knew Johnny Ellis, too, Kathryn thought, and all three men were obviously connected to this Patrick whom Mitch had just called.

'Ric didn't tell me where he was going,' she offered.

The laser-sharp eyes bored into hers again. 'He wouldn't. Not in these circumstances. Fill me in on the whole story, Kathryn, as much as you know.'

His gaze alone seemed to be picking at her brain. Kathryn felt constrained to remember every little detail in case it was vitally important. 'You know Ric's business,' she started.

'Brokering photographs to all forms of media around the world,' he rapped out, tapping the one he'd now laid on the desk in front of him. 'This one was e-mailed in?'

'Yes. Taken at the airport. Dated yesterday. We were checking through the computer file this morning...'

'What time was it when Ric saw this?'

'About nine-thirty. Normally we don't deal in shots that might cause people problems. I was about to delete this one when Ric stopped me. He asked me to print it, give him a copy, put five more copies in the office safe and buy the copyright from the photographer so no-one else could print it. He said he didn't care how much it cost...just get it.'

Mitch nodded thoughtfully. 'Did you acquire the copyright?'

'Yes. After Ric left. Which he did as soon as I'd printed out his copy. He took it with him. I didn't know what he was going to do. He simply said he and Lara Chappel...Lara Seymour...went way back and she wouldn't want that photo published. I felt...' She hesitated, wondering if she should colour the facts with her feelings or not.

'Tell me,' Mitch encouraged.

She sighed. 'All this was out of character. That photo got to him personally. In a big way. It wasn't normal business, if you know what I mean.'

It evoked a wry little smile. 'I guess we all have moments that aren't... normal.'

A flood of heat whooshed up her neck and scorched her cheeks. Kathryn couldn't remember the last time she had blushed. She was thirty years old, a successful career woman, adept at handling all sorts of people and situations. Yet here was embarrassing proof of how *abnormal* her reaction was to this man. Was it horribly obvious that he'd put her in such a spin, even her blood temperature was affected?

Stick to the facts, girl, she berated herself. Best to steer right away from feelings, because she was in a high state of confusion about her own.

'It was just past eleven when Ric called me from his car,' she went on briskly. 'He said he was heading back to the office, should be there in ten minutes. He had Lara Chappel with him and he needed my help. He instructed me to tell my secretary I'd be away for a couple of hours at a business meeting with a magazine editor—nothing unusual about that—and meet him in the basement car park with my bag and car keys.'

'You didn't question what help Ric wanted?'

Kathryn shrugged. 'He's my boss.'

'How did he sound?'

'Very much in command.'

Mitch Tyler nodded. 'Ric has worked in war zones. He'd keep his head.'

Kathryn didn't know if Mitch was reassuring her or himself. Certainly the familiar way he spoke of Ric's past suggested a long and close friendship.

'So you were there waiting for him when he drove into the basement car park,' he prompted.

'Yes. Ric said they'd been followed by a grey sedan—male driver wearing a baseball cap and sunglasses—bound to be hanging around outside since there was no entry to the private car park without an official identification card. He wanted me to drive him and Lara Chappel to Bankstown Airport. They got into my car and scrunched down in their seats while I drove out, and they stayed down until I could assure them we weren't being followed by the pursuit vehicle.'

'Did Lara Chappel say anything to you?'

'Not until we arrived at the airport. She simply did whatever Ric told her to.'

'How did she appear to you? Her reactions to what was going on?'

Kathryn paused, wanting to be accurate in her impressions. 'Nervous, frightened, distracted,' she answered slowly.

Mitch cocked his head to one side, a musing expression on his face.

'Did it occur to you that you could be accused of assisting in an unlaw-ful abduction?'

Kathryn was shocked into protesting. 'It was a getaway, not an abduc-tion. Lara Chappel was willingly following Ric's lead.'

He leaned forward and tapped the photograph on the desk. 'Ric might have used this for leverage.'

'He wouldn't do that.'

The blue eyes glittered mockingly. 'How can you tell what a man will do...when he wants a woman very badly?'

His gaze slid down to her mouth and Kathryn found herself holding her breath while her heart skittered, reacting to what felt like a simmer-ing passion aimed directly at her. Was he just projecting what he thought Ric might feel toward Lara Chappel? Was a clever barrister a brilliant actor, as well? But why target her like this? It felt really personal. And terribly unsettling.

'It wasn't like that,' she burst out in an urgent need to defend herself. 'It was obvious that Lara Chappel trusted him. She was with him will-ingly, anxious to make good her escape. Once we arrived at the airport, she thanked me very sincerely for my help. And I noticed she wasn't wearing any rings.'

It reminded Kathryn of the ring she was wearing herself—the ring proclaiming she'd agreed to marry Jeremy Haynes. Her gaze dropped to the flashy solitaire diamond he'd chosen for her and she told herself once again it was a measure of how much he valued her, not a status symbol of how much he was worth. Of course, money was useful. Life was a lot easier with it than without it. But sometimes...

She twisted the ring around on her finger, wishing it was an emerald, something more personal to her. Jeremy knew she loved green. Yet she couldn't very well argue against his romantic declaration that 'Diamonds are forever.' She heaved a rueful sigh and raised her gaze to the man who was stirring all sorts of troubling confusion in her.

He was staring at her ring, watching the agitated movement of it around her finger. She instantly stilled her hands and spoke very firmly. 'If a woman takes off her rings, it's a very deliberate action, meaning that relationship—her commitment to it—is over. Lara Chappel wanted out of her marriage. I have no doubt of that. Ric wasn't abducting her. She looked at him as though he was performing a miracle for her.'

'A miracle...' Mitch Tyler's mouth twisted with irony as his gaze flicked up to meet hers. 'I see you're engaged to be married, Kathryn.'

'Yes.' Why did she feel defiant about that? He wasn't attacking her on it...was he?

'When is the happy wedding day?'

'We haven't decided yet.'

'No keen rush to the altar?'

She frowned, uneasy with these personal questions. 'It depends on work factors.'

'Your work or his?'

'I don't see how this is relevant to the situation that brought me here,' she flared at him.

'I assure you it is highly relevant,' he retorted, making a languid gesture that denied any attack. 'I'm simply ascertaining how long you want to remain in the position of Ric's executive assistant. Should your fiancé be happy for you to walk out of it today...'

'*I* wouldn't be happy,' she cut in emphatically.

'So you want to keep your job, regardless of any threat Gary Chappel might pose?'

She glared at him. 'You're supposed to take care of that.'

'Ah yes, the miracle worker,' he drawled. 'Ric plays knight to the rescue of his fair Lara, and I'm handed the job of slaying the dragon and keeping you safe.' His eyes beamed hard relentless purpose at her. 'And I will. I will keep you safe, Kathryn. But the legal moves will take a day or two and I'm just wondering how much your fiancé cares about you and your safety.' One eyebrow lifted in challenge. 'As much as Ric, taking his woman right out of reach?'

'I'm not stupid. I can take care of myself,' she protested.

'Not against a man like Gary Chappel,' came the flat retort. Then more softly, insidiously touching a raw memory, 'How did you feel when he confronted you in your office?'

She shuddered.

Mitch Tyler instantly pounced on the response. 'You were frightened.'

'He was in a rage.'

'Breathing fire. He not only has a lot of fire-power, Kathryn, but he has no conscience about using it. If Gary Chappel thinks you're standing in his way...'

The telephone rang. Mitch Tyler snatched up the receiver and listened to the person on the other end of the line.

It was a relief to have his attention withdrawn from her, focused on something else. Kathryn reflected on what he'd said about Gary Chappel, whom she'd found a very scary man, having no regard whatsoever for appropriate or even reasonable behaviour. She'd managed to get rid of him once, but if he stormed into the office again...or came to her home...

A man who had his wife watched and followed...a battered wife... violence toward women...it was beginning to look very ugly to Kathryn. She remembered how he'd repeated her name, committing it to memory for further reference, his contemptuous manner toward her, the sense of threat.

'Okay. So you've agreed to let Lara stay with you. That's fine but Ric can't stay, too.'

Mitch's curt words broke Kathryn's train of concern, alerting her to a new development.

'There have already been aggressive moves made by Gary Chappel to recover his wife,' he continued. 'I have Ric's executive assistant, Kathryn Ledger, here in my chambers, a protective move against further harassment in her office. In all fairness, Ric must become an open target for Chappel to pursue. Best if he flies out of the country as soon as possible—I mean tomorrow—get the heat off his Sydney office.'

*Yes,* Kathryn thought. She certainly didn't want another encounter with Gary Chappel.

A pause for listening, then, 'Get them both to call me when they arrive. I'll talk to Ric first but I also need ammunition from Lara Chappel to make legal moves stick. I have a plan of action in mind but it will only work with Lara's full co-operation.'

A plan of action... Kathryn breathed more easily. She instinctively had faith in Mitch Tyler's ability to counter-punch anything. If anyone had the power to take on a problem and beat it, he did. Ric had trusted him with it. She did, too. And now that communication with the escaping couple could be re-established, everything should be quickly settled.

Mitch put the receiver down. Kathryn tensed as his riveting gaze zeroed in on her again. 'Do you live with your fiancé?' he asked point-blank.

'Yes.'

'He'll be at home with you tonight?'

She shook her head. 'He's in Melbourne on business. He won't be home until tomorrow evening.'

'You can't be on your own, Kathryn. Not with Gary Chappel in a state of raging frustration. Believe me, I know what that man is capable of. Without some restraining force—and I can't even begin to apply that until tomorrow—he's a loose cannon.' He gestured to the phone. 'Want to call your fiancé? Ask him to fly back to Sydney this evening?'

While he was in the middle of negotiations for his future career in financial services? Calling him away from critical meetings to nursemaid her? Because of something that had happened through her job? Which didn't matter as much as his, given that he'd be the main source of financial support when they had children.

'I don't want to do that,' she quickly decided. Jeremy would consider it totally unreasonable.

The blue eyes bored in. 'Aren't you more important to him than business?'

'I can take care of myself,' she asserted again.

'You're a woman...against a man with resources he'll have no compunction in using to get his own way.'

Jeremy would blame her for getting involved with something that was not really her job, bringing trouble upon herself, messing everything up for him. 'I can go to a hotel,' she said, desperately seeking an alternative course.

Mitch Tyler shook his head. 'If you won't call your fiancé to come home and stand between you and any threat from Gary Chappel...you stay with me.'

Her heart skipped a beat. 'Stay...with you?' She could barely get the words out, her mouth had gone so dry.

'Ric made me responsible for you. I take that responsibility very seriously.'

'But...'

'I have a house in Woollahra. It has a guest suite which my sister and her husband use when they come to Sydney. You will be safe with me, Kathryn.'

He wouldn't allow anyone to get to her. She was sure of that. But safe with him? When he seemed to be driving stakes through her relationship with Jeremy with everything he said, everything he was?

*I need to call Jeremy,* she thought. *Stop this now.*

Yet she knew it would only cause an argument...in Mitch Tyler's hearing...and he'd be making silent judgements...stirring her up even more...making her wish...

No.

Better that she did stay with him. If she was so strongly attracted to this man, and the attraction remained strong throughout the evening, maybe she shouldn't be marrying Jeremy Haynes.

Kathryn looked down at the ring on her hand.

And the most troubling thing of all was...she wished she wasn't wearing it.

# CHAPTER THREE

MITCH'S WHOLE BODY was buzzing with adrenaline. He'd thrown down the challenge and every nerve was keyed to piano-wire tension, waiting for which way Kathryn would jump. Her gaze had dropped to the ring on her finger.

*Take it off,* Mitch fiercely willed. *If the guy won't drop everything to look after you at a time of need, he's not worthy of you.*

He was tempted to screw the challenge up another notch, offer to speak to the man himself, make him aware that Kathryn was in serious danger. But that might be tipping the scales which were delicately balanced at the moment. She was not stupid. He'd spelled out what the situation was. The ball was in her court. If she chose to stay with him... well, that choice would be very telling, indeed.

'I don't want to interfere with Jeremy's business,' she said slowly.

His heart kicked with excitement as she lifted her gaze to his, her eyes returning a challenge that demanded he measure up to his own promises.

'You claim I'll be safe with you...'

His groin tingled. It was definitely a sexual challenge. Did she feel the attraction, too? He cocked an eyebrow at her. 'Are you asking me if I'm a man of honour? If you can spend a night under my roof without my coming onto you?'

Heat whooshed into her cheeks, a sure sign that he'd hit a nerve that was pulsing with vulnerability. He smiled, wondering how tempted she was, though he spoke to dispel her unease.

'You're wearing a ring, Kathryn. You can count on my respecting it. Okay?'

The light mockery goaded her into accepting *safe* refuge with him. 'Okay,' she echoed on a long expulsion of obviously held breath. 'If you don't mind, I think it will be less fuss all around if I simply stay with you overnight.'

'Best if you remain in my house tomorrow, as well,' he pressed. 'Take a sick day from work. By tomorrow night there should be safeguards in place so you can resume your normal life.'

'All right,' she agreed, her beautiful green eyes glittering brightly above the scarlet cheeks.

He'd won, Mitch thought exultantly. She'd moved onto *his* ground. And she wasn't *married* yet. Her agreement could very well mean she was interested in finding out more about him, exploring the territory. Within limitations, Mitch forcefully reminded himself. The ring was still on her finger.

Still, his zest for life and all its challenges zoomed into overdrive. While he was waiting for Ric to call from Gundamurra, he took Kathryn through the scene Gary Chappel had made at the office, learning more about her and how she conducted herself in a crisis situation. Very cool and collected. Definitely not someone to be rolled over in a hurry. Yet she wasn't so cool with him, Mitch happily reflected.

Was her relationship with *Jeremy* rock-solid, or could he give it a shake? Was it her own pride insisting on not making *a fuss,* or couldn't she count on her fiancé to respond as he should? As much as Mitch wanted to believe the latter, it was clear that Kathryn Ledger was not a panic merchant and might simply be taking what she saw as a pragmatic course. Security was at hand in the person of Mitch Tyler. There was no need to bother her fiancé. The danger would be over by the time Jeremy walked back into her life.

All the same, Mitch couldn't help feeling elated that she had chosen to spend tonight with him. The thought struck him—*If I were her lover, I wouldn't like this choice one bit.* Yes, she was definitely playing with fire, and Mitch privately determined to stir the embers every which way he could, watching how the wind blew.

* * *

I'm playing with fire, Kathryn thought, feeling more and more unsettled by her decision to bypass Jeremy tonight and go with Mitch Tyler. It might have seemed a safe and sensible option but it wasn't. Somehow he was making her question where she was in her life and why, and the answers didn't feel so right anymore.

When the call came through from Ric Donato, diverting Mitch's attention from her, she told herself she could still change her mind. Yet as she sat listening to the one-sided conversation, she found herself totally captivated by his handling of the situation.

There was no criticism of Ric's actions. Mitch projected both sympathy and understanding for what had been done, and the strategy he outlined for involving Victor Chappel as a powerful restraining force on his son sounded good to Kathryn, as did the threat of negative publicity which would automatically accompany legal action if the restraint didn't hold.

She was particularly touched by the gentle tone he used when he rather hesitantly remarked, 'Patrick said...this is *your* Lara...from the old days.'

The old days... Kathryn wondered what the history was—how these men and Lara Chappel were connected, Ric Donato's enduring caring for her and their empathy for what he felt.

The conversation moved on to Kathryn's safety with Mitch, relating that her fiancé was away and she'd be spending the night with him. Ric asked to speak with her and she ended up promising him she'd do precisely what was planned. Too late to change her mind now. She felt caught up in a juggernaut of action that had to be followed.

Listening to Mitch elicit the information he needed from Lara Chappel was another fascinating experience—a sharp legal mind at work, yet the cross-examination was done sympathetically. Kathryn wasn't sure if this manner of his was simply clever or genuinely sincere, but she couldn't help being impressed by Mitch Tyler's sensitivity to others' feelings—his humanity in a field she would have thought was driven by ego.

On the other hand, she was sure he played to win. It was unimaginable that he wouldn't be a winner—the force of his energy overriding any opposition. If he was representing her in court, she'd have every confidence in his ability to gain whatever outcome was needed. But that was his professional life. What of his private one?

Clearly he couldn't be living with a woman or he wouldn't have offered her a room for the night in his home. He had a married sister and was obviously on good terms with her. No friction in his family as there was in Jeremy's where everyone was hitting off each other, intensely competitive.

She didn't like their habit of putting each other down. Winning meant too much to them. Though it certainly made them top performers in their fields, which was admirable. And as her mother had said, no doubt Jeremy would make a good provider as a husband.

He'd been very successful as a dealer in a merchant bank, drove a BMW Roadster, wore designer clothes, and his penthouse apartment at Pyrmont was very classy. If this next career step—becoming a partner in a very high profile financial services company—came off, he'd assured Kathryn they'd be set for life, riding high, nothing to worry about.

Except... Mitch Tyler had made her question how much Jeremy really cared about her. She'd justified his priorities in her mind, yet her heart felt oddly torn right now. Looking back over their relationship, hadn't she been the one to make all the adjustments, all the compromises?

She came from a caring family and it was natural to her to give what was needed, to create and maintain a happy atmosphere. But if something she needed clashed with Jeremy's ambition, his drive to be number one...would he drop everything to rescue her from a bad situation, as Ric Donato had done for Lara Chappel?

Here she was, staying with Mitch Tyler because she didn't want to put Jeremy to that test. Because...didn't she know in her heart he would fail it? Whereas all her instincts were telling her Mitch Tyler wouldn't. He was like Ric in that sense. Caring with passion. Caring that knew no limits. And Kathryn found herself fiercely wanting to be the object of such caring.

'Hungry?' Mitch shot at her from where he stood by the fax machine, waiting for Lara Chappel's written authorisation to act for her.

She glanced at her watch. Almost seven o'clock. Where had the time gone? 'I'm fine,' she said. 'What are we going to do about dinner?'

'I've got beef strips in the fridge, ready for a stir-fry. Won't take long to cook.'

'You cook?'

'Don't you?' he asked.

'Yes, but...obviously you work long hours. I thought...' He'd be like Jeremy, preferring to eat out. Though, of course, in these circumstances, going to a public restaurant was not a good idea. It wasn't as *safe* as having a private dinner…just the two of them…alone together.

Kathryn took a deep breath, trying to quell the uncomfortable sense of being disloyal to Jeremy. There was no denying Mitch Tyler was different but she shouldn't be comparing, shouldn't feel excited by the prospect of spending an evening with this incredibly mesmerising man.

'I like to cook,' he went on. 'It's relaxing. And I like to go home after a long day at work.' He threw a grin at her. 'Trust me. I'm a good cook. Though I'll let you help if you want to.'

'Okay.' She smiled back, quite charmed by the idea of preparing a meal together. A harmless activity, she decided. Nothing Jeremy could criticise.

The fax came through. Mitch filed it, then arranged for a courier to take the photograph with an accompanying request for a meeting to Victor Chappel. Satisfied that he'd set the ball rolling for a successful outcome, he called a taxi and by the time he and Kathryn emerged from his chambers, the car was waiting for them.

He held the passenger door open for her and waited until she was settled in her seat before getting in beside her. Sharing the suddenly enclosed space with him instantly set Kathryn's pulse racing. He was a big man with a heart-joltingly powerful presence, and far too attractive for her peace of mind. Feeling absurdly nervous about being with him, she fumbled with her seat belt, unable to fit it correctly into its locking slot.

'Let me,' he murmured, leaning over to help.

Rather than appear hopelessly inept she surrendered the task to him and instantly caught a whiff of some seductive male cologne as his face came closer to hers. She stared at his jawline, noting he had a five o'clock shadow and thinking he probably had hair on his chest, too. Would it be thick like the hair on his head, like his eyelashes?

'There. All fastened,' he said, the thick lashes lifting, his eyes locking onto hers, smiling eyes that simmered with warm pleasure in this simple act of looking after her, ensuring her safety.

Or was it more than that?

Her heart was galloping.

'Thank you.' She had to push out the words. They were barely a whisper.

'You're welcome,' he answered—a reply that anyone could have made.

Yet somehow it seemed to encompass the sense that she was welcome in his life. He wanted her there. And it stirred in Kathryn a disturbingly strong desire to be there, too. Which she tried to dismiss as crazy. They'd only just met today. And she was committed to spending the rest of her life with Jeremy Haynes!

Mitch forced himself to settle back in his seat before he did the unforgiveable and kissed those very kissable lips. He'd given his word that she could trust him to act honourably, so any kind of sexual contact was out. Best not to touch her. Or even get too close. He had to keep temptation at bay, concentrate on mind games. Though he didn't want to play games with her, either. He wanted...to immerse himself in Kathryn Ledger and all that she was.

'What's your fiancé's name?' he asked, a streak of jealousy provoking him into finding out more about his rival. 'Jeremy...?'

'Haynes.'

Mitch had never heard of him. 'Where do you live with him?'

'Pyrmont. An apartment overlooking the harbour.'

The guy had money then. Which was to be expected. Kathryn was quite a high flyer herself, running Ric's company in Sydney when he was overseas.

'Actually, the block of apartments does have security,' she added. 'You need a card to get into the elevator. If you just took me home...'

'No.' He flashed her a commanding look. 'Being alone is not a good idea.'

She was fiddling with her ring again, not looking at him.

Mitch cursed himself for reminding her of the man she planned to marry. 'I promised Ric I'd take care of you, Kathryn,' he quickly pressed.

She shook her head slightly, heaved a sigh, then ruefully conceded, 'And I promised him I'd go with you.'

'Is that such a hardship?' he half-mocked.

She grimaced. 'I'm sorry. I guess I sound ungracious. It's very kind of you to offer me the hospitality of your home.'

'It's not about kindness, Kathryn,' he whipped in, hating the remote politeness of her words.

'I know.' She flashed a wry glance at him. 'It would be easier if you were more...'

'More what? I'll try to oblige,' he promised, attempting to tease her out of her withdrawal.

'Older, fatherly, ugly, or just plain obnoxious,' she threw at him in an exasperated rush.

His heart danced with sheer joy. She was admitting an attraction. Beyond any doubt now. A wicked grin broke out. 'I can certainly be obnoxious if it will make you feel more comfortable.'

She laughed, a nervous little gurgle. 'I don't think play-acting will do it. In fact...' Her eyes were seriously curious. '...I'd like you to tell me about yourself. Your family. You mentioned a married sister.'

*She wants to know me.*

Normally Mitch didn't talk about his personal background. Who he was now—a barrister building a formidable reputation with every court appearance—seemed sufficient in itself for most people. If it wasn't, he simply declined to give out information that was none of their business. Yet it was different with Kathryn. He only had this one night to forge a bond that would hopefully overshadow whatever she had with her fiancé.

So he told her about Jenny, how she'd taken on the responsibility of caring for their disabled mother after their father had deserted them, how they'd managed on a social services pension, supplemented by handcrafts done by his mother and whatever Mitch could earn from a paper-boy run and cleaning cars—any jobs he could get after school hours. Tutoring had paid well, when he'd got older.

They'd been a tight-knit little family. Jenny had eventually trained as a nurse and married a doctor who currently had a practice at Gosford, on the Central Coast. Their mother had died of a stroke soon after the wedding, six years ago. Jenny now had a son and a daughter, both beautiful children.

He didn't mention the rape or the assault that had taken him to Gundamurra. That was deeply private, both to him and Jenny. Neither of them ever spoke of it. She'd moved past it, was happy in her life, and Mitch was content with that. Though he'd never forget it himself. One day he might tell Kathryn...if they ever reached that point of intimacy.

The taxi pulled up in front of his house. Woollahra was an old suburb of Sydney, fashionable now because of its proximity to the city centre, but most of the houses were of terrace construction, as they were in Surry Hills which had been considered almost a slum area with very cheap rentals in his boyhood. Though that had changed, too, for the same reason—close to the CBD, renovations upgrading the real estate.

He paid the fare, got out of the taxi and looked up at his home as he rounded the car to open the passenger door for Kathryn. It wasn't a classy apartment overlooking the harbour. It had no view at all, except onto this tree-lined street and the small courtyard at the back. But it satisfied something in him—perhaps a need to be rooted in something old and lasting.

He wondered what Kathryn would think of it.

He wondered what she thought of what he'd told her about his family background.

And he realised...for the first time in his life...he was feeling vulnerable. Not in any physical sense, but in his heart...where it mattered most.

# CHAPTER FOUR

As MITCH USHERED her toward his front gate, Kathryn looked up at the house, trying to distract herself from being so physically aware of him. Where he lived was another expression of the person he was and she could no longer deny she was interested in everything about him. But that was okay, she told herself, as long as sexual attraction didn't start blurring the line that should be kept.

This encounter was out of the ordinary.

Maybe her response to Mitch Tyler, the man, was being coloured by that.

His home was a two-storey terrace, painted a dark blue with white trim. Intricate white lace ironwork decorated the top balcony and lower porch. The street was certainly an upmarket one, every house neat and tidy, the trees along the sidewalk giving it a quietly contained atmosphere.

She knew that renovated terraces in this area were very pricey. Mitch Tyler had come a long way from being a paper boy. All on his own, too. No financial help from his family. Though, there'd certainly been a lot of love and care within that small household. A very impressive amount. *Good people,* her mother would say, warmly approving. Whereas Kathryn was very conscious of her parents' reticence on Jeremy's family.

*Stop comparing,* she berated herself, yet it was impossible not to, especially when Mitch showed her into his home and she instantly fell in love

with it. The whole ground floor had been opened up for maximum living space yet the feeling of the place was still cosy, yet elegant, as well.
No bombardment of fashionable colour and ultra-modern furniture.

The floors were a rich red-brown polished wood and the walls were
all white, apart from the wonderful sandstone fireplace in the lounge
room. Brown leather chesterfields flanked the fireplace and also the
television set which was centred on the opposite wall and surrounded
by bookshelves.

The dining room suite was a lovely mahogany with dark red uphol-
stery, and scatter cushions on the chesterfields were of the same dark
red which was repeated in woven borders on the cream floor rugs. On
the coffee table sat a beautiful chess set carved from black and a creamy
white onyx.

'Do you play?' she asked impulsively, wondering if it was purely a
decorative item.

The blue eyes crinkled in amusement. 'It occupies what might otherwise be lonely hours. I play mostly correspondence chess, for lack of
a handy partner.'

'I'll give you a game later,' she offered, seeing it as a safe activity to
occupy the evening.

'You play?' He looked delighted.

'My father taught me—' she grinned '—for lack of a handy partner.'

He laughed. 'Do you play often?'

'Only when I go home alone. Jeremy doesn't...' She stopped before
saying he didn't have the patience for chess, conscious of it sounding like
a criticism, which wasn't fair. Jeremy worked very intensively. He liked
more social activities in his leisure hours. Which was perfectly reasonable.

'You must tell me about your family while we deal with dinner,' Mitch
smoothly invited, leading her to the kitchen which was the first part of
an annexe built onto the back of the house. Laundry and downstairs
bathroom beyond it, he told her.

The kitchen was white, too, apart from the red-brown granite bench-
tops—much more welcoming than the rather cold and clinical stainless
steel everywhere, which Jeremy favoured because it was modern and the
most expensive. Again Kathryn pushed aside the critical thought, telling herself that she should appreciate Jeremy's choice of state of the art
kitchen fixtures. In fact, she should be grateful for them.

'Red wine okay with you? Or do you prefer white?' Mitch asked, shedding his suit coat and tie and rolling up his shirt-sleeves as he prepared to take charge of preparing their meal.

'Red, if we're having beef,' she replied before realising it might not be wise to drink any alcohol at all.

This was one occasion when she couldn't afford to let inhibitions slip, especially with Mitch's less formal appearance making her even more acutely aware of his sexy physique—taut cheeky butt, muscular arms, broad chest, an intriguing glimpse of black hair at the V end of his opened shirt. Still, one glass of wine shouldn't go to her head and there was no harm in being sociable to that small degree.

'If you want to go upstairs and freshen up while I open this bottle and get organised, the guest suite is directly above this kitchen,' he tossed at her in casual invitation.

It was a considerate way of easing any tension about being shown to a bedroom and Kathryn instantly seized the opportunity for some respite from his overwhelmingly attractive qualities. She needed to get some proper perspective on this situation.

'Thank you. I won't be long.'

'Take your time. There's no hurry.'

The staircase was at the back of the dining room, the treads carpeted in teal-green, a floor covering which extended along the hallway above and into the bedroom she was to occupy. Kathryn was amazed to find the queen-size bed covered by an absolutely gorgeous woollen rug crocheted in multicoloured squares that were bordered by black. It was like a patchwork quilt, beautifully worked. And on the walls were framed tapestries patterned from famous paintings—the best of them, to her eye, a glorious water-lily scene, definitely one of Monet's.

This had to be some of his mother's handiwork, sitting in a wheelchair all day, keeping busy, selling what she could to specialty craft shops. Obviously not everything had been sold, or perhaps these lovely items had been worked after there had no longer been a need to sell. Kathryn liked Mitch Tyler all the more for keeping them, furnishing this room with them—the room his sister stayed in when she came to Sydney.

Family ties...

There was something very heart-tugging about this room. Kathryn swiftly moved into the ensuite bathroom which was far more impersonal—mainly white with rows of teal feature tiles and towels. She looked at her face in the mirror above the vanity bench and wondered what Mitch Tyler saw in her. Was she the kind of woman who appealed to him? If she was free…would he…?

A rush of guilt stopped this treacherous train of thought. She was engaged to be married. Jeremy had been her partner for over a year. Their relationship wasn't perfect but whose was? It balanced out better than most, didn't it? To throw it all away on a chance meeting in extraordinary circumstances…

She lifted her left hand, stared down at the diamond ring on her third finger and once again found herself wishing it wasn't there. Did this mean that her commitment to Jeremy was wrong? Or was this just a passing feeling, a point in her life that was totally out of kilter with all the rest? If she took off the ring, it would signal to Mitch Tyler that…no! This was crazy. Far too fast. She would undoubtedly regret it tomorrow.

Besides, the evening with Mitch had barely begun.

This initial attraction could very quickly wear off.

Kathryn seemed more relaxed when she came back downstairs, happy to sit on the stool on the other side of the kitchen counter and cut up the vegetables he'd laid out for her. Mitch had worked swiftly while she was away, setting the dining table with place mats and cutlery, getting out the wok and various sauces, putting a pot of water on the stove, ready for the two-minute noodles to accompany the stir-fry. Now he could focus on drawing her out about herself and her family.

Though first she asked him if he'd designed the renovation of the terrace house himself. 'With the help of an architect,' he answered.

'And the decor is your choice, too?'

'Yes, it is,' he said a touch belligerently.

She nodded as though she'd guessed it was all his doing and he wondered what judgement she was making of it. Old-fashioned? Harriet had wanted to get rid of his mother's bedspread and tapestries—give them to his sister—but he wouldn't.

Too many hours of his mother's life were woven into them—hours shared chatting to him, caring about what he did, what he wanted to do. Good memories were worth more than stylish decor which invariably went in and out of fashion.

'That's a fabulous rug on the guestroom bed.'

He smiled, relieved by Kathryn's appreciation of it. 'My mother made it.'

'And the tapestries are her work, too?' she asked admiringly.

He nodded. 'She loved doing them.'

'I bet it gave her a lot of satisfaction, too. Like my mother with her pottery, creating something beautiful with her hands.'

It was a natural lead in to asking her about her family. She spoke of her parents with great fondness. Her father was a primary school principal, her mother an art teacher, and they lived at Gosford on the Central Coast. Near where Jenny lived, Mitch thought.

'Dad is a born teacher,' she went on. 'He's really wasted in administration but he does run a good school so I guess that's a worthwhile achievement in itself, all the kids liking and respecting him.'

'A headmaster can make or break a school,' Mitch commented, remembering the one in his own boyhood, who'd never made a stand against bullying. 'I think a good one is worth his weight in gold to everyone under his care.'

Her face lit up with pleasure. 'I agree. Dad's had so many great letters from ex-pupils and parents. He's helped a lot of people.'

They chatted on amicably as the dinner was cooked, transferred onto plates and taken to the dining room. Mitch refilled their wineglasses. Kathryn seemed to hesitate over accepting more wine but let his action go, possibly deciding she didn't have to drink it.

It was interesting to learn that she'd trained as a graphic artist, moved into various promotional jobs, then gradually up the ladder to management, handling accounts in advertising before taking up her position with Ric. Clearly Ric trusted her decision-making, which said a lot about her, too.

Mitch was enjoying her company in every sense. He liked listening to her, watching her, and nothing hit a jarring note with him...except the diamond ring that said she belonged to another man. More and more he felt that had to be wrong. Or was he just too damned late on the scene to change what surely had to be a very serious decision on her part?

She was talking of her two younger brothers—one a pilot who loved flying, the other off back-packing overseas, discovering the world. Did *they* like the guy she'd chosen to marry? Were they confident she'd have a happy life with him?

Mitch wanted to ask these questions but knew they would sound too personal, too critical. Yet her lovely green eyes were dancing at him, sparkling with her own enjoyment in the comfortable rapport they'd established. How many people *clicked* like this?

His intense private reverie was abruptly broken by the sound of his front door opening. Alarm buzzed along his nerves, blowing his mind free of everything but danger signals. He was on his feet in a flash, body pumped with aggression, swinging to meet...

'Mitch...?'

Harriet! Calling out to him from the small vestibule which led into his lounge room. Harriet...using a key she should have returned! Mitch felt his jaw clench as he sensed Kathryn looking questions at him. Of all the people in the world, Harriet Lowell was the last person he wanted intruding on this far too short a time with a woman he really wanted.

Nor did his ex-lover have any right to enter his home uninvited!

The fear that had clutched Kathryn's heart as Mitch had erupted from his chair eased its panicky grip as she heard a woman's voice. It wasn't Gary Chappel breaking in, coming after her. It was someone with a key. A surprise visit from his sister?

Yet Mitch was still tense, and the emanation of violent anger from him was so strong, Kathryn felt herself almost cringing away from it. She tore her gaze from him to see who had stirred such a fiercely emotional response, and instantly felt a weird hollowness as the woman in question came breezing into the lounge room, wearing a slinky black wrap-around skirt with a halter top held together by thin straps, plus carrying a bottle of champagne and a large punnet of fresh strawberries.

'Mitch, darling—' brilliant white teeth smiled as her eyes lighted on him, smoking sexual promises '—quite a victory you had today. I thought a celebration was in order.'

She was tall and blond and beautiful, supremely confident of herself and her welcome in any company. Especially Mitch Tyler's since she had a key to his house. Kathryn wished there was a hole she could sink into.

'Then you thought wrong,' came the harshly cutting reply, jolting

Kathryn into looking back at him. He was clearly furious, his jaw jutting out, black brows lowered. 'I'll see you out again, Harriet.'

Rather than being stunned into acquiescence, as Kathryn would have been, Harriet moved to meet him head-on, battle in her whole demeanour as her gaze zeroed in on Kathryn. 'So...you already have company. Where are your famed manners, Mitch?' she mocked. 'The least you can do is introduce us.'

She'd planted herself too far from the front door for Mitch to force a retreat without manhandling her. He blocked any further progress into his house and presented an open palm to her as he curtly commanded, 'Give me the key, Harriet. You have no right to it anymore.'

'Oh, for God's sake!' she snapped. 'Can't you be civil?'

Pure ice answered her. 'I don't regard entering my home without permission civil.'

'Especially when you're embarking on a new affair,' she threw at him viciously. Her gaze targeted Kathryn again. 'I can't recall ever seeing you before. Definitely not from the upper echelons of legal circles.'

It was a snooty remark, ignored by Mitch. 'The key, Harriet,' he bored in with relentless purpose.

Her eyes poured scorn on him. 'You disappoint me, Mitch. I thought you were a competitor.'

'I choose the ring I stand in,' he stated bitingly. 'I won't be drawn into yours.'

'So you pick up the first bit of skirt you can find in retaliation?'

'Enough! I want you to go.'

'She won't measure up to me,' Harriet jeered.

'Your arrogance is totally ill-founded and this isn't winning you anything. In fact, you're turning into a very ugly loser. Please...give me my key and leave.'

'My hands are full with gifts for you.'

'Tools to get your own way,' he savagely corrected her, grabbing both the bottle and punnet from her hold, tucking the bottle in the crook of his arm so he could still extend his palm. 'Now your hands are free.'

She swung one back and Kathryn tensed, anticipating a violent slap. Mitch Tyler stood like an immovable rock, emanating a power that would certainly intimidate most people. She couldn't see his expression but Harriet had swift second thoughts about hitting him. She moved both her hands to the small shoulder-bag she wore, opening it to submit to his command which undoubtedly wasn't about to be retracted.

'No second chances with you, Mitch?' she commented bitterly.

'As you remarked earlier today, I have a black and white mentality.'

'You judge too harshly.'

'You chose a different bed, Harriet. Don't ever expect to come back to mine. There is no key that will give you entry to it.'

'You're going to regret this.' It sounded like a threat.

'Oh, I doubt it,' he drawled. 'Even if you sleep with all the judges on the bench, they still have to stick to the law.'

She slapped the key onto his palm. 'Going to give it to her now?' Her gaze snapped lofty contempt at Kathryn.

'Have some grace, Harriet. I wouldn't like my respect for you to slip even further.'

She glared at him but obviously found no crack in his armour to attack. Hating defeat, she haughtily turned her back on both of them and headed for the front door. Mitch followed, ensuring her exit from his home and making it secure against any further unwelcome intrusion.

Kathryn remained seated at the dining table, still absorbing the shock of what she had witnessed. No question that Harriet and Mitch Tyler had been lovers and her possession of a key indicated a high level of intimacy and trust, which had been broken, apparently by Harriet's sleeping with a judge.

A mistake she regretted?

A mistake Mitch wouldn't forgive.

An honourable man...dishonoured by infidelity.

And very, very angry about it.

Hurt.

Kathryn shook her head over her own foolishness in thinking the attraction she felt had been mutual. How could Mitch Tyler find her instantly desirable when she was so different in looks to the woman who'd been very recently sharing his bed? Nobody would describe Kathryn as beautiful. *Cute* was the word most frequently applied to her. And *cute* didn't cut it when a man like him could have a Harriet, who was obviously a barrister, too, sharing his world.

The violence of feeling this unheralded visit had stirred was proof enough that his emotions were still engaged with his sexy colleague, despite his decision to end their affair. It was ridiculous to have felt any danger in staying overnight in his home. The fault lay in herself, finding him so temptingly attractive. And that was wrong, too, when her emotions should also be engaged elsewhere. With Jeremy.

Kathryn twisted the ring on her finger, fiercely reminding herself that it promised fidelity—a promise she'd meant to keep. And *would* keep. Just as well Harriet had come, stopping her from possibly making a huge mistake. She should feel grateful to her, but she didn't. The pleasure in Mitch Tyler's company had all been taken away and she simply felt...hollow.

# CHAPTER FIVE

IT GAVE MITCH no satisfaction to lock Harriet out of his home. The action was too similar to shutting the door after the horse had bolted. The damage was done. The rapport he'd established with Kathryn, the pleasant, relaxed mood...both were totally and irretrievably shattered by Harriet's arrogant presumption that she could seduce him into resuming their relationship.

Seeing Kathryn fiddling with her ring as he re-entered the lounge room telegraphed where her thoughts were—right back with Jeremy Haynes—and Mitch knew he had one hell of a battle on his hands to wrest back any ground he'd made with her. The caveman streak in him that had been tapped at their first meeting this afternoon, wanted to sweep her up and stamp himself back into her mind with a kiss that would knock his rival right out of it.

But she would fight him.

She would lose all trust in him.

It was a completely hopeless initiative that would damn him in her eyes and nullify any chance of moving forward with her. He knew this, yet it took enormous control to stop himself from taking some volatile action, to suppress the seething urge and force a reasonable response to what had just happened.

'I'm sorry you were trapped into witnessing what you shouldn't have had to, Kathryn,' he said, trying to keep his intense frustration out of his voice.

She took a deep breath, squaring her shoulders as she turned her gaze to his. There was no warm vitality in her eyes—a dull flat green that left him in no doubt about her inner withdrawal. 'I shouldn't have been here,' she stated, her mouth twisting into an ironic grimace.

'You're here for a good reason,' he countered emphatically. 'And I might add I didn't introduce you to Harriet Lowell for the same reason. Better that she doesn't know your name, nor your connection to Gary Chappel.'

'Of course,' she muttered, nodding as though he'd just confirmed her place in his life—strictly business.

He wanted to yell that it wasn't so.

Heat flooded her cheeks. 'I'm sorry if I was in the way of...of some possible reconciliation.'

Words exploded from him in sheer vexation that she could imagine he might want Harriet back in his life. 'Kathryn, if you discovered your fiancé had cheated on you to gain some perceived advantage in his career, would you still want to be with him?'

Too much anger. He could see her gathering herself to answer him, forced into it.

'No, I wouldn't.' She lifted pained eyes, sympathetic eyes that made his guts writhe. He didn't want *sympathy* from her. 'I don't think cheating is ever justifiable,' she added quietly.

He didn't want her to *cheat* on Jeremy. He wanted her to *break* with him, but he saw little chance of that now.

'Case closed,' he said decisively. 'And may I add, your company is infinitely preferable to hers.'

This claim evoked a wry little smile. 'You've been very kind and hospitable.'

Her guard was up, well and truly, and Mitch didn't know how to reach past it. 'Kindness doesn't enter into it,' he stated flatly. 'Being with you is a pleasure.'

She shook her head. 'I've talked too much about myself. I guess...being a barrister...you're very good at drawing people out.'

'I wanted to know...just as you wanted to know about me, Kathryn,' he shot at her, fighting the barrier she'd obviously decided to raise.

'Yes. Well, it did pass the time and it's unlikely we'll ever meet again, so I don't suppose it matters what we say.' She pushed her chair back and stood up. 'We'd better clear the table now. Do the dishes.'

She was in full retreat.

The half glass of wine she'd left would not be drunk.

Mitch gathered up the glasses and condiments while she took the plates and cutlery. 'I'll make us some coffee,' he said as they headed for the kitchen. The need to prolong the evening with her was imperative. 'I'm looking forward to our game of chess,' he quickly added as she looked about to refuse coffee.

'Oh!' She frowned as though she'd forgotten her offer and now felt cornered by it.

'What do you like to play? Black or white?' he pressed.

Kathryn recalled what Mitch had said about chess occupying what would otherwise be lonely hours. If she retired to the guest suite now, she'd be leaving him to churn over the bitter scene with Harriet...alone with miserable memories. Hardly a kind return for looking after her, caring about her safety.

The embarrassment she felt was her own doing. Mitch Tyler had made every effort to put her at ease in his home and in his company. It would be mean to turn her back on him now. And there was nothing terribly personal about playing chess. They'd be concentrating on the game.

Black or white, he'd asked.

'Let's make it completely fair and toss for the choice,' she suggested.

'You *are* my guest,' he demurred, his face breaking into a grin of relief at her agreement to play.

'I don't want to be given any advantage.'

His eyes twinkled teasingly. 'Confident of winning anyway?'

Her chin tilted up with pride. 'I should warn you I was chess champion at school.'

He laughed. 'So was I.'

She looked askance at him as she rinsed their plates in the sink. 'Don't tell me you're a Grand Master.'

'Okay. I won't tell you.'

He was still grinning as he prepared the coffee-pot. Kathryn decided it didn't matter if he was far more skilled than herself. Playing was simply a means of keeping their minds distracted from other issues. He probably needed to win, given that he'd lost in love, though why on earth the beautiful Harriet had found anyone else more tempting...

Mitch had put it down to ambition.

Would Jeremy put ambition ahead of fidelity to her?

Being successful in his career meant a lot to him and he certainly had a hard, competitive streak, but Jeremy had given her no reason to believe he'd ever cheat on her. She'd been unsettling herself by questioning their relationship. Best to stop it right now.

Having washed and dried the plates and cutlery, she moved back to the stool on the other side of the kitchen counter while the coffee was brewing, putting some comfortable distance between herself and Mitch Tyler. It was difficult to ignore the sheer magnetism of his physical presence and silence made it even more nerve-tingling.

'Talking of winning, what was the victory you had today?' she blurted out, then instantly realised it was a tactless blunder, reminding him of Harriet's excuse for bringing champagne and strawberries to celebrate.

'The Barrington case.' He was preparing a tray with mugs and a plate of chocolate wafers and slanted her a sardonic look. 'If you could call squeezing a decent settlement out of a heart of stone a victory.'

Kathryn knew what he was talking about. The Barrington family dispute had been a rather scandalous case, widely reported in the media, the son having committed suicide, the daughter-in-law blaming the family and seeking compensation. 'I take it you were on the side of the underdog.'

He nodded. 'Harriet represented the family.'

'Oh!' Kathryn felt confused. Why would Harriet want to celebrate *his* victory if...? 'She didn't mind losing?'

He gave a short derisive laugh. 'Harriet hates losing anything. Even me.'

*Especially you,* Kathryn thought. Obviously the beautiful barrister had been bending over backwards to regain some foothold in his life tonight. Which begged the question... 'I realise you feel responsible for me, because of Ric, but if I hadn't been here...'

'It would have made no difference.' The blue eyes stabbed that point home. 'Stop worrying about it, Kathryn.'

She wasn't sure about that. After all, he hadn't asked Harriet to give his key back until tonight. Why the oversight if he was dead against resuming any relationship with her? Barging right in as she had, might well have worked for her if Mitch hadn't been otherwise occupied with what was basically Ric Donato's business—emergency measures in response to his friend's plea for help.

As though he was tuned into her line of logic, he said, 'She knew damned well using that key was an invasion, but it's typical of her. Harriet is a risk-taker. I would have demanded its return before this, except—' his grimace carried distaste '—we've been on opposing sides in this court case. I didn't want to get into personal issues with Harriet when we were in professional conflict. Being a stickler about returning my key seemed inappropriate.'

His curt tone and the steely pride on his face told Kathryn to back off this sensitive ground. Stupid of her to pursue it in the first place. He had to be still hurting over it and here she was, turning the knife in the wound, just to satisfy her own curiosity about his feelings for another woman.

For what purpose?

It wasn't as though she wanted him for herself.

She had Jeremy.

The coffee was poured. Mitch carried the tray into the lounge room and Kathryn followed him, relieved they could now settle down and play chess without any need to make conversation. The silence would be natural, not awkward or tense. She could focus on the game. Relax. Stop questioning what should be...was...beyond questioning.

Mitch couldn't concentrate on chess. He felt totally hamstrung by the situation. He pondered telling Kathryn straight out that meeting her had told him unequivocally that his previous relationship with Harriet Lowell had lacked the more instinctive attraction he felt with her, had even lacked the power to stir him anywhere near as strongly as she did. Could he lay himself on the line that far? Would it hit a chord with Kathryn, or would it embarrass her?

His hands moved the chess pieces in automatic defensive moves to her attack. Before he even saw it coming she had him checkmated. 'I've been blind-sided,' he muttered in self-deprecation as he conceded the game.

Her eyes twinkled both pleasure in the victory and challenge because it was too easy. 'I think you underestimated me.'

'I won't a second time,' he warned, his heart lifting as he felt the connection again. She had to feel it, too. It couldn't be one-sided.

But her lashes swept down as she set up the chess pieces for another game, clearly determined on blocking out anything of a personal nature. 'Would you like to play white this time?' she asked, intent on being fair.

'No. I'm fine with black. I like to come from behind.'

Her gaze lifted in a flash of amusement. 'Making victory all the sweeter?'

'I wish,' he said with feeling.

For one poignant moment she smiled full on and his heart leapt with triumphant pleasure at the instant tug of what had to be mutual attraction—strongly positive. Yet it was far too fleeting to make any capital out of it. The next instant she was staring at the chessboard again, selecting a pawn to move forward, and the shut-out was warning enough not to push for anything beyond her current comfort zone.

He forced himself to focus on the game. He didn't win. He didn't lose, either. They reached stalemate and both of them conceded a draw. He insisted on a third game, just to keep her with him, though he knew it wouldn't change anything. Loyalty—fidelity—to her fiancé was firmly entrenched in her mind.

He won this time and she used his victory as an excuse to retire with equal honours, saying she was tired and thanking him for playing with her.

'We're a good match,' he couldn't resist saying.

'I enjoyed it,' she acknowledged, then rather nervously rushed on, 'About tomorrow, Mitch…'

'I'll be gone early in the morning,' he broke in, knowing she would avoid having breakfast with him, seeing him off. 'Just make yourself at home here. I'll call and let you know the outcome of my meeting with the Chappels.'

'If it's positive, I could go back to work, pick up my car…' She was anxious to be away from him and the intimacy of his home.

'No!' he cut in emphatically. 'Better not to be too confident and hasty, Kathryn. When do you expect your fiancé home?'

She frowned. 'About six-thirty tomorrow evening.'

'I'll feel happier delivering you safely to him myself.' And checking out what he was like. Mitch couldn't bring himself to let Kathryn Ledger go without satisfying himself it was right to do so. Right for her. It was never going to feel right to him.

'Surely that won't be necessary,' she argued, not liking that scenario.

If it made trouble with her fiancé, good! Mitch thought savagely. 'He should be told what's gone on, Kathryn. I'm not sure I can stop Gary Chappel from making a dangerous nuisance of himself outside your business hours. Especially where there are no witnesses. Your fiancé will have to be your watchdog and protector.'

She heaved a fretful sigh. 'All right. But I don't need you to tell him, Mitch. I can do that myself.'

'Okay.' They were fighting words and he had no authority over her life to override them. 'Just let me take you home and pass you over to him. That way I can assure Ric I let no harm come to you. Fair enough?'

The reminder of her work situation with Ric had to have impact on her resistance to his plan. Her boss had made her promise to go along with Mitch's advice and Mitch would report back to Ric. Besides, if her relationship with Jeremy Haynes was all it should be, there was no reason for her not to accept Mitch's escort home.

Her reluctance smacked of conflict.

Which gave Mitch a flicker of hope that she might change her mind about this marriage. Unlikely, he warned himself, yet the desire to have her for himself—at least explore what was possible between them—would not lie down and die.

'I'm sorry if I sound ungrateful...difficult...' She grimaced in apology. 'I guess I'm not used to any need for protection.'

'The need is real,' he gravely assured her. 'Don't dismiss it, Kathryn. In my opinion, Gary Chappel is psychopathic.'

She shuddered, possibly in memory of Chappel's behaviour at her office. 'Okay. I'll wait for you to take me home,' she conceded in a rush.

'The best course,' he said approvingly.

She managed a wry little smile. 'Thanks for looking after me, Mitch. Good night.'

She was off, walking away from him, and all Mitch had from her was a toehold on tomorrow.

It was not a winning position.

But he would not accept defeat until it was staring him in the face. All these years he'd never met a woman who made him feel as Kathryn did.

Ironic that it should happen on the very day Ric had taken charge of Lara's life. Eighteen years...and still Ric cared about her. A one-woman man.

Might Kathryn Ledger be *his* one-in-a-lifetime woman?

Maybe it was just the wrong time for them. Ric and Lara had been separated. She'd married someone else. They'd connected again now. Lara had taken off her rings to go with Ric.

Kathryn had to take off that damned ring.

Until she did...there was no future for them.

There might never be a future for them.

Ships passing in the night...

Everything within Mitch revolted against that concept.

Somewhere there had to be a twist that worked his way.

# CHAPTER SIX

KATHRYN WAS GRIMLY reciting, *Please be home. Please be home. Please be home*...all the way up in the elevator to Jeremy's apartment. She'd deliberately cut her time with Mitch Tyler as short as she could, getting Jeremy to call her once he'd got into a taxi at Mascot Airport so she didn't have to wait until he was actually in residence before Mitch drove her from Woollahra to Pyrmont.

She'd been tense in the car, still disturbed by the powerful attraction of Ric's friend, feeling almost desperate to be distanced from it, get her life back into its normal flow. Here in the elevator, her nerves were literally twitching with dreadful agitation at the thought of being forced to invite Mitch in to wait for her fiancé's arrival. She didn't want any shadow of his presence left behind in the apartment she shared with Jeremy. Bad enough that the two men were going to come face-to-face, making more comparisons inevitable.

At last the elevator halted and opened onto the penthouse floor. She had her key out ready. Just a few more seconds and she could say goodbye to the man accompanying her every step. She pressed the buzzer to alert Jeremy to her arrival then shoved the key in the lock, hoping he would come to the door as it was opened so Mitch would be satisfied about her safety and go. Then she'd be able to relax with everything that was familiar to her instead of feeling hopelessly messed around.

To her immense relief, Jeremy was as eager to see her as she was to see him. As she swung the door wide, he was striding across the penthouse foyer, his handsome face beaming with happy anticipation. He stretched out his arms to wrap her in an exuberant embrace and she rushed in to be wrapped, wanting the comfort of feeling herself loved by him.

'Hey! Have I got news for you, babe!' he crowed triumphantly, hugging her tightly, even swinging her off her feet.

'Um...just a minute, Jeremy. There's someone with me,' she babbled breathlessly.

'Who?' He looked over her head in careless good humour and Kathryn strained against his hold to make one last acknowledgement of Mitch, who was now standing in the doorway, watching her reunion with her fiancé, the blue eyes coolly assessing, his strong face grimly etched.

She had to swallow hard before she got out the words, 'This is...'

'It's okay, Kathryn,' he cut in, apparently not wanting an introduction. 'I can see I'm not needed. I'm off.'

He raised one hand in a brief salute, while using the other to grab the door and close it, making his departure both abrupt and decisive, not even waiting for her to thank him again.

Quick and clean, which was what she'd wanted, Kathryn fiercely told herself, yet that strange hollow feeling attacked her again...like something vital had been ripped out of her.

'Who was that guy?' Jeremy demanded, curiosity piqued enough to forget his own excitement for a moment.

'My protector,' she said wryly.

'What?'

'It's a long story.' Time to concentrate on Jeremy now. She'd left text messages on his mobile phone but apart from the one airport call she'd requested, they hadn't spoken—no communication about his meetings in Melbourne nor the disruption at her own office. She hung her arms around his neck again, telling herself *this* was the man she loved and stretching her mouth into a big welcoming smile. 'I want to hear your news first.'

He was bursting with it. So much so, he didn't even kiss her. His grin was far too wide for puckering up. 'I got the partnership.' His eyes sparkled with delight in the achievement—bright brown eyes, much warmer than blue. 'I'll be heading up the Sydney branch with two other guys, starting next week.'

'But won't you have to work out your notice at the bank?' They surely wouldn't want to lose such a high-powered and immensely successful dealer so quickly.

'Not in my position,' Jeremy declared with supreme confidence. 'They can't risk my tapping clients from them. Once I tell them I'm leaving, I walk the same day. And that day will be tomorrow.'

'Wow! That's really moving,' she commented appreciatively.

'Up and up. With you at my side, babe.' He tucked her appropriately at his side, an arm curled around her shoulders, walking her into the living room and waving to the bottle of champagne he'd set on the kitchen counter. 'I had the taxi stop at a liquor store. Celebration is definitely in order.'

*No strawberries,* she thought, and mentally kicked herself for equating Jeremy's victory with Harriet Lowell's visit to Mitch Tyler's home last night.

'You open the bottle. I'll get the glasses,' she offered eagerly, needing some pleasant bubbles in her head. 'And tell me all about your meetings from start to finish.'

Jeremy was only too happy to give her a blow-by-blow description. Kathryn moved into the stainless-steel kitchen while he popped the cork. She placed his prized crystal flute glasses ready for him to do his skilful pouring, then quickly asked, 'What do you want to do for dinner?'

'Oh, just get a couple of pizzas out of the freezer,' he said with a dismissive wave.

Clearly food wasn't important tonight and he wanted her complete attention, no distraction with cooking. Which she always did when cooking was called for. Jeremy was never going to share that with her. It wasn't in his nature to even think of it or want to do so.

On the other hand, on a great provider scale, he was definitely a ten, so she had nothing to complain about. Just because Mitch Tyler...no, she wasn't going to think about how...*companionable*...it had been with him—sharing the preparation of their meal last night.

She took the pizzas out of the freezer, stripped off their covering, switched on the oven, slid them in, picked up her glass of champagne and focused fully on the man she'd chosen as her future husband. He was glowing; smile, skin, eyes. Clean-cut good looks that any woman would admire, especially when he was full of zappy energy, as he was at the moment, recounting how he'd gone about impressing the other partners in the financial services company he'd targeted.

He wore his dark brown hair in a rather yuppie style, short at the sides, long enough at the top for a natural wave to soften his high forehead and complement the rather acutely angled arch of his eyebrows. Very attractive. Striking. And while his physique was on the slender side, it enabled him to wear fashionable clothes well, which he did with considerable panache. Kathryn had always felt proud to have him as her partner.

And not just for presentation, either. He was very smart, right on the ball with clever and amusing repartee, and she admired his drive to be the best at what he did. Most women would say she'd hit the jackpot with Jeremy Haynes, and she had. Of course, she had.

So why didn't she want to make love with him tonight? Why was she glad he hadn't kissed her in the foyer, with Mitch Tyler watching? Why was she looking at his mouth and thinking of another man's? She should be listening to him with avid ears. This was their future he was talking about. A shining future that would support any family they chose to have.

He described the subtle manoeuvres he'd used, how he'd pressed all the right buttons to win over this person and that person, the top-class Melbourne restaurants where he'd been breakfasted, lunched, wined and dined while all the power-brokering had been done.

Quite a comedown having heated up pizza, Kathryn thought as she took them from the oven and sliced them up for easy eating. Still, the Krug champagne certainly upgraded the meal and fuzzed the tensions she'd brought home with her. She encouraged Jeremy to refill her glass, having downed the first faster than she usually would. There was no need to keep her guard up tonight. In fact, there was every need to start feeling some sexual desire where it should be directed.

They moved to the glass dining table which was supported by two blocks of shiny black granite. The black lacquered chairs were some kind of moulded plastic, the seats and backrests curved for comfort but they were hard and cold to sit on. The design was very modern, of course.

They finished the pizza and were still swilling their champagne when Jeremy finally ran out of steam over his doings and asked about hers. 'So tell me who was the guy at the door, and why did he think you needed protection?' he tossed out in a lightly mocking tone, suggesting he couldn't believe the situation to be a serious one. Or if it had been, it was over and done with, hardly worth mentioning.

Kathryn was niggled by his attitude. It reinforced her feeling that his career was far more important than her safety, and okay...she'd put it first, too, but was that right? Goaded by a sense of her own worth, she started with the status of *her protector*.

'You know the Barrington court case that's been news headlines lately.'

He nodded. 'Heard it was settled yesterday.'

'Well, the man who accompanied me home is Mitch Tyler, the barrister who settled it for the daughter-in-law.'

That raised Jeremy's eyebrows. 'What was he doing with you?'

'Making sure I wasn't accosted by Gary Chappel of the nursing home Chappel family.'

He looked stunned by this news. The shock was swiftly followed by alarm. 'Why would Gary Chappel want to accost you?'

His alarm lifted a considerable weight from Kathryn's heart. Jeremy really did care about her safety.

She proceeded to tell him about the photograph that had turned up on the computer this morning, her boss's reaction to it, his subsequent action in going to Vaucluse and masterminding Lara Chappel's escape from her situation, her own part in evading the pursuit vehicle and driving them to Bankstown Airport.

Jeremy looked aghast as she recounted what she had done to help. 'Ric Donato involved you in this madness?'

She frowned. 'I don't consider it madness to rescue a battered wife, Jeremy.'

'A black eye is not necessarily a battered wife,' he argued.

'Well, it is to me,' she retorted hotly. 'And it wasn't only that. He was having her watched, followed...'

'Maybe for good reason,' Jeremy shot back at her. 'What if she was cheating on him?'

'She was frightened of him, Jeremy. And grateful to Ric for...'

'This is *Gary Chappel's* wife we're talking about,' he almost shouted, then rose from the table in obvious agitation, pacing around, too disturbed to remain seated. 'Does *he* know about your part in this?'

'Not about driving them to the airport. But he did come into the office after they'd gone, demanding to know where they were.'

'And you didn't tell him?'

Kathryn paused to take a deep breath, feeling shaken and confused by Jeremy's reaction which was terribly off-key to her. 'No. I didn't tell him. I wanted Ric and Lara to get safely away. And let me tell you, he's a very scary man,' she added more strongly.

'It's only natural he'd be angry,' Jeremy instantly excused.

'It wasn't just anger. It was...' How to describe the sense of vicious and malevolent threat? 'Mitch Tyler says Gary Chappel is a psychopath and I believe him,' she blurted out.

'Right!' Jeremy snapped. 'So it comes down to you having to be protected from *him*.' He glared furiously at her as he added, 'From the man who's going to be my biggest client when I start my new job next week. I'll be his financial adviser, Kathryn. In charge of the Chappel millions, if not billions. He is a *huge part* of our future.'

She stared at him, seeing how very much he cared about this connection, realising it came ahead of anything else. Jeremy would deal with the devil if there was a big enough reward in it. A chill started in her bones and seeped through her, raising goose bumps on her skin.

'I presume he got your name while you were *blocking* his pursuit of his wife,' he ran on. 'And the fact you're Ric Donato's executive assistant.'

'Yes, he did,' she answered flatly.

'My fiancée.' He threw up his hands as though she'd committed the worst possible evil. 'That's great. That's just great!'

'The solution is perfectly simple, Jeremy,' she heard herself say. 'I can stop being your fiancée.'

'Oh, don't be ridiculous!' he tossed at her, his eyes glittering with the need to find a different option. 'First off, you'll have to leave that job, distance yourself from Ric Donato instantly.'

Her jaw started clenching. 'I won't do that.'

He sliced a dismissive gesture. 'You don't need it. Once I start working as a partner in this business, we'll be on easy street for life. You can be a lady of leisure.'

'I like my work, Jeremy. And I won't walk out on Ric when he has to be somewhere else.'

His furious pacing jerked to a halt as an idea struck him. '*Where* is the somewhere else?'

'I don't know yet. Mitch Tyler advised him to get out of the country as soon as possible. Ric said he'd contact me about his destination before he flew off.'

'*With* Lara Chappel?'

He'd seized on that so fast, Kathryn paused, her instincts warning her she shouldn't give Jeremy this information. He'd use it. He'd use it to somehow further his connection with Gary Chappel, work it to get some advantage.

'I don't know,' she replied, watching him from what felt like a long distance. A very cold distance.

'Where are they now?' he demanded.

'I don't know that, either.'

'You drove them to Bankstown Airport,' he bored in.

'And left them there. I had to get back to the office.' She was glad now she hadn't mentioned Johnny Ellis's private plane. Bad enough that she'd given out the airport clue.

'But Ric must have told you what he had planned.'

'No, he didn't. He said the less I knew, the better. And he trusted me to cover his tracks, Jeremy,' she said very pointedly.

'What Ric Donato wants isn't important,' he stated with breathtaking arrogance.

'It is to me,' she bit out.

Again her feelings and her position were summarily dismissed. 'We give Gary Chappel the information he wants. All we can get that will help him.' He actually grinned as he added, 'In fact, that's the best protection for you, Kathryn. He certainly won't think of harming you under those circumstances.'

Loyalty to her employer didn't matter.

Giving Lara up to an abusive husband didn't matter, either.

This man—the man she had planned to marry—had no sense of morality.

None at all.

Money was his God and he'd serve it, regardless of who got hurt.

His eyes narrowed. 'Best that you do keep working for Ric. Gives you the inside track on what moves he makes.'

'Better still if I'm not your fiancée, Jeremy,' she said with icy preci-
sion. 'Then you have no connection to anyone involved in Lara Chappel's
escape from her rotten husband. You're free and clear of it.'

'No...no...we can use this to our advantage.'

'Your advantage. Not mine. And I won't be a party to your plan which
I find absolutely obscene.'

'Kathryn—' He felt vexed impatience with her attitude '—you don't
understand how power works.'

Oh, yes, she did. There was power for evil and power for good and
Jeremy and Mitch Tyler were at opposite poles of it. Black and white.

She took off the flashy diamond ring, set it on the glass table, rose
from the shiny black chair, looked Jeremy straight in the eye and without the slightest hesitation, declared, 'Our engagement is over. I don't
want to be attached to you anymore, Jeremy. And believe me, you'll be
better off not mentioning any of this to Gary Chappel. You might end
up biting off more than even you can comfortably chew.'

# CHAPTER SEVEN

*Three months later...*

IT WAS FOUR-THIRTY in the afternoon when the case for the prosecution rested. Court was adjourned, allowing the defence to start fresh in the morning. Mitch accompanied his client out, assuring him everything was prepared for tomorrow. His clerk handed him a message and instantly warning bells rang in Mitch's mind.

The message read—'Call Patrick as soon as possible.'

Gundamurra...

Only two nights ago, Ric had telephoned him, wanting advice on returning to Australia, to Lara, and whether Gary Chappel was still a threat?

He'd sounded very stressed.

Had he done something stupid?

Mitch had warned him there was no absolute assurance that Gary was out of the picture. To his mind, a psychopath never dealt straight, even while giving every appearance of it. He also cautioned Ric that Lara might need more time to recover from the ordeal of her marriage.

After Jenny's one traumatic experience, she had shied away from men for years. He knew from the information Lara had given him to sue for divorce that she had suffered much more abuse than a single rape. She

would be grateful to Ric for rescuing her but accepting love from him...
even being with him might cause her painful conflict.

These thoughts raced through his mind as he took off his barrister's
wig and gown, handed them to his clerk and took out his mobile phone. It
wasn't Patrick but his housekeeper, Evelyn, who answered his return call.

'I can't fetch Mr Patrick right now. He's with Miss Lara. But he told
me to tell you what happened here. A plane crashed on our airstrip about
an hour ago. It shouldn't have tried to land. It's all mud here from the
big wet. Only a helicopter can come in. Anyway, the pilot didn't radio
to find out, just brought it down. The plane was a charter from Sydney
and Miss Lara's husband was on it. Gary Chappel. He died in the crash.
Mr Patrick thought you should tell Mr Ric. Okay?'

Gary Chappel at Gundamurra...dead!

Mitch gave himself a quick mental shake. 'Okay. Thanks, Evelyn. I'll
contact Ric and let him know.'

Except he didn't know where Ric was—London? New York? Los Angeles? He hadn't queried where Ric was calling from when they'd spoken two nights ago.

Another shock hit him. Ric had mentioned Gundamurra in that conversation and Gary Chappel had turned up there today. Was there a connection? Could his home telephone be bugged? He'd have to get someone in
to check it out, sweep the whole house for any surveillance gadgets. It appalled him to think that Gary Chappel might have got to Lara through...

But it didn't matter now. The man was dead. Good riddance, too.
Lara was free of him forever now. And Ric could come home without
endangering either her or himself. Or Kathryn.

Kathryn...

*She* would know where Ric was.

He glanced at his watch. She should still be at her office. He could call
her... No, dammit! This was as good an excuse as any to go and see her.
Why not? It gave him the opportunity to check that Jeremy Haynes was
still very much the man in her life.

He called Ric's business number, ascertained from the receptionist
that Kathryn was still at work in her office, and asked for a message to be
relayed that Mitch Tyler was on his way with urgent business and would
she please wait for him to arrive.

As he put away his mobile and headed out of the courthouse to catch a taxi, he smiled grimly over the tactic to force one more encounter with Kathryn Ledger. Probably another exercise in frustration. He remembered only too well how she had rushed into her fiancé's arms when he'd escorted her to the Pyrmont apartment.

A penthouse apartment.

Hard to beat a guy who not only looked like a million dollars but undoubtedly had millions of dollars, as well. Still, the same description could have been applied to Gary Chappel. Money wasn't everything. The problem was...Mitch had no reason to think Jeremy Haynes wasn't treating Kathryn right, looking after her.

He'd instructed her to contact him immediately if there was even a whiff of trouble from Gary Chappel.

She hadn't called.

The message he'd just sent would probably alarm her but he could straighten that out soon enough. And seeing her again might even help him get over the gnawing sense of having missed out on something too good to be missed. Three months...had he been exaggerating the memory of how he'd felt with her?

He flagged down a passing taxi, gave the address at Circular Quay to the driver, and settled back in the passenger seat for the short drive to his destination. Ever since meeting Kathryn Ledger, he hadn't felt a spark of interest in any other woman. Harriet certainly left him cold. He could barely bring himself to be civil to her when they met professionally. Ironic that she'd tried to dig out the identity of 'the mystery woman' in his life, getting no satisfaction because Kathryn was not *his woman,* much as he would have liked her to be.

He wondered if Ric would have any luck with Lara, now that Gary Chappel was gone. Best to get his mind focused on the urgent business before he walked in on Kathryn. No point in nursing any hope that she'd suddenly have a change of heart over marrying Jeremy Haynes. He just wanted to see her...

Kathryn's heart wouldn't stop fluttering. Mitch Tyler, coming to her on urgent business! It had to be something to do with Gary Chappel. Or Ric. Possibly both of them.

There'd been a business e-mail from Ric waiting for her in her office computer this morning. No suggestion of trouble. But that had been sent last night. Now was now, and Mitch was coming in person, which had to mean it was a weighty matter, not something he would tell her over the phone.

Ric had been more or less on the run for the past three months, visiting his overseas offices, but as far as she knew, his safety hadn't been threatened. Neither had her own. Gary Chappel had not accosted her again in this office, nor anywhere away from it.

Jeremy had obviously remained quiet about his past association with her, probably deciding it *was* wiser to have no personal link to Lara Chappel's disappearance. Certainly he'd not tried any contact with her since she'd moved into the small Bondi Junction apartment she now called home. So much for all his professions of love! He'd told her point-blank that *she* was making the mistake in breaking up with him.

A big, stupid mistake.

Maybe he'd thought she'd come grovelling back to him.

Not in a million years!

In any event, her move had not put her in any danger. As far as she was aware, no-one had been following her or checking up on her. No confrontation. No threat. Nothing.

But maybe these past three months had been the lull before the storm—assuring Victor Chappel that the line was being toed, so if anything happened to Ric now...

She was pacing around her office, her mind in a whirl of worry when Mitch Tyler was shown in by her secretary. The sheer physical magnetism of the man instantly scattered her wits. Needles of awareness attacked her body. She stood still, trying to absorb the impact of meeting him again. Her fogged mind did register the fact that he was taking stock of her, too, not rushing into a greeting.

He was scanning her from head to toe, as though matching her to the imprint in his memory. She could feel her blood heating in response to the trail his gaze took. It was totally embarrassing to realise she was reacting sexually, her breasts tightening, her stomach contracting, her thighs going weak.

She desperately tried reminding herself of Harriet Lowell, the kind of woman he found attractive, but it didn't lessen her own response to him one bit. She felt caught up in a dynamic force that drained her of any resistance to the attraction tugging at her. It took an act of will to get her mouth working.

'Mitch...?'

'Kathryn...' He spoke her name on an expulsion of breath that seemed to fan the heat inside her.

'Is there trouble?' she asked, virtually jerking the words out.

'No trouble,' he assured her. 'I've just had word that Gary Chappel died in a plane crash this afternoon.'

'Died...?' The shock of this news served to get her thoughts off Mitch Tyler and her reaction to him. 'Where did it happen? Was it a big plane? Many casualties?'

'No. Small plane. Private charter. As far as I know, he was the only casualty. And probably his fault, not wanting the pilot to radio ahead to Gundamurra to inquire if the airstrip was fit for landing.'

'Gundamurra?' She'd never heard of the place.

'It's an outback sheep station. Where Ric took Lara, Kathryn.'

The outback!

How on earth did Ric know a safe refuge in the outback?

But that wasn't the point.

'Gary Chappel found out?' Her mind instantly spun to Jeremy. Had he told *his client* about Ric's flight from Bankstown Airport? Had Johnny Ellis's plane somehow been traced to its destination?

Mitch grimaced. 'I suspect an illegal tap on my home telephone. But that's irrelevant now.'

Irrelevant...yes, thank God! A surge of relief swept aside the awful sense that she might be responsible, betraying Ric's confidence to a man she'd thought she could trust with it.

'I thought you'd know where Ric is now,' Mitch went on. 'He'd want to know immediately. He's been moving around so much...'

'London. He e-mailed me from his London office last night.' She checked her watch, mentally calculating the time difference. 'Right now he should be asleep in his apartment at Knightsbridge. I have that number. I'll call it for you.'

She moved quickly around her desk, picked up the telephone receiver, flicked open her teledex and proceeded to press the long string of numbers for the international call.

*  *  *

Mitch had walked forward to take the receiver once contact was made. He stood on the other side of her desk, waiting, his gaze dropping to the hand tapping out the numbers.

No diamond ring on her third finger!

He sucked in a quick breath as hope rocketed through him, kicking his heart into a faster beat, blowing all thoughts of Ric out of his mind. Kathryn was free! Unattached!

Or was she? The ring might only have been taken off temporarily for some reason…leaving it accidentally in the washroom, having it cleaned, fixed by a jeweler…

'It's ringing,' she said, holding out the receiver.

So were his ears—ringing with the wild thump of his heart. Ric's voice on the other end of the line demanded his attention. Somehow Mitch managed to impart the critical information in a coherent manner, but the perimeter of his mind was whirling around how best to ascertain the status of Kathryn's engagement to Jeremy Haynes.

Nothing had changed for him. Kathryn Ledger still hit deep basic instincts that no other woman had even twanged before. One look and she'd floored him again. If there was any chance…

Kathryn listened to Mitch's side of the conversation, imagining how relieved her boss would be to know there was no longer any threat to Lara or himself.

No need to wait for a divorce, either.

He could come home and be with the woman he'd risked so much for, a woman he cared about beyond any cost to himself. Kathryn ruefully wondered how it would feel if a man cared for her like that.

Jeremy certainly hadn't.

But Mitch Tyler…no, what good would it do her to fit him into that frame, stirring herself into wishing for a chance with him? Bad enough that she was so susceptible to his exceptionally strong charisma. At least she wasn't feeling quite so shaken by it now and should be able to deal courteously with his departure.

The call ended. The receiver was put down. 'Ric will be on the first flight he can get from London to Sydney,' Mitch informed her. 'No doubt you'll hear from him when he arrives.'

It forced her to meet his gaze directly. The blue eyes were so piercing, she felt hopelessly rattled again. 'Yes,' she said inanely.

'You're not wearing your engagement ring.'

The words were shot at her so fast and hard, her reply tumbled out in a defensive rush. 'I changed my mind about marrying Jeremy.'

'What changed it?' he bored in.

There were so many reasons, yet the only one she could acknowledge to Mitch Tyler without totally embarrassing herself centred on loyalty. 'Jeremy is a partner in a financial services company and Gary Chappel is...was...his client. He wanted me to...to...'

'Betray Ric?'

'Yes. To actually help Gary Chappel find his wife.'

'Gaining an advantage for himself,' came the cynical comment.

'I didn't realise he would trade integrity for ambition. I couldn't live with it.'

'That must have been one hell of a disillusionment, Kathryn.'

She grimaced. 'Better that I found out.'

'True.'

His forceful agreement reminded Kathryn of Mitch's *disillusionment*— Harriet bedding a judge to gain an advantage. It was on the tip of her tongue to make some quip about both of them suffering the same letdown from their partners, until she remembered three months had gone by. For all she knew, Mitch had patched up his relationship with the beautiful barrister. One infidelity wasn't quite the same thing as selling integrity for money.

She heaved a sigh to loosen the tightness in her chest and ruefully remarked, 'You must be very effective at cross-examining people in court, Mitch. I haven't even told my parents what you've just drawn from me.'

His mouth curved into an ironic little smile. 'You knew I'd understand, Kathryn. Not only do I share the background with Ric, but you were also privy to my own experience of something similar with Harriet Lowell.'

'Yes.' She forced her stiff mouth to return his smile. 'I guess that's it.'

There was an awkward silence—bad times swirling between them, memories neither of them could easily dismiss. Kathryn was torn between wanting him to go and wanting him to make some approach to her on a personal level.

His hand lifted in a kind of apologetic appeal as his straight black brows lowered in a frown. 'I'm sorry this business with Ric resulted in...'

'Lateral damage?' she quickly supplied, hating his harking back to Jeremy. 'We've already established it would have been a bad mistake for me to marry Jeremy Haynes, so there's no point in referring back to it.' A rush of hot pride made her add, 'And I'd prefer you not to mention what I've just told you to Ric. It's over. Behind me.'

He nodded. 'No need for him to know. You can trust me to stay silent on that score, Kathryn.'

She did. 'Thank you.'

'Doesn't eliminate the hurt, though,' he said softly, sympathetically.

The heat in her cheeks grew more intense. Impossible to tell him he was far more attractive to her than Jeremy. In every sense. The hurt she was feeling now came from the futile yearning for Mitch Tyler to see *her* as a woman he could get attached to.

'I'm over it,' she stated insistently, fiercely rejecting his sympathy.

'Ready to move on,' he interpreted, his eyes challenging hers with an odd trace of whimsy that had the weird effect of curling her stomach.

'Yes,' she snapped, wishing *he'd* let the whole thing with Jeremy go.

'Want to test that?'

The question confused her. 'I beg your pardon?'

'Well, I really enjoyed your company on the one evening we spent together, Kathryn. I'm thinking...why not have that pleasure again? Providing you're up for it...with Jeremy planted firmly behind you.'

She stared at him in chaotic disbelief. Was he asking her out with him? Challenging her to prove she was moving on?

He smiled. It was a slow warm smile, his eyes teasing her out of any resistance. 'Now that we've got Ric sorted out, why don't we stroll around the quay, drop into one of the bars near the opera house, have a drink together, choose a restaurant for dinner—plenty of them along the concourse—and generally relax.'

He *was* asking her out with him!

It might only be a sympathy/empathy thing.

Maybe a reward for keeping faith with his friend.

A celebration that Ric's problems were now over.

A bit of mutual relaxation because the danger they'd both known and faced was gone.

She didn't care. Her heart was tap-dancing, shooting excitement through her whole body. Happy tingles banished all sense of caution. It might only be one night out with him but no way was she going to refuse it.

'I'd like that,' she said.

'Good!' He positively grinned, pleasure sparkling in his eyes. 'So grab your bag. Let's go and enjoy the evening.'

Enjoy...yes, she would. Just forget everything else and enjoy being with him. There was no ring on her finger. She was free to follow her instincts and it was utterly impossible to repress the hope that they'd lead her somewhere good.

# CHAPTER EIGHT

FOR KATHRYN, IT was a magical evening. Although there was the nip of approaching winter in the air, she was warmed by Mitch's company as they strolled along the concourse toward the opera house. A host of ferries were coming in and out of the quay to transport commuters home to their north shore destinations. The great Sydney Harbour Bridge that towered above the scene was buzzing with traffic. People were rushing all around them, but not she and Mitch. He was giving her his time and attention and Kathryn revelled in it.

It was easy to make conversation with him. She enjoyed listening to details of his life as a barrister, his description of various colourful personalities he'd met. He asked her about Ric's business, how she was dealing with her end of it in the absence of her boss.

He also made it easy to relax with him when they stopped at a bar and he insisted she have a fancy cocktail for fun. The talk gradually moved on to current affairs, personal likes and dislikes. There were no awkward moments. Everything felt like a natural progression.

They dined at a harbourside restaurant, both of them ordering oysters and the fish of the day, sharing a preference for seafood. She had no hesitation in drinking the fine chardonnay Mitch ordered with it. It added to the happy intoxication of being with him and she didn't have to drive home.

Ever since moving to Bondi Junction she'd been catching the train to and from work—easier and faster than being trapped in peak hour road traffic. However, Mitch wouldn't allow her to catch a train home when their dinner was over, insisting on taking her in a taxi and seeing her safely to her door.

It was the act of a gentleman, she told herself, wary of reading too much into it, though he had shown every sign of taking pleasure in her company. She was even beginning to believe he *was* attracted to her. Would he have been so charming otherwise?

Quite a few times her heart had caught when his eyes had seemed to be simmering with more than casual warmth. But he'd made no move on her. No attempt to even hold her hand. And certainly no open suggestion of sexual interest. Yet, as he climbed into the taxi beside her, Kathryn was acutely aware of her own physical—sexual—response to him.

In fact, she was so conscious of it she concentrated very hard on getting the seat belt fastened properly so he wouldn't have to help her this time. Pride insisted that he not sense her vulnerability. So far he had given no indication that he actually wanted to pursue a relationship with her. This might only be a one-off night...an act of kindness, making her feel better about herself.

It was ending fairly early. Though it had started early, too. Five o'clock until ten o'clock was a considerable amount of time together. And he had to be on the ball in the courtroom tomorrow. A late night wouldn't be reasonable. Or was she making excuses because she hoped for so much more with this man?

Her nerves were wound up so tight she couldn't think of a thing to say. It was impossible to sound casually relaxed when she wasn't, anyway. The taxi left Circular Quay, heading up Macquarie Street. It would be fifteen minutes at most to Bondi Junction at this hour. Could she ask Mitch in for coffee? Would that be too forward, too suggestive, too *needy*?

They'd already had coffee.

She'd been out of the dating game so long, having been in an exclusive relationship for almost two years, she didn't know how it was played now. And Mitch Tyler was older, more mature than the men she had mixed with before Jeremy. Surely it was up to him to make a move...if he wanted to. Or was he waiting for some sign from her that she wanted continuance? If he thought she was still hurting over having to break her engagement...

Her fingers were fretting at her skirt. Realising they were betraying her nervousness, she consciously slackened the agitated movement just as Mitch reached across and took one of her hands in his, enveloping it in warmth and causing her heart to slam against the constriction of her tight chest.

'Thank you for what has been a very pleasurable evening, Kathryn,' he said with what sounded like deep sincerity.

Was it an exit line or...?

She had to chance a look at him.

He was smiling.

'I've enjoyed it too, Mitch,' she rushed out, her own mouth breaking into a hopeful smile.

'I was wondering...'

'Yes?' Did that sound too eager?

'You did say you liked classical music,' he went on smoothly. 'I have season tickets for the opera and an empty seat beside mine for the performance of La Bohème this coming Saturday night.'

An empty seat...that Harriet would have filled if they'd still been together?

But Harriet was out of his personal life, just as Jeremy was out of hers.

His eyes appealed for her acceptance as he added, 'We could take in a dinner first...or supper afterwards...'

Relief whooshed through her at what was definitely an invitation. 'I'd like that very much.' Was that too emphatic? She felt so giddy, controlling her response to him was beyond her.

'Good!' He grinned. 'Let's do the lot then. I'll pick you up at six, if that suits.'

'Six is fine. I'll be ready.'

She'd never been to an opera, didn't know if she'd like it or not, but she was ready to embrace any experience with Mitch Tyler. All her instincts said he was special. Very special.

During the rest of the taxi ride he told her that the La Bohème they were going to see was the new Baz Luhrmann production which updated the story to the 1950s—very revolutionary, and causing a sensation, making opera far more accessible to the general public—an experience not to be missed, he assured her. Kathryn happily agreed, though she was far more aware of him holding onto her hand than what he was telling her.

He asked the driver to wait for him when the taxi pulled up outside the block of apartments where she lived. Which meant he was not going to linger over seeing her to her door. She didn't know if she was disappointed or relieved that he didn't expect to be invited into her home tonight.

Did he only want companionship from her?

He caught her hand again as he escorted her inside, causing her pulse-rate to zoom and her throat to tighten up, especially since he fell silent and she didn't know what he was thinking.

It was an old block of apartments, only three storeys high and no elevator. Kathryn couldn't afford anything fancy by herself. The rentals in Sydney were sky-high. The foyer was rather shabby and there was certainly no class about the concrete staircase that led up to her first floor apartment.

Was Mitch noting the obvious status comedown from her living with Jeremy? Or was he as preoccupied as she was with what could come next?

When she stopped at her door he released her hand so she could get her key out of her bag. 'Six o'clock Saturday,' he said as a reminder once the door was unlocked and opened.

'Yes.' She quickly smiled her pleasure in the arrangement.

'Good night, Kathryn.' He leaned down and planted a friendly kiss on her cheek.

The warm, tingly contact brought a tide of heat up her throat. 'Good night, Mitch,' she replied somewhat breathlessly before he could see her becoming flushed. 'Thanks again.'

He nodded and she bolted into her apartment, closing the door and leaning back against it until her heart stopped pounding from the mad rush of excitement. Just a kiss on the cheek! How would she feel if he kissed her with passion?

Mitch returned to the taxi, elated that all his initiatives had paid off and relieved that he'd managed to maintain control over urges that might have screwed up the chance to start building a relationship with Kathryn. He was sure that patience would serve him better in the long run, given that she was still very sensitive about the break-up with Haynes.

Besides, he liked the idea of courting Kathryn in an old-fashioned manner. It had been all sex with Harriet, right from the beginning. Red-hot desire could blind a man to what he should be looking at. He wasn't going to make that mistake this time around, though how he was going to keep holding temptation at bay, he didn't know.

He got back in the taxi, gave his address to the driver and settled back for the ride. As the car pulled out from the kerb, Mitch's gaze was drawn to a man who was getting out of a BMW Roadster directly across the road, a streetlight shining down on his face.

Recognition hit him like a blow.

Jeremy Haynes!

He'd only seen him once before but he hadn't forgotten anything about the man—Kathryn rushing into his embrace, being swung around. Mitch had hated every second of it while the saner section of his mind had acknowledged the physical and material assets that had drawn Kathryn to the guy she'd been intent on marrying.

Past tense!

So what was Haynes doing here?

As the taxi accelerated, Mitch turned to watch Kathryn's ex-fiancé, tension ripping through him as Haynes headed straight for the block of apartments where she lived. Had he been sitting in his car, waiting, watching for her to come home? For what purpose?

It spelled trouble to Mitch.

It might be over for Kathryn but clearly it wasn't over for the guy she'd rejected. And Mitch didn't want what he'd established with Kathryn being messed around.

'Stop!' he hurled at the driver, aggression pumping through him at the thought of Kathryn being stalked. Of course Haynes wouldn't want to let her go. What man would?

'Forgotten something?' the driver quizzed, bringing the taxi to a halt.

Haynes was entering the building, moving fast. 'I've got to go back,' Mitch muttered, his sense of urgency screaming for action. He whipped out his wallet. 'What's the fare?'

'Want me to wait?'

'No.'

'Fare's just on fifteen dollars.'

Mitch handed him a twenty and bolted out of the cab, racing back down the street, determined on running whatever interference was necessary to keep Kathryn on track with him and out of Haynes's clutches.

All his senses were on red alert as he strode into the foyer of the apartment block. He heard nothing coming from the first floor. No altercation. Nothing. The silence alarmed him even further. He raced up the stairs. Jeremy Haynes was not outside Kathryn's door.

Mitch paused at the top of the staircase, churning over what this had to mean.

She had let him into her apartment.

But why would she if she no longer wanted him in her life?

Harriet wouldn't have got past his door if she hadn't kept his key, letting herself in. There'd be no reason for Kathryn to give Haynes a key. She had to have let him in.

He forced his mind to sift through this highly disturbing situation. Haynes couldn't have been bothering Kathryn on any consistent basis. She had too much sense to invite trouble with him. This had to be a surprise visit, taking her off guard.

So why had he come now...after three months?

Time to let her stew over regrets, change her mind about sharing a future with him? Life in a penthouse apartment might be more attractive now that she'd had a lengthy taste of a less wealthy lifestyle.

Mitch dismissed that argument. Money wouldn't sway her.

So what argument could Haynes use to win her consideration?

And why choose tonight of all nights to try for a reconciliation?

Sheer coincidence?

No!

The realisation burst upon Mitch that the same news he had used to get to Kathryn could also be used by Haynes. Gary Chappel's death. Which had undoubtedly been reported on both radio and television by now.

Lara Chappel's safety was no longer an issue.

Haynes could argue there was no conflict of interests any more. He could apologise, say he'd been wrong, express intense regret at having sided with Chappel's pursuit of his wife, explain he'd been anxious about his career, wanting the best possible future for both of them.

Could he sell that argument to Kathryn?

Would she accept it?

Would she *want* to accept it?

Mitch wanted to believe she'd reject it, yet the long investment of emotional involvement with Haynes, to the point of a commitment to marry...impossible to be certain which way she'd jump.

It sickened him to think she was listening to the self-serving bastard, letting herself be persuaded, maybe even rushing back into his embrace as she had the last time Mitch had seen them together.

His hands clenched. He had to fight this. He couldn't bear to lose his chance with Kathryn now. She'd given him positive encouragement. He was not about to give Jeremy Haynes any free ground with her.

He moved determinedly to her door and pressed the buzzer button beside it.

No response.

He jammed the button in with his thumb, frustration mounting, anger stirring. He knew she hadn't gone out again. What excuse could she have not to answer?

Again there was no response.

But he could hear movement inside the apartment. A thump. Then Kathryn's voice raised in panic. 'Stop! I don't want this. Let me up. Let me up.'

A muffled curse from Haynes.

Kathryn shrieking, 'No...! No!'

Mitch beat on the door with his fist, yelling, 'Open up! Open up or I'll call the police!'

More cursing. The door was wrenched open, Haynes glaring at Mitch, breathing whisky fumes as he jeered, 'It's just a domestic, for God's sake! Butt out!'

'No...it's not!' Kathryn cried from somewhere out of sight. She was gasping for breath, frightened, desperate.

Mitch put his shoulder to the closing door and barged in.

Knocked aside, Haynes grabbed at him in belligerent defence. 'Who the hell do you think you are!'

The words floated past the drumming in Mitch's ears. Kathryn was struggling to raise herself from the floor between a sofa and a coffee table that had been knocked over on its side. Her skirt was hitched up, her blouse askew, buttons ripped open.

'Mitch...' She lifted a pleading hand to him, her eyes huge with shock and fear.

'Get out!' Haynes shouted, trying to shove him.

The memory of Jenny's rape seized Mitch's mind. His sister...now another woman he cared deeply about being assaulted. Fury boiled up in him. Reaction came so fast he was barely conscious of violence erupting, his hand pushing Haynes to arm's length, his fist slamming into the lying face of the man who'd abused Kathryn's trust, Kathryn's body.

He felt the crunch of his knuckles hitting bone and it felt good. It felt right. Blood spurted from the slime's nose as he went down. Mitch grabbed him up by the collar and dragged him out of the apartment, down the stairs.

'Stop! Help! For God's sake!' the guy was whimpering.

'Shut up and thank your lucky stars I don't beat you to a pulp,' Mitch growled, barely repressing the urge to hurl him down the stairs, throw him into the street, rub his bloodied nose into the gutter so he'd remember the smell of filth, which was what he was.

Only the memory of months with Patrick Maguire stopped him. The old man's advice rolled through the red haze in his mind...control... discipline...put your energy into making the justice system work. All Mitch had achieved since he'd left Gundamurra would be wiped out if he was charged with another assault and convicted.

Yet the law wouldn't have saved Kathryn tonight. The law wouldn't have got the chance because Haynes was stronger than she was. The law didn't rescue. It worked backwards, after a crime was committed. And then there were victims like Jenny, always carrying the memory.

Mitch grimly set Haynes on his feet in the foyer, then forcibly marched him out across the street to his big money car—the kind of big money that made some men think they could get away with anything. The guy was stumbling, moaning. Mitch didn't give a damn about his pain. The physical pain of a broken nose didn't last as long as emotional trauma, and God only knew what Kathryn was feeling.

They reached the driver's door of the BMW Roadster. 'Get out your keys and go,' Mitch commanded. 'If you ever think of bothering Kathryn again, remember me, and don't doubt for one second that I'll come after you and exact retribution. Understand?'

'Yes...yes...' Haynes sobbed, frantic to get away, the stuffing completely knocked out of him.

Mitch waited until he'd taken off, watching the car move out of sight as he headed back across the street. His body was a mass of jumping nerve-ends, his mind powering in all directions. He tried to calm himself down as he re-entered the building. He had to focus on Kathryn now, move carefully with her.

She hadn't even closed the door to her apartment. A bad sign. He walked in and found her huddled in a corner of the sofa, hugging her arms, looking shell-shocked. Her lovely green eyes were huge. No doubt his violence had added to her distress, but she *had* pleaded for his help, though not anticipating the form it had taken. He hadn't anticipated it, either. That punch had exploded from him.

'I packed him into his car and saw him off,' he stated, letting her know that any further threat from her ex-fiancé had been removed.

She shuddered.

Mitch spotted her suit-jacket and handbag lying on the armchair closest to the kitchenette, obviously dropped there before Haynes had arrived. *Why had she let him in?* Not the time for questions now.

He set the coffee table back on its legs, picked up the jacket and laid it on the table within easy reach if she wanted it for warmth. In her current fragile state, she might shrink from any physical contact from him, especially after seeing what *he* was capable of when stirred into action.

She didn't move.

'I...I thought it was you...at the door. That you'd forgotten...to tell me something,' she said shakily. 'He was in...before I could say no. Then...then...'

'It's all right, Kathryn,' he softly assured her. 'I'm here now. You're safe.'

She shuddered again. The chill of shock. Or fear. Maybe fear of him, too? But he couldn't just walk out and leave her like this. Yet how was he to give comfort without touching?

The jacket was probably inadequate for making her feel secure, protected. A blanket would be better.

It was a small, very basic apartment, the layout quickly scouted—one bedroom, bathroom, living room, kitchenette. He bundled a quilt off her bed and carried it out to the living room. Not daring to risk tucking it around her, he laid it across her lap so she could pick it up and snuggle under it.

'How...how did you know, Mitch?' Even her voice was trembling.

'I was leaving in the taxi when I saw him in the street, heading this way,' he answered matter-of-factly, exerting every bit of control he could muster to resist the rampant urge to grab her up and wrap her in his arms.

'And you...came back?' She finally lifted her gaze to his, her eyes still huge, intensely vulnerable, needing to understand, struggling to find her way out of the wilderness of what had happened.

Before he was aware of it, his hand was out, tenderly stroking her cheek, wanting to impart comfort and reassurance. 'You said it was over, Kathryn. I was worried Haynes might make a nuisance of himself.'

She dragged in a deep breath. 'Thank you. Thank you for coming back, Mitch.'

Relief...gratitude...nothing too negative there.

'I'll get you a hot drink,' he said, forcing himself away from her before he did something stupid.

He wanted her so badly—wanted to crush her to him, warm her body with his, kiss any memory of Haynes right out of her mind—but now was certainly not the time to make his desire for her known. Trust was the big issue here and now, and fraying any measure of trust would be a terribly wrong move. What he wanted might be very unwelcome.

It had to wait.

# CHAPTER NINE

KATHRYN COULDN'T CONTROL the convulsive shivers that kept running through her. Her mind was still trying to grapple with the shock of Jeremy's virulence when she'd denied him any chance of a reconciliation.

Why he'd thought Gary Chappel's death would make any difference... it was all so unbelievable! No appreciation—no understanding—of what he'd revealed about himself or how she felt about it. His ego blinded him to any fault in his own attitude.

*She* was the unreasonable one.

Then his linking of her rejection of him to seeing her come home with another man, and the monstrous possessiveness that had ignored her right to say no...

If Mitch hadn't come back...

Thank God he had! Thank God!

All those assertions that she could take care of herself...impossible against a man intent on having his own way, taking it against all reason, forcing it. And the shock of it happening—the sheer disbelief—so paralysing.

Mitch had rescued her from...her mind shied away from the memory of Jeremy's forcing hands, his horribly marauding mouth.

She almost gagged.

*It's over, over, over,* she fiercely recited to herself.

And Mitch was in her kitchenette, filling the electric kettle with water, preparing to make her a hot drink, looking after her. He'd been so gentle with her, bringing her the quilt from her bed, caring...yet he was so immensely strong...strong enough to knock Jeremy right off his feet, drag him out of the apartment, force him into his car and make him drive away.

Which definitely meant it was over. Jeremy wouldn't return to this apartment. He'd been beaten here, hauled away legless. He would hate any reminder of that humiliation. She was safe. Mitch had made her safe.

Strange that she didn't feel revolted by *his* act of violence...blood spurting from Jeremy's nose. Normally she would hate witnessing such a thing. It had shocked her, yet it had also been an enormous relief to have the whole ghastly situation ended in virtually a moment. Maybe there was a time and place for such primitive action. A slap to stop hysteria. A punch to stop aggression. Especially when the aggressor was taking rights that weren't his to take.

Anyway, she certainly didn't think any less of Mitch Tyler for doing it. In fact, she was intensely grateful to him for stepping in and taking Jeremy out. As for the rough handling of her ex-fiancé...good that Jeremy had a taste of that himself, having dealt it out to her.

Justice...

Though it was bitter.

How could she have been so blind about Jeremy? To even *believe* she loved a man who had no respect for the person she was! What did it say about her to Mitch Tyler? He must think her a fool, completely lacking in any judgement of character.

She was consumed with shame, unable to look him in the eye when he brought her a cup of tea, setting it on the coffee table along with milk and sugar. It was an effort to even utter the words, 'Thank you.' She stayed huddled under the quilt, feeling too raw and exposed to move.

He settled on the armchair adjacent to the sofa. She felt his gaze on her, yet couldn't bring herself to look at his face, the expression in his eyes. The silence tore at her nerves. She was with a man whose good opinion she desperately wanted and her mind was a total mess, unable to function in any kind of positive frame. At least the warmth of the quilt had stopped the shivers but there was a cold empty place in her heart that yearned to be warmed by other means.

'Have I frightened you, Kathryn?'

The quiet question startled her into answering, 'No!'

A quick glance at him picked up his tension, the worried look that stabbed concern at her. It stirred confusion. Why would he think she was frightened of him?

'I'm not normally a violent man,' he explained, one of his hands lifting, opening in a gesture of appeal.

The hand that had punched Jeremy.

Of course.

What had gone down here tonight had to worry him.

He was a barrister, sworn to uphold the law, and hitting Jeremy could possibly get him disbarred. He'd put his professional career at risk for her sake, and here she was, totally focused on herself and how he must view her. At least she could help him on that point.

'I'll swear Jeremy was assaulting me if he goes to the police, Mitch,' she said with determined vigour, pushing her own misery aside. 'But I don't think he will. It would show him up as a loser and obviously——' she grimaced '——he'd do anything not to lose.'

'I wasn't thinking of him. Though I appreciate your offer to stand by my action. I meant...' He paused, his eyes searching hers with riveting intensity. 'My sister was raped a long time ago. It affected her...very deeply.'

'It didn't get that far,' Kathryn quickly assured him.

He nodded. 'Seeing you on the floor...I was remembering Jenny when I hit him. I know I lost control. It must have looked...savage to you. I felt...savage. But I want you to know...I don't go around bashing people on the spur of the moment.'

'I didn't imagine you did.'

'Violence is usually anathema to me,' he pressed on, clearly anxious to emphasise that point. 'I hate it in other people. I fight against it in court. Any form of abuse...'

'I'm sure you do.'

His eyes locked onto hers, driving home his point. 'I don't want you to be frightened of me.'

'I'm not,' she insisted. It was the absolute truth.

His relief was patent. 'I sensed you were withdrawing from me. I thought...'

'Not from fear.' She took a deep breath and unloaded the burden on her heart. 'I'm just so ashamed...'

'There's no reason for you to be,' he shot back at her. 'It wasn't your fault.'

'But I chose him. I was going to marry him,' she burst out, shaking her head in anguish at the terrible mistake she'd made.

'Most of the time, people only let you see what they want you to see,' he argued. 'You were taken in by him, Kathryn, just as I was taken in by Harriet. Both of them very clever people.' His mouth relaxed, tilting into a wry smile. 'And both of them very attractive on the surface. A lot going for them.'

He was excusing her error, trying to lighten her sense of guilt, being kind. Her mind writhed over his kindness, knowing she should appreciate it but hating it. Hating it because brutal honesty would have been infinitely preferable. It would have told her he was feeling more for her than *kindness*.

'I glossed over things,' she muttered. It was what Mitch was doing now. For her sake. Wanting her to feel better.

'Don't we all gloss over things to keep relationships going?' He shook his head. 'Don't be so hard on yourself. Be glad that you're out of it. I think you're well rid of him.'

'No doubt about that,' she said with a mountain of feeling.

'Good! Then don't give him any more space in your thoughts.'

A derisive little laugh gurgled from her throat. 'That's not so easy.'

He hitched himself forward on the armchair, a pained look on his face, his eyes blazing with some strong emotion—anger, annoyance, frustration?

'Kathryn...don't fret over this. He's not *worth* any more of your time.' His voice was forceful, vibrant with the power of all the dynamic energy that emanated from him. 'And *your* value is not diminished because his golden image is in tatters,' he went on. 'You're a very desirable woman.'

'Am I?' Her own frustration welled up. She hurled the quilt aside, not wanting to feel she was Jeremy's *victim*. Not wanting to be treated like it, either, her hurt soothed by the one man she did want. Her feet swung to the floor and she stood up, bristling with the need to sweep aside all this *soothing* and face up to the real truth. She flung out her hands in sheer exasperation, appealing for straight honesty. 'Am I desirable to you?'

The words spilled from her agonised uncertainty. They weren't meant to be a challenge. But they put him so blatantly on the spot, acute embarrassment flooded through her with painful heat. She saw the shock on his face. Then he surged off the armchair so fast her vision blurred, and the next thing she knew, his arms were around her, drawing her hard against him—a distance-shattering impact that left her no room to back-pedal.

'You want to know how *intensely* desirable I find you?' he challenged, his chest heaving against her breasts, his eyes searing hers with a desire so raw it took her breath away. 'I'm barely holding onto restraint, Kathryn. Barely holding on. I realise you're not ready for...'

'Not...ready?' she repeated incredulously. Everything within her was responding chaotically to this physical contact with him. It felt as though she'd been waiting her whole life to be held by Mitch Tyler, and to suddenly learn he'd been wanting her all along completely blew Kathryn's mind. Her inner angst tumbled out. 'I thought because of your connection to Ric and the business with Lara...both of us being at a loose end...I thought you were being kind to me.'

'*Kind?*' The word exploded from him as though he violently hated it. He sucked in a quick breath. His black brows beetled down. 'Is that what you want from me? No more than kindness? A friend in need?'

'No...no...' A wild recklessness whirled through the dizzy realisation that there was far more than friendly caring coming from him. Her hands moved from his broad shoulders, linking behind his neck. 'I want to experience all of you, Mitch Tyler.'

There! It was said.

And she didn't care that it had been said.

It was true.


Mitch's heart was pounding in his ears. Had he imagined what he needed to hear? Her mouth was still slightly parted, tempting him, inviting him. She'd put her arms around his neck. She had to be willing...ready... wanting...

He couldn't hold back. Couldn't. Desire was roaring through him. His mouth crashed down on hers and any seductive persuasion was completely beyond him. He kissed her with all the pent-up passion she'd stirred from the first moment they'd met, and amazingly, she gave it back, as though she, too, was consumed with an urgent, overwhelming need for him.

Her body was soft, pliant under his touch and his hands could not resist finding and learning every lovely curve of it, moving her closer, wanting the warm imprint of her stamped on him...*his woman*. Arousal came fast and hard but there was no withdrawal from her, no attempt to pull away. She was actually pressing herself against him, exciting him further, *wanting* him excited. Whether consciously or instinctively he didn't know.

Didn't want to know.

Didn't want to think.

Just wanted to absorb the feeling of her giving herself to him.

Kathryn could scarcely believe the tumult of feeling that was powering through her. Her mouth was tingling with excitement, revelling in the intense passion of his kisses, craving every erotic sensation he stirred. It was wild, wild and incredibly wonderful, intoxicatingly addictive.

And she loved the tensile strength of his body, the hard muscularity of his broad shoulders, his chest, his thighs, all of them encasing a dynamic energy that seemed to be pouring into her, electrifying her own vitality, pumping her heart faster, making it gallop with sheer elation. No doubting his desire for her any more. She felt his erection pressing against her stomach and exulted in the undeniable evidence of what he was feeling.

Wanting her.

Needing her.

Drawing on her desire for him with dizzying intensity.

She'd never felt anything like this in her life.

His mouth moved from hers, his lips trailing across her cheek. Panic clutched her mind as she thought he was going to speak, to stop. But he didn't. He blew into her ear, sending exquisite tingles right down to the apex of her thighs. His tongue tantalised the sensitive whirls and he blew again, exciting a rush of melting that made her body clench.

He felt the urgent tightening, drew back. 'Have I gone too far?' His voice was furred, more self-questioning than asking her but she answered him with a fierce rejection of any withdrawal. 'No!' But if they were going to make love, and that was what she desperately wanted... 'Let's move to the bedroom, Mitch. Please?'

He sucked in a quick breath, tilted his head back, eyes blazing into hers, a turmoil of questions. Her stomach churned. It would be unbearable if he pulled away now. Had she reminded him of Jeremy mauling her in this room? She wanted to scream that it didn't count. Only what he made her feel mattered and anything less than the full experience of it would leave her in a dreadful limbo, wretchedly empty, deprived.

Driven to stop him from questioning further, she lifted herself on tiptoe, moved her hands to press his head down to hers and kissed him with all the fervour of her desire to hold him with her. His response was instant and gloriously satisfying, swamping her with the heat needed to expel the cold fear of being rejected. Her mind danced with feverish joy.

*It was going to happen.*

*He wanted her every bit as much as she wanted him.*

'Come with me, Mitch. Come with me,' she murmured against his lips, her heart beating like a drum roll of wild anticipation.

She grabbed his hand.

He came with her.

Into the bedroom.

She tore off the blouse Jeremy had ripped open, tossing it onto the floor with a shudder of distaste. She reached around to unclip her bra but other hands closed around her arms and drew them down, preventing her intention from being carried through. Her heart kicked in chaotic alarm. Had Mitch changed his mind?

Then he was kissing her shoulder, the warmth of his mouth chasing away the rash of goose bumps. 'This isn't a race, Kathryn,' he murmured. 'I won't just tumble you onto that bed and get it over with.'

She tensed. Was he having second thoughts?

Yet he was trailing kisses up the curve of her neck, mesmerising her into stillness with that same gentle blow of breath into her ear. 'I want you to know what you're doing.' Even the soft expulsion of his words was thrilling. 'Know it very consciously,' he went on. 'Not an impulse of the moment. And no regrets in the morning.'

'I won't regret it,' she promised huskily, barely able to catch her breath.

'Then you won't mind if I put the light on.'

The light!

Kathryn was instantly attacked by nerve-wracking doubts. What if Mitch didn't find her so *desirable* when he saw her undressed? In the naked light! She wasn't strikingly beautiful like Harriet. Her figure was more petite, her skin paler, freckled where she'd caught the sun. In the dark there'd just be feeling, everything centred on physical contact...man and woman wanting each other.

But if she protested, he'd think...he'd think she wasn't truly ready for him and she was. Her entire being was yearning for him. There was no choice...no choice at all as he lifted his mouth away from her ear, slid his hands caressingly from their hold on her arms, stepped back...

...and switched on the bedroom light!

# CHAPTER TEN

KATHRYN FELT LIKE a rabbit, caught in the middle of a road, spotlighted by the bright beams of an oncoming car. She couldn't move. Her legs had turned to water, the muscles in them quivering like melting jelly. Only her spine stiffened, an instinctive reaction to feeling under threat. And her senses sharpened.

The room smelled stuffy from having the windows shut. At least it was tidy, the bed neatly made, though the quilt was gone and the pillows were slightly awry from its removal. Heat was rushing through her, scorching her cheeks, making her squirm inside. She heard the soft swish of clothes being removed. It jerked her head around.

Mitch was standing by the doorway, only a metre from where she remained rooted to the spot. His suit coat was gone. He was sliding his tie out from under his collar. But his eyes were on her, watching, burning with a sizzling challenge as he tossed the tie onto the coat which had already been dropped on the floor. His hands started flicking open the buttons on his shirt.

'Tell me to stop if you want me to, Kathryn.'

Stop? The word echoed around her mind, losing any meaning it might have had as her fascinated gaze clung to what was being revealed of his body. There *was* hair on his chest but not a lot—shaped like a T, running down to the waistband of his trousers, dipping below it to...she wanted to know, wanted to see, her own poignant sense of vulnerability over-ridden by a compulsion to have this intimate view of him.

He was so very powerfully built, the strongly muscular shoulders and arms emanating a *manliness* that grabbed at her heart—a man who could and would fight for her safety, the ultimate protector. Who was even now intent on protecting her from making an impulsive decision which might feel wrong in the morning.

Kathryn knew it wouldn't.

A man like Mitch Tyler was rare in this world. Not to experience all of him was unthinkable.

Shoes and socks gone.

She turned to face him, deliberately removing her bra to show him she had no intention of stopping anything. Her nipples instantly tightened into jutting hardness. He stood still, staring at her bared breasts. They were reasonably well shaped, if a little on the small side, Kathryn fiercely told herself, refusing to be daunted now, fighting the panicky feeling that she might not measure up to other women he'd had.

His broad chest expanded with a sharply indrawn breath. His gaze lifted to hers, glittering with determined purpose. 'Do I need to use a condom, Kathryn?'

Relief rushed through her. He still found her desirable. He wasn't going to stop. And she trusted him to be safe. He was a protector.

'No. I'm on the pill,' she answered quickly, recoiling from the idea of having any barrier between his flesh and hers. The contraceptive pills she'd been taking had kept her safe from pregnancy this past year. No need for anything else.

She kicked off her shoes, recklessly eager now for what was coming with Mitch Tyler.

He started unfastening his trousers.

Her hands whipped to the zipper at the back of her skirt, determined on matching his undressing, not letting any inhibitions telegraph uncertainty to him. *Intensely desirable,* he'd said. And *he* wasn't hesitating in stripping himself completely free of clothes. As long as she kept watching him, not thinking of herself, she'd be fine.

It was good that the light was on. Without it she wouldn't have been able to see the full length of him...magnificently naked. He was so beautifully male, his strong physique perfectly proportioned, every millimetre of him exuding dynamic virility.

And suddenly it was totally and gloriously irrelevant if her own body lacked some wonderfully stunning feminine allure. The sight of her—or the thought of her—had certainly triggered full sexual arousal in Mitch Tyler, his erection unashamedly blatant, wildly increasing her own excitement.

Yet still there were a few nerve-twanging moments as he simply looked at her, his gaze roving down over her tautly peaked breasts to the small triangle of auburn hair that hid her sex, lingering there, causing her inner muscles to contract at an uncontrollable rush of moist heat.

'You *are* magic,' he murmured, and moved slowly toward her, shaking his head as though trying to free his mind from some spellbound state.

Kathryn shook her head, too, more in incredulous confusion. How could he associate magic with her? What did he mean by it? But there was no time to think. His arms were sliding around her waist and his body was closing in on hers—bare flesh contact—an explosion of sensation bursting through her. He held her tightly to him. She felt enveloped by his strength. Yet he was tender, too, rubbing his cheek gently over her hair.

'I want you to feel good about this, Kathryn.'

His caring for her, over and above his own physical urgency, reinforced all she knew of him, adding a special glow to what she was feeling. It wasn't just sexual attraction, not on her part, not on his, either. The connection went deeper, touching, filling the lonely emptiness in her heart.

'Let me make love to you,' he softly urged. 'Let me experience all that you are.'

The repetition of her own words swept away any sense of inhibition. There could be no holding back if they were ever to reach that mutual satisfaction. This was a time for giving whatever was asked. She tilted her head back to look into his eyes—eyes that bored straight through to her soul with their burning need—and instantly gave him her trust.

'Yes,' she whispered. Such a little word, yet it carried a mountain of consent, a mountain to be scaled however he chose, taking her with him.

His face broke into a smile, pleasure bursting from him, pleasure he transmitted to her mouth in a kiss that was more intent on tasting and exploring an escalating sense of intimacy than stirring an immediate and overwhelming passion. His restraint—control—was both tantalising and incredibly seductive.

He scooped her off her feet and carried her to the bed, his eyes gleaming wickedly as he said, 'You bring out the caveman in me, Kathryn Ledger.'

She laughed, bubbles of wild happiness dancing in her brain. If they were living in primitive times, she thought, sharing Mitch Tyler's cave would definitely be the best place to be in every sense...especially having him come home to her, sweeping her up in his arms, laying her down as he was doing now, hovering over her in all his magnificent maleness, poised to take possession, her own body brilliantly alive with anticipation, humming with joy because *she* was his pleasure.

If he'd taken her right there and then, she would have welcomed him with intense satisfaction, but she quickly realised he meant to keep her waiting, though not because he didn't want her. Desire poured through his fingertips as he caressed her arms, her legs, even her feet, touching with such exquisite sensitivity, following the touch with kisses, making love with a slow, gradual intensity that blew away all her previous experience.

Impossible to even feel shy about what he was doing, not when he looked so entranced with how she felt to him, so completely absorbed in every womanly aspect of her. It gave her the glorious sense of being incredibly special, precious, faultless, even beautiful. The way he kissed her breasts—drawing them into his mouth, tasting, licking, the slow rhythmic suction building an almost feverish pitch of excitement—completely erased any thought of them being anything but loved by him. Adored by him.

And when he moved down to do the same to her clitoris, Kathryn was totally swamped with waves of ecstatic pleasure, driven to fantastic peaks of excitement with the accompanying caress of fingers that knew exactly where to touch and when and how. She had never been made love to like this, not with such awesome, *knowing* sensuality. And she couldn't wait any longer to feel him inside her...this amazing, wonderful man who could stir her entire being into craving him so intensely.

'Please... I need you now,' she cried, grabbing at his arms, frantically urging him to fulfil this last ultimate need.

He responded instantly, and her own body arched in sheer euphoria as the surging power of his own desire—held back for so long—met hers and plunged forward, filling the aching void, reaching her inner-most self, fusing with it. And having achieved that marvellous union, he paused there, letting her savour the bliss of it as he bent down and kissed her, taking her mouth on the same sensational journey of merging with him, increasing the sense of deep intimacy, stirring a passionate yearning for it to go on and on.

She wanted to make love to him, to let him know how she felt about him. She glided her hands up and down his back, over his buttocks, her fingers tracing the tense muscles, finding the erotic zones below his hips. It propelled him into moving, his body rocking over hers as he drove each rhythmic thrust to a thrilling depth, and she wound her legs around his thighs and swung her own body to meet his, squeezing her muscles around him, heightening the delicious friction, and her fingers raked through the hair on his chest, up and down, up and down, inciting the fast action that would bring him to climax.

She could feel his heart pounding, matching the wild beat of her own, and inside her the ripples of pleasure growing more and more intense, white-hot excitement melting around him as he took them both to the pinnacle of absolute bliss—the sweet surrender of all control to a fulfilment that was uniquely theirs, the two of them one in brilliant harmony.

Then just holding each other, savouring the contentment of being so close, intertwined, sharing themselves in a warm silence that needed no other communication, the sense of completion leaving no space for wondering about anything. She lay with her head resting just under his chin. His hand idly stroked her hair.

Eventually her mind admitted the odd train of thought and she smiled over one of them. 'You won't ever have to club me over the head, Mitch.'

'Why would I want to club you over the head?' he asked, sounding helplessly bemused.

'Caveman...taking his woman.'

He laughed and rolled her onto her back, propping himself up one elbow to smile down at her. 'Are you telling me you'd always be willing?'

'Hmm...*always* is a big word,' she teased, although her mind was singing *yes*. She reached out and stroked his cheek, feeling the slight bristle that shadowed his jawline, finding it very masculine and sexy. 'I would expect you to listen to me.'

'I have very good hearing,' he assured her.

'Very good everything.'

'Is that so?'

'I feel extremely fortunate to be with you.'

'Indeed.' He grinned. 'I'm feeling rather lucky myself at the moment. Kind of like Peter Pan. Completely rejuvenated. Must be all your fairy sparkles still swirling around me.'

'Fairy sparkles?'

'I look at you and think...Tinkerbell.'

'You don't!' She laughed at the fanciful thought.

'I do.' He silenced her laughter by grazing his fingers lightly over her lips. His eyes simmered with teasing pleasure as he added, 'A very alluring Tinkerbell. It's the red hair and green eyes, this beguiling mouth that promises a whole world of secret treasure, and the petite perfection of your femininity, right down to your dainty feet. Plus the most provocatively sexy ears I've ever seen.'

He bent down and blew his sexy magic into the ear closest to him, and Kathryn held her breath as the incredibly erotic sensation stirred all her nerve-ends into skittish excitement. It whizzed through her mind that she'd never curse her pixie ears again. If they turned Mitch Tyler on, she was positively blessed with them, especially when what he was moved to do was a madly electric turn-on for her.

It was on the tip of her tongue to say Harriet Lowell had to be brain-dead to allow any other man to supplant him in her bed.

A swift instinctive caution zapped the dangerous comment. Reminding him of his ex-lover would be just as horribly intrusive as reminding him of her ex-fiancé.

This was between them.

Which made it different.

And to her, it was a million times better than anything she'd had with Jeremy. She hoped Mitch felt the same way. *If* he was comparing it to what he'd had with Harriet. A jealous sense of possessiveness drove her onto her side, pressing closer to him as she slid her arm around his back and played her fingers over the tautly delineated muscles that were so much a part of his intrinsic masculinity.

This man was hers tonight, she thought.

How they would fare together in the future she had no idea, aware there was still a lot to learn about each other, but she would never ever regret the experience of this night with him. He had made her feel good about herself. More than good. And she didn't believe it was just *kindness*, though it had followed fast on the heels of Jeremy's gross behaviour with her.

She lifted her face to his and he kissed her.

The quick rise of passion was promise enough that this was no one-night stand.

Not for him.

And certainly not for her.

# CHAPTER ELEVEN

*A month later...*

AS USUAL, HIS clerk handed Mitch a sheaf of messages once court had been adjourned for the day. The top one simply read 'Call Johnny' and gave the telephone number—a *local* number. The afternoon's legal arguments were instantly banished from Mitch's mind. Johnny Ellis was back in town.

He started smiling and the smile grew into a happy grin by the time he was out of the courthouse and calling the number on his mobile telephone. Johnny had been in the U.S. for the past five months, recording an album and doing a tour, and no doubt he was on his way home to Gundamurra, just stopping off to catch up with Mitch and Ric as he always did when he could.

Johnny...the entertainer. And no doubt his nickname in the music industry—Johnny Charm—was well earned. Back when they were boys at Gundamurra, it was he who had invariably lightened any dark moments with his unquenchable good humour. Not to mention the songs he could make up about anything. Even then he'd been brilliant on the guitar Patrick had given him.

A hotel receptionist answered his call and connected him to the man himself. 'Hey, Mitch!' The big voice boomed over the line. 'Do you happen to be free tonight?'

'Where and when?'

'Thought we'd join up at the Italian restaurant under Ric's apartment at Woolloomooloo. *Otto's.* Seven o'clock suit you?'

'Fine! Have you been in touch with Ric yet?'

'Tried at his company office. His chief assistant told me he'd gone out to a lunch appointment and hadn't come back. I'll give his home number a buzz at five o'clock, see if he's there.'

'Do that. See you soon, Johnny.'

Mitch's pleasurable anticipation in the get-together dimmed somewhat as Ric's current situation played through his mind. Gary Chappel was dead, Lara and Ric were both back in Sydney, but she was shying clear of him, using the excuse of the funeral and the publicity around her husband's death in her request for him to stay away from her—a request that had been delivered through Mitch.

And Ric was hurting from it. Badly. He was desperate for face-to-face contact with her. No doubt his heart was still very much engaged there. Almost obsessively so. Kathryn had commented that he wasn't on top of his work at all, his mind very much elsewhere. A whole month had gone by and still no direct word from Lara.

Mitch wondered if he should word Johnny up so he didn't touch on painful areas tonight. Ric had borrowed his plane for the getaway. But if that was brought up it could be quickly skated over and Ric wouldn't like it if Johnny treated him with any special sensitivity. He still had that chip on his shoulder from the old days—a dark wounded pride that drove him beyond where most men would go.

And Mitch was certain now that Lara was at the core of it.

Beautiful, damaged Lara, who was currently taking the steps to put the past behind her, and the hell of it was, Ric had probably become too much a part of that past.

Deep emotional baggage.

Mitch shook his head over it as his clerk waved him to the taxi waiting at the kerb, ready to take them both back to his chambers. As he settled into the car for the short trip, he was wondering how much emotional baggage Kathryn was still carrying from her relationship with Haynes.

Since that first night together, she hadn't once referred back to it, not in all the time they'd spent in each other's company. And he certainly hadn't wanted to remind her. The revelation that Haynes's ambition had no moral boundaries had clearly been a big shock, undermining her confidence in her ability to judge people. His subsequent bullish attempt to claim her back had rattled it even further, causing a complete loss of faith in herself.

At least Mitch had managed to restore a good chunk of that.

And won her trust.

But shame was an insidious thing.

Had she managed to bury it or did it still haunt her?

Was she throwing herself into this affair with him because she wanted him...or because she *needed* him to exorcise the ghosts Haynes had left her with?

Mitch grimaced over his abandoned plan for an old-fashioned courtship. A slow build-up to intimacy would have assured him that what they shared had nothing to do with a rebound effect. As it was...well, it had been totally impossible to reject Kathryn's need that night, especially when he'd been so pumped up from getting rid of Haynes and wanting her himself.

Having taken that step, it was equally impossible to retreat from it. Every time he was with her, whatever they'd decide to do—the opera, a concert, a film, lunch, dinner—it was only a preliminary to satisfying the desire that leapt between them the moment they met and kept simmering to the moment they ended up in bed. Not even making it to a bed sometimes.

Sex was insidious, too. It was such a dominant force—the constant seduction of intense pleasure. Did Kathryn look beyond it when she was with him? How much did she care for the person he was—apart from being the lover who made her feel good?

Time, he assured himself, would eventually answer that question.

It had only been a month.

A month of hell for Ric, which was patently obvious when he joined Mitch and Johnny at *Otto's* for their night out together. He wore the grim look of a man who'd been taken to the brink of total devastation and he was only just hanging onto his determination to survive. Dead man walking, Mitch thought.

Though he did warm up as the evening progressed. Johnny exuded a bonhomie that was irresistible, regaling them with tales from his country and western music world, and Mitch kept the wine flowing. There was a lull in the conversation when Johnny took off to the men's room and Ric's whole demeanour drooped, making it very clear that the effort to maintain a cheerful countenance was draining him.

'Still nothing from Lara?' Mitch asked sympathetically.

A derisive flash from bleak dark eyes. 'As a matter of fact, I met her for lunch today.'

'Not good news?'

His mouth twisted. 'Thank you and goodbye. And nothing I said made a jot of difference.'

'Maybe more time...'

He shook his head. 'Got to put it behind me, Mitch. I'll be off to New York at the end of the week.'

'She did have a hell of a life with Chappel. I can't go into detail...'

'No. It's finished. Let it go.'

The terse finality left Mitch with nothing to say. He knew Ric would hate sympathy yet he keenly felt the death of his friend's eighteen-year dream. He well remembered the nights at Gundamurra when Ric had talked of his Lara, like she was the embodiment of all a guy could ever want in a girl.

It was a sobering reminder to Mitch that a deeply felt attachment did not guarantee a life of togetherness. Timing and circumstances could be big factors in whether or not a happy outcome was reached.

'I hear you've linked up with Kathryn.'

The comment jerked Mitch out of his old memories. 'Yes,' he answered briefly, not wanting to explain how, when and why.

'She's a good person.'

'Yes, she is.'

Curiosity flickered through the dull flatness of Ric's eyes. 'Did she break her engagement because of meeting you, Mitch?'

'No.' He wished it had been so. 'It was a personal issue between her and her fiancé,' he added, not wanting Ric to think it was some fallout from his business with Lara. His friend already had enough grief to deal with. 'I didn't know she'd broken up with him until the day of Chappel's death.'

'Well, at least that's a clean start for you,' Ric muttered.

Mitch didn't disillusion him.

It wouldn't help Ric and it wouldn't help the situation he had with Kathryn.

Johnny returned to the table and the talk moved on to Gundamurra. 'Haven't been home since last Christmas. What about you guys?' Johnny asked.

'I made a flying visit, end of February,' Ric answered casually, no hint that it had been on an extraordinary mission. 'Borrowed your plane, Johnny.'

Johnny grinned. 'Bet you enjoyed flying it, Ric.'

He nodded. 'A real pleasure.'

'And you, Mitch?'

'Haven't had the time.'

Johnny wagged a finger at him. 'You make time this coming Christmas, hear? All three of us together. I know your sister had a new baby last year—fair enough—but this year...no excuses! I'm laying down the law.'

'Getting too big for his boots, isn't he, Ric?' Mitch teased, passing off the pressure of decision, not knowing where he'd be with Kathryn and suspecting it would be a long time before Ric would want to return to Gundamurra and memories of Lara.

'It's all his country and western music and being in the U.S. too long,' Ric quickly chimed in. 'Thinks he's a cowboy now, able to ride rough-shod over both of us.'

'Watch it, brothers,' Johnny mock-threatened. 'I'm bigger than both of you.'

The old camaraderie carried them through the rest of the evening. Ric caught the elevator up to his apartment, leaving Johnny and Mitch to catch taxis to their separate destinations. Though they ended up walking to Johnny's hotel, while Mitch explained why, as Johnny put it, 'Ric looks like he's been through a wringer and hung out to dry.'

Best that he knew before arriving at Gundamurra tomorrow, Mitch thought. Patrick would want to know how the situation had panned out, too, given his close involvement with it.

'So he took her home and it didn't work,' Johnny commented sadly.

*Home*...it was how Johnny always referred to Gundamurra. To him, Patrick was the father he'd never had before, caring about him enough to listen to his dreams and help them come true, telling him he was always welcome at the outback sheep station where their future lives had been shaped. Mitch still had family, but Johnny and Ric had no-one. It meant a lot to them that Patrick had offered his home as their home… their safe place in an ever-changing world. They counted on him being there for them, knowing who they were, liking and respecting the men they had become.

Mitch left Johnny at his hotel, wishing him a safe flight to Gundamurra tomorrow, and took a taxi to Woollahra. As he walked into the home he had made for himself, he was thinking he was different to Ric and Johnny. He'd had a mother who'd loved him, a sister who remained very much a good part of his life. Yet Patrick had still been important to him, too—Patrick and what he'd taught them and brought out in them at Gundamurra.

Mitch knew those six months when he was sixteen were an integral part of who he was now. And Kathryn didn't know that part of him— didn't know what he'd shared with Ric and Johnny, didn't know he had, in fact, been convicted of assault. She only knew what he'd chosen to reveal to her, and even if that did win her heart, he knew that in the long run, everything would need to be told, for his own satisfaction that what she felt for him was real…and solid.

Johnny's comment kept running through his mind.

*So he took her home and it didn't work.*

When Christmas came this year, would Kathryn accompany him to Gundamurra?

And if she did…learning the darker part of his life…would their relationship still work?

# CHAPTER TWELVE

*Two months later...*

'I NOW PRONOUNCE you husband and wife.' The marriage celebrant paused to smile before adding, 'You may now kiss the bride.'

Ric swept Lara into his embrace and the love beaming from their faces brought tears to Kathryn's eyes. Somehow, it was all the more moving because she and Mitch were the only witnesses to this very private wedding.

Lara was over six months pregnant, with Ric's child, not Gary Chappel's as she had feared. The DNA test had relieved her of any further concern on that score. Thank God! Kathryn thought, having seen Ric's torment over Lara's initial rejection of any further involvement with him. If Johnny Ellis hadn't gone to Gundamurra and found out about Lara's pregnancy before Ric had taken off to New York...

'It did work,' Mitch murmured.

'What?' Kathryn whispered, still watching the passionate clinch of the newly married couple and envying the absolute certainty of their love for each other.

'He took her home. And it worked for them,' Mitch answered, nodding at some private satisfaction in his mind.

It touched a highly nervous chord in Kathryn. Once they saw Ric and Lara off on their honeymoon, *she* was taking Mitch home to Gosford with her—his first meeting with her parents—and she couldn't help feeling apprehensive about it.

There had been no real decision made about this step. She'd mentioned it was her mother's birthday this weekend and she was expected home for it. Mitch had said he might as well use the time to visit his sister at Green Point, and since that area was in the vicinity of Gosford, they could travel together in his car, with him dropping Kathryn off and picking her up on the way back.

Given the intimacy of their relationship, it would have sounded dreadfully rude to reject the offer—equally rude not to invite him into her parental home. Yet she felt horribly self-conscious about the visit, knowing how curious her parents would be to meet the man who had supplanted Jeremy in her life, probably wondering if she'd end up being hurt by him, too.

Mitch had accepted the invitation to dine with them tonight but he had stuck with his plan to stay with his sister, possibly sensing Kathryn's inhibitions about sharing a room with him under her parents' roof. Stupid really, given they could barely keep their hands off each other, but her parents didn't know that and she didn't want them to think she was plunging headlong into *another mistake.*

While it had been three very hot and heavy months with Mitch now, and there was no sign of his desire for her abating, Kathryn couldn't help thinking it was all too good—*magic,* as Mitch had called it—and the spell might break. Introducing him to her parents was a scary prospect, especially after getting to the point of planning a wedding with Jeremy.

Maybe Mitch didn't want the open commitment of sleeping in her parents' home, either, keeping his sister as an escape route to slide away when it suited him. Three months...it wasn't a long time, yet Kathryn couldn't imagine ever wanting to be with any other man. She hoped Mitch felt the same way about her. But he hadn't said he loved her, hadn't invited her to meet his sister, and here she was, taking him home with her.

Would it work for them?

He need not have come. He could easily have avoided it altogether instead of offering to drive her both ways. Maybe he was curious about her home life, wanting some more knowledge of her and her background. But what about him and his sister...who had been raped? They had never talked about that.

Because of Jeremy?

It dawned on Kathryn that she'd been floating along in a bubble of happiness where Mitch was concerned, but other things existed outside that bubble. There was nothing hidden between Ric and Lara any more and that was how it should be...everything known, accepted, understood. That was how it had to be for a marriage to work, with love underpinning it all.

She hadn't known enough about Jeremy, hadn't understood, and couldn't accept his attitudes when she had understood. Mitch Tyler was a very different person and she loved everything she knew about him, yet how much more was there she didn't know?

This was weighing heavily on her mind by the time they'd farewelled Ric and Lara. By then it was midafternoon, and since she and Mitch had decided to leave the city early to avoid peak hour traffic, their weekend bags were already in his car—nothing to delay their departure. They were very quickly on their way to Gosford, Mitch in the driver's seat in more ways than one, Kathryn thought.

Had he deliberately manoeuvred a meeting with her parents for some kind of check on her while still holding himself aloof where his own family was concerned? Her uncertainty about his intentions kept her tense and silent as the car headed north.

'I guess you're thinking of the wedding you didn't have.'

The comment startled her—the wedding forgotten, the focus of her thoughts entirely on the destination they were travelling toward. Even more startling—unnerving—was the mocking little smile Mitch flashed at her, especially when there wasn't even a hint of a smile in his eyes. The twin blue laser beams bit into her with hard, purposeful intent.

Kathryn's mind instantly clicked to red alert. This was Mitch's first reference to Jeremy since he'd forcefully taken him out of her life. It appalled her that he might think she regretted her ex-fiancé's departure... for any reason at all.

'I can't imagine anything worse than a wedding where there's no real love,' she said emphatically. 'I was actually envying Ric and Lara. They didn't need any flashy frills to make their wedding into *a big day.* Having each other was more than big enough for them.'

'Would you be content with a ceremony as simple as that?'

She hesitated, frowning. 'My family would be hurt if they were excluded.'

'So what they think is important to you.'

'Yes, it is.'

Another stabbing glance. 'What did they think of Haynes?'

Kathryn's breath caught at the directness of the question. Was Mitch worrying about how he would compare in her parents' eyes? 'They didn't really take to him,' she answered honestly. 'I thought it was…different lifestyles.'

'Are you worried about what they'll think of me?'

Her chest tightened up as her mind whirled through the concerns that had been nagging her. 'Why do you want to meet them, Mitch?' she burst out. 'What's this all about?'

His hands tightened on the steering wheel, knuckles gleaming white. His jaw looked clenched, too, his mouth thinning into a grim, determined line. Kathryn was acutely aware of strong emotion being barely contained. Yet when he spoke it was in a calm, measured tone.

'I'd like to know why you *don't* want me to meet them, Kathryn.'

She winced, hating the idea of explaining her reluctance to expose where she was now with him. Yet if she didn't…what was he thinking? That she was ashamed of their relationship, not prepared to acknowledge it? Treating him like a gigolo who supplied her with sex—a person she didn't want to introduce to her parents because the relationship wasn't *serious* to her? In actual fact, it was so serious, she didn't want anything tainting it. But how to explain that?

'It hasn't anything to do with you, Mitch,' she plunged in, anxious to clear the air of anything offensive or insulting. 'I foisted Jeremy on them and they accepted him for my sake, while all the time they worried that my marriage to him would turn out badly. Though they didn't say that until after…after I broke off the engagement.'

She took a deep breath as she struggled to clarify the conflict in her mind. 'It made me feel worse that they'd seen what I didn't. And here you are—' her hands fluttered in helpless appeal '—driving a classy Jaguar, exuding success, bristling with sex appeal, and they'll think I've fallen for the same package again—you taking over Jeremy's place.'

The ensuing silence felt as though it was loaded with explosives. Kathryn closed her eyes, fiercely hoping she hadn't just ruined everything with her own squirmish guilt for being a blind fool.

'Am I the same package to you?'

Again his tone was calm, almost matter-of-fact, yet the impact of his question sent shock waves through her entire body.

'No!' Her heart sank at the train of thought she'd planted in his mind. She shot him an agonised glance. 'You must know you're so much more, Mitch.'

He didn't answer immediately and his gaze remained fixed on the traffic, making it impossible for her to read his expression. She waited, literally on pins and needles, and when he did reply, it was indirect, putting her on the spot again.

'Then don't you think your parents are capable of sorting that out for themselves?'

His logic could not be refuted. Yet it didn't stop Kathryn from feeling intensely vulnerable about this meeting. 'You didn't answer my question,' she blurted out, needing more than ever to understand his intentions. 'Why do you want to meet my parents?'

He shrugged. 'Because you didn't ask me to. Just the flat announcement that you were off to be with them this weekend.'

A rejection by omission.

A little chill ran down her spine.

They'd been so close these past three months. Of course he'd wonder why she hadn't invited him to go with her. So he'd subtly forced a meeting. No waiting around on a back-step for Mitch Tyler. He went after what he wanted. Yet how *serious* was he about their relationship?

'You haven't asked me to meet your sister,' she pointed out. 'Why don't you do that, Mitch?'

'I was coming to it.' He sliced her a look that sizzled with challenge. 'Jenny would like you to join us for lunch on Sunday, if you can spare the time from your own family.'

He'd already planned it! It was sensing *her* reservations about being accompanied by him to her parents' home that had stopped him from delivering the invitation. She heaved a rueful sigh, realising she'd made a mess of what should have been simple.

'I have no problem with openly declaring an interest in you, Kathryn,' he went on. 'And I don't like being cast in the role of secret lover—kept hidden from your family. I'd much prefer you to feel happy about our relationship. Proud to have me with you.'

'I am!' she cried, horrified at how he had interpreted her nagging sense of failure over Jeremy. 'I'll be very happy to come to lunch with you and your sister's family on Sunday. Please thank her for the invitation.'

He nodded and said no more. But there was no smile from him, nothing to reassure her that he was satisfied with the situation.

Kathryn stewed over what he'd said all the way to Wahroonga where they turned onto the freeway and the travelling would be much faster. She had to get these issues settled before they reached Gosford. If this awful tension in the car was carried into the meeting with her parents, it would go dreadfully wrong. And it was her fault.

'Not inviting you to spend this weekend with me was not about hiding you from my parents, Mitch,' she stated emphatically.

'Good! Because I'm not about to let you, Kathryn,' he said with a hard, ruthless bite that alarmed her even further.

'What does that mean?' she snapped, instantly imagining him claiming intimacy with her in front of her parents...laying their affair out right on the mat, defying her to deny it in any shape or form.

'It means that I won't back off from meeting your parents and I don't give a damn if they spend the whole time comparing me to Haynes because I know I'm a better man than he is.' His eyes stabbed at her apparent lack of confidence in that point as he added, 'I thought you did, too, Kathryn.'

He returned his gaze to the road they were travelling, leaving her to sort out the confused mess in her mind. The really awful truth was she had been proud of Jeremy, happy to show him off as her partner. Which damned her as a superficial idiot. Mitch's sister didn't know that, which gave Kathryn a clean slate to work on, whereas in her parents' eyes... but she was thinking of herself, not Mitch. She wasn't being fair to the person he was—a far better man than Jeremy in every sense.

'I do know that, Mitch,' she said quietly, hoping he would forgive the offence she had clearly given.

He sighed, grimaced. 'I don't want to feel you've taken up with me on the rebound, Kathryn. That I'm fighting ghosts at every turn. You took off his ring but he's still there in your mind, influencing what you do—and don't do—with me.'

*On the rebound...*

That wasn't true. She'd been strongly drawn to the man he was before she'd broken up with Jeremy. But seeing Harriet Lowell in his home that first night had made her think the attraction couldn't be mutual. It was only when he'd openly said he found her very desirable—and proved it—that she could fully believe he actually *wanted* to pursue a relationship with her.

But that issue had all been triggered by the horrible scene with Jeremy, so she could see how Mitch might think that making love with him—then and there—had been an impulsive rebound decision, driven by the need to wipe out the nastiness and supplant it with good feelings. And these past few months with him had been centred on the incredibly wonderful sex they had together. She'd wanted to wallow in it, not think ahead, just let it be.

It seemed...*dangerous*...to think ahead, to even consider a future together. She realised now that she felt *safe* within their relationship as long as it was kept to the two of them. In fact, she *had* subconsciously cast him as her secret lover, clinging to the intimacy of that privateness, not wanting any outside influence to threaten it.

She looked down at her bare left hand. The solitaire diamond ring was gone but what had happened with Jeremy *was* still in her mind. She had to get over it, let it go, or she might lose the man she most desperately didn't want to lose.

'Remember the day we met in your chambers?' she said, determined on changing his view of her feelings for him.

'Vividly,' he answered dryly.

'You affected me so deeply, it made me question whether it was right to go ahead and marry Jeremy. I was still questioning when you took me home the next night. Then Jeremy confirmed how wrong it was. So what I feel with you is not a rebound thing, Mitch. It started before there was anything to rebound from.'

Silence.

Did he believe her?

He was staring straight ahead as though focusing all his attention on the road but she could feel his inner tension as he weighed what she'd said against his own impressions of their first meeting. Kathryn worried over how many times he'd felt *rejected* by her, how much it was eating into him.

A sense of panic hit her as she realised they'd turned off the Sydney to Newcastle Freeway and were heading down the Kariong hill to Gosford. Another ten minutes and they'd be at her parents' home, where she hadn't made him feel welcome. Frantic for him to understand her motivation, she tried to explain further.

'I don't know if you've ever thought of marrying anyone, but it's not a commitment I walked into lightly and I couldn't walk out of it lightly. Having met you, I questioned my choice, but the questioning was painful and I wanted Jeremy to make the pain go away. But he didn't. He made it worse.'

'Fair enough,' came the relieving acceptance of her argument.

Kathryn was just beginning to breathe easier when he hit her with another question.

'You say meeting me caused you to question your choice. You knew I was unattached, so after you'd ended it with Haynes, why didn't you call me, Kathryn? You could have used any number of pretexts to contact me and let me know you were free. As it was, if I hadn't come to you...'

'Oh, right!' she exploded in frustration. 'Here's this powerful man who took care of me for a day because his old friend asked him to. And while I'm in his home, this beautiful tall blonde turns up—a barrister, as well, sharing his profession and clearly having shared his bed. Okay, so he says it's over. Do I look like Harriet Lowell? Do I share his legal world? All I am is an obligation he carried out with charming civility.'

He frowned. 'Did I make you feel like an obligation?'

She sighed at the hopeless error in her reasoning. 'No. You made me feel... I wished I wasn't engaged to Jeremy.'

'I was barely holding onto being *honourable,* Kathryn.'

The black irony of that statement squeezed her heart. He'd wanted her then. Wanted her all along. And she was not answering his need to feel wanted by her.

'I'm sorry, Mitch. Believe me, I thought of calling you many times. But having made such a huge mistake with Jeremy, I just couldn't...open myself to another hurtful mistake. I guess I'm a coward.'

'No. You helped Ric and stood up to Gary Chappel. You fought the big fight over Lara's right to safe refuge while your dreams were crumbling around you. And you walked away from all Haynes offered. Those are not the acts of a coward.'

A red traffic light forced a stop and Mitch reached out and enfolded one of her hands in his. Her gaze instantly sought his, begging forgiveness. 'I do want you with me, Mitch.'

And finally he smiled. It was slow and a touch wry, but at least it was a smile that lifted some of the weight off her heart.

'You'll have to forgive me my black and white mentality, Kathryn. I'm not good at greys,' he said on a dry, whimsical note.

The traffic started moving forward again and Mitch released her hand, returning his to the driving wheel, leaving her with the tingling memory of its warmth and strength. The hand that had hit Jeremy, she thought, rescuing her, fighting for her.

It was now up to her to fight for him, to give him very positive signals because there was much on the line this weekend. No doubt about that. Her parents, his sister...there was no place for any negativity in either meeting. No place for muddly *greys,* either. Kathryn had the very strong sense that this was make or break time in her relationship with Mitch Tyler.

She wanted it to work.

The very thought of losing him...

No. She had to get her head straight once and for all. Mitch Tyler was *her man.* Somehow she had to make him believe she was *his woman.*

# CHAPTER THIRTEEN

*11.30 a.m. Sunday...*

FOR KATHRYN, THE weekend had dragged almost unbearably since Mitch had left on Friday night. The meeting with her parents had gone particularly well, and when she'd accompanied him out to his car to see him off, he'd kissed her with such passion, it had hurt to let him go. She should have trusted what they had together instead of worrying how her parents might view it.

At least this lunch with his sister today gave her the chance to show *his* trust wasn't misplaced. Somehow she would show Jenny that Mitch was not just an attractive package to her, but the man she wanted at her side because he was incredibly special.

'Mitch is here!' her father called from the living room. 'I'll carry your bag out to his car, Kathryn. Say hello.'

She turned anxiously to her mother who was sitting on her bed, watching her last-minute application of fresh lipstick. 'Do I look all right, Mum?'

'Lovely, dear.' She smiled approvingly. 'That knitted jacket looks brilliant on you. Very clever design with all the different blocks of green.'

'Not too dressy on top of jeans? It's a barbecue lunch. Mitch said casual.'

'It's classy casual. Not out of place,' came the decisive reassurance.

Kathryn took a deep breath to settle her madly accelerated pulse-rate and picked up her handbag, ready to go.

Her mother rose from the bed and linked arms with her, smiling indulgently and patting her hand. 'Stop worrying, Kathryn. It's perfectly obvious that Mitch Tyler cares about you. His sister will pick up on that and act accordingly.'

'But I want her to like me...for me.'

'Then just relax and be yourself. Come on. I'll walk you out to the car. Say hello to Mitch, too.'

'You do really like him. You're not just pretending for my sake.'

'Kathryn...' Her eyes were warm, glowing with pleasure. 'He's the best birthday present you could have brought me. I can now stop worrying about you. He's a good man.'

'Much better than Jeremy,' she pressed.

'Chalk and cheese,' her mother declared emphatically. 'Both your father and I feel...intensely relieved and happy for you.'

Mitch had been right. Her parents had had no problem perceiving the differences between the two men. It had been foolish of her to fret over their response to *this choice.* Black and white.

'Kathryn tells me you play chess,' her father was saying as she and her mother emerged from the house. 'We'll have to have a game next time you come.'

'A pleasure I'll look forward to,' Mitch answered, smiling, looking totally relaxed with the situation.

*Next time.*

Kathryn's heart skittered with the happy hope that everything was all right. Mitch had forgiven her for casting him in the role of secret lover. Their relationship was out in the open now—doubly open with its being acknowledged in front of her parents and his sister.

He looked spectacularly handsome, his magnificent physique clothed in blue jeans and a royal-blue skivvy, their colour reflected vividly in his eyes, his strong face as beautifully masculine as the rest of him. Her whole body yearned for contact with him, but he was holding the passenger door open for her, and conscious of her parents watching, she simply smiled her pleasure in his company as she got in the car.

Once they were on their way, Mitch reached across and took her hand, instantly imparting a warm reassurance in their togetherness. 'Just to clear up any doubts that are festering in your mind,' he drawled, casting her a purposeful glance that raised flutters in her stomach. 'I have not taken Harriet Lowell nor any other woman to meet my sister, so you're not about to be subjected to any comparisons, Kathryn.'

'Oh!' Relief surged through her, followed by the stunning realisation that he was letting her further into his life than he had ever allowed anyone else. Which made her squirm even more over her own reservations about introducing him to her parents.

'Mitch, I am sorry about my...my misgivings. Mum and Dad think you're great,' she declared, hoping that resolved the problem she'd raised.

He smiled with a touch of irony. 'So I passed muster.'

'With flying colours,' she assured him.

'They're good people, your parents,' he said seriously. 'They care about you, Kathryn. As they should.'

It reminded her that Mitch's own father had not cared, walking out on him and Jenny, leaving a disabled wife behind, too. A really terrible desertion. Then Jenny getting raped...some horrible man not caring about what he was doing to her, taking what he wanted. Like Jeremy. Only much, much worse.

'Is your sister okay, Mitch?' she asked impulsively.

He sliced her a querying look. 'Why do you ask?'

'You told me...the night you rescued me from Jeremy...you said Jenny had once been raped,' she recalled hesitantly, wondering if she was treading on highly sensitive ground.

'That was when she was eighteen, Kathryn. She's thirty-six now, very happily married, and we don't talk about that time,' he stated firmly, flashing her a look of warning. 'It's long in the past,' he went on. 'She loves her husband, adores her two children and she's looking forward to meeting you.'

Which all proved true over the next couple of hours. Kathryn instantly warmed to Jenny and her husband, Hal, both of them very welcoming and easy to chat with. Their three-year-old daughter was a very cute charmer, all over her 'Uncle Mish' who indulgently gave the attention she demanded of him. He'd be a good father, Kathryn thought, watching him cradle his nine-month-old nephew in the crook of his arm, and talking to him as though the baby understood everything he said.

Hal and Mitch cooked prawns and swordfish steaks on the barbecue, sharing the children between them while Jenny invited Kathryn to help her with salads in the kitchen, having already prepared a big potato bake with cheese and bacon. It was a friendly open plan house with lots of sunlight coming in. A happy house, Kathryn thought, taking Mitch's point that his sister had long moved on from old traumas.

They ate lunch out on a large covered deck overlooking a sparkling inground swimming pool, and the atmosphere was so relaxed, Kathryn thoroughly enjoyed herself. She had no premonition of what was to come after the children were put to bed for an afternoon nap.

The men did the clearing up from the barbecue and Jenny led her down to a lounge setting near the pool, saying they might as well soak up the sunshine while they could. It was a glorious spring day, perfect for being outdoors. They settled down with mugs of coffee, and Kathryn wasn't surprised when Jenny used the opportunity to learn more about her.

'Mitch tells me you're Ric Donato's executive assistant in his Sydney office,' came the casual opening.

'Yes. I guess you must know Ric since he and Mitch are old friends.'

'I know of him. I've never met him.'

That did surprise her. 'You've never met?'

Jenny shook her head and grimaced. 'It goes back to Gundamurra, you see. Mitch was sent there because of me. And that's where he met Ric and Johnny Ellis.'

'Sent there…because of you?' Kathryn was intrigued. It was certainly a piece of background information Mitch had never offered. She swung her feet off the lounge, sitting on the side of it to face his sister who suddenly looked very uncomfortable about having imparted it.

'I thought you knew.' Her eyes searched Kathryn's anxiously. 'Working so closely with Ric…being with Mitch…'

Sensing retreat and eager to persuade Jenny to reveal more, she quickly offered, 'All I know is that Ric took Lara—the woman he's just married—to Gundamurra to keep her safe from her husband. It's an outback sheep station and I gathered that Mitch has been there himself. Johnny Ellis, too.'

Jenny bit her lips and stared into space for several minutes. 'He keeps protecting me, but he can't protect me from my guilt,' she finally muttered.

Definitely a reference to her brother, Kathryn thought, knowing how strong Mitch was on protection. But what was he protecting his sister from now?

'What guilt do you have, Jenny?' she asked softly, wondering if it was related back to the rape that Mitch said they never talked about.

She shook her head but was also frowning as though struggling with a decision, possibly torn between personal need and loyalty to her brother. Kathryn didn't press, sensitive to the fact she had no right to dig into what was none of her business. Curiosity could be taken only so far, especially on such short acquaintance. Better that Jenny didn't tell her anything she might regret letting out. Kathryn wanted her friendship more than she wanted information.

She sipped from her mug of coffee, trying to think of something to say that would ease the tension emanating from Mitch's sister. Jenny was a much softer person than her brother, not the female equivalent at all. She was very feminine, very pretty, with warm brown eyes and curly brown hair and a naturally giving nature. It was easy to see that she would have been a generous carer to her mother, a wonderful nurse, and now a very understanding wife to a busy doctor. Easy to also see she was the kind of person who would stir a powerful protective instinct in her brother.

'I want to know. I *have* to know.'

It sounded like a desperate decision, jolting Kathryn out of her own train of thought and focusing her very acute attention on Jenny as she turned to her, the lovely brown eyes dark and pained.

'How can I help?' The words spilled from Kathryn, her sympathy instantly aroused.

It triggered an outburst of angst. 'When I heard the news reports of Gary Chappel's death...in a plane crash at Gundamurra...and one newspaper said Mitch was acting for Lara Chappel... I knew it had to be all connected. I just knew. But Mitch will fob me off if I ask him. So will you tell me, Kathryn? You must know what went on.'

She had no idea what the connection was in Jenny's mind but clearly Mitch's sister was deeply disturbed by it. There seemed no reason not to tell her the whole story, beginning with the photograph that suggested Lara Chappel was the victim of physical abuse from her husband, what Ric had done about it, how Mitch had handled the legal end, then after Gary Chappel's death, Lara's withdrawal from Ric until Johnny Ellis had gone to Gundamurra and found out about her pregnancy, the DNA test which had proved Ric was the father...

'...and they got married on Friday. Mitch and I were the witnesses,' she finished.

'Did Lara look happy?' Jenny questioned anxiously.

'Blissfully happy,' Kathryn assured her. 'It was abundantly clear that she and Ric love each other very deeply.'

Jenny sighed as though that knowledge gave her some relief. 'Ric's Lara,' she murmured. 'And all three of them contributing to that end after all these years.'

Her words instantly recalled other words Kathryn had heard spoken, Mitch talking on the telephone to Ric at Gundamurra, speaking in a very gentle, sympathetic tone—*Patrick said...this is your Lara...from the old days.*

'Would you mind explaining that to me, Jenny?' she pleaded, feeling left out of something she *should* know.

Jenny took a deep breath and spilled out, 'I'm a coward, Kathryn. That's why Mitch hasn't told you. Always protecting me. I never faced up to it, you see.'

'I'm sorry. I don't see.'

She grimaced. 'When I was eighteen I was brutally raped, and I couldn't bear to testify about it in court...couldn't bear to face the man again.'

'I can understand that. I'm sure Mitch did, too.'

'Yes, but...Mitch couldn't let it go. Couldn't bear that the man should get away with what he'd done. He went after him and delivered...rough justice. He was charged with assault and I didn't...couldn't bring myself to stand up in court and testify why he'd done it. Not then. And Mitch wouldn't say. Wouldn't bring my name into it. For my sake. So he was convicted and given the choice of spending a year in a detention centre or working six months on an outback sheep station.'

'Gundamurra.'

She nodded. 'The man who owns it, Patrick Maguire, had some special program going, wanting to help boys who'd run off the rails. Ric Donato and Johnny Ellis made the same choice at the same time. They were all sixteen. Ric had stolen a car, wanting to impress his girlfriend, Lara. Johnny had been caught dealing in marijuana.'

She paused, again anxiously searching Kathryn's eyes. 'You will keep this confidential, won't you? I don't think any of them would want this background to be public knowledge. Johnny's famous now. And Ric's very respectable. As for Mitch...'

'I promise you this information is safe with me, Jenny,' she returned earnestly.

'I made Mitch tell me everything about Gundamurra. I felt so guilty about him being sent there. He swore it was a good experience, that Patrick Maguire had been like a father to them, and there'd been nothing bad about being with Ric and Johnny, either. Ric was a dyed-in-the-wool romantic who mooned a lot about some girl called Lara, and Johnny was fantastic at making up songs, playing guitar.'

'Well, that must have been true because they've been friends ever since,' Kathryn pointed out.

'Yes. And eventually, years later, when Mitch wanted to study law, I did go to a court hearing to testify on his behalf and his conviction was overturned. I could put it all behind me then. I felt it wouldn't come back to haunt me anymore.'

'Nor should it, Jenny. All these recent happenings have nothing to do with you.'

'But they do, Kathryn.' The haunted look in her eyes poignantly underlined her feelings, however misplaced they were. 'I might have saved Ric's Lara a lot of grief,' she added, clearly unloading the burden of guilt that weighed so heavily on her, yet it made no sense to Kathryn.

'I'm sorry. I don't understand how you could have done that. You didn't know...'

'It was Gary Chappel who raped me,' she cried.

Kathryn felt her heart recoil in shock.

*This* was the connection. The ramifications bounced around her mind as Jenny poured out her grief.

'He sucked me in with his good looks and charm. And he drove a Lamborghini. I was dazzled by him. But by the time he finished with me I knew what he was really like. The things he did to me...' She shook her head, distressed by the memories even now. 'I never told. And I should have done. A man like that...of course, he'd do it to others. He should have been charged. Put away. Mitch would have stood up and done it, but I...I let my brother be put away instead.' Tears welled and spilled down her cheeks. 'And Gary Chappel went on to hurt Ric's Lara.'

'Jenny—' Kathryn reached out and took her hand, squeezing it to impart some comfort '—it's not as black and white as that.'

Perhaps it was to Mitch—possibly why he and his sister never talked about this. But there *were* many greys in the way the world operated. Too many times there was one law for the rich who could buy the best defence, and one for the poor who had to trust they'd be believed.

'The Chappel family is mega-wealthy, Jenny. Victor Chappel would have done everything possible to get his son and heir off a rape charge, including tearing you to shreds on the witness stand. I'm sure Mitch is well aware of that. The way he handled Lara's situation...he knew what he was dealing with and how to bring pressure to bear on their response to it. But that's now. He couldn't have done that eighteen years ago. As you said, he was only sixteen, and I'm sure whatever justice he took into his own hands, he was willing to pay for. You know that, don't you? And Gundamurra wasn't bad for him. You know that, too. You shouldn't feel guilty about any of this.'

'But what about Lara? And there were probably other women...'

'I think for men like Gary Chappel, with great wealth behind them, only death is going to stop them from following their own bent. And he is dead, Jenny. It's over. Over for Lara, too. She's got Ric now and Ric is a really good person. Believe me, I know. I'm sure his love will make up for anything Lara suffered at her husband's hands. And maybe they would never have come together again if he hadn't seen that photograph. So it's really okay. You don't have to worry or feel guilty. Lara's fine.'

Jenny dragged in deep breaths and dashed the tears from her cheeks with her hand, blinked hard to clear her eyes. 'I've always felt wrong about it. Wrong about what I didn't do,' she choked out.

Kathryn knew only too well the shame she'd felt over her huge error of judgement in accepting Jeremy as the man she would marry. Jenny's shame was rooted in a much more dreadful trauma and stirred her deepest compassion.

'Don't feel wrong any more,' she urged. 'You were the victim of what was done to you, Jenny. It wasn't your fault. And it wasn't cowardly not to take on Gary Chappel yourself. I met him very briefly when he came to the office, chasing Ric and Lara. I would have been very frightened if I'd been his target.'

'He had no heart...no pity... I couldn't bear to be anywhere near him again.'

'Mitch wouldn't have wanted you to be. The moment I gave him Gary Chappel's name he had security guards sent to the office to protect me and accompany me to his chambers.'

The bleak memories in Jenny's eyes gave way to a spark of interest. 'You didn't tell me about that.'

'It's how we met.'

Kathryn ran on at considerable length, explaining how Mitch had taken her home with him that night to ensure her safety, adding that he considered Gary Chappel a dangerous psychopath with the resources to get his own way, whatever it took.

'So you see, Jenny, your brother doesn't blame you for anything because he knows the kind of man Gary Chappel was. And you shouldn't blame yourself, either,' she finished with conviction.

Jenny gave her a bemused look. 'So you two met because of him.'

And re-met because of his death, Kathryn thought, but she'd said enough to put the whole set of circumstances into reasonable perspective and Mitch's sister seemed to be considerably less stressed now. She smiled as she answered, 'Yes, we did. And I've got to say, Jenny, your brother is one hell of an impressive guy.'

It drew a smile from her. 'I think he's very impressed with you, Kathryn. In fact, you're the only woman he's ever brought to meet me. I thought it meant...' She gave an awkward shrug. 'I guess he's still protecting me...not telling you about Gary Chappel and Gundamurra. Thank you for...for setting my mind at rest.'

'Put it behind you now, Jenny,' she quickly advised. 'You have a great husband, two beautiful children, Lara is with Ric...'

'And Mitch is with you,' she cut in, sounding very satisfied with that outcome.

But he wouldn't have been with her this weekend if he hadn't pushed for it—all because *she* hadn't put Jeremy behind her. Taking the diamond ring off wasn't enough. She'd made Mitch feel he was fighting ghosts at every turn and that wasn't right, wasn't fair.

Ghosts!

The realisation suddenly struck how very personal those ghosts were to Mitch. Hugely personal!

She'd told him Jeremy—the man she'd committed herself to marrying—had sided with Gary Chappel—the man who'd raped his sister, who'd subjected Ric's Lara to untold abuse...

Then on the night of the very same day she'd told him it was over, he'd seen Jeremy entering her apartment building. What must have been going through his mind when he followed...then found her ex-fiancé forcing himself on her...remembering Jenny's rape, hitting Jeremy as he had surely hit Gary Chappel, feeling intense violence toward both men?

Ghosts...and the long link to Gundamurra where Ric had taken Lara, bringing the past very much to the fore, memories he didn't talk about.

And *she* had thrown Jeremy in his face again because of feeling vulnerable about the meeting between Mitch and her parents. Jeremy, whom Mitch would judge to be in the same class as Gary Chappel! Black and white!

*Am I the same package to you?* he'd asked.

Dear God! The offence was horrific.

She remembered his tension in the car, the sense of violent emotion being barely contained, his white-knuckled grip on the steering wheel.

Yet despite all that, he'd asked her to forgive him for *not being good at greys,* then followed up by completely charming her parents. And today... well, Jenny certainly believed Mitch thought she was special—the only woman he'd ever brought to meet her.

'I'm glad he met you, Kathryn.' Jenny was looking at her as though she answered more than she had already answered. 'Mitch has walked alone for too long. And he has such a big heart...so much love to give. You'll never find a more caring man.' She smiled her own love for her brother. 'Mitch cares with a passion.'

'I know,' Kathryn murmured.

And she did know.

It summed up all her experience of Mitch Tyler.

Yet she had to hear it from his sister to recognise its absolute truth.

It made her feel small, unworthy of him, but she silently vowed he wouldn't feel alone ever again.

He had rescued her from so much.

Tonight she would rescue him from all he'd kept to himself.

# CHAPTER FOURTEEN

MITCH FELT A happy sense of satisfaction as he drove away from his sister's home. Jenny's parting words, whispered as he kissed her goodbye—'She's lovely, Mitch. So right for you.'—and Kathryn sitting beside him now with an air of relaxed contentment…the uncertainties that had plagued him had been largely lifted.

Jenny had felt the magic.

Kathryn's parents had, too.

And the cloud Haynes had left on Kathryn's mind had been dispelled.

He felt far more confident now that he was winning the woman he wanted. Three more months to consolidate their relationship, then…he had to do it…had to take her to Gundamurra for Christmas. He hoped that being there would help her understand, meeting Patrick, feeling how that wise old man of the land and the immense space of the outback had taught him the futility of burning up with anger.

Far better for the explosive energy to be channelled into constructive purpose—achieving, not destroying, pursuing positive outcomes, not giving in to negativity. He'd done that, ever since he'd left Gundamurra. But he had snapped with Haynes, his fist flying out, connecting. Would Kathryn tie that to his earlier assault on Gary Chappel and worry about his capacity for violence? Would she be able to justify it in her mind, let it go, love him…without reservation?

'Thank you for taking me to meet Jenny and her family, Mitch.'

She was smiling at him, her beautiful green eyes lit with gold sparkles. His heart lifted, soaring with hope. 'Jenny thinks you're lovely,' he informed her, returning the smile.

'So is she. And Hal. And the children.'

'I'm glad you had a good time with them.'

'Very good. In lots of ways.'

He threw her a quizzical glance. 'Want to elaborate on that?'

She grimaced but her eyes held apologetic appeal. 'It hammered home what a fool I'd been to worry about this weekend.'

'New steps always carry uncertainties,' he said, knowing the feeling all too well.

'You know what the worst thing about it has been?'

'No. Tell me the worst.'

'Not having you with me all the time.'

It jolted his gaze from the road. Heat was flooding into her cheeks. There was a vulnerable look in her eyes, wanting him to agree, afraid he might not.

'I missed you, too, Kathryn,' he assured her. 'In fact, I was severely tempted to crash your mother's birthday party yesterday.'

'You would have been welcome, Mitch. I would have loved to have you there. We would all have welcomed you,' she said with a fervour that left no room for doubt.

'It's okay.' He reached over and took her hand in his. 'We're together now.' Much more so than on the trip from Sydney, he thought, which was eloquent proof that controlling his anger over Haynes and arguing it through to a winning situation had earned him the result he'd aimed for.

Her other hand covered his, transmitting a desire for more contact with him, instantly arousing the strong sexual urge she'd always stirred in him.

'I want you to stay with me tonight, Mitch.'

His whole body clamoured for instant gratification. His mind dictated that waiting for the right time had to be enforced. Though it was impossible to keep the anticipation of it from simmering through his smile as he answered, 'I was hoping you'd want that, Kathryn.'

She laughed, a delightful gurgle of nervous pleasure.

Mitch wasn't sure how they made it back to Sydney. His driving had to have been on automatic pilot because he only became aware of the outside world when he brought the Jaguar to a halt in front of Kathryn's apartment building at Bondi Junction.

He managed to remember her bag...carried it for her.

She had the key to her apartment ready in her hand, unlocking the door with barely a pause.

They were inside.

He dropped the bag on the floor.

She flung her arms around his neck, her body rocketing against his, and the hunger for her he'd kept contained all weekend exploded through him. He kissed her, needing to draw her into him. His hands took their own urgent fill of her, roving greedily, possessively, over every delectable curve of her femininity, wanting the affirmation that she was his.

They tore off their clothes, her need as pressing as his, exciting him to a wild exhilaration. The caveman in him swung into action, scooping her off her feet, carrying her to the bedroom, and she was laughing with the mad rush of feeling, loving it, kissing him with joy, her hands running over him, inciting him to take her, intensely immediate.

He could not have waited anyway. She wound her legs around his hips, raising her body to meet the thrust of his, arching from the sheer ecstatic pleasure of instant satisfaction, the thrill of her response driving him hard and fast to the centre of her being. He wanted to feel her innermost self embracing him, engulfing, possessing, claiming her man.

It was awesome the feeling she gave him...the sense of utter euphoria. It ignited all the pent-up energy of the past few days and they rocked together in a wild, exultant rhythm, soaring to the crests of waves of excitement, wallowing in the shallows of voluptuous sensuality, revelling in every nuance of pleasure, loving each other.

It went beyond the physical. Mitch was sure of it. It wasn't just a sexual merging. He could see it in her eyes...the total giving of herself, becoming one with him, belonging together. And when he finally climaxed, a sigh of sweet fulfilment whispered from her lips, a sigh that rippled through her entire body, telling him she felt complete in every sense with him.

He hugged her close, savouring this new level of intimacy, believing in it so strongly he wouldn't let himself think anything other than she felt it, too. It had to be. Right from the beginning he'd known instinctively she was the one. And she'd admitted being drawn to him, too, at their first meeting, drawn into wishing she wasn't wearing another man's ring.

He'd buy her a ring.

Not a diamond.

Something that would be special to her.

'Mitch...'

'Mmm...?' He smiled as her fingers played with the hair on his chest, twining it between them, surely another sign of her liking the sense of being joined with him.

'Jenny told me about Gary Chappel and Gundamurra.'

And his heart stopped.

Kathryn instantly felt the tight stillness of his chest. She was lying with her head resting on it, her ear close to the pleasant drumbeat of his heart—a heart fully relaxed from all tension. The beat was suddenly suspended. And the steady rhythm of his breathing came to a dead halt.

Shock, she thought, tingles of alarm racing through her brain. She hitched herself up to plead for his understanding, her eyes frantically trying to break through the glassy stare of his. 'I didn't bring up the rape, Mitch. I swear it. It was Jenny, wanting to know about Gary Chappel and Lara. And it just all came out because she needed to...to put everything together. I had to help her, Mitch. She was so deeply distressed...'

The shock in his eyes gave way to appalled disbelief. 'Jenny...' The name was expelled with the trapped breath released from his lungs. It carried the sound of some completely unanticipated betrayal.

Thinking he was hurt by his sister's choice to confide in her rather than the brother who cared so much, she quickly tried to explain Jenny's reasoning. 'It was the guilt thing, Mitch. She didn't want to lay it on you because she knows you don't want her to feel guilty. And neither she should. I think I convinced her of that in the end.'

'Guilt...' he repeated, seeming to struggle with taking that concept in.

'About not charging Gary Chappel with what he'd done to her, not testifying in court for you, letting you be sent to Gundamurra, then Ric's Lara being abused by the same man who should have been put away instead of going free to hurt other women.'

He stared at her with intense concentration, saying nothing. Kathryn thought he was waiting for more, perhaps still questioning why Jenny had unloaded all this on her instead of him. Deciding it was probably best to recount the whole conversation, how it had happened, she explained that Jenny had thought she knew everything because of her working with Ric and being with her brother.

'I understand what your sister then told me was private stuff, Mitch,' she went on anxiously, acutely aware of how tense he still was. 'But I thought it was more important to help than back off.'

Private stuff...

Mitch could barely get his mind around the shock of Jenny letting it all out to Kathryn, not just her life but his, too. *His,* too, before he was ready to deal with it. Without any thought of how it might impact on his relationship with Kathryn.

Yet as he listened to how the conversation had occurred, it sickened him that he hadn't realised...hadn't answered his sister's need. Chappel was dead. To his mind, that had ended it. Yet it was very clear now why Jenny had connected to Lara's situation. And Kathryn's arguments to assuage all the guilt were good arguments. Mitch doubted he could have done better himself, and possibly they were more cogent to Jenny, coming from an outsider looking at the situation objectively.

*She's lovely.*

An accolade well earned.

He knew he should feel relief that his sister's angst had been so comprehensively settled, should feel grateful to the woman who'd done it. But he felt raw—exposed—not knowing what Kathryn felt about his assault on Chappel, whether she'd linked it to how he'd dealt with Haynes.

Reason told him that she couldn't have made love with him if she had any negative feelings about what he'd done. Did this mean she had justified it all in her mind? Or was it all too fresh for her to assess properly, and the emotional time she'd spent with Jenny had spilled over into a desire to assuage his needs, too?

She was looking to him now for a response to all she'd told him, her lovely eyes troubled because of his silence. He was at a total loss for what to say, acutely conscious that she'd left out any comment on his actions and their outcome.

'I'm sorry if you feel I've intruded on what was none of my business, Mitch.'

'Jenny gave you no choice,' he acknowledged, hearing the terse note in his voice, unable to repress the tension coursing through him. All he could think of was he'd needed more time with Kathryn…more time…

'Does it matter…that I know?'

He forced himself to open up the big question in his mind. 'I guess that depends on whether it matters to you.'

'It gives me a better understanding of where you're coming from, Mitch.'

'What? A juvenile jailbird?' he mocked, wishing he could erase the memory of the violent rage that had once possessed him beyond all reason.

She now knew about Gundamurra, why he had been sent there. He'd disciplined the anger but it still grabbed him when injustices piled up, clawing at him. Even with Kathryn, giving more time to a man like Haynes when she was with him, putting her memories of that relationship ahead of what they had together.

'I don't think Gundamurra was a jail for you,' she said quietly. 'I think it gave you space…from where you were in your life.'

Space…yes. Space enough to make a big difference to where his life might have headed without Patrick Maguire's guidance.

'But I wasn't referring to your time at Gundamurra, Mitch,' she went on. 'I meant your…personal involvement with Gary Chappel.'

*The assault.*

He was not going to excuse it. Pain had been dealt out and pain had been dealt back. He did not regret that act. Never had. Though he didn't want to ever lose control of his own humanity again.

She dragged in a deep breath. Mitch found himself holding his, waiting for her judgement on him.

'I'm so sorry about letting Jeremy get in the way of your meeting my parents, Mitch. That was very wrong of me. Considering how he sided with the man who'd raped your sister, and tried to force me…it must have made you feel…'

*Violent.*

He'd wanted Kathryn to be his from the moment they'd met. And he'd forced himself to act honourably while she was hung up on a man who knew no honour. Where was the justice in that?

'Knowing what I do now,' she said ruefully, 'it must have been very difficult for you to be as you were...with me and my parents on Friday night.'

He'd been fighting for her. It seemed he'd been fighting for her all along. And right now he felt as though the mat had been swept out from under him, leaving him with no control over the outcome.

'I wish...with all my heart...I hadn't made it that way for you, Mitch. It wasn't fair.'

Nothing fair in love and war, he thought savagely. The old adages always held truth. Justice is blind...

'Please forgive me.'

He shook his head. 'There's nothing to forgive. You were being honest with me.'

'If I'd known the background...'

'It would have put a pressure on you I didn't want you to have. Nor do I want you to have it now,' he added fiercely. 'Trying to make up for something that had nothing to do with you.'

'Can't I care about what effect it's had on you, Mitch?'

His jaw clenched. What *effect* was she talking about? Did she think he needed the past raked over like Jenny? Guilt removed? He felt no guilt. 'Kathryn, I've been handling things since I was a boy. What makes you think I can't handle anything that's thrown at me?'

She heaved a long sigh. 'You can. And you do. You handle everything... brilliantly. Except...all this I've learnt today... I feel it goes right to the heart of the man you are...and you've shut me out of it...going it alone.'

Alone...

That one word hit so many chords, vibrating down the years to when he was a little boy starting school, trying to adjust to the fact that being too bright was unacceptable, that being able to read when others hadn't even begun to learn made him separate from them, a target to be beaten in other ways.

Alone and frightened when his mother was hospitalised for months and his father drank himself into a stupor every night, leaving him and Jenny to keep the household running for when their mother came home. Then when his father had deserted all three of them, the lonely responsibility of earning whatever he could so they could make ends meet, ensuring that bills were paid and whatever needed fixing was fixed.

No-one to lean on. No-one to *share* what he'd had to do. The closest

he'd come to a sense of sharing was at Gundamurra, though he'd been different to Ric and Johnny, having a family who wanted him back, needed
him back. But his mother was gone now. And Jenny... Jenny had turned
to Kathryn, not him.

Kathryn...who was sliding down, resting her head on his chest, half-
covering him, an arm around his waist, inserting a leg between his. 'You
have such a big heart, Mitch,' she murmured, kissing him, trailing her
mouth over where that very heart was beating with painful intensity.
'And I love you for it.'

She *loved* him?

'But I want you to let me into it. Not keep things from me any more.
Give me the chance to handle them, too.'

She had handled them!

She wasn't worried about anything he'd done!

His hand lifted and stroked her hair, needing to reassure himself this
wasn't a dream. It was real and he had to make a response that would
satisfy her. His voice came out furred with a turbulent mix of emotion.

'I'm sorry...sorry I didn't tell you about Chappel from the start, but
you were wearing another man's ring and I thought...' He could breathe
easily again. He even laughed. 'It doesn't matter what I thought.'

In a surge of exhilarating energy, he rolled Kathryn onto her back and
leaned over her, needing her to look into his eyes, know he was speaking with genuine sincerity. Deep sincerity.

'Thank you for what you did for Jenny. And you are very much in my
heart, Kathryn. I just wasn't ready to open the doors you crashed through
today, but I'm glad they're open now. Even more glad of the compassion
and understanding you've shown over what has been revealed.'

Happy relief shone back at him. She stroked his cheek, touching, reaching into him. 'So you'll share more of yourself with me from now on?'

Share his whole life with her if she was willing to accept it. But there
was no need to rush. Better not to. She might be wary of making a commitment for life after her experience with Haynes. He wanted her to be
very, very sure of it.

He smiled. 'What are doing for Christmas this year?'

# CHAPTER FIFTEEN

*Christmas at Gundamurra...*

KATHRYN KNEW IT was a big step in her relationship with Mitch Tyler—being invited to the outback sheep station where he had 'done time' with Ric Donato and Johnny Ellis. All three of them were here now, with Ric also bringing Lara and their baby son who'd been named Patrick, honouring the man who still stood tall in their lives.

Patrick Maguire...the strong, caring father none of them had ever had, and Kathryn noted he treated them as much valued sons; welcomed into his home, listened to, enjoyed for the people they were, given respect for what they'd done and were doing with their lives. It was clear that Lara also felt a bond with him, having spent three months at Gundamurra after her escape from her husband.

Kathryn was the only *outsider.* Not that she wasn't warmly welcomed. She was. But the others were clearly at home in this world unto itself, and she wanted to feel that, too, feel part of it as they did.

Maybe she needed more time here to take it in, to understand the unique rhythm of the place which, after three days, was already seeping into her—the sense of there being no hurry to do anything, that the endless land around them would wait timelessly for footprints upon it, that the universe above with its brilliant blanket of stars would still be there, night after night.

No hurry.

Space for breathing.

Time to think.

And Kathryn found herself thinking a lot about where she was in her life and what she wanted in her future.

Patrick's three daughters were amazing people. Jessie, the eldest, had just signed up with the Royal Flying Doctor Service, based in Alice Springs. Emily, who loved flying, was a helicopter pilot. Megan, the youngest, had just come home from an agricultural college, determined on helping her father run Gundamurra. They each had real purpose in their lives and their energy for what they'd chosen shone out of them.

Kathryn felt pale in comparison, just as she had with Harriet Lowell. Her own career had not really been planned. It had been more a series of steps, each one satisfying her for a time before moving on to something else. Her position with Ric was as an assistant, not a driving force. She had no great personal ambition although she was certainly capable of doing whatever she set out to do. Was she lacking in something important? Did Mitch find her lacking?

Had he brought her to Gundamurra to find it?

This concern was playing through her mind on the day before Christmas. Everyone was busy with preparations. All the women were in the kitchen which was a hive of industry. Mitch and Ric and Johnny were putting fairy lights around the trees in the courtyard. Kathryn was surprised when Patrick Maguire drew her out of all the general activity, claiming he was too old for Christmas chores and wanted her company.

'Mitch tells me you play chess. Come and give me a game, Kathryn,' he invited.

He walked her along the verandah to the other side of the quadrangle courtyard which the huge homestead enclosed, and ushered her into his office. Even though they were in the outback, a satellite dish linked them to all modern technology and the office looked very much the hub of business with computers and every other up-to-date aid. However, set beside a window between the desks at one end and the filing cabinets at the other, was a chess table, chairs on either side, the pieces set up ready to play.

It struck Kathryn as odd that it wasn't in the games room, along with the billiard table and the sound system Johnny had installed, plus shelves loaded with boxes of board games that clearly provided plenty of home entertainment. She wondered if chess filled lonely hours for Patrick Maguire since his wife had died and his daughters had been away, pursuing what they wanted to do.

'Did you teach Mitch to play?' she asked as they sat down at the table.

He smiled. 'No, my dear. He taught me.'

'You took the time to learn from him?' It seemed extraordinary to Kathryn—a man of his age learning from a boy of sixteen.

'It helped me understand the power of his mind. And it is, without a doubt, the most formidable mind I've ever been challenged by. Even when he was sixteen,' he added in soft reminiscence, his eyes scanning hers as though gently probing for her understanding of it.

She smiled, speaking her own experience of Mitch. 'He cuts through all the greys and goes straight to the core of any issue.'

'Black and white,' the old man remarked, nodding thoughtfully. Then he asked, 'Does that trouble you, Kathryn?'

She shook her head. 'Not at all. I like it. He has a system of values that I feel very secure with.'

He nodded. 'When they first came here—the three boys—I asked them what they would most like to have that would make their time at Gundamurra better for them. Ric chose a camera, Johnny a guitar. Both items indicated an individual bent that was special to their natures— Ric with the vision to see and capture so much, Johnny with his love of music. But Mitch chose a chess set. Which I thought odd, because to me, it was a game that required two players. He said he could challenge himself, playing both sides.'

'You didn't believe him? Is that why you learnt?'

'No. I believed him. But it struck me he was used to being alone, living in his mind, fighting his own battles. And he'd ended up here because he didn't have the tools to take on the world by himself at the time. Learning chess gave me the time to talk about that with him. And to take some of the loneliness away.'

She looked at him appreciatively. 'You're a very remarkable person, Patrick.'

He smiled. 'They were three very remarkable boys. The most gifted of all who came through here. I always think of them as the three Ps— the passion of Ric, the pleasure of Johnny, and the power of Mitch.'

'The power...yes.' She smiled back. 'It was the first thing that struck me about him.'

'He's a warrior. Always will be. That's Mitch's nature. And the battle-ground he's chosen can be very lonely, Kathryn.'

It sounded like a warning. 'He's not alone with me, Patrick,' she assured him, certain of that in her own mind. 'And I very much support his fight to deliver justice.'

'I was thinking more...' He paused, cocking his head on one side, viewing her curiously. 'What would you have chosen, if you'd been one of the three?'

'Probably a sketch-book,' she answered without hesitation. 'I trained as a graphic artist. Part of why Ric chose me as his executive assistant. He thinks I have a good eye for the best shots.'

'But you're not ambitious for yourself?'

She sighed. 'Is that a terrible flaw in me?'

He laughed. 'We can't all be burning lights. How could they keep burning without a support system? Never underestimate the importance of support, Kathryn. An assistant who cares and shares...whose support one can always trust...there is a huge need for people like that...the nurturers of this world.'

*The nurturers of this world*...it suddenly struck Kathryn that was precisely what Patrick Maguire was—a man who had nurtured many burning lights. It was okay to assist. In fact, it was more than okay. It was a special gift in itself. Support one can always trust. Indeed, it *was* her nature to nurture. Just like her mother. Like Patrick. Except...there was one wrong note in all this...unless it could be explained.

'I noticed in the games room, you have copies of Ric's prize-winning photographs on the walls, and all of Johnny's music he's recorded...'

'But the chess table is here?'

'Yes. I just thought...well, there was nothing of Mitch in that room, and I wondered...'

'Where is he at Gundamurra?' Patrick tapped his forehead. 'In here, Kathryn. And this table is always set up ready for battle to be joined between us. We still play chess by correspondence.' He waved to the computers. 'By e-mail these days.'

'For lack of a handy partner,' she murmured, remembering Mitch's own words on their first night together.

'I'm glad he has you now, Kathryn.'

'And I'm glad he brought me to meet you, Patrick.' The man who had supported him all these years—the touching of minds that Mitch had needed, being known for who and what he was.

Ric and Johnny had shared that, too. Old friends. Special friends who understood what no-one else could without having had the experience here.

'You are very welcome, Kathryn,' Patrick said warmly. 'Very welcome.'

And she finally felt the bond—the knowing, the caring and the sharing—knew why Mitch had brought her here, why it was important to him. In a way, it was the ultimate gift of himself, the one deep insight that made sense of everything else, *if* she had the eyes to see it.

The knowing grey eyes of the old man who had seen so much were smiling at her, making her feel good about herself, good about being here with them all, reminding her what Mitch had said about the name, Gundamurra. In the Aboriginal language it meant 'good day'.

It was.

A very good day.

'Thank you, Patrick.'

He nodded and gestured to the chess pieces. 'Black or white?'

For the traditional Christmas carols session in the courtyard after dinner, Mitch had claimed the absolute centre of the lawn for him and Kathryn. They sat on the rug and cushions he'd set ready, surrounded by all the people who lived and worked on the outback sheep station. The pepper trees on the corners of the quadrangle were strung with masses of fairy lights and on the verandah facing them was a wonderfully decorated Christmas tree, under which lay Patrick's gifts for his staff and their families.

Johnny led them in the singing, playing his guitar like the virtuoso musician he was. Everyone joined in. He even had all the children marching around the courtyard to 'The Little Drummer Boy.' In between the carols, people wandered over to the verandah to fill their glasses from the keg of beer or the bowl of fruit punch, pick up a mince pie or a piece of Christmas cake. It was a very merry evening.

And Kathryn was thoroughly enjoying it, joining in, happily chatting to all and sundry as though she finally felt she fitted in here, and now saw Gundamurra as the special place it was to Mitch. He didn't know what had been said between her and Patrick over their game of chess this afternoon, but her beautiful green eyes had been shining ever since, shooting their magic sparks at him, making his heart dance with joy.

At first he'd worried that it might have been a mistake to bring her—too much to handle with Ric and Johnny here, too. Johnny, in particular, could be overwhelming company. And Patrick's daughters were no shy violets, either, always brimming with positive purpose.

These past three days, Kathryn had been sticking closely to Lara, with whom she obviously felt an empathy. But something had changed this afternoon. He sensed that whatever questions had weighed on her mind—and heart—had been answered and she was happy with the answers.

Which surely meant he could proceed with confidence.

It was simply a matter of choosing the right moment.

The carols were interrupted for Patrick to give his Christmas speech and hand out the gifts. He wore a Santa Claus cap and declared he was standing in for Santa because the kangaroos pulling the sleigh weren't hopping fast enough and wouldn't reach the outback until after midnight. Kathryn laughed and reached out to Mitch, taking his hand and squeezing it.

'He's a wonderful old man,' she said fervently.

'He is, indeed,' Mitch agreed.

'I think it was a very lucky choice...your coming here to him, Mitch. For Ric and Johnny, too.'

'You won't find any argument on that from any of us, Kathryn.'

'Thank you for sharing all this with me. It's very, very special.'

'I'm glad you find it so.'

More than glad. So much more it was impossible to put into words. It was like being reborn into a world where peace and well-being reigned. No dark shadows. No uncertainties. Pure pleasure.

They listened to Patrick, watched him having a personal word with everyone who accepted a gift from him. When that ceremony was over, they joined in a rousing chorus of 'We Wish you a Merry Christmas,' and finally a quieter, but no less feeling rendition of 'Silent Night.'

The station families trailed off to their own homes.

Patrick's *family* cleared away what needed to be taken inside, cleaning and tidying everything, ready for tomorrow. Mitch had deliberately left his rug and cushions on the lawn, and as everyone else was drifting off to bed, he steered Kathryn back outside, insisting it was a night to watch the stars for a while.

They lay together on the rug, looking up at a universe that seemed to be twinkling just for them. For Mitch, it had been a long journey to this moment, but he had no doubts about the decision hovering in his mind. It felt right now. Completely right.

'It's magic, isn't it?' Kathryn murmured, awed by the beauty of the outback night.

'Yes. But for me, the real magic is down here.'

He rolled onto his side, propped himself up on his elbow. She smiled at him. He was tempted to kiss her, but he didn't. Her answer would mean more, coming without any physical persuasion.

'Will you marry me, Kathryn?'

'Yes.' No hesitation. Not the slightest second thought. Her eyes engaged his very directly, serious now, yet glowing with an inner light that touched his soul. 'I love you, Mitch Tyler. And I now know what love is.'

'So do I. It's what I feel for you. Will you wear my ring, Kathryn?'

'Yes. For the rest of my life, Mitch.'

He took the small box out of his pocket, opened it, extracted the ring he'd chosen for her and slid it onto the third finger of her left hand. She lifted her arm to see it and the fairy lights in the trees sparkled through the deep green of the centrepiece which was set in gold and surrounded by star-like diamonds.

'An emerald...' It was a sigh of pleasure, drifting into a smile that transmitted her whole-hearted pleasure in him. 'I've always loved green.'

Then her arm lifted higher, curling around his neck, pulling him down. They kissed, pouring their love out to each other, and to Mitch the whole world felt green, like spring arriving, with all the promise of a vibrant new life taking over from a long, long winter.

His and Kathryn's life...together.

\* \* \* \* \*

265 - 395

# The Outback Bridal Rescue

# PROLOGUE

*Johnny Ellis*
*First Day at Gundamurra*

THE PLANE WAS heading down to a red dirt airstrip. Apart from the cluster of buildings that marked the sheep station of Gundamurra, there was no other habitation in sight between here and the horizon—a huge empty landscape dotted with scrubby trees.

It made Johnny think of the old country ballads about meeting and overcoming incredible hardships in places such as this. And here he was, facing the reality of it for a while. Easy enough to see why the music for those ballads was always slow. Nothing fast going on down there.

'Wish I had my camera,' Ric Donato murmured.

The remark piqued Johnny's curiosity. Apparently the stark visual impact of the place didn't intimidate Ric, though like Johnny, he'd lived all his life in the city. It seemed odd that a thieving street-kid was into photography. On the other hand, the camera comment might simply be playing it cool, making a point of not letting any fear of what was waiting for them show.

Ric looked like he'd been bred from the Italian mafia, black curly hair, olive skin, dark eyes that flashed with what Johnny thought of as dangerous intensity, but if Ric Donato had come from that kind of *family,* some smart lawyer would have got him off the charge of stealing a car and he wouldn't be on this plane with Johnny and Mitch.

'The middle of nowhere,' Mitch Tyler muttered dispiritedly, his eyes fixed on the same scene. 'I'm beginning to think I made the wrong choice.'

More gloom than cool from his other companion, Johnny thought, but then unlike himself and Ric, Mitch had a real family—mother and sister—and family couldn't visit him way out here. But choosing a year in a juvenile jail rather than the alternative sentence of six months working on a sheep station...

'Nah,' Johnny drawled with deep inner conviction. 'Anything's better than being locked up. At least we can breathe out here.'

'What? Dust?' Mitch mocked.

The plane landed, kicking up a cloud of it.

Johnny didn't care about a bit of dust. It was infinitely preferable to confinement. He hoped Mitch Tyler wasn't going to be a complete grouch for the next six months. Or a mean one, blowing up at any little aggravation. The guy had been convicted of assault. It might be true he'd only beat up on the man who'd date-raped his sister, but Johnny suspected that Mitch was wired towards fighting.

He had biting blue eyes, dark hair, a strong-boned face that somehow commanded respect. His build was lean though he had very muscular arms, and Johnny felt he might well be capable of powerful violence. Living in close quarters with him could be tricky if he didn't lighten up.

'Welcome to the great Australian Outback,' the cop escorting them said derisively. 'And just remember...if you three city smart arses want to survive, there's nowhere to run.'

All three of them ignored him. They were sixteen. Regardless of what life threw at them, they were going to survive. Besides, running would be stupid. Better to do the six months and feel free to get on with their lives, having served what the law court considered justice for their crimes.

Not that Johnny felt guilty of doing anything bad. He wasn't a drug dealer. He'd simply been doing a favour for the guys in the band, getting them a stash of marijuana to smoke after their gig at the club. They'd given him the money for it and the cops had caught him handing it over to the real dealer.

Impossible to explain he'd got the money from the musos. That would be dobbing them in and the word would go around the pop music tracks that he couldn't be trusted. Keeping mum and taking the fall was his best move. It was a big favour that could be called in when this stint on the sheep station was behind him, maybe get him a spot in a band playing guitar, even if he was only filling in for someone.

Johnny had learnt very young that pleasing people gave him the easiest track through life. It was much smarter to stay on their good side. Straying from that only brought punishment. He still had nightmares about being locked in a dark cupboard for upsetting his first foster parents. By the time he'd been placed in another home, he'd worked out how to act. It was a blueprint he always carried in his head—win friends, avoid trouble.

He hoped the owner of this place was a reasonable kind of guy, not some bastard exploiting the justice system to get a free labour force, just like some foster parents, taking money from the government for looking after kids who really had to look after themselves, in more ways than just earning their keep in those supposedly *safe* homes.

The judge had rambled on about this being a program that would get boys who'd run off the rails back to ground values, good basic stuff to teach them what real life was about.

As if they hadn't already had a gutful of real life!

And its lessons!

Still, Johnny figured he could ride this through easily enough—put a smile on his face, roll his shoulders, act willing.

The plane taxied back to where a man—the owner?—was waiting beside a four-wheel-drive Land Rover. Big man—broad-shouldered, barrel-chested, craggy weathered face, iron-grey hair. Had to be over fifty but still looking tough and formidable.

Not someone to buck, Johnny thought, though size didn't strike fear in him anymore. He'd grown big himself. Bigger than most boys at sixteen. It made other guys think twice about picking a fight with him. Not that he ever actively invited one, and wouldn't here, either. A friendly face and manner always served him best.

'John Wayne rides again,' Mitch Tyler mocked, making light of the big man waiting for them, yet his body language yelled tension.

'No horse,' Johnny tossed at him with a grin, wanting Mitch to relax, make it easier for all of them.

It won a smile. A bit twisted but a smile nonetheless. It gave Johnny some hope that Mitch might loosen up, given time and if they were treated reasonably well here.

He caught Ric Donato looking curiously at him and wondered what he was thinking. Dismissing him as harmless? No threat? Possibly good company? What did he see?

Johnny tried envisaging himself objectively—a hunky guy who wouldn't be out of place in the front row of a football team, streaky brown hair that invariably flopped over his forehead because of a cowlick near his right temple, eyes that had a mix of green and brown in them and a twinkle of good humour that Johnny had assiduously cultivated, a mouth full of good white teeth which certainly helped to make a smile infectious.

Even so, he was no competition for Ric Donato in the good looks department. Girls probably fell all over him. Which was what had got him into trouble, stealing a Porsche to show off to some rich chick. Johnny had no time for girls yet. He just wanted to play his own music, get into a band, go on the road.

The plane came to a halt.

The cop told them to get their duffle bags from under the back seats. A few minutes later he was leading them out to a way of life which was far, far removed from anything the three of them had known before.

The initial introduction was ominous, striking bad chords in Johnny.

'Here are your boys, Maguire. Straight off the city streets for you to whip into shape.'

The big old man—and he sure was big close up—gave the cop a steely look. 'That's not how we do things out here.' The words were softly spoken but they carried a confident authority that scorned any need for abusive tactics.

He nodded to the three of them, offering a measure of respect. 'I'm Patrick Maguire. Welcome to Gundamurra. In the Aboriginal language, that means "Good day." I hope you will all eventually feel it was a good day when you first set foot on my place.'

Johnny's bad feelings simmered down. It was okay. Patrick Maguire's little speech had a welcoming ring to it, no punishment intended. Nevertheless, a strong sense of caution had Johnny intently watching the big man's approach to Mitch, the first in line.

'And you are...?' The massive hand he held out looked suspiciously like a bone-cruncher.

'Mitch Tyler,' came the slightly belligerent reply. Mitch met the hand with his own in a kind of defiant challenge.

'Good to meet you, Mitch.'

A normal handshake, no attempt to dominate.

Johnny's smile was designed to disarm but it had more than a touch of relief in it as he quickly offered his hand in greeting, being next in line. 'Johnny Ellis. Good to meet you, Mr Maguire.'

The steely-grey gaze returned a weighing look that made Johnny feel he was being measured in terms far different to what he was used to. His stomach contracted nervously as the warm handclasp seemed to get right under his skin, seeking all he kept hidden.

His determinedly fixed smile evoked only a hint of amusement in the grey eyes, causing an unaccustomed sense of confusion in Johnny as Patrick Maguire finally released his hand and moved on to Ric who introduced himself far more coolly, not giving anything away.

'Ready to go?' the old man asked him.

'Yeah. I'm ready.' Aggression in this reply.

Ready to take on the whole damned world if Ric had to, Johnny interpreted, and wondered if Patrick Maguire was looking for that kind of spirit. Had he himself failed some test by appearing too easygoing?

Didn't matter.

All he had to do was ride through the six months here with the least amount of trouble. He might not be a fighter like Ric and Mitch but he knew how to survive, and head-on clashes weren't his style. Reading the lay of the land, adjusting to it, accommodating it...that was the way to go for Johnny Ellis.

Yet as Patrick Maguire stood back and cast his gaze along the three of them, taking in his new recruits for outback tuition, he nodded, as though approving each one. Johnny's stomach relaxed, feeling good vibes coming from the man. Somehow he had passed the test, whatever it was. He was accepted.

So Gundamurra shouldn't be a bad place to be. The old man had said it meant "good day." Johnny decided he could do with a lot of good days. No worries. No stress. No angling for some step that would help him get where he wanted to go in the music world. He could let all that wait for six months, settle in and enjoy the wide open spaces.

Yeah...he was ready for this.

Probably more so than Ric or Mitch.

Though he hoped the three of them could establish and maintain friendly relations while they were here.

It was beyond Johnny Ellis's imagination that a friendship would evolve that would last the rest of their lives, intertwining through all that was important to them...being there for each other in times of need, understanding where they were coming from and why.

The bond of Gundamurra was about to be forged.

And at the heart of it was Patrick Maguire, the man who would become the father they'd never known, a man who listened to the people they were, learning their individual strengths, guiding them towards paths that could lead towards successful futures, encouraging them to fly as only they could...and always, always, welcoming them home.

# CHAPTER ONE

*Twenty-two years later...*

JOHNNY ELLIS RODE into the old western town that had been built for the movie. Behind him was the Arizona desert. In front of him was the film crew, cameras rolling. It was all he could do to keep a straight face, in keeping with the character he was playing—cowboy on a mission.

An inner grin was twitching at the corners of his mouth. On the country and western music scene, he'd made it to the top, selling umpteen platinum albums of his songs, but this was Johnny's first movie and he was having fun, doing something beyond even his wildest dreams.

Having learnt to ride at Gundamurra, he was a natural on a horse, and being big and tall—there weren't many movie stars with his physique—had snagged him the part. Of course, he did have a box-office name, too, a point his agent had made much of. Whatever...he was here doing it, and it sure tickled him to think of himself as following in John Wayne's footsteps.

Mitch and Ric had laughed about it, too.

But he had to be dead serious now. The cameras were zeroing in to do close-ups. Time to dismount, tie his reins to the rail, walk into the saloon, cowboy on a mission. This was the last take of the day, the light was right for it, and Johnny didn't want to mess it up. He was a professional performer, used to being onstage, and getting it right was second nature to him.

He didn't miss a step. The saloon doors swung shut behind him and the director yelled, 'Cut!' Johnny allowed himself a grin as he came back out to the street, confident there'd be no need to do this scene again. The grin grew wider when he spotted Ric Donato lurking behind the camera crew.

His old friend had made the time to come!

Johnny had invited him to the film set, the moment Ric had called to say he was in L.A., checking on that branch of his worldwide photographic business. It was a pity Lara and the kids weren't with him. Ric's wife was one lovely lady and their children had the trick of melting Johnny's heart, they were just so endearing. Little Patrick, who'd turned three just before last Christmas, would have loved a ride in the camera crane.

'Great to see you, Ric!' He greeted his old friend with immense pleasure. 'Want to be introduced around?'

'No.'

The quick and sober reply took Johnny aback. He instantly regrouped, seeing that Ric didn't look too good. In fact, he looked downright pained, something bad eating at him. No happy flash in his usually brilliant dark eyes. They were dull, sick.

'Could we go to your trailer, Johnny? Have some privacy?'

'Sure.'

He gestured the way and they walked side by side, not touching. Any other time Johnny would have thrown an arm around Ric's shoulders, hugging his pleasure in his friend's company, but that didn't feel right, not with Ric so uptight and closed into himself. Johnny's stomach started churning. It always did when he sensed something bad coming.

He couldn't wait until they reached his trailer.

'What is it, Ric? Tell me!' he demanded grimly.

A deep, pent-up breath was expelled. 'I had a call from Mitch,' he stated flatly. 'Megan called him.'

'Megan Maguire?'

A vivid image of Patrick Maguire's youngest daughter instantly flew into Johnny's mind—a wild bunch of red curls, freckled face, eyes the grey of stormy clouds, always projecting fierce independence, spurning his every offer of help with work on the station, defying him to imply in any way that she wasn't fit and able to run Gundamurra just as well as her father did.

Which was probably true. She'd worked towards it, not wanting to do anything else with her life. Johnny knew he'd never made any criticism of that choice. He actually admired her very capable handling of the work she did. What he didn't understand was why she couldn't just ride along with his company whenever he visited, make him as welcome as her father did. She invariably shunned him as much as possible and when she couldn't, her scorn of *his* chosen career invariably slipped out.

Yet she'd liked listening to him play his guitar when she was a kid, hanging on his every word when he sang. Why she'd grown up into such a hard, judgemental woman he didn't know, but be damned if he'd let her attitude towards him keep him away from Gundamurra. Patrick was like a father to him. Best father any guy could have.

'Patrick...' He felt it in his gut. 'Something's happened to Patrick.'

Another hissed breath from Ric, then... 'He's dead, Johnny.'

Shock slammed into his heart. His feet stopped walking. He shook his head, refusing to believe it. Denial gravelled from his throat as it started choking up. 'No...no...'

'Two nights ago,' Ric said in a tone that made the fact unequivocal, and he went on, quietly hammering home the intolerable truth. 'He died in his bed. His heart gave out. No-one knew until the next morning. Megan found him. Nothing could be done, Johnny. He was gone.'

Gone...

Leaving a huge black hole—a bottomless pit that Johnny kept tumbling down. He was barely aware of Ric's hand gripping his elbow, steering him. His feet moved automatically. He saw nothing. It wasn't until Ric thrust a glass of whisky into his hand that he realised he was sitting on the couch in the mobile home provided by the movie company.

'It's a hell of a blow. For all of us, Johnny.'

He nodded. Couldn't speak. Forced a swallow of whisky down his throat.

'I've booked flights to Australia for both of us. I guess you'll need to clear that with your people here. Might mean a delay in their schedule if they can't shoot around your absence.'

The movie...meaningless now.

The deep ache of loss consumed him. Ric had Lara and their children.

Mitch had Kathryn, with a baby on the way. They'd both made homes of their own. For Johnny, Gundamurra and Patrick was home, and with Patrick gone...it was like having the roots of his life torn out of him.

There was no longer any reason for him to go back.

Megan wouldn't want him there.

But he had to go back this one last time...say goodbye to the man who'd always treated him as a son, even though he was no blood relation. Megan couldn't begrudge him that. Ric and Mitch would be there with him. All three of them, remembering what Patrick had given them... the big heart of the man...

Why had it stopped?

He looked up at Ric, his inner anguish bursting into speech. 'He was only in his seventies.'

'Seventy-four,' came the quiet confirmation.

'He was so strong. He should have lived to a hundred, at least.'

'I guess we all thought that, Johnny.'

'It's only been three months since Christmas. He looked well then. Same as ever.'

Ric shook his head. 'There were no warning signs. Maybe the stress of the drought, having to kill so many sheep, lay off staff...'

'I offered help. Whatever was needed to tide them over, see them through the drought however long it went on. You know I've got money to burn, Ric.'

Ric's mouth twisted into an ironic grimace. 'I made the same offer. Most likely Mitch did, too.'

'He helped us, dammit! Why couldn't he let us help him?' Johnny's hands clenched. 'I bet it was Megan who wouldn't take what we offered. Too much damned pride. And Patrick wouldn't go against her.'

'Don't blame Megan, Johnny. She's got enough to carry without a load of guilt over her father's death. I'd deal kindly with her if I were you. Very kindly. Patrick would want you to.'

'Yes, I know, I know...' He unclenched his hands, opening them in a helpless gesture. 'I'll miss him.'

Ric nodded, looked away, but not before Johnny caught the sheen of moisture glittering in his dark eyes. It was a heart-twisting reminder that Patrick had been like a father to all three of them, not just him. Ric was hurting, too. And Mitch...

Mitch was probably already at Gundamurra, giving whatever support was needed, making the legal business of death as easy as he could. Being a top-line lawyer, he'd do that for Patrick's daughters. There wasn't just Megan to consider, but Jessie and Emily, as well. They'd all be in shock. Ric was right. Patrick would expect *his boys* to deal kindly with them.

'We don't know why he died,' Ric said brusquely. 'Maybe it was just... his time to go. No point in railing against it, Johnny. We've got to get moving to make the flights home. Are you okay to do whatever you've got to do before we leave?'

He gulped down some more whisky. It helped burn away the welling of tears behind his eyes. 'Ready to go,' he asserted just as brusquely, rising to his feet. 'Let me make a few calls first, clear the way.'

Helicopter to Phoenix, flight to Los Angeles...many hours passed before Ric and Johnny could finally board the Qantas jet to Sydney and settle in their seats for the longest leg of their journey over the Pacific Ocean. The flight steward offered them champagne. They both declined, choosing orange juice instead. It was not a time for champagne.

A question had been niggling at Johnny. 'Why didn't Mitch call me direct? It would have saved you coming to get me, Ric.'

'We thought it was better this way...the two of us travelling together.'

'Well, I'm glad to have your company but we could have linked up here for this flight.'

Ric slanted him a wry look. 'You might not have co-operated with that plan. You have a habit of doing things your own way. This course ensured I'd be with you.'

Johnny frowned. 'You thought I needed my hand held?'

'No. It's all a matter of timing. There's more, Johnny. Mitch didn't want to load it on you all at once over the phone. He gave that job to me with the advice to let you get over the shock of Patrick's death first.'

The nerves in his stomach started knotting up again. 'So hit me with *the more*. I'm sitting down and locked in. What else do I have to absorb?'

Ric looked at him, decided he was ready for it, and let him have it. 'Patrick's will. Mitch held it. He's opened it.'

'Well, that can't be bad.' Instant relief. 'Patrick was always fair.'

'Prepare yourself for another shock, Johnny. There's a huge mortgage on Gundamurra and you're about to inherit half of it.'

'What?' Incredulity blanked out several million brain cells.

'Not quite half. You get forty-nine percent of Gundamurra and Megan gets fifty-one, leaving her in the driver's seat where she's always expected to be. But she won't have expected to share her inheritance with you, Johnny. The normal thing would be a three-way split with her sisters.'

Co-owner of Gundamurra with Megan?

'Mitch thought you should be prepared...get your head around it before we arrive at Gundamurra,' Ric went on.

Johnny's head was spinning.

What did it mean?

Why would Patrick cut out his two older daughters?

Why make him co-owner rather than Ric or Mitch?

A sense of horror billowed through him. He reached out and gripped his friend's arm. 'I didn't ask for this, Ric. I swear I knew nothing about it.'

'I didn't think you did, Johnny,' Ric assured him. 'I have no doubt Patrick planned it himself.'

'But why me? It's not right, not...' His mind fumbled for words. 'Did he...did he explain to Mitch when he drafted the will?'

Ric shook his head. 'Mitch wasn't in on drafting it. Patrick did it himself and sent it to him sealed for safe-keeping two months ago.'

'Two months...' Johnny shook his head in bewilderment. 'He must have made up his mind after Christmas.'

'Maybe he knew he didn't have long to live.'

'Dammit! Why wouldn't he tell us? We were all at Gundamurra for Christmas.'

'If Patrick thought it was the last one for him, he wouldn't have wanted to spoil it.'

'But...' Johnny lifted his hands in helpless frustration.

'Want to know what Mitch thinks?'

He waved a go-ahead, completely beyond imagining what had motivated such an extraordinary step.

'Patrick elected you to save Gundamurra. It's highly unlikely that Megan can do it by herself. The way things are going with the drought, she won't be able to service the mortgage. And it was you who always thought of it as home. Not me. Not Mitch. You.'

Johnny frowned. 'Mitch had a home with his mother and sister, but I thought you...' He searched Ric's eyes.

A very direct gaze accompanied his reply. 'You needed it more than I did, Johnny. And you can't deny it touches something in your soul. It comes out in your songs.'

Need...yes. There was so much hype and superficial crap in the career he had chosen, so much touring to make his success stick, it was the thought of Gundamurra that kept him sane, grounded, and going back there always put his world in perspective again—what was real, what wasn't.

'It won't be the same without Patrick.' Grief squeezed his heart. '*He* was the soul of Gundamurra.'

'You're forgetting Megan.'

*Megan.*

His mind shied away from thinking of her right now. Already he could see those stormy grey eyes hating him for being given half of *her place,* wishing he'd never set foot on Gundamurra, let alone have any claim on it.

'Patrick forgot his other daughters, Jessie and Emily,' he said, tearing his mind off the one daughter who'd become such a nagging thorn in his side.

'They've both made their lives away from Gundamurra and Patrick financed their ambitions,' Ric reminded him. 'I think they'll feel they've had their share. Jessie has her medical degree and the women's clinic she wanted at Alice Springs. Emily has her helicopter business at Cairns. The money to set them up was taken out of Gundamurra, probably contributing to the current debt. They can't be unaware of that.'

True enough, Johnny silently acknowledged, yet the family home was the family home. Leaving them out and putting him in might very well stir a sense of injustice. He couldn't help but feel uncomfortable about this inheritance on many counts. On the other hand, *Patrick had wanted him there* and it was impossible to discount a decision which would not have been taken lightly.

'It's up to you and Megan to pull Gundamurra through this bad patch and revive it, Johnny,' Ric gravely assured him. 'Patrick got it right.' He sighed and softly added, 'He always got it right.'

It was some relief that Ric thought so.

Mitch, too, apparently.

But no way was Megan was going to accept it gracefully.

Jessie and Emily might not, either, though Ric was right about their interests lying elsewhere and Patrick had put large investments behind their chosen careers. Besides which, both of them were married to men who shared those interests, Jessie's husband being a doctor for the Royal Doctor Flying Service, and Emily's husband a fellow helicopter pilot.

Only Megan was unmarried.

Not surprising with her bristling form of feminism, Johnny thought, wishing she'd stayed in the sweetly amenable little sister mould that he'd always found so engaging. *That* much younger Megan had never minded him stepping in and helping.

The flight steward came and took their glasses. The plane was about to take off. Johnny leaned back in his seat, closed his eyes and tried to relax. Fourteen hours to Sydney. Then the flight to Gundamurra in the far north west of New South Wales...the outback.

He felt the pull of it in his mind...the vast, seemingly empty land, wide-open space, searingly blue sky. It had a rhythm all its own—one that always felt good. The only jarring note was Megan standing in the middle of it, waiting for him, furiously frustrated because she had to share Gundamurra with *him*.

Had Patrick got it right?

The financial part, yes. Johnny could pour millions into Gundamurra without a pang of personal loss. Mortgage gone with a simple transfer of money. Plus all the investment Megan needed to maintain the sheep station, eventually making it into a thriving concern again. But she certainly wouldn't welcome him into the life there. Over the past few years, her eyes had been branding him as an unwanted intruder, wanting him out.

*But I'm in,* Johnny thought on a surge of grim determination to keep what Patrick had granted him, regardless of Megan's reaction to it. He was co-owner. That gave him the right to be at Gundamurra whenever he wanted to and Megan would just have to stomach having him as her helpmate. Maybe, given time, he could whittle away whatever prejudice she had against him.

The leaden weight of grief eased as a strong sense of purpose grew. The outback was primitive—man against nature—a constant challenge that had to be won, just to survive, let alone prosper.

Above all else, Johnny was a survivor.

He wanted this challenge. Maybe he needed it. So come what might, he was going to hold his ground on Gundamurra. Patrick had entrusted it to him.

# CHAPTER TWO

MEGAN FINISHED DOING her morning rounds, ensuring her work orders were being followed, checking for any problems, chatting to the families who still lived on the station, subtly assuring them that the status quo was not about to change. They were to carry on as usual.

She should have felt relieved that the sombre mood hanging over everyone for the past few days had lifted this morning, but the reason for it was a major irritant. *Johnny had arrived.* Never mind that Ric Donato and Mitch Tyler were also here. It was Johnny who put smiles on everyone's faces. Just the thought of him was enough to do it.

Charm...

It was as natural to him as breathing.

And it always reminded her what a hopelessly naive little fool she'd been to see it as something else when applied to her. There was no differentiation. He ladled it out to one and all—his trademark in the pop world where he was a big star, a master of light entertainment. It meant nothing. Absolutely nothing.

Having finally recognised that, she'd tried to bury the hurt of it and move on. It would have helped if he'd gone completely out of her life—out of sight, out of mind—but he kept coming back, making her feel bad about herself because it was stupid, stupid, stupid to still feel attracted to him. His interests lay elsewhere, wrapped up with his glittering successes overseas. Their lives did not mix. Never would.

Why hadn't her father seen that?

Why?

Had he only thought of the money needed—choosing the one person who could probably shed a few million dollars without even noticing it was gone?

Money as meaningless as charm.

Megan grimly determined to accept only what she absolutely had to in order to keep Gundamurra running. There was no avoiding confronting Johnny Ellis over what was to be done. He was here now, having come yesterday with Ric, flying his own plane in as he always did.

No doubt Mitch had told him about the will. Though even without that pressing business, he wouldn't have stayed away, not from her father's funeral. She could only hope that having started a new career in movies, he might be content to be an absent shareholder in Gundamurra. After all, her father was gone. No more *mentoring* readily available from Patrick Maguire.

As she walked back to the homestead, tears blurred her eyes. She didn't want to feel betrayed by what her father had done, yet the grief of losing him was so much harder to bear because he'd left her in this intolerable position of having to accept Johnny Ellis as co-owner of Gundamurra.

Her shock at the terms of the will had been followed by a wild surge of rebellion, a violent need to fight it. She'd argued fiercely with her sisters, but Jessie's and Emily's flat refusal to go against their father's decision left her without any support from them in a legal action to have it overturned.

In sheer desperation she'd broached the issue with Mitch Tyler, putting to him that Johnny might well have unfairly influenced her father. After all, she'd argued bitterly, he wasn't known as Johnny *Charm* for nothing.

Those laser-blue eyes of Mitch's had cut her down for even suggesting it, and his subsequent words had shamed her. 'Is that worthy of your father, Megan?'

He'd waited for her answer.

When she'd maintained a stubborn silence, squirming inside at the pertinent criticism of her viewpoint, Mitch had flatly stated, 'If you want to dishonour his will, I'm not your man. I'm here on Patrick's behalf, to help facilitate what *he* wanted. It's the very least I owe him for all he did for me.'

His high-minded integrity had goaded her into trying to bring it down a peg or two, force out some human weakness in him, make him empathise with what she was feeling. 'Why Johnny? My father took you in, too. And Ric. The three of you stayed in his life. Don't you feel slighted that he passed you over for...for a pop-star?'

It wouldn't have been so...difficult...having to share the property with either of his other *boys*. And there was no denying she needed help in these current circumstances. Ric would have dealt delicately with the problems, caring about her feelings. Mitch would have handled her needs from the city with efficiency and absolute integrity. But Johnny Ellis...whose whole life was about playing to an audience who loved him?

Mitch's straight black brows had beetled down. 'You don't understand your father's choice?'

'Do you?' she'd challenged.

'Yes. So does Ric. I think you need to talk to Johnny before taking any hostile step, Megan. You might not ever appreciate where he's come from, but...'

'I know what he is now,' she'd snapped.

'You've just pasted a label on the man which I know to be very superficial, Megan. Johnny has not yet reached the fulfilment of the person he is. I think...' He'd paused, his gravity giving way to a gleam of whimsical irony. 'Did Patrick teach you to play chess?'

'Yes. We played sometimes.'

'He always favoured a knight attack.'

'What has that got to do with anything?'

'It was a strategy, Megan. Your father thought out his strategies very carefully. Don't devalue the thought he put into his will when you talk to Johnny. Remember that Gundamurra was Patrick's life, as well as yours, and he knew how to share it.'

The sting of those words still hurt. She wasn't mean-hearted. She hadn't felt jealous of her father's pride in his three bad boys who'd made good. Nor of his affection for them.

She just didn't want Johnny Ellis constantly trampling through her life. She wished he'd married one of the gorgeous women he mixed with in his star-studded world so he wasn't free to drop in on her world whenever he liked.

At least, after the funeral, he'd have to go back to his cowboy movie. Hopefully he'd ride off into the sunset—anywhere else but here! She didn't begrudge him the fulfilment he was still looking for, as long as he stayed away and left her free to hold the reins at Gundamurra.

Maybe he could be persuaded to do just that.

With this purpose burning in her mind, Megan headed for the homestead kitchen. If Johnny was not still sleeping after his long trip from the U.S., he'd be there, being fed by Evelyn who'd be fussing over him with sickening adoration.

The housekeeper had been with the Maguire family all her life, born on the sheep station, and trained by Megan's mother to run the household with meticulous efficiency, just as she herself always had before cancer had taken her life. Everyone loved and respected Evelyn, but her attitude towards Johnny Ellis—as though the sun shone out of him—grated terribly on Megan.

It was bad enough that she never tired of listening to his songs, playing them over and over again. No doubt she'd be cooking up all his favourite foods, regardless of the current strict budget. Megan tried not to feel too critical of this indulgence as she opened the kitchen door... and came to an embarrassed halt, finding the highly dependable housekeeper weeping on Johnny Ellis's big, broad shoulder, his cheek rubbing the top of her head, one brawny arm holding her while the other was engaged in delivering soothing pats on her back.

It was instantly clear that the grief Evelyn had held in the past few days had suddenly overflowed and Johnny was comforting her. Megan stood rooted to the spot, realising that she and her sisters, wrapped in their own loss, had taken Evelyn's services to them for granted, not really considering that she, too, might feel devastated by their father's sudden death. It was Johnny who was giving her what she needed, sympathetic understanding and a shoulder to cry on.

*What I need, too.*

A painful loneliness stabbed through Megan's heart. Jessie and Emily had their husbands. Ric and Mitch had their wives. With her father gone, she had no-one to hold her, soothe her pain. And the sight of Johnny Ellis embracing Evelyn made it worse.

It wasn't fair that he looked like a strong, steady rock to lean on. His life was all about *image,* Megan fiercely told herself. Her gaze fixed scornfully on his riding boots—still playing the cowboy role—then noted how the denim of his jeans was tightly stretched around his powerful thighs, showing off how solidly built he was.

No doubt his female fans swooned over his macho sexiness, imagining his private parts were the ultimate in virility. Megan wondered just how many women didn't have to imagine, having known him intimately. Did he have a different one every night? Two or three a day?

It would have to be so easy for him, a mere crook of the finger. His star status would assure him of groupies everywhere. Though strictly on a male appeal level, he had the lot anyway; impressive physique, a very masculine face accentuated by a squarish jawline, a strong, almost triangular nose with its flaring nostrils, wickedly twinkling greenish eyes which were quite strikingly complemented by tanned skin and toffee-coloured hair, and, of course, the wide mouthful of white teeth that flashed winning smiles everywhere, not to mention the million-dollar voice.

Which suddenly crooned, 'I think this is the time for me to make *you* a cup of tea, Evelyn.'

The weeping had stopped.

With a choked little laugh, Evelyn lifted her head. 'No...no...' she said chidingly, reaching up to pat his cheek as he gently released her from his embrace. 'Thank you for letting me unburden my sorrows, but don't be taking away my pleasures now. You sit yourself down and let me get busy.'

Megan hadn't gathered wits enough to effect a swift retreat before the two of them moved apart and Johnny's swinging gaze caught her in the open doorway. Her stomach lurched as their eyes locked and she felt the sympathy he'd given to Evelyn being transmitted to her. She didn't want it from him. Didn't need anything from *him.* And be damned if she'd cry on his shoulder!

'Megan...come on in,' he invited, his hand beckoning her forward, taking charge, assuming control!

*Not of me! Never!* Megan silently and savagely vowed.

'Evelyn was just telling me about your father...how he'd been clutching your mother's photograph from the bedside table in his hand when you found him,' he went on softly, sadly. 'I guess—'

'Yes.' She cut him off, feeling tears welling up again. 'I hope he's with my mother now. He missed her very much.' Fighting her way out of a storm of emotion, she waspishly added, 'I wonder if you'll ever know that kind of love, Johnny?'

His face tightened as though she had slapped him.

Evelyn gave a shocked gasp.

Acutely aware that the personal remark had slipped out of her previous thoughts and was totally inexcusable, Megan almost bit her tongue in chagrin. She had to deal with this man. That was best done by keeping as much *impersonal* distance from him as possible.

'I think finding that kind of love is rather rare in today's world,' Johnny answered in a measured tone.

'Especially yours,' flew out of her mouth before she could stop it.

'Miss Megan…'

Evelyn's reproof faded into a heavy sigh.

Megan gritted her teeth, refusing to take back what she believed. She glared defiance at the man who'd probably slept with thousands of women without giving any one of them any serious commitment. Her words had clearly struck a nerve and she took fierce satisfaction in the way his eyes glittered at her. No sympathy now.

'Rare in your world, too, Megan,' he countered, using his voice like a silky whip. 'Unless you've met the man of your dreams since Christmas.'

'Too busy,' she loftily retorted.

'Which reminds me…'

'We need to talk,' she leapt in before he could take charge of their *business* meeting. 'When you've finished your breakfast, perhaps you wouldn't mind coming to the office.'

'Whatever suits you,' he returned obligingly.

'That will be most appropriate. You'll find me there.'

She quickly closed the door and strode outside, marching off a mountain of turbulent energy as she headed for the front entrance of the homestead and the steps leading up to the verandah which skirted the huge house—a verandah that welcomed people out of the sun that could too often be pitiless in the Australian Outback.

She hadn't welcomed Johnny Ellis.

Couldn't welcome him.

Having reached the top of the steps she turned, her gaze skating around all the outbuildings that made Gundamurra look like a small township from the air; the big maintenance and shearing sheds, the prize rams' enclosure attached to the lab, the cottages for the long-term staff, the bunkhouse for jackaroos, the cook's quarters, the supplies store, the schoolhouse.

She was twenty-eight years old and this was her life—the life she'd chosen—the life she loved.

She didn't *need* a man.

Certainly not a man who peddled charm.

What she needed was this whole area to be an oasis of green again. Even the foliage on the pepper trees looked brown, coated with dust. All the land to the horizon was brown, and above it the sky was a blaze of blue, no clouds, no chance of rain.

If only the Big Wet had come this year, breaking the drought, her father might not have decided to write that will, making Johnny Ellis a permanent fixture in her life. The pressing question now was…how was she going to pry him out of it? Or at least, minimise his presence to next to nothing.

He didn't belong here.

With this thought firmly entrenched in her mind, Megan went inside, passing through the great hall that bisected this section of the homestead, moving onto the verandah that skirted the inner quadrangle, heading straight for her father's office.

Once there, she found herself drawn to the chess table by the window, remembering what Mitch had said, that her father thought through his strategies very carefully. The black and white pieces were set up ready to play, which had to mean his last game with Mitch—played by e-mail— had been completed.

Game over, she thought, and on a deep wave of sadness, laid the black king down. She stared at the white knight, fretting further over why her father had thought Johnny Ellis was the right man to ride in to the rescue, then gave up on trying to figure it out and moved on to sit in the large leather chair behind the desk.

It was a big chair made for a big man. Physically she didn't fit it, never would, but at least her father had granted her the right to sit here in his place, and no way in the world was she going to let Johnny Ellis occupy it while they talked.

He was ten years her senior but that didn't give him any authority over her or what was to be decided in this room. It was she who owned fifty-one percent of Gundamurra...she who had the whip hand...and all the millions he'd made as a pop-star could not change that!

# CHAPTER THREE

*DEAL KINDLY WITH her...*

Ric's admonition was playing through Johnny's mind as he approached Patrick's office, but Megan's attitude towards him made it damned difficult to keep it fixed there. Icy politeness from her last night and the least possible amount of contact. This morning, rejecting his sympathy point-blank, actually turning it into one of her snide hits on him, not even caring that Evelyn heard it, too.

All the same, he shouldn't have let himself be goaded into hitting back. Especially about the lack of any special love in her life. That was a low blow, especially when she'd just lost her father. Johnny grimaced over the insensitive lapse in his control. He had to do better in this meeting, not let Megan get under his skin. He was older than she was, had more people skills. It was up to him to...*deal kindly with her.*

At least he didn't have to worry about Jessie's and Emily's feelings. The two older sisters had welcomed him warmly last night, making it clear that their only concern was Megan's future on Gundamurra. The situation on the sheep station was grim. Like Patrick, they were counting on him to ensure there was a future here for her.

And he'd do it.

Even against Megan's prickly opposition he'd do it.

Though he hoped she'd be reasonable.

The situation demanded she be reasonable.

He paused at the office door, took a deep, calming breath, gave a courtesy knock to warn of his imminent entry, allowed Megan a few seconds to get her mind into appropriate gear, then moved in with every intention of being at his diplomatic best.

But he wasn't prepared for the scene Megan had set and his sense of rightness was instantly jolted. She was sitting in Patrick's chair, taking Patrick's place before he was even buried. It was too soon. It was...

Johnny checked himself, took stock of the woman he had to deal with.

The defiance in her eyes could mean she was making a statement by taking her father's chair—a statement of empowerment that she might feel a need for in this situation. And being seated there put the desk between them, a decisive distance that possibly suggested she was feeling vulnerable about having to deal with him.

They were the kindest thoughts Johnny could come up with.

'Megan,' he acknowledged softly, nodding for her to take the lead in this meeting.

'It was good of you to come, Johnny...'

Which was a pleasant enough greeting until she added, '...being in the middle of shooting your first movie.'

Kind thoughts flew out the window. He eyeballed her in furious challenge, every muscle in his body taut with aggression at this belittling of his feelings for her father. Patrick had been the most important person in his life and Megan could not be ignorant of how very much their relationship had meant to him.

Not one word passed his lips, but the force of his anger obviously got through to her. A tide of heat burned up her neck and scorched her cheeks, lighting up the freckles that added a cuteness to her pert little nose. Except Johnny wasn't thinking *cute* right now. He was thinking *little*. No way was she big enough to take over from her father, not in any sense.

She gestured to the chairs at the chess table, her gaze shifting from his. 'Please take a seat.' The words were husky, as though she was pushing them through a very tight throat.

Satisfied that he'd wrung some shame from her, Johnny stepped over to the chess table to move Mitch's chair—not Patrick's—into a face-to-face position with Megan. The fallen black king caught his eye. What was this? The king is dead...long live the queen?

Johnny pulled himself up again. Mitch might have laid the chess piece down—a symbol of Patrick resting in peace. Leaping to hasty and possibly false conclusions was not conducive to a fair meeting. He rolled the chair out from the table and closer to the desk, then sat down, telling himself to watch and listen, refrain from stirring any more hostility in Megan's mind. Though what he'd ever done to earn it was a total mystery to him.

He stared at her, waiting for her to start. The scarlet heat had receded from her face, leaving her skin pale and the freckles more prominent. She wore no make-up, hadn't done for years, though he remembered her experimenting with it in her teens. She'd been a happier person then, enjoying his company. They'd had fun together, laughing easily, chatting easily. Then she'd gone away to some agricultural college and something had changed her.

She could have been quite strikingly beautiful if she'd put her mind to it...good bones, big expressive eyes that could twinkle like silver or brood like storm clouds, a full-lipped mouth when it wasn't thinned with disapproval of him, and a glorious mane of red curls, currently pulled back into some tight clip at the back of her neck. A lovely long neck it was, too.

Apparently she didn't care how she looked. Being a woman was not her thing. When had she last worn a dress? A checked shirt and jeans was her usual garb, as it was today. Maybe she wanted to look like a man in them but she didn't.

As much as she might try to minimise her femininity, her figure was too curvaceous for anyone to mistake her for a male. In fact, her antagonism towards him over the past few years had made him acutely aware of her as a woman, especially when she turned her back on him, her taut cheeky bottom wagging her disdain of what he stood for in her eyes, stirring feelings in him that were entirely inappropriate, given she was Patrick's daughter.

Did she resent having been a daughter instead of a son?

Was that why she looked so sourly on him...because he had a similar physique to her father?

Johnny hadn't meant to speak first, yet the question that rose in his mind seemed imperative, at the very core of the situation that had to be settled between them. The words tumbled out, seeking the answer that might make sense of Megan Maguire's attitude towards him.

'What happened to the girl who used to like me?'

*I grew up.*

Megan wasn't about to give that answer, nor explain the milestones that had marked her passage to where she was now. She looked at Johnny Ellis, knowing he was thirty-eight, yet the years sat so easily on him, she could still see the sixteen-year-old boy who'd made up songs for her when she was just a little kid—songs that had generated dreams that were never going to come true for her.

The monumental crush she'd had on him in her teens had finally bitten the dust when he hadn't come home for her twenty-first birthday. She'd planned for him to see her as a woman, but her coming of age had obviously meant nothing to him. He'd stayed in the U.S., busy with his career, and no doubt involved with the kind of woman who shared his limelight. She was just Patrick Maguire's youngest daughter, someone he was nice to when it suited him to visit Gundamurra.

Facile charm.

Meaningless.

It was her father who'd drawn him back to Gundamurra...her father who had given him almost half of it in his will, trapping her into this ridiculous and frustrating partnership with a man whose life was aimed at adding more stars to his celebrity status.

'Do you need everyone to like you, Johnny?' she lightly taunted, hoping he'd hightail it back to Hollywood where everybody probably fawned on him.

He shrugged, his eyes holding hers in challenge. 'Usually I know why not. Where you're concerned, I'm at a total loss, Megan. What have I done to you to warrant your dislike? Best spit it out now before we get into business together.'

'What reason could I have for disliking you, Johnny?' she countered. 'You've always been charming to me.' Which was absolutely true. 'As for doing business together,' she quickly ran on, 'I don't imagine you'll want to take an active part in running Gundamurra. You do have a movie to finish and probably many more in your pipeline.'

'No. Just the one. Which I'm committed to by contract,' he stated drily. 'Undoubtedly, people will wait to see how well I perform on screen before other offers come in.'

'Oh, I'm sure with your star quality—'

'Let's not speculate on a hypothetical future, Megan,' he cut in. 'We're here to discuss the far more immediate future of Gundamurra, are we not?' He cocked a challenging eyebrow at her. 'Can we be honest about that?'

She felt herself burning again. She'd thought a bit of flattery—pandering to the ego that stars of his magnitude had to have—would set the scene she wanted to play through with him. But his eyes were seeing straight through that ploy, mocking her attempt to manipulate what she saw as his push to be loved by more and more fans through the movies he could make.

'You need not be concerned about the running of Gundamurra, Johnny. I'll be doing that,' she stated with grim determination.

'I don't doubt you're capable of it, Megan, given enough resources to ride through the drought. That's where I come in.'

The lack of resources…there was no denying that, though there'd been no mismanagement. Her father had taken out the first big loan from the bank to finance Emily's helicopter business, before the drought started biting deep. Then to keep the sheep alive, keep paying wages, more loans…and wool prices had dropped. The mortgage now was so big, Megan didn't know how she could service it with no relief from the drought in sight. Even if it rained tomorrow, she'd need recovery time.

A rescue package had to be accepted from Johnny Ellis if she was to keep Gundamurra. Except it wasn't entirely hers to keep. It was his, too. And she still didn't know how he wanted to work their partnership. He'd just denied her any sense of security about him going away and staying away.

'We need an injection of funds,' she admitted flatly.

He nodded. 'I'll wipe out the mortgage today, get the bank off your back.'

Just like that! Megan instantly bridled at how easy it was for him while she had sweated over every dollar being spent. 'No, you won't!' The denial exploded from a deep well of pride.

He frowned. 'I have the funds, Megan.'

'I don't want to owe you fifty-one percent of the mortgage.' She glared defiantly at him. 'If you pay off forty-nine percent of it, I can get another loan from the bank which could see me through...'

'Why put yourself through that worry when you don't have to?' he argued, waving an impatient dismissal of her counterproposal.

'Because I won't take your charity,' she shot back at him.

'Charity?'

He rose from his chair, glaring down at her from his formidable height, a big man, as big as her father had been, emanating a power that wanted to blast her point of view to smithereens. He raised a clenched fist, shaking it as he spoke with more passion than she'd ever heard from Johnny Charm.

'I owe *my life* to this place. I don't want to see it go under. I didn't like seeing it struggle to survive. I offered your father...'

He closed his mouth into a tightly compressed line, shutting down on the vehement flow of emotion.

What had he offered her father, Megan thought wildly. What? Had it influenced the terms of the will?

Johnny stepped forward, pressed his hands on the desk, leaning forward, his eyes firing bullets at her. 'I now have the right to do what I'm going to do. Patrick gave me the right.'

'He didn't give you the right to interfere with my share,' she fired back, refusing to be intimidated into being indebted to him.

'You can pay me back when you can, Megan. If you must. But the bank is not going to have any claim on Gundamurra.'

'Even if I let you do that, I'll have to borrow again to keep going,' she pointed out, mocking his ignorance of what had to be done.

'No. I'll set up an account for you to draw from,' came the swift reply. He was all primed to fix everything with his money.

Her jaw set stubbornly. 'I won't accept that.'

'You don't know how long this drought will last.'

'I'll manage it my way.'

Frustration boiled through Johnny. Megan would put Gundamurra at risk again and there was no need for it. He wanted to pick her up and shake some sense into her, but there was steel in the grey eyes so fiercely defying him—Patrick's eyes—and he knew he had to find another way of convincing her to use the money he could provide.

He straightened up, turned away, walked over to the window, stared out at the one patch of green left on Gundamurra—the homestead quadrangle. Not all the millions of dollars he had available could turn the rest of the vast sheep station green. Only rain could do that. Lots of rain.

However, an unencumbered supply of funds could pay for feed to be trucked in. It could pay wages. It could make life absolutely secure for everyone here, bring back those who'd had to leave. They could comfortably wait out the drought, be ready for the good times to come again.

'Would you prefer me to buy you out, Megan?' he tossed at her with little hope.

'No,' came the firm and predictable reply. Her eyes said she'd have to be forcibly dragged off Gundamurra, no letting it go of her own free will.

He shrugged. 'I thought, since you dislike having to deal with me so much…'

'You overstepped the line, Johnny,' she informed him rigidly. 'By all means wipe out your share of the mortgage. That's your right.'

'Fine!' he snapped. 'Do you want to draw a line through Gundamurra, divide it up so I can pour whatever funds I like into salvaging my forty-nine percent of it?'

*Treat her kindly…*

Maybe there was truth in the old adage that one had to be cruel to be kind.

Her jaw clenched. 'My father wouldn't have wanted that,' she grated out.

'Have you stopped to think of what your father did want…instead of what *you* want?'

'He didn't accept your money while he was alive.'

He pounced on that statement, inflamed by her antagonism towards him. 'Because *you* argued against it?'

'No. I didn't know about any offer. You just mentioned it yourself, Johnny.'

Her eyes were clearly weighing its effect on Patrick's will. He blasted her calculation by informing her, 'Ric and Mitch offered help, too. All three of us, Megan.'

Confusion looked back at him. 'Then why choose *you?*'

It was eating at her. 'Would Ric or Mitch have been more acceptable to you?' he tested, wanting to know if his friends were equally unwelcome in her life.

'That's not the question,' she snapped evasively.

'I think it's pertinent. Why not me?' he challenged.

Intriguing to watch the flush come again, sweeping into her cheeks with blazing heat. She dropped her gaze and fiercely claimed, 'I can manage on my own. With the mortgage reduced, I can...'

'What if you can't? Why risk it?' He paused, sure now in his own mind that *he* was the problem. 'Is your dislike of me so great that you can't bear to let me help?'

'I don't dislike you! It's just not right!' she burst out, banging her own hands on the desk as she leaned forward to deliver this declaration with vehemence.

'Then what would make it right for you, Megan?'

The storm of feeling in her eyes gave way to a dull bleakness. Johnny read the answer in her mind— *Nothing.* Was she looking down a black pit, too, with her father dead?

'I don't know. I don't know,' she muttered, shaking her head over the wretched admission and sagging back in the chair, shoulders slumped in defeat.

She looked so miserable, for the second time this morning, Johnny felt the urge to pick her up, but not to shake her, to wrap her in a comforting embrace and promise her he would make everything better. He remembered doing that when she was a little kid. She'd been running to tell him something and fallen over, scraping her knees—such a sweet little girl, clinging to him, trusting him to make the hurt go away.

He'd loved that little girl.

Patrick's youngest daughter.

Maybe that was what Patrick's will was about...taking care of Megan. But how was he to do it?

His gaze dropped to the chess table.

What was the phrase used where no-one could win?

Stalemate.

He had to start again, adopt a strategy that would get past Megan's pride. If she really didn't dislike him, there had to be other factors involved in her attitude towards him, perhaps a love affair gone wrong when she'd been at that agricultural college, seeding some drive to prove herself completely independent, basing her whole future on taking over from her father. If she was stuck in that groove, how could he ease her out of it?

Not by anything she perceived as charity.

Slowly, accompanied by a weird sense of many factors pushing it, an idea came to him.

It was totally wild. Absurdly quixotic. Yet the more he thought about it the more it appealed to him. On many levels. Especially the prospect of wearing down Megan's resistance to it, winning her over.

Though that mission could well prove impossible.

Still, something was needed to break this hopeless impasse and the shock of his offer might open Megan up more, give him an understanding of how she viewed him. He certainly had nothing to lose by putting it on the table. In heaping more scorn on him, she would have to give reasons for it, reasons he could work on.

He pasted an ironic little smile on his mouth and aimed it at her. 'You know, Megan, you'd have the right to all I could provide...if you married me.'

# CHAPTER FOUR

*MARRY HIM...*

Megan felt her jaw drop in sheer shock.

Incredulity blanked her mind for several seconds.

Her heart rocketed around her chest in some stupid manic excitement until the words that had preceded Johnny's proposal hit home, firing up a surge of anger that lifted her right out of her father's chair to hurl a furious rejection at him.

'You think I'd marry you for your money?'

She didn't wait for a reply, so totally incensed by the suggestion, she flew straight into attack. 'How dare you lump me with the kind of women who hang off you for what you can give them?' Her arms scissored a dismissal of absolute disgust. 'Which just goes to prove how tainted your thinking is by the life you lead. Buy a woman here. Buy a woman there. Have one in every port of call.'

Her mocking hands landed on her hips, planting themselves there in a belligerent flaunting of her own femininity which wasn't for sale. 'Well, not at Gundamurra. Not even if I was reduced to eating dirt would I join that queue for your favours.'

He had the gall to look amused, his eyes twinkling unholy mischief at her as he observed, 'So, you see me as some indiscriminate sex machine, churning through women at a rate of knots, probably not even remembering their names.'

She glared back at him, wishing she hadn't let her tongue loose on this theme.

He strolled towards her, gesturing an open invitation to continue. 'I'd like to hear what evidence you have that formed this picture of me.'

'Oh, don't pretend there haven't been swarms of groupies after you,' she snapped, folding her arms across her chest to contain herself against the strength of his attraction as he came at her. 'Anyone in a sweet shop gets tempted to taste,' she fired to pull him up short.

It didn't so much as make him pause. He hitched himself onto the other side of her father's desk, bringing his eye level down to a very direct line with hers, holding her gaze with a mocking intensity that squeezed her heart, making it thump in painful protest.

'Did you ever make these comments about me to your father, Megan?'

'No. Why would I? I'm sure he understood where you were at, Johnny,' she returned with acid emphasis.

'Yes, he did. He took the time to understand exactly where I was at when I was sixteen.'

'Sixteen.' She rolled her eyes. 'You weren't a huge star then.'

'No. I was a street-kid, whose only knowledge of how life worked was firmly planted in being used and using back, perpetuating a system of abuse.'

She frowned, not relating to this picture at all. 'I remember you as always being a happy person.'

He shrugged. 'I'd learnt that a smile could ward off many evils, as well as hide what no-one wants to know about.'

'Huh!' she pounced. 'I knew the legendary charm was all a pose.'

The satisfaction in her voice drew a quizzical look from him. 'It began as a survival tactic. But now I like to make people feel good. Is that so wrong to you?'

'It's deceptive.'

'Deceptive?' he repeated critically, goading her into ignoring a defensive caution.

'It draws people into thinking they're special to you and they're not. They don't really touch your life at all.'

'Every person is special, Megan.' His eyes bored into hers, rattling her deep box of resentments as his voice gathered an emotional vehemence. 'Didn't your father teach you that? Didn't your father show, by example, that he believed it? And lived by it?'

His gaze moved to the chair she had vacated in her anger, and the look on his face—the raw anguish of wanting to see her father there and knowing he never could be again—made her realise how offensive it had been to him to find her sitting in it, assuming a place that was irreplaceable in his mind.

He nodded to the chair. 'Patrick taught me to value my own individuality. He explained why I shouldn't let myself be used, why I shouldn't accept any more abuse, how allowing it diminished the person I could be, and if I held on to a strong belief in the music I personally loved and trod my own path, I could climb out of the belittling pattern of use and abuse which had been my life for as long as I could remember.'

*Abuse...* She hadn't thought about his life before he came to Gundamurra. Mitch had said something about her not appreciating where Johnny had come from. Had he suffered a traumatic childhood? But that was so long ago. He'd become so successful, it couldn't still shadow his life...could it?

He turned a fierce glittery look back to her. 'So I am who I am, Megan. I don't have to belittle anyone else to make myself bigger. I don't abuse the position I have by taking what is offered to me for all the wrong reasons. Far from being *tempted by the sweet shop,* I feel sorry for the people who populate it because they have never learnt to value themselves. They think if they get a piece of me, it will make their lives better. But it won't. Any change for the better has to come from within.'

It was an impressive speech, forcing her to reassess how she'd painted his life in her mind. Okay, he'd stepped away from continuing a cycle of abuse. Yes, she could see her father's hand in that. But rejecting every attractive 'freebie' that came his way?

'I don't screw my fans, Megan,' he went on, obviously reading the doubt in her eyes. 'But they do touch my life and I try to touch theirs through the lyrics of my songs, which carry the same set of values that your father taught me. Patrick knew that. I don't know why you think otherwise.'

Oh, great! Now it was Saint Johnny, as well as the king of charm. 'You're a man!' she flashed at him, unable to swallow such a pinnacle of nobility. 'As for your songs, isn't it simply clever commercialism to tap into the dreams people nurse for themselves? That's street smart, Johnny.'

His eyes raked her derisively. 'And you want to put me back in the gutter where I belong. Is that it, Megan?'

'No. You're perfectly welcome to the brilliant heights of Hollywood.'

'As long as I leave Gundamurra to you. To an embittered woman who'd rather let it die than accept the help of *a man*.'

The sudden counterattack shocked her into hot denial. 'I am not an embittered woman!'

'What happened to you? Did you feel *used* by a man? Did he only want sex from you instead of the whole package?'

'That's none of your business!'

'Oh, yes, it is, Megan. You've made it my business by the way you treat me, giving me the low-life status of a rutting animal that doesn't care what body he uses for sexual release.'

'Okay! So you don't do that,' she granted, though some defence was called for. 'You can't blame me for thinking it. Pop-stars are notorious for taking what they can.'

'Except I don't have that reputation. Yet you lumped me with it anyway. Because I'm *a man?*'

'Because you're Johnny Charm,' she jeered, hating the way he was turning the tables on her, digging into her life. 'And you can't deny that draws a lot of women to you.'

'But not Megan Maguire,' he mocked. '*She* won't be one of the herd. *She'll* stand aloof and scorn his company.'

That was too close. Far too close. She lashed back. 'What's the matter, Johnny? You can't stand not having everyone worship you?'

He bored in again. 'Why have you been so ready and willing to give me feet of clay, Megan? I haven't used you or abused you. Did the guy you fell for at agricultural college turn out to be a womaniser, charming his way into one bed after another?'

'Why haven't you married if you're not a womaniser yourself?' she retorted, fighting for any foothold that would exonerate her attitude.

He grimaced, his expression changing to an inner musing. 'There wasn't anyone I could bring here. Not one in all these years.' He shook his head, shifted off the desk, a wry look on his face as he turned away from her and strolled back towards the chess table. 'Ric had no hesitation in bringing Lara here...'

Megan couldn't see the relevance. Lara had needed a safe refuge. What better place than an outback sheep station?

'...Mitch brought Kathryn...'

He picked up the black king she had laid down on the chess table, his thumb running over the carved wood as though he wished he could bring it to life. Was he remembering that her father had played chess with Kathryn, as well as Mitch?

'They understood about Patrick. About Gundamurra,' he went on, his voice dropping to the soft deep timbre that invariably stirred an emotional response in his songs. 'They could take it on board, accept it, appreciate it, live with it.'

But they didn't live here, Megan corrected in her mind. Their lives were centred in the city.

He placed the king back on the chess table, standing it upright, nodding to it as though in respect, then swinging around to face her with a rueful little smile. 'The companions I've had from time to time were happy to share Johnny Charm's life, but they wouldn't have wanted Johnny Ellis.'

She shook her head in confusion. 'You've lost me.'

'Oh, I lost you a long time ago, Megan,' he drawled, cocking his head to one side as he looked her over in a distant, objective appraisal. 'I think you lost yourself, as well. You do your utmost to deny that you're a woman, neutering your femininity in men's clothes, scraping back your hair...'

'That's purely practical for the work I do,' she defended hotly.

His gaze dropped to her folded arms. 'Whole body language telegraphing *keep away*. That guy at college sure must have done a number on you. I would have thought Patrick's daughter would have had guts enough not to be a victim, to know her own worth...'

'I do, dammit!' She flung out her arms in defiance of his reading. 'Which is why I won't be bought with a marriage proposal from you!'

'That was more a provocative thought than a proposal, Megan.' His mouth curled in sardonic humour. 'And it did provoke quite a lot, didn't it?'

She burned over how much she had revealed. He hadn't even been serious. He'd set a trap and she'd leapt right into it. The urge to return to her father's chair, regain the authority she needed, had her swinging towards it, but the realisation hit her that Johnny would despise her if she claimed that seat again in these current circumstances.

Somehow she had to snatch some initiative. Reversing direction, she rounded the desk, placing herself against the front of it, hands propped on the edge, adopting a commanding though relaxed position, and tossed out the only thing she could think of to put Johnny Ellis on his back foot.

'What if I'd said I *would* marry you?'

He had the nerve to grin at her, a grin she wished she could smack right off his face. Topping that irritation came his totally rocking reply, 'Then we could very well be planning a wedding.'

He didn't mean it. Of course, he didn't mean it! He was watching her, watching for a chink in her armour through which he could draw more blood. She tossed her head disdainfully and scoffed, 'You've got to be joking.'

'Am I? It wasn't so long ago that marriage was all about consolidating property.' His eyes seemed to sizzle a challenge at her as he added, '*And* having heirs to it.'

Her stomach contracted at the thought of Johnny Ellis fathering her children. Her mind savagely denied any desire for a sexual connection with him and snatched at a pointedly mocking reply. 'We don't live in feudal times anymore and I would hate being stuck in a loveless marriage while my husband gallivanted around the world doing his thing.'

His eyebrows lifted in equally mocking surprise. 'I thought you'd settled on Gundamurra as the love of your life. Why would you care what your husband did as long as he provided you with a future here?'

He was twisting everything around to make the unacceptable sound reasonable. She had to end this ridiculous conversation. 'I'll make my own future,' she stated emphatically.

'Which you'll have to share with me, anyway,' he reminded her.

'Not...intimately!'

'It could be productive.'

'Oh, stop it, Johnny!' she burst out in frustration, pushing off the front of the desk and almost folding her arms again, stopping herself by clenching her hands at her sides and flaming at him, 'Don't play this stupid game with me!'

He instantly sobered. 'Not so stupid, Megan. It uncovered a prejudice you've been nursing for years. An unjust prejudice. I hope you'll now lay it aside so we can be friends.'

She didn't want to be *friends* with him. She wanted...

'Friends with a common purpose,' he went on. 'To save Gundamurra. It doesn't matter where I'm coming from. It doesn't matter where you're coming from. We both care about this place. So just let it be, Megan. I supply the money. You put it to good use. It's as simple as that. And what your father wanted.'

She looked at Johnny Ellis and saw a mountain of unshakeable purpose.

He wasn't going to go away until she agreed.

Fighting him was futile.

Worse...it stirred up all she had to keep hidden from him.

Her father had ordained this.

Her father...

A huge lump of emotion blocked her throat. Tears pricked her eyes. She jerked into action, walking around the desk again, pausing by her father's chair, her hand sliding up the worn leather of the back rest, gripping the top of its wooden frame, wanting the strength that had been embodied in this chair to seep into her. She swallowed hard and forced out the words that had to be said.

'All right. You supply the money and I'll use it however it will best serve Gundamurra. If you'll go and get Mitch now, we'll sort out the necessary financial arrangements.'

'Megan...'

The soft caress of his voice shivered down her spine. 'Please...just go.'

She heard him heave a long sigh. 'I just wanted to say... I know you consider Gundamurra as your birthright and you see me as an intruder. But in a very real sense, I was reborn here. It's home to me, too. It always will be.'

*Always...*

A shudder ran through her. Every muscle in her body tensed as she heard him move, relaxing only when she heard the office door being opened and shut.

Gone.

But he'd be back.

And if this was home to him, even without her father here, he might always come back. He had every right to. He owned forty-nine percent of Gundamurra. There was no escape from sharing it with him.

What if she said she would marry him?

Would he really marry her...forsaking all others...till death do they part?

A pipedream.

A stupid, stupid pipedream!

The reality was he'd go off about his business whenever it suited him—a business *she* couldn't share because Gundamurra needed all her time and attention—and she'd be left wondering who *was* sharing his life away from her.

A great marriage that would be!

But if he was unfaithful to her, she could divorce him and maybe get his share of Gundamurra in the settlement.

Dear God! She was thinking like a bitch! A horrible, nasty bitch! All because... She closed her eyes and dredged up the real truth...the truth that had been festering behind all her responses to Johnny Ellis since she'd been old enough to acknowledge the deep down craving. She wanted him to love her. Love her as the one and only woman he wanted.

# CHAPTER FIVE

IT HAD BEEN a long tension-filled day for Johnny and he was glad when Mitch and Ric suggested a stroll down to the jackeroos' bunkhouse after dinner. The women were occupied, going through the funeral arrangements for the following day. Jessie's and Emily's husbands had retreated to the games room for a quiet game of billiards. Soon they would all go to bed, make it an early night, because tomorrow...was the last farewell.

It was a relief to be outside under the outback sky with its brilliant canopy of stars—a relief for it to be just the three of them for a while—old friends who'd forged an understanding that didn't need words. They'd come here for six months when they were sixteen, and here they were again, twenty-two years later, silently sharing memories that belonged only to them...and the man whose spirit they carried in their minds.

'Is Megan okay with you, Johnny?' Ric asked.

'She has accepted my financial help,' he answered.

'I told Ric the rescue package is in place,' Mitch put in. 'That's not what he's asking, Johnny.'

He heaved a rueful sigh. 'She's moved from hostile to passive neutral. I'm working on it, Ric. Given time...'

'You don't have much time,' came the quiet reminder.

'It's hard for Megan to see past my...other interests. But I think we broke some barriers today.'

'I'm worried about her,' Mitch said. 'She looked and sounded...defeated.'

Johnny frowned over the description, not liking it.

'Megan is Patrick's daughter. She'll fight her way up again.'

'Be good if you could make it to friends before you leave, Johnny,' Ric observed.

'I'm working on it,' he repeated.

'Problem is...she's so young,' Mitch commented.

'Not young for what she does here. She can handle it. I have no doubts on that score,' Johnny said with certainty.

'I meant...young...for understanding about you. You're a bit of a cowboy, Johnny. I hope you didn't ride too roughshod over her this morning.'

'Roughshod! Let me tell you, if I'm a cowboy, she's one hell of a prickly cactus.'

Ric laughed. 'Got under your skin, did she?'

More than Johnny was prepared to admit. 'I told you... I'm working on it.'

'Smooth it over,' Mitch advised. 'You're good at that.'

Except his *charm* didn't work with Megan.

Ric had the final word. 'Make friends with her.'

*Friends*...

Johnny was having severe problems with that concept.

Easy enough to say it as a pacifier—*friends with a common purpose*. It had been the safest thing to say to Megan in the circumstances. And he had to give her credit for trying to proceed on that basis. She'd stopped her snide attacks on him, been amenable to the financial arrangements he and Mitch had set up—absolutely no argument there—and after lunch, she'd willingly laid out to him the most urgent problems to be dealt with at Gundamurra.

Yet there was a sick distance in her eyes, a dull flatness to her voice, and while Johnny could respect the consummate knowledge and experience she'd displayed where the running of the sheep station was concerned, he'd been constantly distracted by the urge to cosset and comfort her. Not as a child, either.

He'd found himself becoming more and more conscious of her as a woman, studying her mouth, her ears, the few little curly tendrils of hair that hadn't made it into the tight confinement of the clip at the back of her neck, the shape of her hands, the nervous mannerism she had of running her thumb over her fingerpads, making him want to wrap his own hand around hers and smooth away the fretting.

All the talk about sexual experience this morning had its influence, as well, stirring a host of tantalising thoughts, and urges that weren't so high-minded. Had she ever known real pleasure with a man, or had the guy—guys?—she'd known at college been the crass sort who cared only about their own satisfaction? He suspected she'd been tightly buttoned up for years and that wasn't right. He wanted to free her from those bad memories, make her stop wasting herself.

Or did he simply *want* her?

Certainly her fiery pride had stirred a caveman streak in him that itched to carry her off to bed, strip her of the clothes she wore to deny her sexuality, and force her to acknowledge she was a woman with needs that could be answered if she'd submit to letting it happen with him.

But she was dead against him as a man.

Much less a husband...

And there was no denying he had to get back to Arizona to finish the movie, leaving her in charge of Gundamurra. This was not the time to make any move on Megan. His top priority was to establish and reinforce a working relationship that benefited the drought-stricken sheep station. When he returned—and that was months away—she might look more kindly on him. It would be good to see warmth in her eyes. Oddly enough, he'd preferred the sparks of scorn to bleak grey.

The bunkhouse was empty—no jackaroos in residence. Gundamurra was operating with only permanent staff who lived in cottages on the property.

The three of them automatically headed for the bunks they had once occupied, flopping onto them, stretching out, remembering the fears and griefs and dreams they had shared in the darkness of long-ago nights.

They talked about Patrick, as only they could.

For Johnny, it reinforced all he felt about Gundamurra.

He made up his mind to take time out from his career once the movie was finished, come back and stay, find out if it held enough to keep him happy here. His life had moved a long way since he was sixteen. It had been quite a journey with many satisfying milestones, yet the tug of home had never been diminished.

And now Patrick had called him home.

His last will and testament.

Share Gundamurra with Megan.

Or should he give it up to her? Save it from bankruptcy, ensure it could continue running without any insurmountable disaster laying it completely to waste, then leave it to his daughter—a gift in return for the gift of life Patrick had held out to him.

What had been in Patrick's mind when he'd written that will?

Johnny felt honour-bound to get it right.

But what was right?

His mind was torn in many directions and he couldn't bring himself to talk them through with Ric and Mitch. The feelings he had about Megan were too private. And very possibly it would be wrong to act on them.

Eventually they left the bunkhouse, said goodnight to each other. Johnny felt a stab of envy as his old friends went off to bed where the women who loved them would be waiting—women who knew and understood all about them and loved who they were. He walked alone around the verandah that skirted the inner quadrangle of the four-winged homestead, stopped at the door to his bedroom, felt too restless to go inside.

He moved over to the verandah railing, leaning on it as he gazed out at the one square of lawn on Gundamurra that was still alive, watered by an underground bore, piped in especially to keep this grass green. Patrick's wife had insisted on it. She was happy to live in the outback, as long as she had one square of green to look at. Pepper trees had been planted at each corner of the quadrangle to provide shade for the bench seats placed under them.

This was where everyone on the station gathered on Christmas Eve, singing carols, making merry. Johnny usually led them in the singing, playing his guitar, sitting on that bench...

He jolted upright.

Someone was sitting there now.

Megan.

He knew it instinctively.

Megan alone...as he was.

He didn't stop to think she might want to be left to herself. His feet moved straight into action. The compulsion to close the distance between them pounded through Johnny's heart. She didn't have to be alone. He didn't want her to feel alone. Patrick had willed him to be here for her.

Megan's pulse rocketed into overdrive.

Johnny had seen her.

He was coming.

She'd meant to speak to him, had sat out here in the hope of catching him before he went to bed, yet courage had failed her when the opportunity had come. He'd been with Ric and Mitch, revisiting the bunkhouse, and she'd suddenly felt hopelessly young, having understood nothing of their backgrounds—how bad it had been for them—because she'd only been six years old when they'd first come to Gundamurra.

Maybe the age gap was too big for her ever to cross.

Stupid dreams...

Why couldn't she let them go?

'Mind if I join you, Megan?' His voice was soft and deep, seeming to carry the dark loneliness of the night.

She looked up. A big man. As big as her father. Broad shoulders. Ready and willing to carry the weight of Gundamurra on them. For her father. For her.

But *with* her? For the rest of their lives?

Her chest tightened up. She took a deep breath, fiercely told herself she had to be fair, and said, 'I'd like you to, Johnny.'

He settled on the seat beside her, leaning forward, his forearms resting on his thighs, hands linked between his knees. 'I miss him, too, Megan,' he said softly, 'though I guess your sense of loss encompasses much more, having been with your father every day, working with him...'

'Don't!' She swallowed hard to press back the swift welling of grief. 'I need to talk to you about...about something else,' she rushed out.

'Whatever you want,' he gruffly offered.

*Want*... He didn't have a clue what she *wanted* of him. Was it so hopeless? He hadn't married. Hadn't met anyone he felt right about bringing here. If she showed him she understood something of what he felt... though she didn't really. His pop-star life kept getting in the way.

He turned towards her, reached across and took her hand from her lap, wrapping his around it, holding it still. 'You'll wear your fingerprints out doing that,' he gently chided. 'Come on, Megan. Spit it out. You had no hesitation in letting me have it straight between the eyes this morning.'

'But my aim was wrong, Johnny. I wanted to shoot you down in flames and...and I had it so screwed up...'

'It's okay,' he soothed.

'It's not okay!' she flared, not wanting to be *indulged*. 'Mitch told me I didn't know where you were coming from and I just brushed that aside because I didn't want to see...didn't want to know any good reason for Dad choosing *you.*'

'I'm sorry it was such a bad shock, on top of everything else.'

His thumb caressed her palm, sending warm tingles right up her arm. It was difficult to keep her mind focussed on what had to be said. All her defensive instincts were urging her to reject his touch, not let herself feel this treacherous thrill of pleasure in it. Yet if she stopped being negative, stopped fighting...

'I never asked Dad about you...' she blurted out, determined on at least clearing the air between them. '...about your life before you came here. You were just Johnny to me. Then later on you were Johnny, the star, making a big name for yourself.'

'All through your childhood and teen years, I liked the fact I was just Johnny to you, Megan. I would have liked it to stay that way. I had more than enough people only seeing me as a star,' he said drily.

She was glad he couldn't see the angst stirred by that statement. 'I'm sorry I took a...a bad view of you.'

Whether he sensed the angst, she didn't know, but he instantly injected some humour into his tone, trying to lighten the conversation. 'Well, it was certainly a change from the usual reaction I got from women. Brought me down to earth with a thump every time I came back to Gundamurra.'

'Stop it, Johnny!' she cried in exasperation. 'I don't want your charm. I'd rather know what's behind it.'

She sought his eyes but he looked away, his gaze lifting to the stars in the sky. His hand started to squeeze hers, then relaxed again, as though he was very conscious of not transmitting tension. Yet she sensed it was coiled inside him, wound tightly around whatever it was he didn't want to reveal.

'When the three of you went off to the bunkhouse tonight, I had a talk with Lara and Kathryn,' she pressed on. 'I didn't know what any of you had done to bring you here to Dad in the first place. I learnt a lot about Ric's background. And Mitch's. But they couldn't tell me anything about you, Johnny.'

'They had nothing to tell about me because there is nothing,' he stated tersely. 'Both Ric and Mitch have a family history. I don't.'

'But you must have a history,' Megan persisted, determined to know. 'Even an orphan has a history.'

'None that I remember.' He shot her a glittery look. 'I was told my mother was a prostitute who died of a heroine overdose when I was two years old. No-one claimed me and I was placed in foster care. Whoever my biological father was—' he shook his head '—no way of knowing.'

A two-year-old. Megan wondered how long it was before someone had found him after his mother had overdosed. Probably best that he didn't remember.

'Your father was a father to me, Megan.'

Yes, she understood that. Yet… 'What of your foster parents, Johnny?'

Again he shook his head. 'There are people who should never be put in charge of children. I dropped out of the system when I was twelve. Went on the streets.'

Megan was shocked. He had spoken about abuse this morning, but how much abuse? What kind? She sensed he wasn't about to tell her. He was brushing over the bare facts as it was. She moved on to what he might answer.

'What about your education?'

'The best education I got was from your father. It has served me far better than any academic learning could.'

Her father again. She hadn't realised how very much he'd meant to a boy whose life had been empty of caring. Worse…a life that had surely been coloured by total mistrust of anyone—a smile to ward off evils.

'Where did you learn music?' she asked.

'The technical stuff from musicians. Guys in bands. But I made music in my head from very early on. It blocked out other things.'

And she had mocked his music as clever commercialism!

From what he'd said, even his songs were linked to what her father had taught him. Probably everything Johnny was now could be linked back to her father.

'Dad gave you a guitar,' she remembered.

'Yes, he did. I still have it. It's the one I play for our Christmas carols.'

What he'd been given here meant so much to him. So much. And her father had known it.

Why choose Johnny Ellis?

Because Johnny had been more *his adopted son* than the others?

Was she more his daughter than Jessie and Emily?

She liked to think so, yet she had no doubt he'd loved them all, each for her own different and very individual qualities. She hadn't ever really appreciated how lucky she and her sisters had been—brought up in an environment where caring for them was taken for granted, parents who loved them, listened to them, did their best to provide whatever was needed so they could pursue their interests.

Her childhood had been very happy. Her teens had been mostly a fun time, though she'd missed Gundamurra while she was at boarding school. It was only her fixation on Johnny that had blighted her later years.

Not his fault.

She'd acted like a spoiled bitch because he hadn't come to her party, hadn't fulfilled the role she'd cast for him. So she'd cast him in another role that didn't fit him, either.

Well, her perception of him had certainly been changed today. The problem was…it made him even more attractive to her.

'I haven't said I'm sorry…for *your* loss.' She squeezed his hand to impress her sincerity on him. 'I am, Johnny.'

His gaze swung back to her and it seemed to hold the dark intensity of eternal night—no stars. 'Will you stand with me tomorrow? At the graveside? Patrick put us together, Megan. I want us to be together.'

Her own desire for togetherness with him—far beyond what he was asking—zinged through her entire body, twisting her insides, heating her blood. She hoped he couldn't see the rush of heat to her face. 'Yes,' she whispered, her throat almost too tight to speak.

'Thank you.'

For a moment the air seemed charged with a sense of closeness that wildly fired up all Megan's hopes and dreams. Johnny rose to his feet, pulling her up with him. Her heart started galloping. He dropped her hand and she thought he meant to draw her into an embrace. The yearning for it inside her swamped any cautious thought she might have had.

She heard his sharply indrawn breath, saw his broad chest lift, expand,

and looked up to find his head bent towards hers. His hands clamped around her upper arms. His gaze fastened on her mouth. Her own pent-up breath parted her lips. Anticipation kicked through her mind, scattering all her wits. He was going to kiss her. Johnny Ellis was going to kiss her.

But he spoke instead.

'I always used to think of you as my little sister, Megan.'

No-o-o-o... The silent scream reverberated around her head.

'If you could think of me...as your big brother...standing by you...'

No...no...no!

'...I think your father would like that.'

Rebellion cried this had nothing to do with her father. Nothing!

'You should go to bed and try to rest now,' he said, his smile a twist of brotherly caring. And he dropped a kiss on *her forehead.* 'Goodnight, Megan.'

He released her arms, backed off, turned, and headed across the lawn to the guest wing which housed his room.

She clenched her hands, the urge to fight, to hurl herself after him and beat out every shred of brotherly feeling, was barely containable. Pride forced her to hold still. Common sense directed her to go to her own room, shut the door and wait until tomorrow.

Tomorrow she would show him she was a woman, not a little girl. Her femininity would not be *neutered* by men's clothes. As for her hair...

She would *show* him.

No way was she going to let him pigeonhole her as *his little sister!*

# CHAPTER SIX

JOHNNY WAS TOTALLY stunned by Megan's appearance the next morning. Not only was she wearing a curve-hugging black suit with a flirty little frill at the bottom of her skirt—drawing attention to the feminine shapeliness of her calves, fine ankles, and feet shod in sexy black high heels—but her hair was...positively mesmerising.

All throughout breakfast he could not stop looking at it. Usually she wore it in pigtails or scaped into a knot, tightly confined, with a hat crammed over it more often than not. He could not remember ever seeing it like this—lustrous red-gold waves springing softly from her head, cascading into curls that bounced alluringly around her shoulders. It looked so vivid against the paleness of her skin, and formed an amazingly rich, sensual contrast to her sombre attire.

Her face seemed different, too. Maybe it was the startling beauty of her hair framing it, or the subtle touches of make-up—brows pencilled a shade darker, a smoky shadow applied to her eyelids, enhancing the shape and size of her eyes, lending a more feminine mystique to their sharp directness, and the red-brown lipstick certainly added an enticing lushness to her mouth. He had imagined she could look quite striking if she tried. He simply wasn't prepared for...stunning!

She wore a double strand of pearls around her throat. They looked like the pearls he'd chosen for her twenty-first birthday. A grown-up

necklace he'd thought at the time, something really good to commemo-
rate her coming of age, Patrick's youngest daughter. He'd bought them
in Broome, Picard pearls, the best in the world. He'd meant to present
them himself at Megan's birthday party, but Liesel—leaving her had
been impossible just then.

Seven years since Megan had turned twenty-one.

He'd sent the pearls and forgotten about them.

There had been Liesel's death...and all the promise of her talent lost.
Now Patrick's death.

He should be thinking of the man, not his daughter.

Johnny tried to keep his mind focussed on paying his last respects to
Patrick Maguire. Yet even at the funeral service his attention was split.
Megan sat beside him and every time she bent her head he was distracted
by the rippling flow of her hair, the scent of it reminding him of fresh
lemons, slightly tart but light and refreshing, completely unlike the erotic
muskiness of other women's perfume.

And she stood beside him as Patrick was buried in the designated plot
beside his beloved wife. With the extra elevation of high heels, the top
of her head came up to his chin. Not as little as he had thought her. She
held herself with very straight and tall dignity. Patrick would have been
proud of her.

Afterwards, when they returned to the homestead, Johnny could not
stop his gaze from following her every move—greeting the guests who'd
flown in to attend the wake, graciously listening to what they wanted
to say, serving them with drinks or food. Many people *he* didn't know
had come, but *she* knew them all and their connections to her father. It
brought home to Johnny that this was her life and he had only ever been
a visitor to Gundamurra, not an integral part of it.

The people who lived on the station knew him, welcomed his company, chatted to him. Somehow it wasn't enough. He wanted to be at
Megan's side, sharing the responsibilities of outback hospitality, familiar with everything that was familiar to her. The sense of being an outsider—*the pop-star*—grated on him, especially when Megan's attention
was courted by young men attached to other pastoral properties.

Men who were smitten by the way she looked today.

Men who won kind smiles from her.

Men who might be eager to offer themselves as partners, given some sign of encouragement.

Johnny's charm started to wear thin.

A previously unknown possessive streak hit him, driving him to insert himself into the private little *tête-à-têtes* these men sought with Megan, making his presence at her side felt and forcibly acknowledged. Though that didn't work too well. He found himself viewed as a curiosity, not a threat to their interests.

He managed to hold himself back from crassly declaring that *he* now owned forty-nine percent of Gundamurra, which he'd saved from the brink of bankruptcy, so Patrick's daughter was not quite the attractive prospect they might imagine her to be. Futile move anyway, he argued to himself. How she looked today was drawcard enough.

Perhaps he was less than subtle in cutting out one guy who was definitely coming on to her. Megan threw him a look of exasperation and grittily declared, 'I do not need a big brother standing over me, Johnny.'

He'd never felt less like a big brother.

'Seems like you're not sour on all men after all,' he shot back at her.

Her eyes widened.

Johnny realised he sounded jealous. He *was* jealous. He wished he'd given in to the temptation to kiss her last night, kiss her so hard she wouldn't be thinking of giving any other guy the time of day. He wanted to grab her arm and haul her away from everyone else right now, have her to himself, convince her that he was the man for her.

But was he?

And what damage might he do to the working partnership they had to have, if he made the move and it was wrong for her?

'I'm just trying to be as good a hostess as my mother,' she said, her chin lifting in defiance of his criticism.

'Right! Well, I'll leave you to it.'

He backed off, sternly reminding himself of the company they were in—people here for Patrick. However, he spent the rest of the wake simmering with frustration, though he took considerable satisfaction in the number of glances Megan threw his way. She'd well and truly disturbed him. Let her be disturbed, too!

He was glad when all the guests were gone and he could busy himself helping with the cleaning up, chatting with Evelyn in the kitchen, feeling *at home* again. There was no formal dinner tonight. The family picked at leftovers, flaking out in the sitting room once the homestead was back to normal. The consensus of opinion was that the wake had been all it should have been for a man of Patrick Maguire's standing—a man who would be sadly missed by many.

Emotional and physical fatigue gradually took its toll, people trailing off to bed until there was only Johnny and Megan left in the room. He was sprawled in an armchair. She was on a sofa, one elbow propped on its armroll, legs up, her stockinged feet bare of the shoes she had kicked off. It was a pose that seductively outlined the very female curve of waist, hip and thigh, and Johnny found it difficult not to let his gaze linger on it.

He expected her to leave. She usually did avoid being alone with him. Any moment now those legs would swing off the sofa, take her away to the privacy of her room, and it was probably better that they did, save him from making a fool of himself. He watched her feet, waiting for them to move. She wriggled her toes. His gaze dropped to the shoes lying beside the sofa, noting the long, narrow shape of them.

'Cramped feet?' he asked.

'They're not used to wearing fashionable shoes,' she drily admitted.

'Want me to massage them?'

'Is that a big brotherly thing to do?'

The mocking taunt whipped his gaze up to meet the smoking challenge she was directing straight at him.

Megan could no longer contain the furious frustration that had been welling up in her all day. 'I am not your little sister and I do not need you to watch over me,' she threw at him in seething protest over how he had acted with her—last night, holding her hand and kissing her forehead as though she were a baby, keeping close to her today, ready to be supportive at any falter on her part, inserting himself at her side whenever he thought she might not be able to handle what he interpreted as possibly unwelcome attention.

He hitched himself forward in his chair, gesturing for understanding, frowning over her reaction. 'It was just a friendly offer, Megan.'

Friendly!

For him to now sit on the other end of the sofa and nursemaid her to the extent of massaging her toes... It would drive her so crazy she'd probably end up needling his crotch with them! She swung her legs off the sofa and stood up, viewing him with bristling *hauteur*.

'I'm fine. What's more, I'm all grown up, Johnny, in case you haven't noticed. Which you should have, since I made the effort not to *neuter* myself today.'

He grimaced. 'Impossible not to notice.'

'So what did I get wrong?'

'Wrong?'

'You weren't moved to make any positive comment.' She lifted her arms and tossed her hair back over her shoulders in angry impatience with it hanging around her face—hair she'd spent over an hour shampooing and blow-drying so it would look fluffy and feminine. 'Still not good enough for you!' she muttered, mocking herself more than him.

'Not good enough?' he repeated incredulously, shaking his head as though hopelessly confused by her attitude.

Of course her words made no sense in the context of his *little sister* mind frame. Totally incensed by his insensitivity to this major attempt at changing his view of her, Megan clenched her jaw and headed for the liquor cabinet at the other end of the room, determined on blotting out the stupid futility of trying to change anything where Johnny was concerned.

'Well, I'm certainly old enough to get drunk tonight,' she tossed at him derisively. 'Entitled to, what's more. So why don't you go off to bed, Johnny, and leave me to drown my sorrows?'

He suddenly exploded off his chair, grabbing her arm as she moved past him. 'What do you mean by...*not good enough?*' He bit out the words as though they were killing him. His eyes slashed at hers, trying to cut through to her soul.

The intensity coming from him pumped Megan up to defy him further. 'You didn't even notice I was wearing the pearls you gave me for my twenty-first birthday,' she rattled out recklessly. 'On the other hand, why should you? You probably got some aide to buy a suitable gift and send it to me.'

'I did notice them,' he fiercely refuted her. 'I chose them myself. And I was pleased to see you wearing them.'

'You didn't *say* anything!'

'What do you want me to say? That you look fantastic? That I could hardly keep my eyes off you? That I wanted to beat every other man away?'

A sense of wild triumph zinged around Megan's brain. She had succeeded in getting to him as a man. Johnny Ellis had actually been *jealous* of the guys who'd shown her some admiration. He *had* seen her as a woman with the power to attract male interest.

It was a huge step forward, but where did it get her if he wasn't prepared to act on it? 'So you think I need your protection now?' she flung at him.

'It's the last thing on my mind.'

The emphatic beat of his voice was like thunder in her ears, thunder in her heart. And she got action aplenty. He stepped closer, scooping her body around to face him. The hand that had seized her arm lifted, its fingers raking through her hair, dragging her head back so that it was tilted up to his. The raw desire flaring from his eyes made her stomach quiver in anticipation.

Johnny Ellis wanted her.

His mouth crashed down onto hers in a passionate plundering that incited an equally passionate response, years of wanting pouring into her need to taste *this* man, have him tasting her, wanting more of her. She wound her arms around his neck, stretched up on tiptoe, pressed closer, trying to lock in every possible physical contact with him, revelling in the exciting heat of his big strong body, the tension in his muscles.

He kissed her as greedily and urgently as she kissed him. When he sucked in air, she did, too, her pulse racing, her breasts heaving to the same rise and fall of his chest. Though even the slightest pause in this hectic intimacy hit a panic button. She didn't want him to stop, to pull away from her, have second thoughts about what he was doing. She kept a tight hold on him, her fingers thrusting through his hair, curling around his head, rabidly encouraging continuance.

He kissed her some more, with a deepening eroticism that stirred her desire for him into a chaotic frenzy, every nerve in her body sizzling for the fulfilment of all he promised. His hands roved over her back, following its curves, curling over the taut mounds of her bottom, squeezing, lifting, fitting her more closely to him. No doubt about how strongly he was aroused. She felt his erection against her stomach and exulted in the blatant physical power of his desire for her.

Then he tore his mouth from hers and buried his face in her hair, rubbing his cheeks over it, breathing in the scent on it, tasting it with hot sensual kisses. And she pressed her own face into the warm hollow of his neck, savouring the smell of him, her sensitised lips picking up the rapid throb of his pulse beat there, enclosing it, sucking on it, excited by his excitement and wildly wanting to drive it higher and higher.

'Megan...'

The hoarse whisper carried the sound of raging need, making her heart leap with fierce exhilaration. His throat moved in a convulsive swallow.

'Megan...' A stronger tone, harsh with urgency. 'Tell me—' intense command '—is this right for you?'

'Yes...yes,' she answered, every fibre of her being affirming its rightness for her.

'You know I have to leave tomorrow,' he said in strained argument.

'I don't care,' she cried recklessly.

'Then neither do I,' he muttered savagely, and Megan found herself abruptly swept off her feet, her legs hanging over his arm, the rest of her clamped to his chest, and he was carrying her out of the sitting room. 'Better than drowning your sorrows in a bottle,' he bit out, apparently still needing to convince himself he wasn't doing wrong by her.

'Yes,' she agreed emphatically. 'Much better.'

'Your room or mine?'

'Mine.' Where she had dreamed so many times of Johnny Ellis coming to love her. Years of dreams. Never any substance to them. At least she was about to experience some physical reality of all those secret desires, even if it was only sex.

When he stepped out on the verandah, he hesitated. 'I don't have any protection with me.'

'I told you I don't need your protection.'

'Right!'

Relieved of any worries about getting her pregnant, he surged forward again, striding out, legs pumping with driven purpose as he headed straight for her room. Megan had no protection at all against the possibility of conception, but she didn't care. She hung on to him, recklessly abandoning every care.

It didn't matter what was said.

Didn't matter what was done.

As long as she had Johnny Ellis in her bed tonight!

# CHAPTER SEVEN

JOHNNY'S MIND WAS in total ferment, but his body kept moving, driven by its own physical need to satisfy the desire roaring through him. As he'd stepped out on the verandah, the cooler air of the outback night had hit him in the face, sobering him enough to realise what he was doing... taking Patrick's daughter to bed with him. Yet Megan wanted it, too. She was clinging to him. No second thoughts from her.

And she *was* grown up. Well and truly grown up. Even prepared for sex, having her own form of protection since she didn't need him to use anything. Which meant he'd been completely wrong about her attitude to *all men*. She couldn't have been sour on them. Only him. So why was she letting him do this? More than that, actively stirring him into it.

Pride stung by the comments he'd made about her yesterday?

Using sex to take away the bitter taste of her father's death?

Using *him* because he was here and she thought he was the kind of man who would view it as meaningless?

He reached her door, opened it. His heart was rocketing around his chest as he carried her inside. The ache in his groin demanded that he stop thinking and simply take what was being offered. He closed the door, switched on the light, his mind fiercely dictating that Megan not hide him in darkness.

He set her on her feet, cupped her face in his hands, forcing her gaze to meet his. 'It's *me*... Johnny,' he said, searching her eyes with gut-wrenching intensity for answers he could live with. 'Sure you want this, Megan?'

Angry defiance sparked. 'Getting cold feet, Johnny? Want to put me back into the *little sister* box?'

'No, I don't!' exploded from him.

The sparkles changed to glittery challenge. 'Then don't treat me like an idiot child. We're here. And yes, I'm sure.'

He stopped caring about what was in her mind. The desire burning inside him flared up, took control, directing the paths it wanted to take. His hands slid slowly down the long elegant neck that held her head so high. Her skin was warm, soft, silky smooth. She stood absolutely still, watching him, absorbing his touch without the slightest flinch. The sensual trail of his fingers was interrupted by the necklace at the base of her throat.

*His* pearls.

Leave them there.

He wanted her stripped of everything else but not them. The pearls were a link to him. They had meaning. He lifted them, rubbed them between his fingers, knowing their lustre was increased by contact with flesh—her flesh—his.

'Why did you wear them today?' he asked, wanting it to be significant.

Still the challenge sizzling at him. 'Why not? You gave them to me to wear. They looked good with my black suit.'

Denying them any personal meaning yet all his instincts insisted it was there—if only as a weapon in her armoury to get at him. Flaunting her hair, her figure, *his* necklace...was it just some sexual battle she was waging?

The primitive survivor in Johnny stirred.

Regardless of what was driving Megan, he would win out in the end.

And get it right.

Megan sucked in a quick nervous breath as the skin-tingling pads of his fingers glided down the edges of her jacket's V neckline. Panic was still blurring her mind. She'd thought he was going to stop, back off. The white-hot need for intimacy was no longer outrunning control and she couldn't bring herself to force it by throwing herself at him. They were here in her bedroom. He had to want her...want her so much nothing would stop him.

She shouldn't have hit out with that negative stuff, reminding him of the years between them, pretending that his necklace was just a necklace.

But he wasn't backing off.

It *was* happening.

And she was scared stiff that he'd find her hopelessly inadequate at meeting him as an equal when they were finally in bed together, that he'd realise how relatively inexperienced she was and wish he hadn't been tempted into having any sexual connection with her.

She'd only been thinking of satisfying herself before.

But that wasn't enough.

She wanted Johnny to love her, need her, come back to her.

With tantalising slowness he undid the top button of her jacket. Then the next. And the next. Her breasts seemed to swell with a terribly tight feeling. Yet her legs were turning into wobbly jelly. He slid her jacket off her shoulders, caressed her arms as he pushed the sleeves down. Her skin broke out in goose bumps. She had to *do* something or she'd end up paralysed by inhibitions.

His coat and tie had been discarded after the visitors had left, the sleeves of his shirt rolled up when he'd been helping in the kitchen. As his hands moved around her back to undo her bra, the thought of being stripped naked while he was still dressed galvanised Megan into action. She attacked the buttons on his shirt, needing to rip it off him as fast as she could, keep some kind of equality between them.

Once he'd dispensed with her bra, he helped, tossing his shirt on the floor to join the other discarded clothes, then removing her skirt while she hesitated over touching his trousers. She'd seen Johnny naked to the waist before—washing up outside many times. The beautifully sculpted masculinity of his chest and arms held no surprises for her, but close up like this, with the taut muscles and smooth hairless skin barely a heart-beat away from the tips of her bare breasts, she was too caught up in breathless anticipation to even attempt stripping him further.

Besides, he did it fast enough, revealing himself without any worry whatsoever about her reaction to *his* completely naked body. No doubt he was perfectly comfortable in his own skin. And why wouldn't he be?

On any male scale he was magnificently built. Impossible for him to feel any sense of inadequacy with so much blatant power in his physique.

Her stillness, her staring, evoked a gruff taunt from him. 'Not freezing up on me, are you, Megan?'

Her chin jerked up, eyes flaring a bold challenge. 'Just looking.' This was no time for backing down!

'Satisfied?'

'I hope I will be.'

Something like an animal growl issued from his throat. His hands spanned her waist. She was lifted off her feet, carried swiftly to the bed, laid down so he could stand back and look at her. Which he did, taking in every detail of her from the spill of her hair on the pillow to the uncontrollable curling of her toes. Megan wanted to close her eyes but she couldn't allow herself that weakness. It would betray the nervous fear pumping through her. She watched him, waiting for his response, her heart drumming in her ears.

Johnny could barely contain himself. She lay there in seductive abandonment, her hair a fiery halo, her arms lying loosely across the bed, waiting to wrap around him when he came to her, the lushly full breasts peaking their invitation, her pale skin gleaming like sensual satin. He'd lose himself in her in no time flat if he wasn't careful.

No way was he going to leave Megan thinking of him as a rutting animal. If she wanted that kind of perverse satisfaction, she wasn't about to get it. Nor would he let her dismiss him as just another man. God only knew how many lovers she'd had but he was all fired up to be the one who lingered longest in her memory, the one she'd want more than any other.

She was still wearing the sheer black pantihose that had drawn his attention to the shapeliness of her legs. He leaned one knee on the bed, hooked his thumbs under the waistband and rolled the garment down, slowly easing it over her hips.

She lifted herself slightly to allow it free passage past the sexy cheeks of her bottom. He smiled at the natural triangle of red-gold pubic hair, glad it hadn't been subjected to a bikini or Brazilian wax. The fiery arrow, pointing to the apex of her silky thighs, was much more exciting.

He caressed the erotic curves of her legs as he removed the black nylon, her feet, her toes, and there was certainly nothing *brotherly* about what he did. The slight twitches and gasps from Megan told him the prolonged sensuality was getting to her. He wanted to weave such an enthralling web of it she'd be totally captivated, aware of only him and how he was touching her, making love to her.

He trailed kisses up and down her inner thighs, revelling in the revealing quiver of her flesh under his lips as he moved her legs apart. He caressed the soft folds of her sex, feeling the moist heat that telegraphed her readiness for him. Not yet, he told himself, fighting the urge to take, to sate his own almost bursting need for her.

He grazed his mouth over the erotic little hollows under her hipbones while inciting her need to a higher pitch with his hand, his thumb gently rubbing her clitoris, fingers circling, diving inside her, working a teasing rhythm as he pressed hot kisses over her stomach. And her body arched up to him, inviting, inciting.

But he wanted her wild for him.

He ran his tongue around the tips of her breasts and she broke into chaotic movement, hands clawing at his back, urging an upward surge. Excitement flooded through him but he denied her demand to hurry the pace, surrounding the taut thrust of her nipple with his mouth, drawing on it, reinforcing the rhythmic caress he'd maintained, building an arc of throbbing pleasure.

She grabbed his head, fingers tugging his hair. He moved to her other breast, determined on having her whole body acutely aware of him, craving and wallowing in every nuance of sensation he could give her. Her body thrashed from side to side in a chaotic offering that drove him to almost frenzied action. Impossible to hold out much longer.

He drew himself up, hovered over her, his eyes seeking affirmation of all he felt in hers. Shards of silver were fiercely shot at him. Her legs curled around his thighs, convulsively pressing. Her hands linked around his neck, trying to pull him down to her. She was panting with the primitive passion he had stirred.

Whether it was pride or possessiveness or some dark streak of male domination driving him, Johnny didn't know, but the powerful need to stamp himself in her mind overrode everything else.

'Say my name,' he commanded, resisting the compelling pressure to perform at her instigation. 'Say it!'

'Johnny...' It burst from her as though her mind was filled to over-flowing with it.

His heart leapt in exultation. He positioned himself to enter her, pausing to feel the pulsing welcome of her inner muscles closing around him, sucking him in.

'Again,' he insisted.

'Johnny...' It was an anguished plea.

He picked up her fluttering hands and slammed them above her head as he drove himself deeply into the sweet hot cavern of her innermost self. He lay on the soft cushion of her breasts, his face directly above hers. He wanted eye contact but her lids were shut, her mouth open, dragging in quick shallow breaths.

'Look at me!' he commanded.

The lashes flew up. Her eyes seemed unfocussed, inwardly concentrated, but they swam back to seeing him squarely.

'Know me as you feel me, Megan,' he said more softly, and kissed her, wanting to engage her in a sense of total intimacy with him, with the Johnny Ellis she had scorned for so long but was now accepting with all her being.

Megan was swamped with tidal wave after tidal wave of incredible sensation. The unrelenting swell of it had crashed through any inhibitions she might have had long before Johnny had finally plunged into this ultimate joining with her. Now she simply rode with it, incapable of doing anything else, marvelling at the exquisite peaks of pleasure, the ripple effect through her entire body, the almost torturous tension of anticipating more and more, the ecstatic feeling of letting herself go, melting around him.

In the hazy recesses of a mind drowning in intense feeling, there lurked the exhilarating satisfaction that this was, indeed, Johnny Ellis making love to her. And if she'd been waiting her whole life for this, it was worth the waiting. She didn't question why he'd demanded she say his name. Her thought processes were far too adrift for questioning anything. She'd wanted to say it, anyway, wanted to taste it, savour it, shout it, identifying and claiming him as the only man who had ever moved her this deeply.

As for knowing him...it was knowledge she had craved, knowledge she was now exulting in, knowledge she would hug to herself forever. It was awesome, fantastic, the glorious sense of rolling from one climax to another, pinnacles of creamy pleasure, then finally the faster pumping of his need, spilling into wild spasms of release, Johnny letting go, surrendering control to her as his powerful body shuddered into relaxation, accepting her readily loving embrace.

Conscious of his weight on her, he rolled onto his side, but he didn't disentangle himself from her. She stroked him, adoring his strength, wanting to touch as she hadn't dared touch before. It dawned on her how passive she had been while he did...everything!

Absorbing the feelings he'd aroused had stunned her into a weird submission, as though she was in a time and place where only what he was doing to her had any reality—an immediate and overwhelming reality that compelled intense concentration.

Only now did she realise she hadn't made any effort to pleasure him. Hadn't even thought of it. Was he satisfied with how it had been? Would he want more of her when he hadn't been given any active demonstration of desire *from* her?

She hadn't exactly been a log, but...

'Content?' he asked.

It sounded as though he'd been working hard to give her satisfaction and wanted to be assured of it.

'Are you?' she tossed back, worried about not matching up to his previous sexual partners.

He shifted, propping himself up on his elbow, smoothing her hair away from her face with his other hand, eyeing her with brooding frustration. 'What is it with you, Megan? You can't concede a straight answer?'

Aware that she was being defensive again, she tried a rueful smile. 'Sorry, Johnny. You're a fantastic lover. Thank you for being so...so giving.'

He returned her smile. 'Then you do feel content?'

'How could I not? You've completely rocked me with a truly brilliant experience,' she said flippantly, wary of placing too much weight on what could very well be a one-night stand.

*Rocked her...* Was that another hit at his career? Johnny's sense of satisfaction that he had reached Megan deep down was instantly shaken by insecurities.

Maybe she had just been using him... Johnny on the spot.

And he had performed his heart out for her.

Brilliant...

'Well, I'm glad I'm good for something...apart from money,' he mocked.

He saw her eyes blank with shock, then spark with alarm. Her hand lifted swiftly to his face, cupping his cheek, instinctively needing to reach into him as she rushed into earnest speech.

'I'm sorry if that came out wrong, Johnny. It's just that...you're going tomorrow...and I have to let you go...so...'

'Easier to put me back in the box you've had me in for years, Megan?'

She grimaced. 'That is where you live most of your life. No point in my wanting it otherwise.'

He asked the crucial question. 'Do you want it otherwise?'

Her lashes dropped. She watched the trail of her hand as it slid down his throat and over the bunched muscles of his shoulder. She drew a deep breath and wryly said, 'Let's be realistic, Johnny. You're here tonight, gone tomorrow, and I don't know if you'll ever be back.'

'I'll be back,' he stated unequivocally. 'As soon as the movie is wrapped up.'

'Mmm...'

To his ears it was the hum of disbelief. Why wasn't she prepared to accept his word for it? He'd never lied to her, never given false promises. Still, there was no way to prove he would return until he did.

She was gently rotating her palm over his nipple, seemingly fascinated by the fact that it could respond like hers to caressing. It surprised him when she leaned over to take it in her mouth and her hand glided down, over his stomach, touching him, stroking him. Excitement instantly buzzed. This was hard evidence that she still wanted him, no matter what the future held.

He rolled onto his back, carrying her with him, letting her do whatever she wanted with his body, letting the pleasure of it stream through him. He played with her beautiful hair, running his fingers through its silkiness, winding it around them, wishing he could bind her to him just as easily. But the reality was...only time could do that. So he wanted to make the most of now.

He was fully aroused again, teetering on the brink of climax. He quickly lifted her to sit astride him, wanting her to do the taking, want-ing to watch her loving him, if only physically. The necklace of pearls swung back and forth as she settled into a rhythm—a metronome mea-suring the escalation of excitement. He cupped her breasts, wanting to feel the beat of her flesh on his everywhere…soft, hot music to his soul.

She paused, her eyes glittering with stormy feeling. 'Say *my* name, Johnny.'

He smiled at the echo of his primal need to be known by her. 'Megan…'

'Again!' she fiercely insisted.

'Megan Maguire,' he rolled out like the rich chord of a song that gripped his heart—a song he was yet to write but it was beating through his mind.

'Yes.' It was a hiss of satisfaction. 'I am my father's daughter and don't you ever forget it, Johnny Ellis,' she added proudly, tossing her hair back over her shoulders as though it was a mane.

Then she rode him hard, and Johnny was racing with her, exhilarated by the frenetic energy behind making him come, loving the sight of her driving them both to an intense climax, the pearls whipping around her throat. His pearls…his woman… Patrick's daughter…

It felt so good to hold her afterwards. No tension. No sense of conflict running between them. It was as though she gave herself to him with-out reservation, her body folding into the curve of his, spoon-fashion, happy with being close, relaxing into languorous contentment. No ques-tion about that now. There was a sense of peace in the silence, though Johnny knew there were other questions that would have to be answered in the future.

Had Patrick foreseen this connection between him and Megan?

Had he made his will with a marriage in mind?

Home is where the heart is, Johnny thought, but Megan didn't believe his heart was in the life at Gundamurra. He had to show her it was so.

She heaved a deep sigh, then quietly asked, 'If you chose these pearls for me personally, Johnny, why didn't you come to my party and give them to me?'

He raised his head from the pillow, looked over her shoulder. She was fingering the necklace as though wondering if it really did mean anything.

He kissed her shoulder. 'I planned to, Megan. I'd booked my flight home. Then I learnt a close friend of mine had been taken to hospital, overdosed on heroin. I hoped I could talk her into wanting to live.'

'Her?'

'I don't know if the name would mean anything to you... Liesel Furner?'

'No. It doesn't ring any bells.'

'Liesel had some brief fame as a torch singer. Her voice was very powerful, very emotional, very passionate. A great talent...but also a deeply screwed-up person. She...gave up on herself...and I couldn't pull her out of the darkness.'

'You cared about her.'

He paused before answering, looking back, remembering how he'd felt. Impossible to explain an experience to someone who had never been driven into those dark prisons of the mind by the abuse of others. Mitch and Ric would have understood, but Megan? He didn't want her to take her there. Not tonight.

He used a simple parallel. 'I would have liked someone to care about my mother, Megan.'

Another deep sigh. 'I'm sorry, Johnny. I guess you're saying Liesel died, too.'

'It didn't matter what I said...what I did...she didn't have the will to survive.'

'But she must have known you cared. At least she had that.'

While Megan had thought he didn't care about her.

No difficulty in reading that equation.

And the truth was... Liesel's life had meant more to him than anybody's birthday party. The childhood abuse she'd suffered had struck a strong empathy in him. He'd wanted to give her what Patrick had given him, get her head around all the negatives, lead her into...

But he'd failed.

And it had taken him a while to get past that failure.

When he'd come home again, Megan had gone off to agricultural college. And ever after that, she'd removed herself from him, actively driving him away from any sense of closeness with her.

'I'm sorry I disappointed you. It wasn't that I didn't care...'

'You were dealing with your own life,' she finished for him, a wry touch of resignation in her voice. 'And that's how it is, Johnny—you dealing with your life, me dealing with mine.'

*We've shared tonight,* he wanted to argue, but he knew one night wouldn't carry much weight with her.

It was a beginning, he told himself, and settled back down to hold her as long as he could.

# CHAPTER EIGHT

STRANGE HOW CALM she felt the next morning after Johnny had left her to go to his own room, mindful of the untimely aspect of their intimacy if it were known. It had been a very private interlude, just between them, and they'd agreed it should stay private. Especially since he was leaving today.

Megan wryly wondered if she had finally grown up, accepting what couldn't be changed, respecting what should be respected. The rebellious turmoil incited by her father's will was gone. The bitter scorn she'd nurtured towards Johnny and his career had been ill-founded, fed by her own self-absorbed needs and totally unfair. It, too, was gone. In its place was a far more sympathetic appreciation of the person Johnny was and what drove him.

She still wanted him. More than ever after last night. But she knew she had to let him go, release him from any sense of responsibility towards her. What had happened between them had been more her doing than his. She'd made the decisions, pushing him into giving her a very real taste of the man he was.

A generous lover...a generous person in every sense...and it was time for her to be generous to him. No snipes. No clinging. Just let him go to be whatever he wanted—needed—to be.

She put the pearl necklace back in its jewellery box, then washed and dressed in her usual shirt and jeans, conscious of feeling no need to be aggressive or provocative about anything today. The sense of putting away her life to this point before embarking on the next phase was very strong.

Her father would not be with her anymore. Johnny was going this morning. Mitch, Ric, their wives, her sisters and their husbands...they were all flying out, as well. She would be left to get on with the task of managing Gundamurra as best she could, with the financial backing Johnny had set up and put at her disposal. This was what all her life had been building towards...following in her father's footsteps. It was time to take it on now and make a success of it.

Everyone came to the dining room for breakfast, probably conscious of its being their last meal in each other's company for a while. Possibly a long while. Megan wondered if Mitch and Ric would ever return to Gundamurra, now that her father was gone, though both of them were very solicitous towards her.

'If any problem arises that I can deal with, call me,' Mitch urged earnestly. 'No hesitation, Megan. Just call me. Okay? Any legal thing you want explained, or you're worried about, or something you want cleared with Johnny...'

The message was loud and clear. He was there for her. As her father had been for him.

It was the same with Ric, though his concern was more personal, taking the chair beside her at the table to speak privately. 'Megan, if Johnny starts treading on your toes, taking over what he should leave to you, let me know and I'll talk to him. I have no doubt he'd mean well, but Patrick made you the boss here and that's how it should be. So any time you need a mediator, I know Johnny will listen to me. Just lay it out and I'll handle it. Okay?'

All three of them, determined on giving support—her father's *boys*. And although there was no blood relationship between them, they truly were a band of brothers, Megan thought, probably closer than real family in their knowledge and understanding of each other.

They were her father's legacy, too, she realised, not just Gundamurra. Stepping in as brothers to her, as well, except she'd never wanted Johnny as a brother. Had her father known that? Had he written his will with the deliberate intent of forcing both of them to deal with each other, hoping for an outcome that would at least sort out her feelings, one way or another?

He'd known far more of Johnny than she had.

Maybe he'd simply aimed for her to learn who Johnny was—the real person behind the image. A major lesson about making judgements, not letting emotions rule, standing back and using informed reason, putting herself in another's shoes, treading gently instead of blindly stomping. *Being worthy of her father...* Mitch's words...finally struck home to her.

Johnny had seated himself directly across the table and she was acutely aware of him watching her over breakfast—concern in his eyes, too. 'I'd like a private chat with you before I go, Megan,' he pressed.

'Sure, Johnny.' Her smile was to show everyone they were *friends* now, no acrimony souring the partnership they had to have. 'Let's walk down to the airstrip together. Mitch can take the Land Rover to carry the luggage and everyone else. I'll see you all fly off in the plane, then drive back to the homestead.'

There was a hard moment, filled with the nervous tension of wanting him to understand it was better to skip past the physical intimacy they'd shared, just leave it behind them. Meeting in a room would make that difficult for her. His attraction was too strong, the sexual memories too fresh.

His eyes searched hers with a sharp intensity that suggested he wanted to fight this arrangement, seek a more exclusive time of closure with her. It was a huge relief when he nodded, conceding to what would be a far less fraught situation for her, being out in the open with the evidence of the drought all around them, a pertinent reminder of what their partnership was essentially about—rescuing Gundamurra.

Thankfully Evelyn provided some distraction, coming in to fuss over him, as usual, ensuring he was served with the crispy bacon he liked. For once, Megan could smile at the housekeeper's desire to indulge his preferences. How many people did care about Johnny Ellis at such a basic level, expecting nothing back except the pleasure of giving him pleasure? He'd never had loving parents. It was good that Evelyn added to his sense of being home here at Gundamurra.

Megan wanted him to come back.

He'd said he would.

She hoped her blatantly *wanton* behaviour last night would not cause him to reconsider. If he thought she expected a continuing affair with him...

The bottom-line truth was she did want it.

But did he?

Somehow she had to make him feel free to choose. Her heart cringed at the thought of him nursing any sense of obligation towards her, especially in a sexual sense.

This was very much on her mind when the time of departure came. Jessie and Emily weren't leaving until after lunch, so they and their husbands had joined her on the front verandah to say their farewells to the others. Everyone hugged and kissed. The Land Rover set off for the airstrip where Johnny's Cessna was waiting for them, ready to fly them back to Sydney. Megan waited for the dust to settle in the vehicle's wake before setting off with Johnny, who seemed perfectly relaxed, amiably chatting to her sisters.

Charm, she thought, wishing she knew what it was papering over today.

'Time to go,' he finally said, shook hands with the men, kissed her sisters' cheeks, then caught Megan's hand to lead her down the steps.

He kept possession of it, his strong fingers tightly enveloping hers as they began their walk together. Megan made no attempt to extract them from his hold. She didn't even care if it was a big-brotherly link. It was good to feel his touch again, good that he wanted to touch her.

What she had to project now was dignity and grace. Never mind that her insides were churning with the need to hang on to this man. He was under contract to finish his movie. Begging him to stay was not an option, anyway.

'Megan…you *will* use the money,' he said forcefully, his tone strained with uncertainty.

Why would he doubt it? Because of having sex with her last night? Did he think that might have somehow tainted his investment? That her pride would stop her from using it?

'Yes, I will, Johnny,' she assured him. 'Gundamurra needs it,' she added to put everything in its proper perspective.

'Right!' he agreed, relief obvious.

He cared about Gundamurra. That, at least, they had in common. But would he come back? They had walked past most of the buildings before Megan screwed up the necessary courage to say, 'I don't want you to feel bad about last night, Johnny. It's nothing for you to worry about.'

'Nothing?' He repeated the word as though it was intensely offensive.

Megan inwardly cringed. The last thing she wanted was to sound scornful of what he'd given her. Her mind whirled, seeking ways to fix his impression. 'I just meant...it was good for me.'

'But this is the cut-off line,' he muttered derisively.

She tried again. 'You're leaving. I don't want you to be concerned about it. That's all.'

'Over and done with.'

'I hope it was good for you, too,' she rushed out, hating the way he was bringing down the curtain when she desperately wanted him to keep caring about her.

His fingers almost crushed hers before he realised what he was doing and relaxed his grip. 'Will you e-mail me? Give me reports on how things are going here? I want to know, Megan,' he said tersely.

If it was a test for how she really felt about continuing a relationship with him, Megan was only too happy to comply with what he required. 'Yes, I will,' she said firmly.

'Good!' Again he squeezed her hand, but not as tightly as before.

Her head was almost giddy with relief. He was inviting her to have regular contact with him...if he replied to her e-mails. She couldn't really count on that. Once he was back to making his movie, caught up in such a different world over there...but he couldn't completely forget her. Even if he got involved with another woman, making love to her would trigger memories...wouldn't it?

Her stomach felt like a worm farm.

She fiercely told herself she had no personal claim on him. Had no right to make one. Yet everything within her burned with a deeply primitive desire to have him as hers and hers alone.

The Land Rover stood just ahead of them, Johnny's Cessna behind it, ready for take off.

'If the shooting of the movie runs to schedule, it should be finished in three months,' he informed her. 'Do you have any problem with my coming back then, Megan?'

'No,' she shot out, elated that *he* had no problem with it. 'You'll always be welcome home, Johnny,' she added as warmly as she could, acutely aware of not having welcomed him for far too many years.

He stopped, pausing her, as well. Drawn by the mountain of tension emanating from him, Megan half-turned, steeling herself to glance up at him. He stepped to face her full on, his free hand lifting, tilting back the wide-brimmed Akubra hat she always wore outside to protect her fair skin from the sun. His eyes were a piercing green, scouring hers for truth.

'Do you mean that, Megan?'

She held his gaze with determined steadiness. 'I do, Johnny. I'm deeply sorry I was such a mean bitch to you.' She managed an appealing little smile as she finally acknowledged, 'My father knew best.'

His face relaxed, returning a smile that held whimsical irony. 'Patrick...yes... I think he did.' His voice was furred with feelings, instantly stirring up her own.

A huge lump of emotion welled into her throat. Tears pricked her eyes. Desperate to keep this leave-taking on some kind of even keel, she babbled, 'I hope your movie goes well.'

Still the whimsical half smile. 'More important is the movie of my life.'

She didn't understand.

He saw the confusion in her eyes and quoted...

"'All the world's a stage,
And all the men and women merely players:
They have their exits and their entrances:
And one man in his time plays many parts."

Shakespeare.'

He gave the credit drily, then added, 'I'm not entirely uneducated, Megan.'

'You've taken out honours in the school of life, Johnny,' she quickly replied, wanting to acknowledge how wrong she'd been in her judgement of him.

He shook his head, as though his successes were irrelevant. 'I wish I didn't have to make this exit, leaving you with so much work to carry through alone.' His voice gathered an urgent intensity and he took both her hands in his in pressing persuasion. 'Promise me you'll let me know if you run into difficulties that seem insurmountable.'

And he'd come running to the rescue?

Maybe he would...for Gundamurra.

But for her?

'Okay. But this is my stage, Johnny,' she felt compelled to remind him. 'I know how to play it. And I don't want other roles. This is who I am.'

He nodded. His eyelids lowered to half-mast, thick lashes veiling the expression in his eyes. He took a deep breath as though inwardly gathering strength for what he had to say next. All Megan's senses were on sharp alert, anxious to glean some hint of what he was thinking. Yet when he spoke, they were simple words of farewell.

'Until next time.'

He leaned down and kissed her cheek, then stood back, smiling a full blast of Johnny Ellis charm.

'I like your hair loose. They say a woman's hair is her crowning glory. Yours outshines all the rest, Megan.'

His hands slid from hers and he was off, striding for the open door of the waiting plane.

Was her cheek better than her forehead? Megan wondered as she watched him go. Her hat would have made her forehead a harder place to reach. Better that he hadn't kissed her mouth, she told herself. It would have been too tempting to cling to him, turn it into more than a friendly goodbye kiss.

*Next time,* she kept repeating in her mind.

The door of the plane was closed.

She waited for Johnny to make this exit from her life, listening to the plane's engines starting up, watching the wheels begin to roll, picking up speed, lifting off the dirt airstrip, her eyes following the flight of the Cessna until it was a distant speck in the sky.

Only then did she realise she'd been winding her hair around her fingers—hair she'd left loose this morning because she hadn't wanted to look *neutered.*

*It outshines all the rest,* he'd said.

She wanted to believe it wasn't just charm, that his last smile to her meant that he did see her as a very special woman in his life.

Uniquely special.

But she'd have to wait for his next entrance to know if that was true.

# CHAPTER NINE

MEGAN'S ASSURANCES THAT she was okay with what had happened between them did little to relieve the turmoil in Johnny's mind. Her dismissive attitude had made him feel…unimportant to her, as though she'd only been using him to make herself feel better. Certainly she'd been closing the door on it, letting him know she wasn't expecting nor inviting a repeat performance.

Was wishing him well with the movie her way of putting him back in a pigeonhole that had nothing to do with her life? At least there'd been no scorn attached to it, more a straightforward acceptance that this was what he did. Nevertheless, even that seemed to emphasise the distance she seemed intent on establishing, telling him unequivocally that—*unlike him*—Gundamurra was *the only stage* for her.

Fair comment, Johnny told himself, though everything within him wanted to fight it. However, the current circumstances were wrong for making any headway on that ground. On any ground. And maybe *he* was wrong for her in any long-term sense. Johnny felt he couldn't be certain of anything until he returned to Gundamurra and put in a lot of time on the sheep station with Megan.

Back in Arizona, the movie wasn't fun anymore. He grew annoyed with the script, especially in the scenes he had to play with a rancher's widow. They didn't sit right with him. Neither did the ending. He kept

thinking of how it would be for Megan if she were the widow, struggling to survive and having to make the choice of helping a cowboy who
would inevitably leave her.

He argued with the director, insisting that the whole feel of the scenes
was wrong, that they should be stark and powerful, pulsing with tension over the conflict of interests, not just some token female interest in
the movie, and the cowboy should feel compelled to return to the ranch
once his mission had been accomplished.

He won his point.

The female lead was very grateful to him for the meatier role. Too
damned grateful, making a nuisance of herself. He had to explain he was
seriously involved with another woman. What woman? she demanded
to know, since there was none in evidence. Johnny kept his mouth shut,
only too aware of what the media would do with a name. He couldn't
bring that circus down on Megan, especially when there was nothing
but a business partnership settled between them.

She kept her word, e-mailing him reports on what she was doing at
Gundamurra, how his money was being used, accounting for every dollar put into the place. He both welcomed and hated her messages which
were totally devoid of anything personal. It was as though the intimacy
they had shared was a brief aberration, best forgotten.

He kept his own replies matter-of-fact, trying not to impinge on what
she clearly saw as her authority, trying not to beg more interest in him
from her. It was clear that what he was doing had no real existence in
her life. He understood this but found it uncomfortably belittling. Was
all he had achieved so *useless* to her mind?

He didn't mention the movie, apart from counting the schedule
down—two more months, six weeks, four, two, a few more days. He
didn't stay for the wrap-up party. He didn't care that the director seemed
impressed with his acting ability. The moment he was no longer needed
for any more scenes, contract fulfilled, he packed up and moved out,
heading home to Gundamurra and Megan Maguire.

The land was in no better shape than when Johnny had last seen it—still
no rain—but the sheep definitely were, Megan thought with satisfaction.
There were more watering holes for them, thanks to the extra artesian
bores his money had made possible, and the feed they were trucking in

made a huge difference. Besides, she didn't anticipate any problems with Johnny over her management. His replies to her e-mailed reports had held nothing but approval.

Her only problems with him would be personal, and it was impossible to know how to handle them until she was with him again. She checked her watch as she headed towards the homestead kitchen for morning tea. Only a few more hours and he'd be flying in. Once he arrived... Megan told herself she had to remain calm, wait and see how he behaved towards her, keep reassessing the situation as she gathered more information.

She found Evelyn alone in the kitchen, vigorously grating carrot for Johnny's favourite cake. No doubt the housekeeper's two helpers, Brenda and Gail, were polishing up his guest suite, ensuring everything was in perfect readiness for his welcome home. Megan brushed off Evelyn's offer to make tea, munching some dry biscuits to settle her stomach while she brewed the tea herself. As soon as she sat down at the table with a steaming mugful, the grating stopped and Evelyn faced her with a determined air of confrontation.

'Are you going to tell him?'

Megan shrugged her bewilderment. 'Tell...whom...what?'

Evelyn wiped her hands on a cloth, the dark brown eyes of her aboriginal heritage measuring some goal she had in mind before speaking again. 'Don't think you can be fooling me, Miss Megan. I've seen the signs too many times.'

The nausea she'd been fighting every morning for weeks rolled around her stomach.

'Reckon I knew Miss Lara was pregnant even before she did,' Evelyn went on, leaving no doubt about the subject she was bent on tackling.

Megan realised it was useless to deny it. 'Have you told anyone?' she asked anxiously, alarmed at the thought that everyone on the station was aware of her condition and holding to a conspiracy of silence until she was ready to admit it.

'No. But I'll tell Mr Johnny if you don't,' came the challenging reply.

'You mustn't do that, Evelyn,' Megan instantly cried, panic welling up at the thought of any premature disclosure which might undermine her plans for the future.

'No good comes from keeping secrets that shouldn't be kept,' Evelyn bored in with absolute conviction. 'Especially from the man who fathered the child.'

'What makes you think Johnny's the father?' Megan shot back at her, desperate to raise enough doubt to give herself more time.

Evelyn clucked her contempt for any other possibility. 'No-one else it could be. Think I didn't know what you were up to...day of Mr Patrick's funeral...wanting to turn Mr Johnny's head? All these years...watching how you are with him? One way or another—nice or nasty—you've been set on making him take notice of you.'

Humiliation burned through her. Had her feelings been so horribly transparent to everyone? No, they couldn't have been, she frantically argued to herself. Johnny had believed she disliked him. Her sisters had been worried about her reaction to their father's will. They had simply been anxious that she not be hostile to Johnny and the help he could give. Mitch and Ric had taken that stance, too. Only Evelyn... Evelyn who cared about anything relating to Johnny...

'It's not his fault I'm pregnant,' Megan blurted out. 'It's not fair to load it on him.'

'Takes two to make a child,' came the firm rebuttal. 'Accepting the blame for it makes no difference, Miss Megan. The child belongs to him, as well as you.'

'I let him believe I was protected,' she pleaded. 'I'm the one who's responsible for this pregnancy. He would have ensured it didn't happen.'

Evelyn shook her head, disappointment and disapproval stamped on her expression. 'If you wove a web of lies to get Mr Johnny into your bed, you'll only make the situation worse with more lies. Time you faced up to yourself and to him.'

'I don't want him to feel trapped. That's not fair, Evelyn,' she repeated emphatically, gathering strength to fight any interference with whatever she decided to do.

'You think he'd want *his* child to be as fatherless as he was? No way, Miss Megan. No way. You just pile injustice on top of injustice if you keep this from him.' Her eyes narrowed in grim judgement. 'You're thinking of yourself. What you want. Always been that way. But I won't let you cut Mr Johnny out of what is rightfully his. You tell him or I will.'

'It's not your business!' It was a desperate cry of protest. This was between her and Johnny and she needed time to work out how best to approach the future…what arrangement to make with him.

Evelyn seemed to puff herself up with even more determination. 'Your dear mother's gone. Your father whom I admired and respected more than any other man on earth is gone.' She lifted a hand and shook a finger at Megan. 'They put me here. They trusted me to get things right. And neither of them would ever have planned to cheat a good man.'

*Cheat*…that was a totally unacceptable word. Megan recoiled from it. She'd been carrying a wretched load of guilt for weeks. That was nothing new. Yet mixed in with the guilt was an insidious streak of exhilarating pleasure in having Johnny Ellis's child—a part of him he couldn't take away from her. But *cheating* him…that didn't sit at all well.

Evelyn planted her hands on her ample hips. Her big bosom heaved. Her chin was thrust out in belligerent pride. 'I've lived at Gundamurra all my life. Over fifty years now. Served your parents best I could. Always followed their example. You can sack me if you want, Miss Megan. Your father gave you the right to do that…'

Gundamurra without Evelyn?

Shocking thought…even more shocking than cheating.

'…but as long as I'm here, I won't stand by and let you pull the wool over Mr Johnny's eyes, not on something as important as this will be to him. His child…'

Mine, too, Megan thought, fiercely possessive.

'You can't expect me to hit him with it the moment he steps off his plane,' she swiftly argued.

'You should have told him already,' came the damning retort. 'Every minute you leave it makes it worse. More underhand. More *unfair*,' she hammered home.

A relentless drive for truth was looking Megan straight in the face—impossible to ignore—impossible to even bend. Evelyn would serve Johnny with it along with her carrot cake if she was not satisfied with immediate action on this issue.

Strong loyalties had been stirred.

To Evelyn's mind, Patrick's daughter had not been acting as Patrick's daughter should, letting down the tradition of justice at Gundamurra, lying to a man who had learnt trust here, trusting her father, trusting himself. And perhaps the very longevity of her service did give her the right to feel she had to be the keeper of that trust, regardless of whether it served Megan's interests or not.

'I'm sorry you feel...so let down by me, Evelyn.'

She heaved a troubled sigh. 'It's your parents I'm thinking of, Miss Megan. They'd be telling you the same as I am. Lay it out in the open and deal with it.'

No other choice now.

'Tonight. I'll tell him tonight,' Megan promised.

Evelyn weighed that answer and finally conceded to it. 'I'll know tomorrow morning if you haven't done it,' she warned. 'Hard enough to look Mr Johnny in the face today, holding back what he should know.'

A brief reprieve.

At least she'd have a little time to gauge Johnny's attitude towards her, find out how long he intended to stay at Gundamurra this time, what career commitments he might have made while working on the movie, how much of his future was tied up elsewhere.

She'd wanted to feel prepared for every contingency before laying out the fact that would inevitably have a far ranging effect on the rest of their lives, wanted to have answers ready for whatever was Johnny's reaction to it.

However, Evelyn's words had stung her conscience. There was no denying the truth of them. Johnny would not want his child to be fatherless, as he himself had been. Which meant she had to share. No cheating him out of the role he'd want to play—a role he'd insist on playing.

Roles...exits and entrances...

What had she done in her own selfish desire to have her needs answered?

One careless act.

A reckless lie.

Though even acknowledging she hadn't been fair to Johnny, she couldn't regret doing it.

She *wanted* this child.

# CHAPTER TEN

Something was wrong.

Even Evelyn's superb carrot cake with the cream cheese icing did not settle the churning in Johnny's stomach. Fair enough that Megan was tense about his homecoming, but never before had Evelyn been uncomfortable in his presence. Both women's responses to him seemed strained and they avoided eye contact with each other, focussing on him with a kind of forced eagerness to make him feel welcome, rushing to fill any brief silence with a host of questions about the movie, his trip, whether or not he'd stopped over in Sydney to see Ric and Mitch.

Something big was hidden in the silence they rushed to cover.

Trouble at Gundamurra?

Johnny had to force himself to eat the cake, drink the tea, all the time waiting for the axe to fall, whatever it was.

Weird how quickly everything could change. His heart had been dancing with pleasure when he landed. Megan had been standing by the Land Rover, waiting to drive him up to the homestead from the airstrip. Although a hat was jammed on her head, her glorious hair was loose, tumbling around her shoulders, surely a sign that she wanted to please him... as a woman.

Once he'd emerged from the plane, his legs had eaten up the distance between them, every fast stride pumping with anticipation. But she'd thrust out a stiff, formal hand, and he'd felt constrained to hold back the pounding urge to hug her tight and keep holding her until the warm imprint of her body had assuaged the need to feel her flesh and blood reality again.

Her smile had been stiff, too.

*Okay, let her get used to having me here again,* he'd told himself. *Give her time to relax in my company.*

Now she was babbling on, trying to sound bright and natural while Evelyn was plying him with afternoon tea, her dark eyes empty of their normal sparkle at seeing him. He could feel the worry in their minds. It was like an invisible monster, growing bigger every minute, claws out ready to grab him, like the monsters of his childhood lurking in the cupboard his foster parents had used for punishing bad boys. He'd made up music in his head to drive them away, but no music was going to drive this away.

Finally he could stand it no longer.

Just as with Ric, holding the news of Patrick's death from him, Johnny could not wait for what he knew to be something bad. 'Tell me what's wrong!' he burst out in urgent demand.

It jolted them both into a silence that was clearly fraught with hidden concerns. No denial from either of them. The monster grew bigger in Johnny's mind.

Evelyn looked at Megan.

Megan had frozen into shocked stillness. Her hat was off now and even her vibrant hair was motionless, her grey eyes suddenly like opaque glass, nothing shining through.

'Evelyn...' he appealed.

The motherly housekeeper, who usually enjoyed indulging his every wish, shook her head, not even the hint of an appeasing smile on her face. 'It's not for me to say, Mr Johnny.' Grave, decisive words, accompanied by another anxious glance at Patrick's daughter, her employer.

There had always been a free and easy mood in Evelyn's kitchen. The heart of a home, Johnny had thought.

What had Megan done to change that?

Patrick wouldn't like it.

This wasn't how Gundamurra should feel.

Johnny instantly determined to change it back to what it should be. Whatever was going on had to be stopped, turned around.

Megan stirred out of her stunned state. His eyes bored into hers, demanding enlightenment. No way was he going to let her evade giving it. She might own fifty-one percent of Gundamurra but he had rights here, too.

'Let's go——' heat whooshed into her cheeks, vitality returning in an embarrassed rush '——to the office, Johnny.'

The office.

It was business then.

'Okay.' He could handle that.

He stood up.

Evelyn instantly busied herself at the sink, not looking at him, washing her hands, which Johnny couldn't help thinking was somehow symbolic.

Megan led off, leaving him to follow. Even when they reached the verandah that skirted the inner quadrangle of the homestead, she didn't pause to let him fall into step with her, marching on in a driven fashion, back straight, head high, not glancing at him when he caught up with her. He noted that her cheeks were still scorched with heat. And her hands were clenched. Whatever the problem was, she found it painful, being forced to impart it to him.

Pride badly hurt, he decided. Some huge mistake in managing Gundamurra. She'd hate to fail or be found wanting with anything to do with the sheep station. Whatever the crisis was, Johnny was determined to get around it, one way or another. Surely there was nothing that couldn't be fixed.

She didn't wait for him to lean past her and open the door to the office. She barged straight in, assuming he would follow and close the door behind them, which, of course, he did. It surprised him that she didn't go directly to her father's desk, take his chair, protect herself with some sense of authority. She veered off to stand over the chess table, hugging herself tightly as she stared down at the black and white battleground.

It was a stance that bristled with spiky tension, insisting on space around her. Johnny trod softly, moving over to the desk, propping himself against the front of it, trying to establish a relaxed, non-critical air. He hadn't come home to beat her over the head with anything. He wanted her trust. If she'd just place some confidence in him...but there was none forthcoming at the moment.

'It's okay,' he soothed. 'I'm not going to bite, Megan. Just tell me...'

Her head tilted back. She swung around to face him. Her expression seemed torn between intense inner conflict and a need to rise above it.

'I lied to you, Johnny.'

The bare statement held both guilt and defiance.

His mind clicked instantly to the e-mailed reports of what she'd done at Gundamurra. Had she baulked at using his money, after all? He hadn't checked, believing everything she'd told him. Surely she wouldn't have carried out such an elaborate deceit. From the air, the vast sheep station had still looked drought-stricken, but since there'd been no rain, he hadn't expected to actually *see* a difference. Tomorrow, he'd thought, she would show him.

'What did you lie about?' he asked, doing his utmost to keep calm.

Her lashes fell. Her mouth twitched into a rueful grimace. She took a deep breath, forced herself to meet his gaze squarely, then laid it out. 'The night we spent together... I told you I was protected...and I wasn't.'

It took him several moments to unscramble his mind which had been totally focussed on possible problems at Gundamurra. Then it took several more moments for the implication of her words to sink in. The shock of it robbed him of any ready speech.

'I'm pregnant,' she shot at him in case he hadn't put it together.

*Right!* he thought, still unable to produce a verbal response. He simply stared at her as understanding flooded through his mind. Evelyn knew. No hiding a three-month pregnancy from Evelyn. She'd known about Lara's pregnancy. Probably remembered his reaction to that piece of news, too, letting Ric know immediately so his old friend understood Lara's position and could act on it if he wanted to.

Evelyn would have advised Megan that Johnny had to be told. But what did Megan want of him?

That was the big question.

Though instantly overriding it was *what he wanted.*

Megan was pregnant with his child.

There was no question about what should be done.

'We get married,' he said, pushing off the desk to stand tall and determined against any opposition she threw at him.

'Married,' she repeated, as though she couldn't believe he had made that leap.

'I think Mitch told me it can't be done under a month. We can fly to Bourke tomorrow, sign whatever papers have to be signed for legal notice...'

'Johnny, people don't get married over a pregnancy anymore,' she cried, her arms unfolding, hands flapping in agitation. 'Especially when...'

'It was just a night of sex?' he finished for her, all his doubts about Megan's motivation for that night crowding into his mind.

He watched her flounder, so many emotions flitting across her face, it was impossible to decipher what she was thinking. Johnny decided it didn't matter. The only important end to this conversation was to give the child she was carrying—*his child*—the kind of security every child deserved to have.

'Look!' she finally pleaded. 'I did something stupid...wilful...'

'We're all guilty of rash acts from time to time, Megan,' he said sympathetically.

'I'm responsible for the consequences, not you, Johnny,' she shot back at him.

'That's beside the point. Whether planned or not, I'm the father of this child,' he stated simply.

'It doesn't mean you have to marry me.' Wild pride in her eyes.

'Do you have a problem with being my wife?'

No answer.

Anguished uncertainty in her eyes.

The sex between them had been good, Johnny argued to himself. She couldn't deny that. And he was co-owner of Gundamurra. Difficult for her to marry some outsider when she had a child by the man who would continue to share her home.

'I'm here, Megan,' he pressed. 'You can't send me away. I'm not going away. Why not accept—'

'But you *will* go away,' she broke in vehemently. 'You always do. Career opportunities will come up...'

'I don't have to take them. I can afford to retire from the whole entertainment circus right now.'

'You won't want to. Not in the long run.'

'Don't tell me what I want, Megan. More than anything I want to be a good father.'

'You don't have to be married to fulfil that role, Johnny.'

'You'd prefer us to be single parents?' His mind buzzed around what advantage Megan might see in that situation and zeroed in on the worst possible scenario. Connected to her insistent belief that he would go away... 'If I have to fight you for custody rights, I will,' he fired at her in grim challenge. 'Just because you're the mother doesn't make you the arbiter of what's best for our child.'

She looked appalled. 'You wouldn't drag him—her—around the world with you.'

'Why not? Gundamurra might be the centre of your universe, but would a fair judge rule that a child can't experience anything else? If you don't want to be my wife and work at being a harmonious couple...'

'A good father would want a stable life for his child,' she fiercely argued.

'Yes. And also want the child to feel loved by both parents. Not one cutting out the other. Was that what you intended to do with me, Megan? Cut me out?'

'No!' She paced around, pumped up with too much turbulent energy to remain still, though her arms folded across her chest again, projecting a need for self-containment, excluding him by action if not by word.

Johnny kept his distance, watching her deal with the pressure he had mounted for the outcome he wanted. Anger was still burning through him. If she had imagined he'd just waltz off about his business and leave her to bring up their child any way she wanted, she could certainly dismiss that idea right now.

She paused, shooting him a measuring look. 'You said Gundamurra was home to you. I want it to be home to our child, too.'

'So why not make us a family, Megan? What objection do you have to marrying me?'

'If I marry you...will you leave our son or daughter here with me when you take on career commitments overseas?'

Johnny knew that being a hands-on father would always come first with him. However, his career was clearly a big stumbling block to Megan, had been for a long time and still was, though he'd thought he'd answered the prejudices she'd held about it. The arrangement she wanted to put into place seemed very one-sided to him, and certainly not to his liking.

'Should I take on work that requires me to be elsewhere, I would want my family to go with me.'

'No!' Scarlet pride in her cheeks. 'I will not compete with...' Her mouth clamped shut, but her eyes held a violent storm of feeling.

'Compete with what?' he probed.

'The women in your world,' she flung at him, hating having to say it yet unable to hold it in.

He shook his head. The absurdity was...*she* was the only woman he wanted. Nevertheless, the realisation finally dawned that Megan was consumed by an intense sense of vulnerability, fighting him to keep herself and their child on the only secure ground she knew.

'There is no competition,' he said gently, wanting to erase her fears. Rank disbelief stared back at him.

It propelled him forward, his hands spread in an openly inviting gesture. 'You *can* trust me, Megan. As my wife, you'll have my absolute commitment and loyalty.'

Still the rigid stance, arms folded in stubborn resistance, but there was a wavering in her eyes, perhaps a wanting to believe that couldn't quite be suppressed.

He curved his hands over the tense muscles of her shoulders. 'I promise you Gundamurra will always be our home, the big constant in our lives. But if I ask you to leave it sometimes, to share something else with me for a while, aren't you brave enough to try that, Megan?'

'*This* is my life, Johnny. You can't expect me to leave it. I don't want to be a fish out of water. I'd hate it.'

His hands instinctively slid up to cup her face, forcing her gaze to hold his while he pushed for a resolution. 'This is fear talking, Megan. And what we need here is a leap of faith. The reality is we're going to have a child. We should live together as a family. And marriage is about giving to each other, not laying down conditions that will limit—if not wreck—the relationship we should have as husband and wife. I'm not even asking you to meet me halfway. Just give a little. At least...give it a chance.'

He dropped his hands and backed off. 'Think about it. My position is not going to change. Either we get married and we both try to make it work as best we can...or I'll fight you for my fair share of fatherhood. I won't be kept dangling on this, Megan. You have until tomorrow morning to decide.'

Johnny left the ultimatum hanging and walked to the door. As far as he was concerned, there was nothing more to discuss. Whichever way Megan chose, his own course was clear. His child was going to have the kind of father he would have wanted himself—a father like Patrick— always there for him. Or her. If Megan didn't ever come to love him, at least their child would. No way was he going to miss out on that!

'Wait!'

His hand was already on the doorknob when her call whipped through the tense silence, halting his exit. Johnny gritted his teeth and half-turned, conceding a few more moments but not prepared to enter into further argument.

She'd dropped the folded arm posture and her hands were now fretting at each other, revealing how very nervous she was. Her eyes held a fearful pleading that he found painful. He'd never done anything to hurt her. Never would. Her throat moved in a convulsive swallow, as though her thoughts sickened her.

'Dammit, Megan!' he muttered fiercely. 'Can't you see...?'

'I'll give it a chance.'

'Give what a chance?'

'I'll marry you.'

# CHAPTER ELEVEN

'WILL YOU, Megan Mary Maguire, take this man...'

While the marriage celebrant intoned the traditional vow with all due solemnity, Megan was still struggling to believe it was really happening, that she was standing here in full bridal regalia, about to say the words that would make her Johnny Ellis's wife.

*This man...*the one she'd always wanted...her wedding to him more a teenage fantasy than an adult reality, yet here they were, standing on the green grass of the inner quadrangle, everyone who worked on the homestead in attendance along with her family and Johnny's closest friends, bearing witness to the marriage. This was how she'd dreamed of it, although her father should have still been alive, giving her away.

Perhaps he was in spirit.

Certainly it was his will that had started the very personal situation between her and Johnny rolling. If only the baby hadn't forced this end, if she'd been sure of Johnny's love for her, Megan knew she might have been a deliriously happy bride. As it was, her stomach was full of butterflies and all she could do was hope that everything would turn out right. Or right enough to live with this decision.

The celebrant looked expectantly at her.

'I will,' she said.

A leap of faith.

'Will you, Johnny Ellis, take this woman...'

No doubt about his reply. He'd been the driving force towards this wedding from the moment she'd agreed to marry him. No quick civil ceremony in a register office. A proper celebration of their union in front of those closest to them. At Gundamurra, because it was the most appropriate location—home to both of them—and it would keep the wedding contained and private. Ric would do the photographs, some of which would be released to the media afterwards, making the marriage publicly known.

At first, she had protested the idea of a photo of her—Johnny Ellis's bride—being splashed around the world, becoming part of the publicity machine that surrounded his career. His reply had made any argument impossible—

'I'm not going to hide you, Megan. And I am not entering you into a competition. To me you are the most beautiful woman in the world and I want other women to know it. To know I'm married to you.'

She'd never thought of herself as beautiful. Not anything like the celebrities he had mixed with socially. Had he said that simply to quell the panic she felt at being compared to *them?* Whatever the truth, Megan had desperately wanted to live up to Johnny's stated view of her, at least on their wedding day.

She'd asked Ric's wife, Lara, who'd once been an international model, to help her choose the wedding dress, a fabulous design in ivory silk with lace and seed pearls, making it possible to wear the pearl necklace, and a wonderful long veil attached to a pearl tiara.

Evelyn, with sentimental tears in her eyes, had declared she looked just like a princess, and her dear mother and father would be very proud of her today, but most of all Megan wanted Johnny to be proud of her, proud to have her as his wife.

'I will,' he said, very firmly.

Then they were exchanging the gold rings he had chosen. She was glad he wanted to wear one, too, the symbol of his commitment to their marriage.

This past month he'd devoted most of his time to catching up on all the work being done at Gundamurra, proving to her that he had a deep interest in it, even making suggestions for improvements that should be considered when the climate was right. But how long would he stay here before his career called him away? And how was she going to cope with his life?

*Don't think about it.*

*Not today.*

'I now pronounce you husband and wife.'

Johnny was smiling at her.

She could hear the clicking of Ric's camera.

Her heart was rocketing around her chest in anticipation of the kiss that was to come. It was impossible to move her facial muscles into a responding smile. Her mind was wildly sorting out the expression in Johnny's eyes. Pleasure in her appearance, yes. Also a flash of triumphant satisfaction, possibly in having carried through what he'd decided was right, even to holding off having any intimate connection with her until their wedding night. But mostly, she saw a simmering desire, revelling in the promise that she was his, to have and to hold from this day forth.

Sweet relief.

At least he did want sex with her.

He kissed her with a slow, seductive sensuality, his mouth certainly seeming to suggest that passion was just lying in wait for the privacy of their honeymoon. No problems in bed, Megan assured herself. Maybe her pregnancy actually made her more desirable to him. She hoped so, acutely conscious of the more rounded tummy hidden by the clever design of her wedding gown.

He steered her to the table where they were to sign the marriage certificate. Once that was done, everyone came up to congratulate them, wishing them a long and happy life together.

It amazed Megan how genuinely given these sentiments were, as though no doubts about the success of this marriage were being harboured. They knew she was pregnant. Neither she nor Johnny had tried to keep that a secret. Yet it seemed irrelevant to them. It was as though they had all decided that this match had been made in heaven and it met with their heartfelt approval.

Whether Ric or Mitch had raised any questions with Johnny, she didn't know. They gave no sign of it. Her sisters had thought it marvellous that Johnny wanted to marry her. Not one hint of criticism from them. Apparently they were perfectly confident that a workable future could be achieved between the two of them, probably on the principle that love conquers all.

Except the only *love* Megan was sure of was Johnny's love for their unborn child.

A huge barbecue dinner had been organised. Fairy lights had been strung around the pepper trees, just as they always were for Christmas, and the mood was just as merry. Speeches were made. Johnny played his guitar and sang a song he'd composed especially for her. He called it 'Coming Home' and everyone was moved by it, including Megan, who fiercely wished that the lyrics were a true expression of how he felt, not merely a string of effective sentiments that stirred emotions.

It prompted Lara to ask if he'd sing at a charity concert which was being organised in Sydney, all the proceeds to be used for drought relief, wherever it was most needed. 'Your name would pull in more people, Johnny,' she pressed. 'The concert won't be for a couple of more months. We have to fix a date for all the artists we want to be available. The idea is for them to donate their talent for the cause.'

'I'm taking time out from that scene, Lara,' he excused apologetically.

*Because of me,* Megan instantly thought. 'It's okay, Johnny,' she leapt in. 'I won't mind if you do it.'

He frowned at her, puzzled by her apparent eagerness for him to move back into the limelight.

'It will help people who are in desperate need of help,' she rushed out, needing him to see she could be fair.

'Lara said the concert will be held in a couple of months, Megan,' he reminded her, still frowning over her impulsive urging. 'I won't want to leave you at home alone at that point in time, being so pregnant, possibly needing my help.'

Was he worried about the baby? She'd only be six or seven months along, dependent on the date of the concert. Her pregnancy would definitely be showing by then, but Johnny had said he had no intention of *hiding* her.

'I could go with you,' she argued, determined not to appear selfish. Besides, this performance was to be staged in Australia, not overseas, and should only take up a week or two with rehearsals. 'It will give me the chance to buy baby things in Sydney,' she added eagerly.

'And I can guide you to the best shops,' Lara offered with her lovely smile. 'We'll have great fun shopping, Megan.'

'I'll come with you,' Kathryn chimed in, smiling at Mitch who was proudly carrying around their new baby son. 'Josh will be needing bigger clothes by then.'

'The mothers' club,' Johnny commented with an indulgent shake of his head.

'Yes. And I can just see you and Mitch and Ric forming the fathers' club in the not too distant future,' Kathryn retorted laughingly.

'You could be right,' he acknowledged.

If he really did base himself in Australia from now on, Megan thought hopefully.

'About the concert, Lara,' he went on. 'Send me the paperwork on it and I'll let you know.'

No promise.

Megan was disappointed that she hadn't won his approval. She silently resolved to find out what his reservations were about committing himself. There was still so much about Johnny she didn't know, despite having known him for most of her life.

But he was, without a doubt, the most handsome man in the world to her, breathtakingly so in his formal black dinner suit. And now, for better or for worse, he was her husband. Megan told herself to stop worrying about the future and just concentrate on tonight, being with him in every sense.

Tomorrow they were flying to Broome for a week's honeymoon—a week of making love and sharing intimate thoughts, she hoped. Tonight she wanted to convince Johnny that it wasn't *just sex* for her, banishing any thought that she'd only been *using* him to make herself feel better on the night of her father's wake.

She wanted *him*.

Only him.

She tried to transmit this while Ric was posing them for the photograph he'd envisaged being the definitive one of their wedding. It was late in the evening—time for the party to break up—and everyone had followed Ric out to the setting he had chosen, away from all the buildings. He stood Megan and Johnny facing each other, holding hands.

Behind them was a dark empty landscape, seemingly flat to the horizon, above it the brilliant stars of the outback sky.

They had to wait for him to get the lighting just right. Johnny joked about the exacting eye of an artist but he seemed happy to co-operate with his old friend's concept.

'That sure beats a cathedral,' Mitch murmured, almost reverently, looking up at the canopy of stars. 'Now I know why you won all those photography prizes, Ric.'

'To me, nature always beats anything man-made,' Ric answered. 'And this shot is meant to be totally primal, the imprint of greatest human faith in each other against the stark might of the outback.'

A convulsive little shiver ran through Megan at the all too perceptive truth of those words.

Johnny squeezed her hands, instantly imparting warmth and strength. She looked up into eyes that blazed their searing message into her heart... *believe in me.* She didn't hear the camera click that captured her own surge of emotion, the huge welling of need and desire to believe their marriage would survive anything life threw at them. Survive and thrive here at Gundamurra, because this was where she belonged, where she wanted Johnny to feel he belonged, with her and the children they would have.

Home...

And that overwhelming wave of feeling was still sweeping through her when they were finally alone together in the room where their baby had been conceived. She was no longer nervous, nor apprehensive, nor worried about convincing Johnny of anything. A blissful sense of union with him permeated every kiss, every touch, building a deep passion for all the intense pleasure they could give to each other.

They were married.

On this—their wedding night—all other realities were left to be met when they had to be met.

# CHAPTER TWELVE

THE HONEYMOON WAS pure sensual bliss—a week of hot days and balmy nights in Broome—time out from the drought problems at Gundamurra—nothing to do but enjoy themselves in any way impulse took them.

Megan found that sexual pleasure with Johnny was extremely addictive. He was a marvellous lover and there was certainly no doubting his desire for her. It seemed to constantly simmer in his eyes, flaring into passion when she dared to provoke it, and twinkling with wicked satisfaction when she lay contentedly in his arms afterwards.

Though occasionally she felt a stab of jealousy at the look of entranced love on his face when he felt the baby move. Not once did he speak of loving her, and Megan could not bring herself to admit to the feelings she'd always had about him. She was the mother of his child. That was what their marriage was based on. And Johnny certainly did his best to be a husband she could be happy with.

And she *was* happy for the most part. When they returned to Gundamurra, Johnny threw himself into working with the sheep, going out with the men to do whatever chores were scheduled, coming home to her each evening with the air of a man well satisfied with jobs done. She couldn't fault his commitment to their partnership. The only problem that arose between them centred on the charity concert Lara had mentioned on their wedding day.

The paperwork had been sent for Johnny to peruse. Megan fretted over his reluctance to make a positive decision, acutely conscious that her negative reaction to his career might be at the root of his aversion to the idea. Wanting to make amends for her previous attitude, she kept pressing him, reasoning that drought relief was the best possible cause for donating his talent, and very appropriate since he was now person-ally connected to the land.

She did not foresee that the agreement she finally won from him would almost immediately throw them into conflict. A request for a publicity interview at Gundamurra came in and Johnny was strongly opposed to granting it.

'You said you weren't going to hide me,' Megan argued.

'It's not hiding you. It's protecting you,' Johnny argued back. 'You've had no experience of dealing with the media. Anything you say can be skewed to fit into the story an interviewer wants to do.'

'But I'm a first-hand authority on the drought.'

'They won't be after a story on the drought.'

She didn't believe him.

She suspected he didn't want to expose her to his career so soon after their marriage. Yet to her mind, it had to be faced, and the sooner it stopped being a hurdle to be avoided, the better. Besides, a story on how the drought was affecting Gundamurra would surely make city people more aware of the problems in the country. How could it possibly hurt her? What was he protecting her from?

'You can't control what people write, Megan,' he stated, impatient with her stubbornness on this issue. 'The only kind of interview you can control is on live television, and it takes a lot of practice to get that right, believe me.'

All she could see was he didn't want to share this part of his life with her. Johnny Ellis was the star, the crowd-puller. She was just his wife in the background.

To close the rift that had opened up between them, Johnny gave way on granting the interview at Gundamurra. The story was subsequently headlined—The Outback Bridal Rescue—with a half page photograph of Ric's special shot of them on their wedding night.

The only comment on the drought was that without Johnny Ellis's investment in Gundamurra, even this well-established sheep station would not have survived it. The rest of it was about Johnny's career and speculation about its future now that he was supposedly married to the land. Or was he simply carrying over the cowboy role he'd played in the movie which was yet to be released, in real life for a while?

Megan hated it—hated the doubts it raised in her mind, hated the way every *important* thing she and Johnny had spoken about had been virtually ignored.

'How do you live with this?' she raged.

'Megan, you chose to let them invade our privacy here, to let yourself be exploited. Will you listen to me now?' he answered quietly.

She listened.

He laid out his plan, explained the reasons for it and Megan ended up feeling she had no choice but to accede to it, given that she was pregnant and Johnny's schedule would be hectic with rehearsals and handling the media coverage expected of him to get maximum publicity for the concert.

So here she was, being mollycoddled by Ric and Lara in their lovely home at Balmoral Beach, while Johnny held court from a top-class city hotel with top-class security guarding him from unwanted attention, escorting him to and from wherever he had to be.

She went shopping with Lara and Kathryn, unaccosted by anyone. She had the freedom of the city to enjoy in any way she liked, with good company readily available. Except it wasn't Johnny's company. And it was lonely in bed at night.

Johnny called her on his mobile phone frequently. She could hardly complain he was excluding her from his life, yet she did feel excluded. Mostly they talked about what she'd been doing, where she'd been, what she'd bought. It seemed to her he deliberately minimised his activities, perhaps believing they would be of no interest to her. Even when she pressed him on them he was dismissive, not allowing her any sense of sharing.

'Will it always be like this?' she cried in exasperation during one call. 'You there, me here?'

It evoked a silence that suddenly crawled with black irony. This was what she had initially wanted, to have no part of his career, for her and their child to occupy a separate place in his life. But now Megan was desperate to believe that the intimacy they had forged during the past two months together at Gundamurra *could* be transplanted elsewhere. Or didn't Johnny believe that was possible?

She cursed the narrowness of her previous attitude, worrying that it was still casting a shadow on Johnny's thinking, despite her attempts to show him it was different now. Her nerves tightened up as she waited for his reply, wanting him to say something she could get her teeth into and tear apart.

'No. You won't always be pregnant, Megan.' Strained patience in his voice, making her feel like a petulant child. 'As I've already explained to you, I just want to save you unnecessary stress in your condition. It will only be another week and we'll be home again. Okay?'

Eminently reasonable.

But in Megan's already stressed mind it translated to Johnny's judgement that she wouldn't cope with the demands of his career and he didn't want the hassle of looking after her, having to mop up her inexperienced errors of judgement which made her more a hindrance than a help, especially when he should be focussing on putting his best professional foot forward.

I'm being selfish again, she told herself, and let the issue drop, privately vowing to learn how to handle his world better the next time around, listening to him instead of barging forward with her own ideas.

Yet Johnny's emphasis on her pregnancy kept niggling—the child who meant so much to him. Megan couldn't help thinking he wouldn't choose to be in a hotel room by himself if the baby had been born. He'd want *his family* with him. And while their marriage might have seemed reasonably safe and solid while living together at Gundamurra, maybe she'd been living in a fool's paradise and deep unbridgeable gaps could open up at any moment.

Ric and Lara were indulgently amused by her desire to watch Johnny's spot on each television show that featured him, to listen to the talk-back radio programs he participated in, to read every interview printed in the newspapers. They thought she was besotted with her new husband. The truth was her secret insecurities compelled her to know precisely how Johnny performed, whether *she* was mentioned and what Johnny said about her and their marriage.

For the most part he diverted any questions about his private life, speaking with surprising passion about the plight of farmers and pastoralists, many of whom had worked the land for generations, benefiting all Australians. He reminded people of all the traditional poetry and songs that epitomised the hardships of country life, the culture of survival that was at the core of our patriotism.

'You've got to hand it to Johnny. He hits straight at the heart,' Ric commented appreciatively, while they were watching him perform on one current affairs program.

Yes, right at the heart of the anchorwoman who was interviewing him, Megan thought, watching the body language that shouted how very attractive she found him in every sense. And he was...charming, sincere, his voice an incredibly seductive tool, and all of him emanating so much sexual magnetism, the woman was turning into a melting marshmallow instead of living up to her reputation for being sharp and tough.

It left Megan with the certainty that he could have married anyone, but didn't have to. They'd fall at his feet, anyway. It was only because she was having his child that he'd decided to marry her. All his love-making, caring... If she hadn't been pregnant, would he have given so much? Any of it?

On that one fateful night of sex, he would have used protection.

Now he was protecting *her condition.*

Protecting his fatherhood.

Megan's emotions were in a total mess by the time the night of the concert arrived. Lara, who was on the charity committee, had obtained tickets for what she considered the prime position in the Sydney Entertainment Centre. They were in the front row of the central tier of seats facing the stage.

'Above the floor level,' she explained, 'with a barrier between us and any madness that might break out.'

'Madness?' Megan queried.

'You've never been to a pop concert, Megan?'

'No, I haven't.'

'The area closest to the stage is usually called the mosh pit. Fans can totally spin out, especially when the music gets them going. We'll be safe where our seats are situated.'

*Safe*...that word grated on Megan's jangling nerves. Yet when they did take their seats in the huge auditorium which was jam-packed with thousands of people all buzzing with excited anticipation, she appreci- ated the choice Lara had made. Even more so when the first pop band onstage swung into action and the sound assault of their music was in- creased by almost incessant screaming from fans jumping up and down and carrying on like lunatics.

It was certainly an education to Megan about Johnny's life. She knew he'd done many concert tours throughout his career, more in the U.S.A. than here in Australia. He was a megastar on the country and western music scene, though his popularity was not limited to only those fans. His songs had universal appeal, which was why he was billed as the star act tonight, the last one onstage, bringing the concert to an end, leaving everyone happy and uplifted.

Clearly the performers got a huge kick out of the wildly enthusiastic response from their audience. Their energy level was amazing and there was certainly a sexual buzz in their strutting. Was all this adulation ad- dictive? Would someone who was used to it find life boringly flat with- out regular doses of it?

As the evening's entertainment progressed, security guards had to stop some fans from climbing onto the stage. Others had to be carried away for medical attention, having fainted from the crush or their own hyperexcitement.

Just before Johnny was to make his appearance, a girl with long blonde hair and a tight scarlet mini-dress was actually tossed by her companions onto the stage and she thrust a note into the retiring singer's hand before leaping off to escape the guards.

'Groupie,' Lara drily remarked. 'No doubt she'll want to be picked out from the crowd backstage once the show is over.'

Megan was relieved the girl hadn't targeted Johnny.

Not that he'd be swayed by it. His view of groupies had convinced her that he would never take that kind of sexual advantage from his celeb- rity. She simply didn't need any more evidence of how desirable he was to other women. As it was, her nerves were on edge, waiting for his per- formance—live—in front of this massive crowd of people.

*Definitely my last concert,* Johnny thought grimly, waiting for the guys to vacate the stage. They were still prancing around, all pumped up from the wild response to their music, eating up the frenetic crowd energy while they could. The buzz didn't last. After the adrenaline rush came the let-down because it was all about the music and the event itself, not the person. Johnny knew he didn't want this anymore. Especially not the empty hotel room afterwards.

Tomorrow he could go home with Megan. To Gundamurra where he was genuinely liked for the man he was. Put all this artificial *love* behind him and raise a family where the love would be real. Megan would be happy about that. It was just too difficult for her to be faced with everything celebrity involved.

'Something for you, Johnny.' A photograph was thrust into his hand by the main vocalist of the band, now bouncing off stage. The guy winked at him. 'Blonde bomb in a red mini-dress, front row. Great tits.'

Johnny was about to toss it away when the guy added in a mocking drawl, 'Oh yeah! Said to tell you she was your long-lost sister. Try anything, some chicks.'

*Sister!*

The idea thumped into Johnny's heart.

It had never occurred to him that his mother might have had another child. He couldn't remember one but he didn't recall anything about that time. And he certainly hadn't been told he had a sister somewhere. But would he have been informed if the child had been adopted out? Maybe a baby. Which meant she'd be thirty-six now.

He stared at the photograph. Definitely not a teenager. Could be in her thirties. Difficult to tell a woman's age. He saw no likeness to himself but that meant nothing. She would have had a different father.

*Long-lost sister...* His stomach started churning. He'd never thought to do a search himself, believing he'd been the only one left abandoned by his mother's death.

What if he wasn't?

'Your turn to wow 'em, Johnny,' one of the backstage guys prompted him.

He heard the MC doing the introduction.

There was nowhere to stash the photograph except under his shirt. He caught sight of writing on the back as he turned it over to slide it down his V-neckline.

*Please let me get to you—your sister, Jodie Ellis.*

Jodie... Johnny...

Had she tried before and been turned away by his minders?

Or was it simply a groupie scam?

No time to think about it now.

He was on.

Blonde in a red mini-dress. Front row.

Megan was totally stunned by Johnny's performance. The screaming of the fans stopped the moment he began to sing. He just seemed to command the rapt attention of everyone in the auditorium, his strong, beautiful voice carrying waves of emotion that swept out and grabbed people by the throat.

He didn't need to gyrate around the stage. He didn't need to whip up excitement. He simply stood and delivered and there were sighs of pleasure as people swayed to his rhythm, happy clapping with the upbeat songs, thunderous applause when he finished each number and flashed the charismatic smile that would have charmed love out of a stone.

Megastar.

Of course, the fact that he was spectacularly male—a man's man—a woman's man—added immeasurably to his powerful attraction. Megan couldn't help noticing the blonde in the scarlet mini-dress doing everything she could to draw Johnny's attention to her. Apparently she had changed her mind about the main object of her desire tonight. No contest, Megan thought, but she didn't like it.

She particularly didn't like the fact that Johnny seemed distracted by the woman, his gaze returning to her again and again throughout his performance. What was she doing that Megan couldn't see? Why was Johnny zeroing in on her so much?

It stirred up all the insecurities Megan was struggling with, especially since she couldn't make eye contact with him herself. Impossible for Johnny to actually see her so far back from the brilliantly lit stage. The major part of the audience had to be a dark blur to him, simply a presence he heard and felt and responded to.

At least he *knew* she was here, with his old friends and their wives. When he announced his final song, he did look directly to where they were seated and it gave Megan considerable relief to hear him say he'd composed this song for his wife on their wedding day—a very public acknowledgement of their marriage.

He already had the audience completely in his hands, but his rendition of 'Coming Home' was incredibly moving, heart-tugging, so much so that there were several moments of poignant silence at the end of it before the crowd erupted into huge prolonged applause, everyone on their feet, clapping, shouting, not wanting to let him leave the stage.

But with a simple hand salute to the crowd, he walked off and did not return. The audience eventually accepted that the concert was over. People started to move towards the exits, still buzzing with pleasure despite not having persuaded Johnny into an encore.

Megan would have been happy to leave, too, but she caught sight of a security guard escorting the troublesome blonde with an air of set purpose. The action unsettled her again. Lara, Kathryn, Ric, and Mitch were enthusing over Johnny's performance as they all moved out to the aisle, ready to make their way out of the massive entertainment centre, but Megan was too distracted to voice any sensible comment herself.

'Can we go backstage?' she asked, impelled to settle the nagging sense of not knowing what was going on with Johnny, needing to be with him.

It wasn't planned.

But they went.

And were ushered into a dressing-room where the blonde in the scarlet mini-dress had her arms wound around Johnny's neck and her body plastered to his!

# CHAPTER THIRTEEN

SHOCK HELD THEM all silent.

Except for the blonde.

Megan burned with humiliation as the woman rubbed her body provocatively, invitingly, against Johnny's and babbled on about how fantastic he was and she'd do anything—*anything* he wanted—just to be with him.

A blatant groupie.

And Johnny had to have given instructions for her to be brought to him.

Well, he was certainly caught in a spotlight now!

Yet there was no guilt on his face.

With an air of grim self-containment, he reached up and forcibly pulled down the arms that held him, stepping back out of body contact as he spoke with biting distaste. 'You picked the wrong mark.'

'But you sent for me,' the blonde protested.

No escape from that truth.

Megan's heart died.

If she hadn't come backstage, seen this for herself…

'Please…just go.' Johnny nodded to Megan. 'My wife is here.'

The blonde whipped around to see. Her gaze skated over the group who'd entered, fastened on Megan, raked her from head to foot in angry frustration, pausing at the now obvious bump of her pregnancy. 'So, you got him with that trap,' she said nastily.

'Go!' Johnny thundered, as though he could barely tolerate the offence, his expression fighting both pain and fury.

*Trap* was right, Megan thought miserably.

Having realised there was no choice but to accept defeat, the blonde flounced around them to the open doorway, jeeringly tossing back, 'You don't know what you're missing, Johnny.'

A stony pride settled on his face as he muttered, 'I do. I know exactly what I'm missing.' But he spoke to empty space. The blonde was gone. And his eyes had emptied of all feeling, too. There was suddenly a sense of dreadful emptiness permeating the whole room.

No-one spoke.

Megan sensed they were all hanging out for an acceptable explanation, possibly embarrassed at being witnesses to a scene none of them liked. Her hand instinctively moved to spread over the hump which held her baby, a fierce protective love welling up and choking her.

Wretched thoughts jumbled through her mind. There'd been no need for Johnny to marry her. She hadn't asked him to. Nor had she wanted him to feel he was missing out on anything. She hated that he did. How could she hold him to their marriage, knowing it got in the way of... *his life?*

Johnny visibly regathered himself and flashed a derisive look at Ric and Mitch. 'She claimed to be my long-lost sister.'

As though *they* would understand.

Not his wife.

'I thought...it was possible,' he added with a grimace that somehow expressed a world of loss.

A sister? Megan's mind whirled, trying to fit this idea into the train of circumstances she had watched, trying to understand how Johnny could have believed such an unlikely claim...what it might have meant to him.

'We're your family, Johnny,' Mitch said quietly.

'You'll always have us,' Ric backed up.

The three men...who'd been boys at Gundamurra...a brotherhood... but not linked by blood.

Johnny nodded, acknowledging the bond between them, yet his eyes were still bleak as his gaze fastened on the hand Megan had placed over her tummy and she intuitively knew what he was thinking. This baby was the only blood link to him…flesh of his flesh. No sister. But he would have a son or a daughter.

It was her baby, too, but she didn't think that counted to him. He wanted this child. Regardless of the cost to himself on any other level, *he needed to have this child in his life,* filling a hole she could not really imagine because she'd never been in his situation. Mitch had a sister and a son. Ric had a son and a daughter. Johnny was still alone in the world in any biological sense.

'Will you come back to the hotel with me tonight?' he asked her, a hollow quality in his voice that seemed to expect nothing, just a yes or no.

'Yes,' she said, all her nerves knotted with apprehension, yet the need to know what was on his mind was paramount—how their marriage really was for him, good or bad. He could put all his willpower behind a commitment, but feelings were something else.

He heaved a tired sigh. 'Ric, Mitch…' A wry appreciation flitted into a brief curl of his mouth. 'Good of you to be here for me, but…' He gestured an apologetic appeal.

'We'll leave you to it,' Mitch swiftly interpreted.

'Don't let this get you down, Johnny,' Ric quietly advised. 'We have to let the past go.'

'Guess it got up and bit me tonight, Ric.' He shrugged. 'Took me off guard. I'll be okay.'

He made a dismissive gesture and his two old friends moved out, taking their wives with them, closing the door to give him privacy with Megan.

Feeling totally ill-equipped to deal with emotions Johnny had never revealed to her, and painfully aware that she had not been invited backstage, she couldn't bring herself to go to him. Hopelessly tongue-tied, she stayed where she was, waiting for some sign that he actually welcomed her being here. Although he'd asked her to stay, the request had been made in front of others and might only have been some kind of test for loyalty from her, trust in his word.

Johnny seemed to be viewing her from a great distance, perhaps weighing her silence, her stillness, perhaps seeing a chasm between them that he didn't have the energy to cross. Was it up to her? Panic seized her mind, inducing a terrible torment of indecisiveness.

Finally he spoke, his mouth taking on an ironic twist. 'I guess you thought it was something different.'

Megan inwardly writhed over the doubts and suspicions that had driven her backstage to check what was true or not. After what had just unfolded here she couldn't confess to them. It felt too wrong. As though it might be the end of any possible relationship between them if she did. Yet she had to say something. He had surely noticed her shock on seeing him with the blonde.

With a helpless little gesture of appeal she weakly offered, 'I'm sorry, Johnny. It looked...'

'As though I'd lied to you,' he drily finished for her. 'I haven't, Megan. Not about anything.'

He turned and picked up a photograph from the make-up bench behind him. 'This was passed to me by the singer who came offstage just before I went on. I would have tossed it away, but for what was written on the back.'

He held it out to her, making her feel forced to step forward and take it, forced to read the words that had swayed him into checking out the woman who had claimed to be *his long-lost sister.* She looked just as tarty in the photograph as she had in real life, heavily made up, sexily dressed, provocatively posed.

'Did you want her to be your sister, Johnny?' she asked, unable to hide her distaste.

'You mean she might be a prostitute...like my mother?'

The derisive remark whipped heat into Megan's cheeks—shame at having forgotten what was clearly unforgettable to him. She scrambled to excuse the slip. 'I meant...she doesn't look anything like you.'

'How could I know what *a half-sister* would look like, Megan?'

She took a quick breath, feeling she was drowning in waters too deep for her to wade through. His mother probably hadn't known who *his* father was, let alone...

'I'm sorry, Johnny,' she repeated in frantic appeal. 'I guess... Ric and Mitch are more...more attuned to where you've come from. To me you're just you. And you're such a big person...'

She stopped, shaking her head at the realisation she was denying his past any importance, precisely when he was feeling it very badly. 'What can I do to help?' she cried, horribly conscious of how inadequate that sounded even as the words tripped out of her mouth.

His shoulders squared, his broad chest expanding as he tilted his head back and dragged in a deep breath. 'Let it go.' It was a command to himself. He sighed and his gaze came down to meet hers, eyes bitter with self-mockery. 'Ric has it right. Just let the past go. Stupid of me...in my position...to let myself be sucked in. Sucked back to it.'

He snatched the photograph out of Megan's hand and tore it into smaller and smaller pieces as he stepped over to a wastebin. He dropped the fragments into it and turned to her with a savage look. 'I will never do another concert, Megan. Don't ask it of me again. Not for any reason.'

'I'm sorry...' It sounded so dreadfully ineffectual—as meaningless as a parrot's repetition—but what else could she say?

'Let's get out of here!'

Security guards escorted them to a limousine.

Security guards rode in the car with them, inhibiting any private conversation, not that Johnny's closed-in demeanor invited any. Megan felt hopelessly inhibited about making any contact at all. She wished he would hold her hand...anything to link them again...but he didn't, and the tension emanating from him seemed filled with a fierce impatience to get this whole business over and done with.

Security guards accompanied them every step of the way up to Johnny's hotel room, checking it was empty before they finally withdrew. Even then, Johnny forestalled any move by Megan to break into his insulated mood, muttering, 'I need a shower,' and heading straight for the bathroom. 'Make yourself at home. Order up some supper if you like. Just call room service,' he added carelessly.

She was left standing in a very spacious, very luxurious hotel suite, overwhelmingly conscious of how lonely it could be, despite being surrounded by what great wealth could buy.

Had Johnny felt this kind of loneliness here? Putting up with it to protect her? Did he feel even more alone now because she hadn't given him her complete trust, had stood back from him when she should have moved forward to offer comfort, assuring him that while he had missed out on much in the past, she could make up for it?

Megan didn't know if she could or not, but the strong fear of losing any chance of deep intimacy with him compelled her into trying to reach out to his heart.

With trembling hands, she stripped off her clothes. Johnny might simply be washing off the sweat from performing under a blast of hot lights, but her imagination saw him washing off the dirty sense of being tricked into facing the murky circumstances of his birth, the horrors of his childhood which he'd never shared with her, drowning out the loneliness that her lack of understanding had undoubtedly made sharper.

She forced her legs to walk into the bathroom, her mind gripping on to a fierce determination not to panic, not to react wimpishly to any suggestion of rejection from Johnny. He didn't hear her enter. He stood under the drenching spray of the shower, eyes closed, head bent, and she saw that the packets of soap provided by the hotel lay unopened, the facecloths still folded on top of the towels.

Grabbing one of the soap packets, she ripped off its wrapping, opened the door to the shower and stepped into the spacious cubicle—plenty of room for two, even with a big man like Johnny. His head snapped up, eyes jerking open.

'You must be exhausted,' Megan rushed out, her own eyes shooting sympathetic appeal as she wildly lathered up her hands. 'Let me...'

She swiftly transferred the suds to his shoulders, spreading them over the tautly bunched muscles, watching them trail down his chest under the beat of the water because she couldn't pluck up the courage to look at his face again, frightened of seeing that he was suffering her touch, not wanting it.

He said nothing but made no move to stop her from running the soap over him. His stillness and his silence drove her into working quickly, down over his chest, his stomach, lower. The rapid pounding of her own heart drummed in her ears. A desperate desire for him to respond positively slowed her hurrying hands, dictating a more sensual slide over his naked flesh.

*I have to make him feel loved,* she thought frantically, *not alone, not missing out...*

How could she answer his needs?

Before she could think better of it, a thought slipped out of the anxious jumble in her mind. 'You used to think of me as your little sister.'

She was instantly mortified, realising it sounded like she was linking herself to the blonde who would have done anything to be with him, and here she was caressing him intimately, and he was becoming aroused...

'Megan...' His voice was harsh.

It had been a plea for him to return to caring about her, not...

'You're my wife—' His hands tore hers away from him. *'My wife!'*

'Then let me be your wife,' she cried, her eyes pleading against the angry torment in his. 'I'm sorry I got things wrong. I'm sorry I had no real idea of what the concert involved. I didn't know how it was for you.'

He shook his head in anguish and from his throat came an animal groan of pain. Too bewildered and distressed to fight for anything more, Megan was intensely relieved when he released her hands and pulled her into a fierce embrace, almost crushing the breath out of her. He rubbed his face over her hair. Never mind that it was soaking wet—they were both soaking wet—the action echoed her own craving for him and sent a flood of warmth to her fear-chilled heart.

'You don't need to know,' he growled. 'You'll never need to know. I'm done with it.'

His fingers tangled through her sodden curls and dragged her head back. His eyes blazed into hers. 'But don't you ever think again that I'd choose any other woman over you. Do you hear me, Megan?'

'I'm sorry…'

'No, dammit! Just say yes…yes…'

'Yes.'

His mouth swooped on hers as though he had to taste the word as well as hear it, and Megan poured all her own chaotic emotions into a kiss that pulsated with passionate need—a hot, urgent acceleration of desire that seared away any doubt that Johnny wanted her.

He slammed off the shower faucet, swept her out of the shower cubicle, wrapped a huge bath towel around her, and carried her out to the king-size bed in his hotel suite. There were no pleasure intensifying preliminaries. He came into her hard and fast and Megan welcomed the instant union with as much savage satisfaction as he took in it, a tumultuous fever of possession gripping both of them, whipping them on to a world-shattering climax.

Afterwards she clasped him to her, stroking his hair as he lay with his head resting just above the valley of her breasts, his breath warm against her skin, the tension gone from both of them. He shifted slightly, gliding his hand gently over her rounded belly.

'I forgot the baby,' he murmured incredulously.

'It's all right,' she soothed, smiling over the wonderful fact that he had wanted her so absolutely, not thinking of his child until now. 'I would have told you if it wasn't.'

And right on cue a ripple of movement under her skin reminded them of the new life that would soon be born.

'See...he's kicking me for it,' Johnny said fatuously, a smile in his voice.

'Might be a she.'

'Mmm...' It was a contented hum.

Contentment was good.

Her whole body was humming with it.

Megan didn't want to say anything that might spoil the sense of peaceful harmony, of very real togetherness. She believed Johnny didn't want to be with any other woman, and right now, that was enough.

Whether he really was *done* with his career, or just the concert part of it, she didn't know. Time might change that view anyway. She did know she would respect whatever decision he made about it, no argument, no criticism, no complaint. There might be more needs in Johnny that neither she, nor Gundamurra, nor even their child could ever answer.

He fell asleep, still in her embrace.

She stroked his hair, loving him, determined to be *his wife* in every sense—partner, lover, best friend and confidante. She didn't want him to feel alone...ever again.

# CHAPTER FOURTEEN

'HOME...'

So much heartfelt satisfaction in Johnny's voice.

And his grin was pure pleasure.

They were still in the air, flying over the woolshed, the name of the sheep station—Gundamurra—painted in large letters on its roof.

*Coming home* was all Johnny had talked about ever since they'd woken up in the hotel room this morning. No mention of the concert, nor its traumatic aftermath. It was clear to Megan that he was determined on letting it all go, blocking it out. She wasn't sure if that was right for him, but she wasn't about to cast shadows on the happy twinkle in his eyes.

She grinned back. 'You've still got to get this plane down safely.'

He laughed and brought it in on the airstrip, a perfect landing but for the inevitable bumps along the ground. 'Need to get this strip graded again,' he remarked as he switched off the engine.

Which meant he'd hire a grader in the coming weeks, cost no object to Johnny. Megan didn't worry about what he spent on the property anymore. As long as he was happy.

'Another thing,' he said as they went about disembarking. 'I'm going to buy a helicopter. Emily can teach me how to fly it.'

'Why do you want a helicopter?'

'It would be more handy for checking out the property than a plane.

It can land anywhere. And who knows? The Big Wet might come next year and break the drought. It could be raining in January when the baby is due and I want to be able to get you out in time. If the airstrip turns into a bog, we'll need a helicopter.'

She laughed, pleased that he was looking ahead, making plans. 'By all means get yourself a helicopter. And I'm sure Emily will be delighted to give you lessons.'

'Right! Now for Evelyn's superb carrot cake,' he said with relish.

Of course, Evelyn had it ready for him.

And Johnny was in such high good humour he gave her a hug and a kiss on the cheek to thank her for it. 'I love being in your kitchen, Evelyn,' he declared, sitting down at the table, ready to enjoy his afternoon tea. 'This is where I really feel I'm home.'

'Oh, go on with you, Mr Johnny.' She was bridling with pleasure, beaming love right back at him. 'You're just proving the old adage—the way to a man's heart is through his stomach. Here you're served with good home-cooking instead of all that hotel stuff.'

'Only you, Evelyn, can make a cake like this,' he declared, hoeing into the huge slice in front of him.

'Well, that's nice to know. Now tell me how the concert went?'

He shrugged. 'Did its job. Full house. Lots of money for drought relief.'

Evelyn sighed her frustration at what was to her a totally inadequate report. She shot an appealing look at Megan, who knew where Johnny's dismissive attitude was coming from. Nevertheless, it was measly fare for his greatest fan. Impulsively she jumped into the task of giving satisfaction.

'He was wonderful, Evelyn. He had the whole audience—thousands of them—in his hands. The way he used his voice was just magic. They didn't want to let him go when the concert ended, standing up and cheering and clapping. I've never heard anything like it. Absolutely amazing!'

Her warm appreciation of his performance seemed to startle Johnny, jerking his head towards her, but he frowned, too, as though he didn't want to hear it.

'So they should want more,' Evelyn happily declared. 'He's the best singer I've ever heard.'

'Well, they can buy my music anytime they like,' Johnny said carelessly, then switched to a charming smile. '*You* will always have it free,

Evelyn. Now please…we're hanging out for news of what's been happening here while we've been away.'

*Over and done with,* Megan thought.

And Johnny kept it that way.

The weeks rolled on towards Christmas. Megan became more heavily pregnant. Johnny bought his helicopter and learnt to fly it. He took
over more of the running of Gundamurra, insisting that she had to slow
down and rest, look after herself and the baby.

Quite frequently e-mails came in from his agent who was based in Los
Angeles. Johnny read them, answered them, deleted them. He did not
discuss them with her, didn't even refer to them. Which Megan found
disturbing. The block-out on his career seemed too extreme.

Eventually she felt driven to question him. 'All these e-mails…are you
getting offers for work, Johnny?'

'Nothing I want to take up, Megan. I'm finished with all that.' He
smiled with grim irony. 'Sooner or later my agent will believe me.'

She let that ride, leaving the decision completely up to him, though
she wondered if he would remain content with their life here. Times
changed. Currently he was looking forward to being a father, but later
down the track…

He shrugged and added, 'Most of the messages are about outstanding
business which will roll on for years. Contracts with recording compa-
nies and sponsors running out, being re-signed…stuff like that. Nothing for you to worry about.'

'I'm not worried.'

'Good!' He smiled. 'I don't want you to be. I like my life just the way
it is, right here with you.'

He meant it and she accepted it, not raising the issue again.

Johnny invited their extended family home for Christmas and they all
came. Tradition was upheld with the Christmas Eve party held around the
homestead quadrangle, everyone who worked and lived on Gundamurra
attending. Johnny took on the role of Santa Claus, giving out gifts he'd
bought personally and piled under the Christmas tree with almost child-
ish delight, anticipating the surprise and pleasure they'd give when un-
wrapped.

It made Megan wonder how many miserable Christmases he'd spent
as a boy. Empty times. Lonely times. And she thought how much her fa-

ther's understanding had encompassed when he'd opened his heart and mind and home to his three bad boys, turning their lives around, teaching them there were different paths to take—paths far more rewarding to their true inner selves.

'If anyone can fill Mr Patrick's shoes, it's Mr Johnny,' Evelyn whispered to Megan, almost bursting with pride in her personal favourite, watching him charm the children with 'Ho-ho-hos' as he made much of selecting just the right gift for them.

But would filling those huge shoes answer what Johnny truly wanted for himself?

Megan remembered what Mitch had said when she'd been so angry over the terms of her father's will, carrying on about Johnny being a pop-star—

*You've just pasted a label on the man which I know to be very superficial, Megan. Johnny has not yet reached the fulfilment of the person he is.*

And yes, it had been a superficial label, meanly judged. Her father, Mitch and Ric had known Johnny far more deeply. She was still learning about the person he was, knew that fatherhood would be something big in his life, but where true fulfilment lay for him, she didn't know. Perhaps he didn't know himself yet. She could only hope it lay in their life at Gundamurra.

Regretful of her lack of generosity towards him in the past and far more aware of his childhood background, she'd bought him many gifts for Christmas; a new Akubra hat, a leather belt with the letter *G* for Gundamurra worked into the buckle, a coffee mug with Daddy printed on it, a big enough possum harness for him to wear if he wanted to carry the baby with him as he walked around the station, a box of chocolates to feed his sweet tooth. She had another, more important gift for him, waiting for when they could be alone together.

Johnny gave her a beautiful pearl ring which he'd bought secretly while they were on their honeymoon in Broome. Megan loved it. Somehow it made the gift of the pearl necklace for her twenty-first birthday far more personal and special.

After the usual massive feast on Christmas day, when everyone else was tottering off to have a siesta through the heat of the afternoon, she drew Johnny along the verandah to the office. Although she felt nervous that he might feel pressured to be what she wanted him to be, the gift still felt right to her.

She handed him the prepared envelope.

In it lay the deed to two percent of Gundamurra from her share, giving him the controlling hand.

He stared at it, frowned, and panic instantly played havoc with Megan's taut nerves. He turned an uncomprehending look to her. 'Why?'

'Without you, Gundamurra would not have survived. And you're my husband, Johnny. It's...it's more fitting that you be the boss.'

He shook his head. 'Patrick's will...'

'My father chose you to play the role of knight to the rescue and you did it very generously. But it's moved beyond that now, Johnny. We're married. I think Dad would give his blessing to this gift.' Her argument faltered into uncertainty. 'Do you... Do you mind?'

He threw out his hands. 'How could I mind?' Yet he still frowned, searching her eyes. 'Are you sure you want to give this, Megan? I know how much inheriting Gundamurra meant to you.'

A painful flush scorched her cheeks. She'd been so hateful to him over the will, scornful of all he'd stood for in her eyes, fiercely rejecting any encroachment by him on what she saw as her territory.

'I was wrong, Johnny. Wrong about so many things...' Her apologetic smile was tinged with irony. 'You've shown me how wrong I was and I want to make up for it.' Her eyes begged him to let her.

'Megan...' He sighed, then moved to curl his hands around her shoulders, his eyes warmly reassuring. 'You're Patrick's daughter. You didn't need to do this. I don't feel less of a man because you own more of Gundamurra than I do. This gift is too big for me to accept. I can't feel right about it.'

'But I feel right to give it,' she pleaded. Or was she subconsciously tying him to her? Loading him with a responsibility to stop him from ever walking away? Trying to balance out her own secret insecurities?

He hesitated, assessing her need, weighing it against what he felt. Finally he said. 'Then let it be one percent. Equal partners.' He grinned. 'I can live very happily with that.'

Relief poured through her. 'Partners. Yes,' she eagerly agreed, winding her arms around his neck, pulling his head down to draw him into a kiss which would seal their partnership—a kiss that very quickly led to Johnny sweeping her off to bed.

They gave Mitch the job of fixing the percentage for them.

Their baby was born three weeks after Christmas—an adorable little girl whom they named Jennifer, instantly shortened to Jenny by her doting father.

The drought had not broken. Johnny's helicopter wasn't needed to transport Megan to and from the maternity ward in Bourke hospital. However, they were no sooner back on Gundamurra when the rain did come, and it was a Big Wet, raining on and off for the next two months. The parched country, that had seemed so lifeless for so long, started to bloom again.

'It's like a miracle, isn't it?' Johnny remarked with awe as they stood on the front verandah one morning, looking out on grassed land that reached to the horizon.

'Rebirth,' she murmured, loving how it always happened—what looked like dead ground coming to life again.

'Two miracles,' Johnny crooned down at their daughter who was cradled in his arms. 'You came into the world and brought the rain with you, Jenny. Now we'll be able to build up a whole army of sheep. Lots of lambs for you to play with.'

She gurgled back at him, perfectly happy with her father's plan. And Megan, too, was perfectly happy. No doubts at all that Johnny was happy to make his life on Gundamurra with her and their child.

No doubts...until she watched Johnny's movie on the night before Good Friday.

The weather had turned fine enough for the family to fly in for Easter, an invitation pressed by Johnny so he could show off his daughter. Ric brought the surprise with him—a video copy of The Last Cowboy Standing, which had already been released in the U.S. and according to Ric, was grossing huge box office profits.

'You're slaying them, Johnny,' he said with huge pride in his old friend. 'I've just been in L.A. on business, and believe me, even the diehard critics are hailing you as an actor who should be up for an Academy Award for this performance.'

'That's just hype,' Johnny demurred.

'Well, let's see,' Mitch drawled, grinning from ear to ear as he added, 'Can't wait to watch John Wayne riding again.'

Everyone stood up, eager to go to the TV room. They'd finished dinner. The children were in bed asleep. There was no reasonable excuse not to watch the movie and it would be like another rejection of Johnny if she didn't, yet Megan could not quell the fear that Ric's report had stirred. If Johnny's acting was so good...she didn't want to see, didn't want to know.

He'd put aside his singing career. She could accept that because he had already achieved his ambitions in that arena, but this might be another career pinnacle he'd want to climb. They'd been so happy together these past few months. She didn't want anything to threaten what they now shared, but wasn't that being mean again, thinking only of what *she* wanted instead of considering Johnny's needs?

If she had to, she'd go with him anywhere.

He caught her hand as they were heading out of the dining room, pausing her while the others moved on, squeezing it hard as he murmured, 'Are you okay with this, Megan?'

She looked up into eyes that were sharp with concern, caring about what she felt, caring which was undoubtedly fed by the bad memories she'd given him.

'Of course,' she replied, smiling to show they would not be in conflict over this movie or anything arising out of it.

Still he hesitated, apparently reluctant to see himself in the movie, anyway.

'Have you got a problem with it?' she asked, wondering if he'd been intent on blocking out everything he'd done before their marriage.

He grimaced. 'I've never watched myself perform.'

Embarrassment that he might not live up to the hype?

'You're brilliant onstage, Johnny,' she assured him, squeezing *his* hand to inject her support and confidence. 'You have a talent for emoting that I'm sure will come across on film, too.'

'Emoting...' He looked quizzically at her for a moment, then shrugged. 'Well, might as well see what the director did with all the scenes he shot. Just remember it's only a movie, Megan. Okay?'

'Okay,' she repeated firmly.

There had to be a woman in it, Megan thought, as they followed the others to the TV room. The tension emanating from Johnny probably meant there were love scenes. But she was not going to be jealous. The movie had been made before they were married. Johnny's commitment to her since then had been rock-solid. She fervently wished she hadn't doubted it over the blonde at the concert. So many wrongs...still to be righted.

One of the sofas had been left vacant for them. As soon as they were settled on it, Ric started the video rolling. The credits zigzagged over a long shot of a cowboy riding towards a ranch. Ric and Mitch tossed a few teasing remarks at Johnny which he took good-humouredly. However, everyone was stunned into silence when the cowboy finally reached home and entered the ranch house.

Silence from the movie, too. No music track. No speech. Just the stark images of a wife who had been beaten, raped, and killed, and two small children lying broken and dead on the floor, blood on the wall showing where their head injuries had happened. The shock and grief of the cowboy were heart-gripping and everyone watching could see—feel—the surge of savage need to find the perpetrators, grim purpose mixed with a terrible tenderness as he removed a red and white polka dot neckerchief from his wife's dead grasp.

He crushed it in his own hand and that image was instantly transferred to the cowboy standing at three graves, slowly turning away and walking to his horse. Then the music started—music that seemed to reinforce the relentless beat of the horse's hooves, riding out on an unshakeable mission.

'Hell!' Ric breathed. 'That's powerful stuff, Johnny.'

To Megan every scene that followed was powerful; each gang member being hunted, confronted, punished with raging violence, then killed, until there was only one left, the leader who'd worn the neckerchief. No longer having the support of the others, he panicked and rode away. During the chase, the cowboy was shot and badly wounded, though he managed to keep riding and reach another ranch house where he collapsed at the front door.

When he swam back to consciousness, two small children came into view, clearly stirring anguished memories, then the woman who'd taken him in and was tending his wound, a widow who was struggling to survive on the ranch.

She let him know he was an unwelcome intrusion, an extra burden she resented, but he gradually thawed her hostile attitude with how kindly and caringly he treated her children who lapped up his attention. Sexual tension grew as the cowboy recovered and on the night before he was to leave, the widow decided to have him, well aware that the probability was he'd never come back.

It was an extraordinary scene—the cowboy's sense that it wasn't right to take what she was offering, the torment on his face, the widow goading him into succumbing to the desire they both felt, a kind of desperate passion in the lovemaking. It gave Megan goose bumps, reminding her of her own feelings on the night Jenny had been conceived.

The next morning the children followed the cowboy to his horse, pleading for him to come back soon, but the widow simply stood in the doorway, watching him go with a bleak look of resignation on her face.

He hunted down the gang leader, but there was no explosion of violence, no fury, more a grim execution. The cowboy dropped the polka dot square of cloth over his dead face with an air of sick finality. His expression clearly telegraphed—done, but what to do with his life now? He rode back to the graves of his family. More poignant grief and a sense of saying goodbye as the crosses of the graves were silhouetted by a beautiful sunset.

The final shot was of the widow's children, spotting a cowboy riding towards their ranch, calling out to their mother, running to meet him and the widow coming to the doorway, a frown gradually lifting to an expression of wonderment as the cowboy dismounted, took the children's hands, and walked towards her.

Megan was still mopping up tears when Ric turned the television off. Her sisters and Lara and Kathryn were, too. Even Mitch had to clear his throat before speaking.

'No hype, Johnny. You made me live that with you.'

'Yeah,' Ric agreed, shaking his head in bemusement. 'There's nothing new about the story-line—probably been done a thousand times—yet you made it so personal. It's your movie, Johnny. You carried it all the way and made it a great movie. A *tour de force.* No wonder you're getting rave reviews!'

'Probably surprise more than anything,' Johnny mocked.

'How do *you* feel about it?' Lara inserted quietly.

He grimaced. 'Makes me feel I've been caught naked, to tell you the truth. I shouldn't have done it.' He pushed up from the sofa, drawing Megan to her feet, as well. 'If you don't mind, you guys, I'm taking my wife off to bed. Jenny still wakes up at night.'

*My wife...and Jenny, his child...*

Megan was acutely conscious of the silence they left behind them, even more conscious of Johnny's rejection of his acting which had been so good it could very well lead him to be a megastar on the screen.

He was closing himself off from it because of her and their child. Megan had passively accepted his decision to retire from the entertainment field, but now she felt very strongly that it wasn't right for him to turn his back on so much talent. It was too big a sacrifice...a terrible waste.

She had to talk to him about it.

Had to open the doors.

She remembered him quoting Shakespeare the morning after her father's wake—

*'And one man in his time plays many parts.'*

If anyone should, that person was Johnny Ellis.

# CHAPTER FIFTEEN

MEGAN SAT ON their bed, watching her husband strip off his clothes, re-membering the scene he'd played with the widow in the movie—the raw conflict and the caring.

'Why are you embarrassed?' she asked.

He shot her a wary look, eyes guarded, watchful, assessing.

Anticipating trouble with her?

'Mitch was right,' she asserted warmly. 'You made us live it with you. I don't think many actors can grab people by the throat like that. You deserve the accolades, Johnny.'

A wry little smile twitched at his mouth. 'I wasn't really acting, Megan. I just channelled what I felt about...other things...into the role.'

'What other things?' she probed, her pulse skipping into a faster beat at the implication that parts of the movie had parallelled his own life experience.

*Caught naked...*

He shook his head. 'None of it relates to our life now.'

Putting in the block again.

Megan gritted her teeth, determined to fight it this time. 'I want to know all of you, Johnny, not just the part you think is suitable for me.'

He flashed her a hard look. 'No, you don't, Megan. You've spelled out many times that Gundamurra is your world and you don't want to be a part of any other.'

Damned by her own words!

'I'm sorry that the movie has disturbed you,' he went on. 'Just remember it was made *before* we were married.'

Her own thoughts before she saw it!

Her heart sank as she realised Johnny had taken on board all the parameters she had drawn and because he wanted their marriage to work, he was doing what he had to do to keep it within them. In a burst of shattering insight, she understood it was the mind-set of a survivor. Cut away anything that might put their life together at risk. Keep everything steady and on course. Don't invite trouble. Be charming. Smile.

The abused child in Johnny Ellis was still there—buried deep but still inside him, doing what had to be done to survive and prosper in a hostile world!

Having shed his clothes, he landed on the bed, pulled her down beside him, and *smiled* to set her at ease as he started unbuttoning her shirt. 'You must be tired...'

'Stop!' she cried.

He frowned at the sharpness of her protest.

'Stop patronising me, Johnny.' Her eyes begged his understanding as she rushed to explain. 'I did see your career as a threat to anything we could have together, but I have grown up this past year and I know to put someone like you in a cage is terribly wrong.'

The frown returned. 'I'm not caged at Gundamurra, Megan. There's plenty of space here. Different challenges. More than enough to happily occupy me.'

She reached up and stroked his cheek, wanting desperately to get under his skin, the self-protective layers he'd grown over too many years. 'I love you, Johnny. I want you to share your life with me. All of it, not just the part you think is acceptable to me. I promise you, I won't turn away from any of it, just because it's unfamiliar to me. So please...put down the barriers and let me into your mind.'

His eyes studied hers quizzically. 'You've never said that before.'

'I've been a frightened fool, holding back because I didn't believe I could ever have all of you, but if you'll truly share with me, Johnny, I swear I'll always be there for you, wherever you want to go and whatever you want to do. I'll never take your family from you, nor...'

He placed gentle fingers on her lips, halting her speech. 'You love me?' he repeated gruffly, as though that was all he'd heard.

Appalled that he had gone all this time with her in the intimacy of their marriage and not felt loved, Megan spilled out the truth of her long fixation on him, from when she was a little girl—her hero-worship, her teenage crush, the self-protective rejection that had taken the form of scorn, the wild intensity of her need to have him *once,* the guilt of *trapping* him into marriage, the fear of not ever being enough for him. She laid her heart absolutely bare, desperately hoping he would open up, too—good or bad.

She had to know.

Only with knowing could she feel truly married to him.

No secrets.

No forbidden areas.

Honesty.

She saw her revelations strike chords of recognition in his eyes, saw them provoke expressions of bemusement, tenderness, regret, irony, and her nerves were screwed into a complete mess by the time she'd laid it all out to him, but she didn't care. It was the truth.

For several heart-churning moments he made no reply, simply stroking the wild mop of her hair away from her face, seemingly entranced by the curly tendrils. Or the colour. Her crowning glory.

'We always had that gap between us, Megan,' he remarked ruefully. 'You captured my heart when you were a little girl. In my mind, I adopted you as my little sister, just as I adopted Patrick as my father. Crossing that line was unthinkable. Though I certainly thought about it in recent years.'

'You did?' she queried incredulously.

He nodded.

'You never showed it.'

'Inappropriate. Firstly, you were Patrick's daughter. Secondly, you wouldn't have a bar of me, anyway.'

She sighed. 'I thought you were out of my reach, Johnny.'

'I realise that now. But once you agreed to our making love on the night of Patrick's wake, I was hell-bent on bridging that gap.'

That startled her into saying, 'It wasn't...just sex?'

A whimsical little smile. 'Did it feel like *just sex* to you?'

'Johnny, I was so caught up in my own feelings...and I'd baited you, tricked you...'

'I was where I wanted to be, Megan. And nothing was going to stop me from coming back and winning more from you.'

'Like...in the movie?' she asked, wanting to know if he'd transferred his feelings for her to the scene with the widow.

He grimaced. 'I didn't think of you ever seeing that movie. When I went back to Arizona, I had them rewrite the part with the widow. I could see she should be thinking the cowboy had too big a commitment to his previous life, that he'd go and never come back. You were in my head all the time, Megan.'

'The cowboy was torn by the situation, too, Johnny—between her and what he'd set out to do,' she reminded him. 'I don't want you to feel torn.'

'It was something he had to finish before he could move on. And he did finish it. I feel the same way. There's no conflict in me about what I want.' He smiled, a beautiful, happy smile. 'You've just given it to me.'

Her love...

Such a powerful thing if it wasn't hemmed in by constrictions.

'It's free, Johnny,' she promised him. 'You don't have to perform for me. No matter what you choose to do, or have done in the past, I love you.'

'What still bothers you about my past, Megan?'

'The children...what you felt in the movie. You said you channelled it...from what?'

Sadness clouded his eyes. 'When you're a little kid, you can't stop what adults do,' he said quietly. 'I remember Ric telling Mitch and me—back when we were sixteen—how his mother was regularly beaten up and eventually killed by his father, how he'd tried to get in the way, only to get hurled aside and beaten himself. I knew how that was. I learnt very young that you can't win against adults. They're too strong. And they have answers for everything—for the bruises and the broken bones and the bed-wetting...'

'What was the worst for you?'

He hesitated, not wanting to pull it out.

'You told me about Ric, Johnny,' she quickly pressed. 'Please...tell me about you.'

It came reluctantly, almost as though he was ashamed of it. 'Being hit wasn't so bad. I hated being locked in a cupboard. Alone. In the dark. No escape. Days, nights... I never knew how long it would last. Or if they'd forget I was there. I had to stay quiet or I'd get pulled out, beaten, and put back even longer.'

'My God, Johnny! No wonder you ran away when you could.'

'It's a long way behind me now,' he said dismissively. 'But playing that initial scene in the movie—the terrible waste of lives that promised so much—it wasn't hard for me to call up grief, nor a savage desire to balance the ledger. Though, in the end, as Ric says, it's best to let those feelings go and move on. You just don't ever forget...how it was.'

'No,' she murmured. 'I can't imagine you would. Thank you for telling me. It helps me to bridge the gap...knowing why you think and feel as you do. And I don't want you to ever feel alone again, Johnny.'

He smiled as she wound her arms around his neck, the desire for more unifying action simmering into his eyes as he hopefully asked, 'Have I said enough?'

'No.'

'What more?' His patience was being tested.

'I want to hear you say you love me.'

He laughed, and to Megan's ears, it was the heady laugh of freedom. His eyes sparkled wild pleasure as he bent to brush his lips over hers and whisper, 'I love you, Megan Maguire. I love having you as my partner in all things. I love sharing your life—'

'You've got to let me share yours, too,' she cut in breathlessly.

'Everything. I love everything about you.'

Then he proceeded to show her how very much he did, and she loved him right back...openly, wholeheartedly, blissfully secure in the certain knowledge that she was every bit as special to him as he was to her... and always would be.

# CHAPTER SIXTEEN

JOHNNY WAS COMPLETELY at peace with his world the next morning, looking benevolently on everyone, not the least bit perturbed when Mitch and Ric wanted a private meeting with him in the office. As the three of them strolled along the verandah which skirted the inner quadrangle of the homestead, he inquired about his old friends' contentment with their lives.

'I'm a happy man,' Ric declared.

'Couldn't have it better,' Mitch said decisively.

'Sorry if I did wrong, bringing that video, Johnny,' Ric slung at him with an edge of concern. 'Didn't mean to upset things.'

'You didn't,' Johnny assured him. 'It cut a bit close to the bone in places, but that's all right.'

'You're okay with it?'

'Sure.'

'Megan?'

'No problem. Sorted a few things out for us, actually. Guess I was a bit too tight-lipped about stuff I've carried with me for a long time.'

'I was with Kathryn, too,' Mitch admitted ruefully. 'Hard to open up. But makes a big difference when you do.'

'Makes sense of everything for them,' Ric remarked knowingly.

So they had held back, too, Johnny thought.

*We all felt vulnerable. . .guarding ourselves.*

Trust was such a huge thing, coming from their backgrounds. They'd learnt to trust Patrick. Yet even he, at the end, had confounded Johnny with his will. Probably Mitch and Ric, too, though they'd set it aside, making up their own reasons for it.

'So what's this meeting about?' he asked as he ushered them into the office.

'A letter from Patrick,' Mitch answered.

Johnny was stunned. He closed the door on automatic pilot, staring at the other two. It was clear they both knew about it. No surprise on Ric's face. And Mitch was drawing an envelope out from inside the jacket he was wearing.

'He left it with me, Johnny,' he explained. 'To be opened a year after his death when the three of us were together.'

Fair enough, Johnny thought. Mitch was the lawyer. Of course he would obey Patrick's instructions. Yet if it explained the will, why a year later? It would have saved a huge amount of heartburn and worry if they'd all known Patrick's reasoning in the first place.

Mitch held out the envelope. 'I think you should read it out, Johnny.'

'No. He put it in your keeping, Mitch,' he asserted, his stomach already churning over what its contents might be, whether Patrick would have wanted what he'd ultimately done. The other two had nothing to worry about. They could be at ease, while he... No, he fiercely told himself. He'd done right. It felt right. Megan felt it, too. Partners, in every sense.

'You read it, Mitch,' Ric agreed.

None of them moved to sit down. Somehow, it was a mark of respect to Patrick to keep standing. Mitch opened the envelope and withdrew a sheet of paper, slowly unfolding it. He cleared his throat.

'Just let me read it through. Leave any discussion of its contents to the end. Agreed?'

Johnny and Ric nodded.

Mitch took a deep breath and read—

*My three sons,*
*That's how I think of you. I could not have loved you more, nor been more proud of you, if you had been born to me.*
*I get so tired now. I can feel my body slowing down, time running out.*

*Ric and Mitch, both of you have found what you needed to fulfil the rich promise of your lives. I believe you know this and will understand I want the same for Johnny. To some measure, I think I stood in the way of that happening, so the will I have written is meant to correct that.*

*There's Megan, too. I've made provision for Jessie and Emily but Megan will need help to get past this drought and rebuild. I know all three of you would step forward to ensure her future on Gundamurra, but I have singled out Johnny, not because I favour him above either of you, but because it gives him my approval and blessing to make his home at Gundamurra with Megan, if he so wishes.*

*I sit here thinking of the bond that has always been between them—a natural gravitation towards each other which has never lessened, though it has been much strained in recent years. I believe the tension I have observed between them is the tension of barriers raised which neither of them feel able to cross.*

*I could be wrong. A year is long enough to break those barriers if the desire to do so has the strength of love behind it. If this has not proved true, I now put it in the hands of the three of you to correct the inheritance, returning it all to Megan, and sharing the financial onus I put on Johnny to rescue Gundamurra for her.*

*You each offered help. I know it's in your hearts to give it. Let Johnny go free to seek what I hope he will find one day—the peace of coming home to a woman he loves, who also loves him. And Johnny, please forgive my trespass on your life. I trust the year was not too hard on you. On all three of you, wondering why I did what I've done.*

*Stay brothers to each other. And thank you for all you have given me through the years.*

*Patrick.*

It took Johnny a while to swallow the lump in his throat, to feel composed enough to speak. 'Did either of you realise what the will was about?'

'We didn't know for sure, Johnny,' Ric answered. 'We just figured Patrick knew what he was doing.'

'Knight attack,' Mitch murmured, waving to the chess table. 'Patrick wanted you to capture the queen. That seemed to be the logic of it. And you did, Johnny.'

'Well, I wouldn't put it like that to Megan,' he said hotly. 'We're partners.'

'All the barriers down?' Ric quizzed, a satisfied twinkle lurking in his brilliant dark eyes. 'Seemed that way to me this morning.'

A quick train of realizations clicked through Johnny's head. 'That damned concert! Lara's idea. And bringing a video of the movie home, shoving it in our faces...'

'You helped me with Lara, Johnny,' came the quick retort.

'You *knew* something, Ric.'

'I swear I just put two and two together.'

'We were both here for Megan's twenty-first birthday,' Mitch slid in. 'It was very clear that we didn't make up for your absence.'

'Right! So I'm an idiot for not seeing it before this.'

'No, Johnny. Megan was ten years younger than you. And Patrick's daughter,' came the sympathetic reply. 'They were big blinkers to see past. Both Ric and I wore the same blinkers until Patrick's will was read. Then for the most part we stood back and let the two of you fight it out.'

'Which brings us to the critical question...' Ric paused, then pointedly inquired, 'Have you come home, Johnny?'

'Yes. Yes, I have.'

And he laughed because they were both grinning at him, and their grins plainly said, 'Welcome to the club!'

'In fact,' he went on, 'I was discussing with Megan last night—I'd like to start up an opportunity program for street-kids here on Gundamurra. I probably won't be as good as Patrick at it, but I want to give it a shot.'

'No question kids would relate to you, Johnny,' Mitch said warmly. 'It's a great idea.'

'Very fitting,' Ric agreed. He nodded to the big leather chair behind the desk. 'If anyone can fill Patrick's chair, it's you, Johnny. I wish you well with it.'

'I'll second that,' Mitch said, smiling. 'I can see that chair fitting you like a glove as time goes on.'

It embarrassed Johnny that they thought so much of him, but he was intensely grateful for their support and understanding. 'Thanks, guys. I'll do my best to live up to it. And Mitch, I was thinking since you're high up in legal circles, you could help me organise the program.'

'You can certainly count on my help.'

'I take it you're not thinking of doing any more movies?' Ric posed.

'No. It's not real life. What I have with Megan here on Gundamurra *is* real. And it's good. I wouldn't swap it for anything.'

'So there's nothing to discuss,' Mitch said decisively. 'I think we should do what all brothers would do at such a time. Arm ourselves with a drink and raise a toast to the man who got it right for us.'

Which they proceeded to do.

'To Patrick Maguire, who gave us the lives we now have,' Ric said.

'To the best father we could have had,' Mitch said.

'Rest in peace, Patrick. It was indeed a *good day* when we arrived at Gundamurra,' Johnny said. Then with deep feeling, 'Your mission is complete. We've all come home.'

\* \* \* \* \*

# talk about it

Let's talk about books.

Join the conversation:

 on facebook.com/harlequinaustralia

 on Twitter @harlequinaus

www.harlequinbooks.com.au

If you love reading and want to know about our
authors and titles, then let's talk about it.